Diaries
1987–1992

Also by Edwina Currie

FICTION

A Parliamentary Affair
A Woman's Place
She's Leaving Home
The Ambassador
Chasing Men
This Honourable House

NON-FICTION

Life Lines: Politics and Health 1986–88
What Women Want
Three Line Quips

EDWINA CURRIE

Diaries
1987–1992

LITTLE, BROWN

A *Little, Brown* Book

First published in Great Britain in 2002
by Little, Brown

Copyright © Edwina Currie, 2002

A CIP catalogue record for this book is available
from the British Library.

Unless otherwise stated, all photographs are from
the author's private collection.

ISBN 0 316 86024 7

Typeset in Berkeley by M Rules
Printed and bound in Great Britain by
Clays Ltd, St Ives plc

Little, Brown
An imprint of
Time Warner Books UK
Brettenham House
Lancaster Place
London WC2E 7EN

www.TimeWarnerBooks.co.uk

Contents

Author's Note

The full text of this diary runs to some 225,000 words. My warmest thanks are due to Time Warner's editorial director, Alan Samson, and to Adam Sisman, who undertook the immense task of editing.

When I started the diary in the summer of 1987, just after the General Election, I made myself two promises: that I would always write down exactly my opinions and feelings at the time, and that I would never go back to alter anything, however unpalatable or wrong my judgements might subsequently prove to be. During editing we have maintained these principles; nothing has been changed, except where necessary to make sense of the abridged script.

The originals will, I hope, eventually be placed with supporting papers in the archives of the Women's Library in London as part of their collection of twentieth-century women in politics.

Edwina Currie Jones,
September 2002

List of Abbreviations

CCO	Conservative Central Office
CMO	Chief Medical Officer
COHSE	Confederation of Health Service Employees
CPC	Conservative Political Centre
DHA	District Health Authority
DHSS	Department of Health and Social Security
DoH	Department of Health
DSS	Department of Social Security
DTI	Department of Trade and Industry
EMS	European Monetary System
ERM	Exchange Rate Mechanism
FPC	Family Practitioner Committee
GATT	General Agreement on Tariffs and Trades
GDP	Gross Domestic Product
MAFF	Ministry of Agriculture, Fisheries and Food
MEP	Member of the European Parliament
NACODS	National Association of Colliery Overmen, Deputies and Shotfirers
NFU	National Farmers' Union
NHS	National Health Service
NUPE	National Union of Public Employees
PPS	Parliamentary Private Secretary
PUS	Parliamentary Under-Secretary of State (junior minister)

RCN   Royal College of Nursing
RHA   Regional Health Authority
SDP   Social Democratic Party
SLD   Social and Liberal Democrats
UDM   Union of Democratic Mineworkers
WEU   Western European Union
WHO   World Health Organization

Foreword

In 1987, Edwina Currie was a junior minister in Mrs Thatcher's Government. The Conservatives had won their third successive election victory in June. In the subsequent reshuffle, John Moore was appointed Secretary of State for Health and Social Security, replacing Norman Fowler, who became Secretary of State for Employment. EC remained in the post she had gained in 1986, as Parliamentary Under-Secretary of State for Health, now serving under John Moore, with Tony Newton as Minister of State.

All three of the principal offices of state continued to be held by ministers who had been in those positions for some years: Nigel Lawson as Chancellor of the Exchequer; Sir Geoffrey Howe as Foreign Secretary; and Douglas Hurd as Home Secretary.

When she began these diaries, EC was forty. From 1975 to 1986 she had been active in local government in Birmingham. In 1983 she was elected Conservative MP for South Derbyshire. She and her husband Ray, a chartered accountant with Arthur Andersen, had been married for fifteen years. They had two daughters: Debbie, born in 1974; and Susie, born in 1977.

They divided their lives between the Tower House, their family home in EC's South Derbyshire constituency in Findern, a village near Derby, and a flat in Victoria, within easy reach of the House of Commons. When Parliament was sitting, EC and her husband tended to spend the working week in London, travelling to Derbyshire for the weekends.

The secret springs of events are seldom known. But when they are, they become particularly instructive and entertaining . . . the greatest actions have often proceeded from the intrigues of a handsome woman or a fashionable man, and of course whilst the memoires of those events are instructive by opening the secret workings of the human mind, they likewise attract by the interest and events of a novel . . . If some people would write down the events they had been witness to . . . the meaning of an age would be transmitted to the next with clearness and dependence . . .

I have been in the midst of action . . . I have seen parties rise and fall – friends be united and disunited – the ties of love give way to caprice, to interest and to vanity . . .

Georgiana, Duchess of Devonshire, September 1782

1987

Victoria, Monday 31 August

Just finished reading papers in preparation for my visit to Gravesend tomorrow: they're proposing a complicated reorganisation of local health services and we're being bounced into it. In the long run the Health Authority wants a huge new £60 million single hospital, all on one site, but I'm against that – inhuman, cold, unattractive and fiendishly expensive.

Holidays marvellous. Thank God we got three weeks in Majorca. Still can't believe we had endless sun (90°+), sea, beaches, etc. I put on weight – 10½ stone – fortunately lost half a stone since we came back. I can close my eyes and we're still on the beach at Cala de St Vincente, going brown, or running on the front at Puerto de Pollensa. Ray moaned the whole week he was there, got his feet badly burned through ignoring advice. He's looking fat and was clearly tired. I had long and sombre thoughts through the night, but since we got back here he's been friendly enough. I'm more amused than distressed by his recalcitrance and sullenness. So glad I have alternative ways of spending my time. We talked about misery and expense of the Tower House – leaks, repairs, pool not used, lights fusing, etc., and he telephoned Mike, his drinking pal (an electrician at Rolls-Royce), who came round and said whole top floor needs rewiring and offered to do it in spare time. Mike is a typical South Derbyshire craftsman: clever, practical, honest, hard-working. I am lucky to represent people like that.

Spent an hour going through diary up to Easter. I must be busiest minister outside the Cabinet (and more than some in it, I bet), in the busiest department. No free Fridays and Saturdays till June '88. If I'm not careful I won't see anything of the family, and then they are right to moan.

Debbie in state of great excitement about going to Denstone.[1] Bit frantic getting her ready. She has grown enormously recently, and now weighs a fraction under 7 stone and has size 6½ feet – even though she's not yet thirteen. All her kit has to be bought from school shop, so I'm tied to going there, which is a real pest. Also trying to arrange routine check-ups for both with dentist in Birmingham, *and* Deb is due to see consultant at dental hospital for last bit of brace asap. She will be so very beautiful in eighteen months when all steel gone; we joked that I'd have some photos taken and see if a model agency was interested – she could earn money in holidays. Susie also lovely, but different: blonde, sharply intelligent and hard as nails. She has talent for needing little sleep (reading at 11 p.m., up at 7 a.m.) and catnapping, e.g. in car. Will find it very useful if she enters politics! – and she may, as she continues to be interested in much of my activity. Great amusement on holiday when some woman recognised Deb, not me – made a change from endless approaches (all friendly) all over the island. Poor woman couldn't understand why the Currie family fell about laughing at her!

What do we think of my colleagues? Moore[2] is Kennedy. Clean looking and (apparently) clean living; clever, pretty, ambitious wife. But he was forty-eight before he made Cabinet (compare Rifkind,[3] who really does have a good brain, or Harold Wilson for that matter). He is keen on teamwork, which suits me. Fowler[4] was a

1. A private boarding school, about 15 miles west of the Curries' Derbyshire home.
2. John Moore, Secretary of State for Health and Social Services; Conservative MP for Croydon Central.
3. Malcolm Rifkind, Secretary of State for Scotland; Conservative MP for Edinburgh Pentlands.
4. Norman Fowler, Secretary of State for Employment; Secretary of State for Social Services 1981–7; Conservative MP for Sutton Coldfield.

man of cliques, sucked people dry and then discarded them (Wardle, Hayhoe, Whitney, Newton and others). But Moore's political judgement is hasty – he tried to ditch the Social Fund[1] after all those hours we put in (two hundred plus) on the Bill, and all the commitments given by Willie Whitelaw[2] et al. He wrote letter to John Major[3] (who put Bill through) saying Social Fund was politically indefensible! Then he found himself opposed in Cabinet by Major, Fowler (ditto) and Whitelaw amongst others. If he had thought twice he would not have tried it on, but he's angry at Fowler for leaving so many blank cheques – promises to Treasury about savings, which are (1) vague, and (2) difficult, especially with AIDS problems – and he wants to show he's smarter. I'm not sure he is. Portillo,[4] who has worked with him before, says he's 'sold as seen' – there is no secret man. In that case, Moore is also intolerant and somewhat arrogant, despite the carefully offered charm; but he's also insecure, and surrounds himself with evidence of his already achieved high office, e.g. the toys we are presented with on official occasions. His office is full of them (mine are languishing in a box in the kitchen!).

Portillo is impressive and will go far. Really able, thoughtful, and neither left nor (I suspect) right wing. Made a good speech to the Canadians which he circulated (got no publicity at all), in which he showed he had *read* Adam Smith – most unusual – and understood. *And* J. K. Galbraith and a few others. But I couldn't say the strong

1. A fund administered by the DHSS to make grants and loans to families receiving social security payments for the purchase of basic items like beds, cookers, etc. It foundered because it cost more to administer than was disbursed, and involved pettifogging decisions of a tyrannical nature.
2. Lord Whitelaw, Lord President of the Council and Leader of the Lords.
3. Chief Secretary to the Treasury; Parliamentary Under-Secretary of State for Social Security, 1985–6; Minister of State (Social Security), DHSS 1986–7; Conservative MP for Huntingdon.
4. Michael Portillo, Parliamentary Under-Secretary of State (Social Security), DHSS; Conservative MP for Enfield Southgate.

things he says (e.g. 'doctors and nurses conspire to arrange over-manning') – the press would go bananas. Not fair really!

Tony Newton[1] is a sad case. Now in his sixth year at the DHSS and really fed up with it. Did all Norman Fowler's legwork for years and got no thanks or reward. But he's disorganised and poor at taking decisions. He spent two and a half hours at the National Health Service Management Board last week discussing how to handle prevention; it needed forty-five minutes to an hour at most. But he hadn't made up his mind or even worked out the options in advance. Bit Keith Joseph-like at times, but that's not conducive to good government. He's *always* late – even when he's in the building – and that really annoys Moore. Tony looks old and tired much of the time, heavy smoker; the cigs are doing him no good at all and I am concerned about him.

Nick Scott[2] is fat, cheerful and lazy. Bit 'hail-fellow-well-met'. It will help Portillo, of course, who *is* a hard worker. Well, it is easier if you have a small constituency on the doorstep, instead of a huge one halfway across the country. Scott's wife – pretty, sexy, Sloane-ish blonde – was once married to someone else. John Moore says he knew Jocelyn Cadbury[3] well and once tried to pair him off with the current Mrs Scott!

Tony is a good friend, one of a long string of older, clever, platonic friends. Wish I could talk more to Ray, but non-political spouses don't understand our love affairs with politics, and simply mutter that we asked for it. I remember B[4] saying his wife was same. But the

1. Minister of State (Health), Department of Health and Social Security; Parliamentary Under-Secretary of State for Social Security, 1982–4; Minister of State (Social Security and the Disabled), 1984–6; Conservative MP for Braintree.
2. Minister of State (Social Security), Department of Health and Social Security; Conservative MP for Chelsea.
3. The former Conservative MP for Birmingham Northfield.
4. EC's highly placed lover.

brotherhood of politics – and of the Commons – does create intimacy and exclusiveness.

Tower House, Wednesday 9 September, 11.40 p.m.

Yesterday we at last got the children off to school. That is the toughest job of the year – comparable only to doing four hundred plus Christmas cards. Debbie's uniform is a plain unsmart grey. She's in two houses, one to sleep, one to work, which I found very confusing. We took her on Monday evening and were subjected to a pep talk by headmaster – Susie[1] listening hard! I was bored, and spent most of the time observing the new parents hanging on every word. I suppose Ray and I have different attitudes to the role of school and authority; he (and Deb) thinks it's important that her house should win all its matches, for example, while I think that sort of thing is silly. They are teamworkers, I'm not; I look at the rules and obey those I think are valuable, and ignore (or seek to change) the rest. Susie is more like me. I wonder what she'll make of it next year?

Once they had gone the house seemed empty and the tension vanished. Deb rang up later to say that, after all the fuss and effort, she had only two pairs of knickers – one grey, one navy on! – so I'll have to send some. Now I'm pottering round doing constituency work, appearing in local papers and doing boxes in a half-hearted fashion. Some DHSS visits tomorrow and Friday, including a curry in a restaurant in Leeds with the disc jockey James Whale, followed by a phone-in on his late night radio programme. Apparently he's been talking about it for weeks.

Found myself wondering about Tony Newton. Most of the stuff in my boxes has been through his hands and he seems to find it increasingly difficult to take a decision. He will have completed

---

1. Susie was due to go to Denstone in 1988.

seven years in DHSS by the next reshuffle: maybe all I have to do is sit tight. But we need his brains. So far I doubt if JM has the same quantity. Last week he made a speech on privatisation in the USA which caused a stir here, leading articles, etc., partly because he claimed to be sole begetter of this jewel in Margaret's crown ('I' everywhere, not 'we') and partly because it's seen as bid for the leadership when there's a vacancy. *But*: he's got probably four years at DHSS and he's not going to be able to privatise it. A real thinker would be looking ahead, not claiming the past. Ken Baker[1] is brainier, I think, and has greater vision and so far still has my preference.

The SDP vanished in a puff of smoke last week too.[2] Maclennan[3] (new leader!) just about symbolised the whole sweet-natured, narrow, naive and indecisive set-up. Roy Jenkins wanted them to join the Liberals after a decent interval, Owen wanted (and still wants) his own party. They are a shower. It is sad, really – they split the Labour vote nicely in '83, and '87 was thus much harder to fight. And there is room for a non-socialist anti-Tory party. I suppose that the future depends now not on third parties (or fourth) but on the leftward tendencies of the Labour Party. This week it's the TUC Conference, and they sound more like dinosaurs than ever. John Prescott[4] on TV tonight explaining that no, they knew it was unrealistic to take back shares without compensation, but that 'compensation' will be at the shares' original price; and Alan Tuffin[5] pointing out that nine million shareholders will vote against that,

1. Secretary of State for Education and Science; Conservative MP for Mole Valley.
2. The Social Democratic Party (SDP) voted to merge with the Liberals; Dr David Owen, MP for Plymouth Devonport and former Labour Foreign Secretary, started his own breakaway party.
3. Robert Maclennan, leader of the Social Democratic Party (SDP); the long-serving MP for Caithness and Sutherland (Labour 1966–81; SDP since 1981).
4. Member of the Shadow Cabinet; Labour MP for Hull East.
5. General Secretary, Union of Communication Workers.

won't they? Meanwhile, Scargill ranting again and drawing cheers, while younger, smarter men struggle to bring the movement into the twentieth century.

Ray has just phoned from London. He's clearly been out for the evening, though he denied it – he wasn't making much sense. Wish he wouldn't do that. Oh yes, and then snoring like a motor mower with TB. If I'm already awake I have to move to another room to get away from it. Giving up smoking has not improved the quality of the sound. We had a good weekend – he was in lively mood both Friday night and Saturday morning, which is unheard of!

Victoria, Sunday 20 September, very late

Just a quick note while I drink a small glass of Drambuie! Then I'll sleep like a log. Then 7 a.m. breakfast TV to talk about our new alcohol policy, followed by inter-Government group with representation from seven or eight ministries, chaired by John Wakeham:[1] that effectively gives it a very strong voice in Cabinet. The PM didn't want this group – her first reaction was that there was a proliferation of such groups (not true, there's only one, on drugs) and that it was only OK if it was informal and low-level. Someone has been reading her the riot act, as the proposal has just come out in the form agreed by Douglas Hurd[2] and John Moore, and a good thing too. I remember her telling the Smoking Room loudly in June that she disapproved of advertising condoms on TV – someone sat on her on that, too, and the ads started in August. I suspect Willie Whitelaw has a big influence and is very skilled at persuading her.

1. Lord Privy Seal and Leader of the House of Commons; chairman of various Cabinet committees; Conservative MP for Colchester South and Maldon.
2. Home Secretary; Conservative MP for Witney.

Victoria, Sunday 27 September, very late

Got up at 7 a.m. to do boxes (all done!), then collected to go to Glasgow to record *Open to Question*[1] with an audience of teenagers. In preparation I borrowed a tape and saw their efforts last year with Heath (November '86) and Healey. Heath was asked what he thought of me and was very rude – he's never exchanged a word with me, never, the arrogant beggar – and said he thought it was quite wrong for me to have a go at people about their smoking. Well, if I've achieved anything, it's the elimination of that attitude: most people now would say I was quite right, it's part of the job. The kids asked whether that applied to Lord Whitelaw too – and there's another one who felt it was OK to criticise a fellow minister. But, my God, they take umbrage if I say anything. Douglas Hurd was apoplectic last October when I said on TV that his *audience* had wanted something with a bit more sparkle at Conference. Be better than your critics, my dear! The only problem is that it's going out on the Tuesday, right in the middle of this year's Conference, where I'm already speaking on the Wednesday to Age Concern and then from the platform on Thursday, so even without opening my mouth at Conference I would have a column inch or two. They asked if I'd like to be PM and I said no, in all honesty I wouldn't like it; I guess I'd like to be leader, but that's different – the sheer scale of the PM's job is terrifying. Anyway I doubt if anyone would ask, but I do hate it when the media speculate – it reminds me of the Northfield by-election[2] and I didn't get that either. When I look at the children (Debbie home this weekend), I feel that they are my best work and always will be; and I've no doubt that whatever I may do, Susie in particular will do more and

1. A television programme.
2. In 1982, EC failed to be adopted to succeed Jocelyn Cadbury as Conservative candidate for Birmingham Northfield.

better. So my task in life is to do my best for them, and to do my duty for everything else.

Someone with his eye firmly on the leadership is John Moore, who made a strong speech on social security and getting away from the welfare state this week. There's a naivety about him, and an arrogant intolerance, that comes from a man of not excessive ability in a hurry. One adjective I should *not* use to describe him is 'wily' – but Baker is and so is John Major. Hurd wants it too, but he's *so* boring. Moore will come up against what Boyson[1] called the 'dog and bone' syndrome – you can't take a bone from a dog that's already eating. There are only three groups/benefits Moore can tackle: pensioners (but they paid, and there are ten million of them), child benefit (but the Tory ladies like it) and the disabled (he hasn't encountered them yet. Just watch!). Let it be recorded that the origin of his thinking is Charles Murray's *Losing Ground*, sent to him after the election by Keith Joseph. If Moore were the brains he thinks he is, he'd have read it before – it was published three years ago. The same goes for me too, of course! The book is fascinating and devastatingly accurate in its view of why more welfare makes things worse, particularly in its destruction of the status rewards of being respectable, law-abiding, etc. Chilling reading. Where it's hopeless is in suggesting what to do about it. Just abolishing the system won't work – and in a democracy it requires a vote or two in a free Parliament to do that. Well, we shall see.

There was an interesting discussion about diaries on Radio 4 yesterday. Why have I started this one? Because I need someone to talk to; because I have a ringside seat and I'd eventually like to share my view of events, if only with myself when I'm a self-indulgent ninety-year-old, or with my daughters or grand-daughters, if they are

---

1. Sir Rhodes Boyson, Conservative MP for Brent North and a former Minister of State.

interested. And because history only exists if it is recorded, so I have something of a duty to put down facts – otherwise the wrong person gets the credit or the blame.

Spoke to B this evening – I'm so glad he was in. Oddly enough, I need the diary more now that he's so busy. I wonder if it will start to fade? It's so hard when I don't see him. Still, I've thought that every year and we're still at it. Maybe he feels the same way – he said this evening that he enjoys our chats. It feels somewhat disloyal discussing my boss with him, as clearly they are rivals, but oddly it does not feel disloyal to be involved with a man who isn't my husband! If I didn't phone B, then it would stop. But I don't want it to.

Victoria, Monday 5 October, 8 p.m.

Writing this quickly before Ray comes in. We had a weekend minus children, which was very enjoyable. On Thursday night I spoke to Ray on the phone, and he told me that he had something to talk about. It turns out he's going to leave Arthur Andersen & Co. after twenty years, because he has got fed up with the partners who supervise him (who have been promoted over his head mostly). In my view they treated him very badly by not making him a partner. He'll be better off elsewhere – but asked for 'no advice for six or seven weeks', and then told me he needs to lose 3 stone! I wonder whether he will get himself in hand? He said himself he's the wrong side of forty (forty-two in fact), but currently he looks over fifty and will be competing for jobs with people half his age. Anyway, I'll do whatever I can to help, and that includes spending as much time as possible with him, so we'll drive up to Blackpool[1] together tomorrow and perhaps leave other fields fallow for the moment, perhaps for good.

---

1. The 1987 Conservative Party Conference was being held in Blackpool in this week.

I need to concentrate my energies on a limited number of objectives: doing my job well and looking after, and encouraging Ray, in what will be a most difficult time for him, and I doubt if I will have much energy for – or need of – anything else.

Victoria, Sunday 11 October, midnight

A short entry tonight; I'm beat. I drove down via Lord Hesketh's extraordinary house[1] in Towcester where I spoke at a 'Patron's Club' meeting: I was expecting something very grand as the invite came via David Smith at Conservative Central Office, but the only grand thing was Alexander in black tie, and his magnificent house. Otherwise it was standard local Tory stuff and not that well attended. I had to stand on a stool and kept losing my heels in it – felt badly as it was a lovely old embroidered thing – but they insisted. Also discovered yesterday that I've lost my cheque book (presumably at Blackpool) which is a real nuisance – can't pay cleaning ladies, will have to phone bank, etc.

Conference was great, one of the best I've been to. John Moore's speech was disappointing in the end – there was so little 'claptrap' in it that the audience's attention wandered. The story about Moore's trying to change the Social Fund was in the *Guardian* on Wednesday. Every word true, of course. It was put under my nose at breakfast TV and I wasn't going to say so; but it named a civil servant who was leaving the department, so I implied that the story could have come from him, a disgruntled employee. Now the Permanent Secretary is cross that I have been impugning the honour of one of his staff who (it turns out) is going to the City on secondment only. Please will I apologise? Well, certainly old boy. But I'm not too pleased at having

---

1. Easton Neston; Lord (Alexander) Hesketh was active in Conservative Party politics and was a Government whip.

to lie on behalf of my boss, who should have been more clued up in the first place.

Victoria, Wednesday 28 October, late

The week before Parliament reassembled was exceptionally busy, and I could hardly speak for tiredness at the end. On the Tuesday (13th – my birthday) I travelled up to Oxford for 'Look After Your Heart' – with yet another grotty meal of cold bean sprouts and vinegar – this time I protested and at least got some meat – plastic ham; and challenged them to produce a hot meal next time. The journalists all cheered! Anyway, we had super cover in the local press next day. Then on to Oxford Union that evening for debate, 'That the Labour Party is irrelevant to the 1990s', proposed by Bill Rodgers[1] (mechanical) and me (first time there in nineteen years – and it hasn't changed at all, but better now – more kids, more enthusiasm). Opposed by Ken Livingstone[2] and Paul Boateng,[3] both fine speakers, Boateng especially – with his upmarket background he fits the Oxford Union perfectly. We lost, but gallantly, 380 to 281: in my day we'd have lost hands down. It was packed and exciting, with kids hanging from the chandeliers. David Ashby[4] told me later that his daughter was present and the general view among the students was that it was 'splendid'. Livingstone stuck to 'We must persist, the voters will understand eventually', but Boateng went for 'We must listen to the electorate'. Ambitious and able, he. They missed the last train back (the debate started late), so I offered them a lift in the official car on condition they didn't gas all the way home.

1. Co-founder of the Social Democratic Party; formerly a Labour MP and minister.
2. Labour MP for Brent East; formerly Leader of the Greater London Council.
3. Labour MP for Brent South.
4. Conservative MP for North-West Leicestershire.

The following day was an early train to Leeds, then late-night drive over the Pennines to Lancashire, stayed in Nelson, opened a square crumpet factory. 'These are designer croompets,' the owner kept saying. It reminded me of Willy Wonka's chocolate factory and I was helpless with laughter most of the time, but the owner and John Lee,[1] the local MP, were serious and anxious. I do have fun! Visited a private home for severely handicapped adults in Barnoldswick (pronounced Barlick – 'To rhyme with garlic?' I said brightly to one resident. 'Ay?' she said.). I escaped at 2 p.m. and went for a quick walk around the town: it was all dinky terraced housing, built for an age when life and people were shorter. We went into the village school and the head proudly showed us round: lovely children, shy and sweet-natured, loved and cared for with good staff, but no reading, no written work on the walls, no maths, no science. All we saw were children playing. Even the craftwork was unprepossessing – all as if designed by a robot, with similar bits of silver paper stuck on in the same places. They don't realise how they encourage conformity and discourage initiative. It seemed to be functioning barely above the level of a good playgroup.

The week Parliament returned was also busy. I've started clearing the diary and cancelling outside things with a vengeance. I'm booked in for far too many events: I'm everyone's favourite after-dinner speaker. I grind my teeth when I realise the others may well be picking up a fee of £1000 for doing the same job!

Questions today went well – almost too well. I had a lot, and to my horror the Speaker decided to plough on and they got faster and faster, so I was bobbing up and down on Bridlington, maternity, physiotherapy in Birmingham, ambulances in London, etc. – all done pat, of course, to everyone's amusement. They started to cheer

1. Conservative MP for Pendle; Parliamentary Under-Secretary of State for Employment.

as I answered our James Cran,[1] and then the Speaker called the PM for her questions. James protested that he hadn't had his supplementary, so the Speaker made the PM sit down again and called me again – very embarrassing and very funny really (though I doubt if *She* was amused. She's always uptight at Questions). When she got to her feet at last, Dale Campbell-Savours[2] shouted, 'No, we want the new leader'. I think God was teasing me, but it was fun.

Two adjournment debates this week, then Robin Day and *Question Time* on Thursday. Ray is home most of the week with the girls for half term, but I'm too busy for anything else anyway. The field lies fallow, whether I like it or not . . .

Victoria, Sunday 8 November, 10.35 p.m.

I'm in London to have breakfast tomorrow morning with a group of American ladies – looked like fun to do. Came up on 6.37 p.m. train – very crowded, you'd think British Rail would put more coaches on but no, they designed them for eight coaches so that's what we get, full or empty. Now, I would rather enjoy running BR! At least this time they didn't close the buffet early, maybe because I was on the train – they know I complain if they don't give a good service. Then I had a silly row with the government car service driver who came to get me. Normally my driver waits on the platform and helps with bags, etc., but he's not on duty on Sundays (ninety-five hours a week is quite enough), so it's always someone I don't know, in a different car. The only clue is, nobody else drives Montegos these days! Last time I couldn't find the geezer at all and the police drove me home; this time he was waiting on a different platform because that's what the indicator said (the platform had a

---

1. Conservative MP for Beverley.
2. Labour MP for Workington.

mail train on it). He doesn't use his head! I could go by taxi but I'm skint, and I could go by Tube but I'm scared. Even though I'd much prefer the freedom from jams and the cheapness, going by Tube is difficult and a bit dangerous, especially alone. I was jumpy this evening; a big bomb went off in Enniskillen and killed a lot of people on a Remembrance Day parade. The pictures on TV were awful, mostly old people, many injured. We have to be so bloody careful – you need a very deep commitment to democracy to keep at it.

I did Remembrance Day in Chellaston[1] this morning; nice, rather old-fashioned Royal British Legion, short march, nice service in very old St Peter's church (packed) and only a short time outdoors which was a blessing; but no band, so it felt very low key. Golly, I am lucky to represent such nice, good, ordinary people in such a lovely place.

PM announced Peter Brooke[2] as party chairman on Monday. 'Peter who?' seems the main response, but I've had contact with him, first as Parliamentary Under-Secretary at Education, when we saw him about having a polytechnic in Derby; and then when he was on the Ministerial Group for Drugs, as Treasury minister. He's nice, bright, friendly, self-effacing: thoroughly likeable and utterly forgettable. If his Daddy hadn't been Home Secretary he wouldn't be a minister. I'm mostly relieved, and not surprised, that I wasn't asked (the *Guardian* and other papers had flights of fancy about it). Firstly, I'm OK where I am, and doing useful work. Secondly, whatever my talents for rabble-rousing, they are not needed at the beginning of a Parliament. Thirdly, though I'm a good organiser and get things done, they don't know that (yet), and fourthly, I have no business contacts and the main part of the job at present is raising donations. I don't envy Peter his task at Party Conference, following

1. A suburb of Derby.
2. Conservative MP for City of London and Westminster South; formerly Minister of State at the Treasury and Paymaster-General; son of Henry Brooke, Home Secretary under Harold Macmillan.

Norman Tebbit (who can't seem to make up his mind whether he has left frontbench politics or not). The job will destroy him as it did Gummer,[1] so I'm very glad it's him and not me.

Ray was somewhat downcast last week and this weekend, and left to go home on Wednesday afternoon. He's been going home on Thursday for some time; running away from the job and problems here isn't a good habit. He's now looking regularly at job ads, but not yet applied for any. At least he's getting some good advice, e.g. from Charles Theaker (Shirley's[2] husband, a head-hunter) and he will see Caroline Portillo (Michael's wife, another head-hunter) tomorrow. He needs a job paying around £35,000 plus car to pay the bills; after 1 January my salary, including the living allowance, will be over £40,000. I asked him if he minded that I earned more – he has teased me about this for seventeen years – and he said no, but it can't be easy. If men knew how it hurt to be put into an inferior position like that, they wouldn't tease, so I shan't. But we have over £80,000 coming in now, and still can't manage. I have so little attachment to goods I would sell the car (I did in '71 to raise a deposit and again in '74), and I'd move home, but Ray has got himself attached to that huge leaky old house in Findern which we really can't afford. The children's schooling comes first in my view: everything else is secondary, though I would dearly love to have money in the bank instead of *endless* overdrafts. It has occurred to me that no sooner will the girls have finished college than we'll be paying for old people's homes – my mother is likely to outlive all of us! – and when we've done that, we'll have retired. So much for enjoying the fruits of hard work.

I think we've broken the smoking culture: biographies now mention whether someone is a smoker as a weakness of character,

---

1. John Selwyn Gummer, Minister of State at the Ministry of Agriculture, Fisheries and Food since 1985; Conservative Party chairman, 1983–5; Conservative MP for Suffolk Coastal.
2. Shirley Theaker, EC's constituency secretary.

whereas not long ago, 'nonsmoker' was synonymous with 'fanatic'. Nice to be on a moving bandwagon. I got headlines this week at a Royal College of Nursing conference when I had a go at nurses smoking. I had agreed this beforehand with Trevor Clay, the General Secretary, who feels strongly about it and has tried more than once to have an RCN 'no smoking' policy. This time he'll succeed. The other reason for doing it was as a smokescreen: it stopped them talking about pay quite effectively, and in fact the speech – which also covered stress, nurse management, status, etc., – was well received.

Only seen John Moore briefly this week: no meeting on Monday as he was preparing for the Second Reading of the Social Security Bill that day, and no meeting Wednesday – no reason given. But as I see his comments on policy papers he goes down in my estimation. I don't think he understands the NHS, its scale, its problems. He failed to get enough capital for the breast cancer programme, and has been sending out petulant memos saying that with a £1 billion capital programme it should be easy for the Regional Health Authorities to find the money needed. But that £1 billion is already committed.

Moore wants the NHS actively to compete with the private sector (why? Seems illogical to me). Tony and I have both pointed out that this will bring criticism from enemies and friends, but in another petulant little note he says it's the scheme he wants. So much for working as a team. Perhaps like many people from a very difficult background he is so insecure that praise and glory are all he wants to hear. B is very critical of him too, and gave me to understand that Moore could have had more money in the recent PES round[1] if he'd boxed cleverer. B was on good form, both talking and everything else – I am *very* lucky, and we agreed to carry on: the information is fascinating! One piece of good news: Michael Portillo

---

1. Public Expenditure Survey round, when Government money is allocated for the coming year.

and I (and Lord Skelmersdale[1]) are to have a PPS. We've chosen David Amess.[2] He's nice, bright, friendly and sensible. Only problem – he's anti-abortion. I asked the ladies at Duffield on Friday night how they felt about David Alton's Bill[3] and they didn't like it: nice middle-aged Tory ladies!

I've been writing for an hour and must stop – need to look at papers for tomorrow.

Victoria, Sunday 29 November, 6.30 p.m.

Surprised to find it's three weeks since I did my diary. A lot has happened, particularly in last two weeks, of which most important is that John Moore keeled over with pneumonia (bacterial) two weeks ago. After much press comment and speculation about mystery illnesses he came out of hospital on the Thursday and was back at work Monday, looking flushed and wheezing and rubbing his heart. On Tuesday morning he flaked out – at Number 10, if you please, during a discussion about nurses' pay. That can't have pleased the PM too much! Much tea-room sniggering over whether she gave him the kiss of life, etc. It explains a lot, including his generally lacklustre performance recently; and if he's got any sense (which I am now beginning to doubt) he'll be off till after Xmas. I sent flowers on 17 November and we all sent a Fortnum's hamper for his birthday on 26 November; fruit naturally.

It has been a ghastly week for the Government on the NHS. The District Health Authorities have done their sums, the Regional Health Authority chairmen met us in Cambridge the previous Wednesday when we outlined PES to them, and everyone is feeling

---

1. Parliamentary Under-Secretary of State, Department of Health and Social Security.
2. Conservative MP for Basildon.
3. The Liberal MP David Alton was sponsoring a Bill to restrict abortions.

very pessimistic. We've been given £700 million next year, 1.7 per cent in real terms, and it's nowhere enough. We now spend 5.2 per cent of GDP (net) on the NHS, 5.9 per cent if private care is counted: one of the lowest percentages in the developed world. When I was preparing a speech ten days ago for the Healthcare Financial Management Association (erstwhile treasurers) I naturally assumed the percentage was rising; to my amazement no, it's due to go down to 5.1 per cent by 1990. So I thought, sod it, I bet Moore intended that, and everyone should know: so I said it, and it was picked up by Nick Timmins, the bright lad who writes for the *Independent*, and now they do. On Thursday during the debate I was checking with officials in the Box[1] (the Press Office had backed off and said the remarks were 'unscripted' which is crap. I wish they would stop apologising for me). I asked them, wouldn't it be possible to negotiate PES the other way round? Instead of starting with this year's budget and then hassling over additions, why not start with the figure we thought we should be aiming at, e.g. 5.5 per cent of GDP, and make comparisons with other countries? Yes, they said, we did suggest that to Secretary of State but . . . How very interesting. We should like to boast that we fund the NHS better than everyone else: yet the Secretary of State wants to be macho by *not* pleading for more money. At the same time demand for health care has had a hefty hike recently, as transplantation is so successful, as new anaesthesia makes surgery safe even for the frail, and as we head for 4½ million over seventy-five. I know (and said it in debate) that there's no cash figure which is 'enough', but I suspect there are some years, e.g. 1985–7, when it is closer to 'enough' and others like now when the gap is widening. The crux of the row this week was over a hole-in-the-heart baby in Birmingham who had his op cancelled five times, because of lack of intensive care nurses. Fortunately, some

---

1. The seat behind the Speaker, occupied by civil servants.

came back off sick leave and he was done on Wednesday, but it's an old story at Birmingham and Leeds and many other places – they don't train enough specialised nurses, then they don't manage them properly, so they get tired and disillusioned and clear off. They had the same problem at Birmingham ten years ago, of children being refused admission: then the Intensive Therapy Unit was full of kids with whooping cough, dying. In ten years' time it could be AIDS or God knows what: but it will be something.

And so to the PM, of whom I've seen a lot this week. Lunch at Number 10 on Monday (23 November): five Cabinet ministers (Whitelaw, Young,[1] Wakeham, PM and Waddington,[2] with Peter Brooke) and one Minister of State (Ian Stewart, Defence, who hardly got a word in) and four Parliamentary Under-Secretaries (Richard Needham, Northern Ireland; Colin Moynihan, Sport; John Lee, Employment – also fairly silent; and me). Archie Hamilton, her PPS, was at the far end of the table. Mostly she went *on* about the NHS and how we are going to have to reform it quicker than expected, in this Parliament. She did not specify what she had in mind but she's wide open to the ideas of people like John Redwood[3] and David Willetts[4] (blond prat), all young, fit, wealthy and ignorant, and, where they're not wealthy yet, at least trying to forget their poor past. Some of the ideas are inconsistent, e.g. why not pay hospitals per operation and then they'll have to be efficient? (This is like the diagnostic system in the USA, which has resulted in the wholesale sacking of nurses.) But Prime Minister, I ventured, we do that with dentists now; it does not guarantee efficiency, it discourages

---

1. Lord Young, Secretary of State for Trade and Industry.
2. David Waddington, government Chief Whip since 1987; Conservative MP for Ribble Valley.
3. Conservative MP for Wokingham.
4. Director of Studies, Centre for Policy Studies; and Consultant Director, Research Department.

prevention and it conflicts with the cash limit controls. I think she's after a 'money follows the patient' idea; certainly you could use a voucher system for a few limited things, but God help the bureaucracy if we did it on a grand scale. Anyway it doesn't *by itself* create more resources, and if we're not careful it just means a drain of NHS money into the private sector. She also told me gaily that you can't prevent a heart attack, to which I said, 'Well, they did in the USA, and strokes', so she changed the subject. Maybe she realised she was talking nonsense. She also said at lunch that all the world leaders have low blood pressure; she herself has low blood pressure. I said those with high blood pressure keeled over years ago. As it happens, she felt faint the following evening at Buckingham Palace and had to go home early.

Meanwhile there are genuine souls like Tony Newton, slaving away, teeth gritted, on proposals to charge everyone through the nose for their teeth, and defending the Government's handling of the NHS against the screaming mob which is the modern House of Commons (doesn't bother me, I just shout back). As he sat next to me on the bench three times this week, he reeked of cigarettes, and of that strange mixture of sweat and fear of a man *in extremis*. I hope he doesn't keel over too, but then I thought he might in '86 when we were together on Social Security Bill, all two hundred hours of it, and he not only recovered but found time to get married.

And then the PM turned up for my speech closing the debate on Thursday. Some surprise. Kinnock[1] and pals were at the premiere of Richard Attenborough's film on Steve Biko,[2] so maybe she decided to show them up. She acted like my whip during the debate; listening to Harriet Harman[3] drone on, she said, 'You'll make mincemeat of

---

1. Neil Kinnock, leader of the Labour Party; MP for Islwyn.
2. *Cry Freedom.*
3. Labour spokesman on Health; MP for Peckham.

her', and then during the speech I could hear, 'Four minutes left. They've pinched your time . . . Two minutes. Keep going. Speak to the mike', etc. I wore a white wool suit which we bought in Paris a while back and an emerald shirt, and I was gunning for them. The speech read better in *Hansard* than I expected, although my timing was thrown to the winds. Having to shout gave me a real sore throat next day, but we survived, with an unexpectedly large majority of over 120.

Tower House, Friday 25 December

Life got even more 'exciting' after my last entry. On the Monday evening (30 November) we had the Second Reading of the Health and Medicines Bill. Bits and pieces, but we are charging for dental and optical tests for the first time. Partly to raise revenue to do other good works and to bribe GPs to be more efficient, and partly to repay the Treasury some very large sums which were promised by Norman Fowler several years ago. He left some important back-dated cheques around – only they really were backdated, the money goes to the Treasury. Some wheeler-dealer. I had to do the closing speech and this time I timed it beautifully, got in my closing punch line – 'The opticians earn over £30,000 per year. We think they'll compete to give free eye tests. And financially, we think they'll manage.' Jill Knight,[1] whose late husband was an optician, has made a terrible fuss about the eye tests, just as she did about the ending of free specs in 1984, but she was very cross with the opticians on the phone the next day after hearing this, and was relatively easily per-suaded not to serve on the Bill committee. Since then Tony Newton has written an excellent 'Dear Colleague' letter explaining what we

1. Dame Jill Knight, the long-serving Conservative MP for Birmingham Edgbaston.

are up to, and I don't think we'll have too much trouble in committee. There were a dozen abstentions on a two-line whip, none against: not a real rebellion, unlike the row over the community charge last week, with a dozen against on a three-line whip, including Ted Heath. He complained that the PM treats dissenters as 'scum', but I don't think he gives her the chance to do much else. And his little army were all 'has beens' and 'never weres'.

The rest of the week was ghastly for me. Tuesday night was Consolidated Fund Bill – all through the night – with debates on the NHS at 3.30 a.m. and 5 a.m. Then I had the adjournment debate that night, and another on Friday. I managed to do SE Thames RHA review as well, and prepare for Cheshire FPC review. Very difficult discussions, partly because I was tired, partly because I knew Tony was deep in conversation with John Major about money. I had told Major that matters were serious, that half the DHAs were in trouble and that it was going to get worse. Tony confirmed this to me again, that John Moore would not increase the bid, even though he knew that £707 million more would be very tight. Mr Moore called it 'the bloody NHS' when he talked about it at ministers' meeting on Monday. He is still not well, and would in my humble judgement have got better quicker with some decent treatment at Bart's on the NHS! Willie Whitelaw had what was called a 'mild stroke' and was treated at the Westminster on the NHS, but then Willie has nothing to prove and (at sixty-nine) far more to fear than our Secretary of State, who is, I am rapidly concluding, a fool and a prig, and intellectually not up to the job.

Well, we got more money – £100 million extra for this year – and in fact it was more than that, for £44 million due to be 'paid back' was set aside. The deal was done by two wets, Major and Newton. No more for next year, though: on that basis I would not have accepted it, as they will reopen the wards only to close them again in July. Most of the Health Authorities have neither the foresight nor the courage to close whole hospitals. Knowing that the PM wanted 'no more closures', I'd have reopened the PES agreement and dug out another £250 million. Or at least I would have tried – or like to think I would. It has been a really nasty few weeks and I don't want to live through it all again, but I fear this 'patching up' – a typical Tony Newton exercise – will simply mean it happens again next year.

Christmas at home. I don't like Christmas. There's too much of it, and I don't believe it: the paganism, the rebirth in the depths of winter, etc. B asked me what I believe (I was in the bath!) and I said I had religion and ritual stuffed down my throat when I was a kid and want no more of it, don't like priests and set words; don't go to church unless it's a special occasion, and communion makes me feel left out; it's an exclusion device. And the message is important, but not more important than the messenger – claiming he's God just distorts it, distracts people from what he was trying to say. The commercialism always makes me nauseous. Long ago I did a 'deal' with the kids: no presents, but I'll take them to the sales afterwards. I did the works – turkey, etc., and we cleared the table in the study and ate there. Debbie is so gorgeous now, really beautiful: she'd like to have a go at part-time modelling and she is the right shape, so I'll see what we can do when she's a bit older – it would certainly be more lucrative than working in Boots as I did! Susie has exams for Denstone in March and is working well at school; her report was excellent for her, she shows considerable promise, but neither of them work with real drive. They don't need to like I did.

Ray still isn't settled and managed to reduce me to tears after the meal when I said '87 had been a good year. He said it had been a terrible year for him, with a broken neck most of the year and likely to be in pain all his life. He hurt his neck (not broken) in March when he went to Spain to play golf with his mates and got knocked about in a car crash; and then he invited one of them and his girlfriend on our holiday in Paris at Easter. I was livid and very upset (B said I was right), mostly because he had been claiming he had so little time and money. It transpired he paid £300 in a sub to the Reform Club earlier this year so he could play snooker with the same bunch. They are all divorced and drink a bit too much and leave their children at home with their wives. So forgive me if I'm not too sympathetic. I said I hoped '88 would be a better year for him, trying to conciliate, and he'd have the job he wanted, well paid and enjoyable. 'I've got the job I want,' he said belligerently. 'I just want a change. So don't lecture me.' Well, I can't talk to him now. Not that I ever could. Makes me so sad inside. All I want is arms round me and a cuddle and some encouragement: and I don't get it from him. God bless B. I hope he is having a good Xmas.

Tower House, Wednesday 30 December, 11.40 p.m.

Things have been quiet this week, partly because the department packed up on 22 December for the move to Richmond Terrace.[1] Much criticism of us moving to decent premises (cost nearly £40 million), but oh, they should try working in that wasteland at the Elephant & Castle. John Moore said last week that he blamed that building for our illnesses; I remarked that maybe the volume of work had something to do with it (both Ministers of State with bad colds, Michael Portillo had one too and I was shaky), but John said no, 'that kind of remark irritated him'. Prat. There's a frailty about him, and he seems to look after himself out of necessity. When you sit close to Nigel Lawson there's a vigour, a sensuality about him: but John Moore has the air of a delicate boy; he moves carefully, he

---

1. The DHSS was moving from Elephant & Castle to Richmond Terrace, just across Whitehall from Downing Street.

conserves energy and yet he gets very tired easily (he was beat by October). Perhaps it is not surprising, considering his terrible childhood. It could explain why he's so small – not much taller than me.

Some work has popped up, however. We have a continuing fuss about the gypsy site in Chellaston. Goodness knows why we didn't repeal the 1968 Caravans Act – there are now ten thousand approved places. I have two sites in South Derbyshire and I don't want three. In all honesty I have no sympathy for these layabouts and was pleased to see the steady way local people have taken on the fight. David Bookbinder[1] called me a racist which made everyone *very* angry; even the local paper, which tends to be Labour, said we get a better class of protester in Chellaston! I phoned Nick Ridley's[2] office and got back the most officious letter from Marion Roe[3] saying he would intervene only in exceptional circumstances. She didn't even bother having a word with me, even though she has the room next to mine in Star Chamber Court. And she has been nagging me daft for a year about her local hospital. Not impressed. The letter has gone back with a message saying it won't do.

1. Labour leader of Derbyshire County Council.
2. Secretary of State for the Environment; Conservative MP for Cirencester and Tewkesbury.
3. Parliamentary Under-Secretary of State, Department of Environment; Conservative MP for Broxbourne.

1988

Tower House, Sunday 24 January, midnight

Sitting up in bed doing this; Ray has driven down to London tonight. It's been a beautiful spring-like day, sunny and mild. I went for a long splashy muddy run down by the canal this morning. That feeling when you slide into a hot bath afterwards is simply fantastic. It had snowed on Friday and we were all set to be snowed in; I had a five-hour journey from London to get to Shropshire for *Any Questions*, then another miserable two hours on slushy roads to get home, but when we woke up today it had all gone.

One of the questions was about the Liberal Assembly's decision to vote for a merger with the SDP. Quite extraordinary how easily they kissed goodbye to their party after such a long history, and with so little on offer. After all, there are still seventeen Liberals in Parliament; it was the SDP that was massacred in the last election, with only three million votes to the Liberals' seven million; and the five SDP MPs are split several ways. Maclennan went round to David Owen's house and begged him to join them; Owen threw him out after five minutes! Then Maclennan confessed to the press that he'd wept over the whole business. The truth is that the Liberals hang out to the left and the SDP to the right: they won't see eye to eye on policies, and without Owen they don't have a strong leader. His future will be interesting. I saw him in the middle of the week with Rosie Barnes,[1] looking as pleased as punch. We hope he'll put fifty

1. Rosemary Barnes, SDP MP for Greenwich.

candidates into the fray next time to take votes from Labour (hope one of them will be here in South Derbyshire), so we are being nice to him, apparently. How are the mighty fallen.

But the main story since Parliament came back has been more hassle over the NHS. There's an inter-union battle for membership going on between NUPE, COHSE and RCN, and so out they came on strike from Manchester, and now they are threatening further 'action' on 3 February. This will be a lively year – they are spoiling for a fight in the frustration after the election. It has all the feel of the miners' strike in 1984. And they have cause. We met the RHA chairmen in Eastbourne for one of our regular meetings on Wednesday: they are expecting bed closures of around *six thousand* this year. Moore said, 'That was a most useful discussion. I do find these discussions valuable. Thank you for your interesting contribution.' Don Wilson[1] stared at him in undisguised fury. Tony went white. And I was heard to say, 'Jesus Christ'.

B came round on the 14th. Still marvellous. Aren't I lucky!

I'd better put down my role in all this. It became apparent during the first ten days back that John Moore just didn't know what to do. He looks OK, but his speech in yet another Opposition day debate was not well received. He almost broke down in the middle. After the Eastbourne meeting I asked Tony what was happening; the answer was, 'Not a lot'. Poor John has been unable to put a foot right recently. He met the Presidents of the Royal Colleges, and soothed them by announcing 'action to increase the resources for health care'; this was misunderstood, so he faced headlines saying that he was giving more money to the NHS. She was furious, his name was mud, and John Major stamped on it the following day in the debate on the Autumn Statement. Then he tells the *Telegraph* he's interested

1. Sir Donald Wilson, chairman of Mersey Regional Health Authority.

in tax relief for BUPA subscriptions – which got reported as 'Moore on collision course with Maggie' – and she ruled *that* out in public too.

So I asked my friend in Treasury what he would do, and he said we should get a position statement drawn up across the country, with a careful and rigorous estimate of what's needed. Then Moore should present it to her with an ultimatum, with the clear intention of buying time. I phoned Chris France[1] late at night and told him what was suggested. It is, of course, a deep secret that it comes from our sympathetic friends in the Treasury! Anyway, the suggestion was such plain common sense that I 'bagged' it and added some ideas of my own. As it happens, I had reason to return a call from Trevor Clay of the RCN. They have asked to see the PM, so I suggested they draw up the same kind of report for her. It won't have identical figures, but it should show the same trend. Anyway our data collection is so poor that we can't contradict them, and the PM thinks the RCN are goodies because they are refusing to strike.

What else have I done? Well, I've made sure the Treasury know the position, quietly; John Moore doesn't know, though Tony realises I'm doing some informal briefing. For example, I gave my notes from Eastbourne to our friend. The Chancellor wrote a very helpful minute to Number 10 outlining schemes he could support in very measured tones, and without a 'secret' classification. Everyone in Cabinet is giving his opinion: Geoffrey Howe made a speech on Friday about the NHS, Norman Fowler spoke on Radio 4 yesterday morning most authoritatively, with just a hint of a gloat in his voice. He's getting his own back for the nasty things John Moore said about him when he first came in. Moore is like a grey ghost at the moment.

---

1. Christopher France, Permanent Secretary, Department of Health and Social Security.

I don't think he'll last. Certainly he faces a tough time, even more so after Easter as the social security reforms come in. We shall see!

Victoria, Friday 29 January

It's getting harder to do this even on a weekly basis and try to remember what happened each day, there's so much going on. Since I left home on Monday I've clocked over ninety hours' work – and I'm expecting still more over the weekend, as we have the debate on the Warnock Report next Thursday and I've never read it, let alone the White Paper.

So let's start with Monday morning, on the platform at 7.45 at Derby, opening the *Daily Telegraph*, where there's an NHS story on the front page (there always is, these days). And it says John Moore is pulling things together, and Tony Newton is doing very well, and yours truly is regarded as not pulling her weight. I was both surprised and angry. Just for the record, since October I've done over 3000 yellowjackets (Private Office letters), seen 17 delegations, done 1000 written Parliamentary Questions, taken part in 5 major debates (and since I started in October 1986, 43 adjournment debates). At a Downing Street lunch on Wednesday Peter Lilley,[1] whom I can't stand – real 'Dr Fell' stuff – was boasting about how much he gets involved in policy making. I asked him about the adjournment debates, etc., and he admitted that he'd done only one. I told him my total and his mouth fell open! Oh yes, and the MPs' letters are rolling in, at a rate of 350–400 per week. I have a backlog (mostly post-November, and partly because of moving office) of 2500. Michael Portillo's is one thousand. They are all in the typing pool, where the typists are working till 9 p.m. and on

---

1. Economic Secretary to the Treasury; Conservative MP for St Albans.

Saturdays! So I hauled in the office manager, told her to get some agency staff, and gave her a fortnight to clear them. The only problem is how I'm going to sign two thousand letters in the next fortnight . . . Anyway, to this stupid story. I went into John's office, waved the *Daily Telegraph* at him and said, 'Is this your considered opinion?' and he says, 'Isn't it terrible what the press are doing? They've been treating me so badly.' I nearly thumped him. Tony was off sick that day, but later in the week, when I mentioned that I was still hurt and livid, he said all the right things, bless him – and typically he hadn't even seen it.

But things have certainly been moving. What JM wanted from me on Monday was encouragement, not a moan on my own account. Immediately after 'Prayers'[1] he was to go to Downing Street to thump the table, and tell her to stop messing about: he was the only one who could reform the NHS, no one else in Cabinet could or would, he was her only chance. 'I'm going to be angry this time,' he said, 'or else . . .' but didn't specify. I wondered then and since whether he would have offered to resign, but no hints. It's too dangerous to do that; in her current volatile mood she might just accept! Anyway I saw him later that evening and he was very chipper – leaned across, grinned and said, 'I got what we wanted today – the lot!' Subsequently we were told via Ingham[2] (i.e. on the front pages again) that there's to be a full review of the NHS, apparently to be supervised by a Cabinet committee chaired by the PM, with Lawson, Major, Moore and Newton (not enough), with 'no holds barred' – including backtracking on election pledges against hospital charges and charging for GPs. Uproar. So on Thursday at Question Time she

1. Monday and Wednesday morning departmental meetings attended by the entire ministerial team, including PPSs and political advisers, and others by invitation, often preceded by departmental meeting of civil servants.
2. Bernard Ingham, the Prime Minister's Press Secretary.

makes it clear that election pledges stay, and no major changes will take place till after the next election (i.e. until they have been trailed in the manifesto). Trying to puzzle it out, Tony and I reckoned that we are allowed to think about and discuss any changes, but some things we can't do in this Parliament. All very confusing; Ingham says we'll have a consultative document by summer, then we hear it's a White Paper at the end of the year, then she says the review will take most of this Parliament. Frankly, I don't think they know what they want, except votes and less trouble.

The Number 10 lunch followed an hour and a half's discussion: all Parliamentary Under-Secretaries (including Lords); whips; Lord Young sitting at her right hand, David Waddington on her left, Robin Butler[1] and Nigel Wicks[2] in attendance, no other senior minders. I was embarrassed to find she and I had similar suits in the same bright blue; I sat on the second row of green velvet chairs. Peter Bottomley[3] sat in the middle of the front row and argued with her, somewhat incoherently but good-naturedly, about the Civil Service. Robert Jackson,[4] sitting elegantly right in front of me, asked a muddled question about the restrictive practices of professions, then spoiled it by having a go at the police. Tim Sainsbury[5] surprised me by asking a silly question about how junior ministers don't get involved enough in decision taking, the Civil Service runs everything. 'Nonsense,' she said. 'You go and see the Permanent Secretary.' I thought of Chris France and Michael Partridge[6] in our office: that's

1. Sir Robin Butler, Secretary of the Cabinet and Head of the Home Service.
2. The PM's Principal Private Secretary.
3. Parliamentary Under-Secretary of State, Department of Transport; Conservative MP for Eltham.
4. Parliamentary Under-Secretary of State, Department of Education and Science; Conservative MP for Wantage.
5. Hon. Timothy Sainsbury, Parliamentary Under-Secretary of State for Defence Procurement; Conservative MP for Hove.
6. Second Permanent Secretary, Department of Health and Social Security.

not how I do it, they come to me! Patrick Nicholls,[1] now rather handsomely going grey, surprised us all by arguing that we had to buy time for the NHS and put in more money. She tried doing her 'Space Invaders' act, but just like the little ghost he kept popping up again, and she got rather annoyed. Richard Needham,[2] Ian Grist[3] and I had got together beforehand in my office – Michael Forsyth[4] was supposed to come but couldn't – at RN's suggestion to discuss tactics and decided to talk about pay. Grist is so thick that he didn't manage it, but Richard and I had a go, with both of us urging regional pay (which is OK because it's being suggested in our evidence to review bodies for nurses' pay), and I had a go at central bargaining and Whitley Councils.[5] She started hedging about the limited role of the Nurses' and Midwives' Remuneration Board, but I said, 'You started it, Ma'am, and you can change it', and I think she liked that. She's easily flattered but doesn't miss a trick. Peter Lilley wants to abolish the Homeless Persons Act 1977: 'They are all single girls trying to jump the queue and getting pregnant to do it.' I don't think I'd like him as PM. I get the same feeling about John Redwood, who interrupted the adjournment debate on Thursday evening. Those staring eyes, those faces inappropriately young (Lilley is older than me) without smile lines or wrinkles, those unlived-in bodies. Not my kind of people.

On Tuesday I went to Southampton, first to Southampton General Hospital where we discussed breast cancer and cervical screening,

1. Parliamentary Under-Secretary of State, Department of Employment; Conservative MP for Teignbridge.
2. Parliamentary Under-Secretary of State, Northern Ireland Office; Conservative MP for Wiltshire North.
3. Parliamentary Under-Secretary of State, Welsh Office; Conservative MP for Cardiff Central.
4. Parliamentary Under-Secretary of State, Scottish Office; Conservative MP for Stirling.
5. Pay negotiating bodies for public service employees.

then on to the Post House Hotel for a black tie dinner. The unions (and Socialist Workers Party) staged a demo all afternoon: my staff and the security guards, etc., were all very twitchy, but in fact although it was noisy and there was some shoving it really didn't worry me too much: keep smiling! The press were the real menaces as far as I was concerned, as they were shoving and in danger of tripping me up or knocking my eyes out with their cameras. I gather it looked quite nasty on television this evening.[1]

My speech (cleared by Number 10) went down well. And the midnight news was (1) the SDP assembly; (2) EC's speech; (3) John Moore's demo in Portsmouth (smaller than mine); (4) Tony in Epping, and only then (5) the PM!

Victoria, Sunday 7 February, p.m.

Outside it's wet, cold and miserable, but inside it's hot because I left the heat on full blast over the weekend, didn't I? Money to burn, that's us. In fact I came up tonight to do the bills, as the last time was six weeks ago and everyone is sending us red reminders. The East Midlands Electricity Board is threatening to cut us off in Findern, despite the fact that we got into a muddle last time and paid twice, and they overestimated the meter, so now they owe us money. Odd how Ray assumes it's my job to do it, even though he now has more spare time than I do. He's still job chasing, in an alternately desultory and excited way. The firm had its worst accountancy exam results for ten years (i.e. since he took on the responsibility for these), so I imagine it isn't too matey there at present. I wish he'd get settled.

By Tuesday morning nothing had happened about my outstanding letters and I was feeling really fed up, especially as I had a snotty

---

1. In this speech EC outlined some ideas for the future of the NHS, and suggested that better-off patients might contribute to the cost of their treatment.

note from Peter Morrison[1] saying when he went to his department he demanded a turnaround of eight to nine days on correspondence and got it. And I gather he's been moaning elsewhere (e.g. to Nick Scott). Well, that's easy when your whole department gets less mail in a year than I get in a month. I called in Partridge, showed him the letter; he called in Geoffrey Podger, John Moore's Private Secretary, who smarmed around – he's almost the only person in the DHSS who calls me minister – told me how sorry he was, etc., it was all Mary's[2] fault – and then things started moving and they are coming through for signing at three hundred per day. My arm is aching, but I'm determined to shift that lot and beat them into the ground!

The papers being put to the Ministerial Review Group are disappointing – I hope I get a chance to say so, perhaps to one or two brighter friends on it. They seem to be solely concerned with financing methods. No one is attempting to forecast demand, or to look at outcomes, i.e. health, and thus evaluate *input* methods by any reasonable *outcome* measure. If you switch from taxation to insurance, and take into account that in the UK (partly because we have the NHS) the bulk of demand is uninsurable, what progress have you made? Only to increase admin costs and to frighten a lot of people, without improving health. And if you switch to payment by unit of service, to encourage efficiency in the hospitals, you get excessive service, no incentive to save or do prevention, and no control over cost limits and cash limits – or you have an arbitrary cash limit plus queues, as now. If you expand the private sector by giving tax relief on subscriptions, you don't save money, you spend it, and there needs to be some evaluation as to whether that is the best way to spend the extra. For the long-term disabled the incentives at present are to dump them in hospital (no costs) or dispose of assets and

---

1. Deputy chairman of the Conservative Party and Minister of State, Department of Energy. Conservative MP for City of Chester.
2. Mary Grafton, EC's DHSS Private Secretary.

dump in a nursing home (DHSS pays – over £700 million at present). There's no incentive to care for them at home, where allowances are miserable and physical assistance, e.g. nightwatch service, almost nonexistent or very difficult to obtain. Lady Jenny Cooke, whose husband Sir Robert[1] died of motor neurone disease, came to see me recently with a hair-raising tale of mistakes and mismanagement among all the services during the twelve months he took to die, mostly at home. How would changing the financing system help them? Yet if we look at outcomes, we can include prevention and choice and quality of life. That is, in the end, what we are in politics for, not just to employ accountants and quote statistics.

The Southampton speech caused quite a stir and I'm now 'Scotchifying' it for the visit to Glasgow and Edinburgh on 19/20 February. The 'nurses' strike' on Wednesday was a big flop; in the whole country only two hundred operations were cancelled that day and nine thousand were performed, though a couple of London hospitals panicked and cancelled operations for several days. A march down Whitehall with banners was highly nostalgic, right down to the long hair and clenched fists, which upset some of the nurses to the point of tears. A meeting held at St Thomas's and addressed by left-wing Labour MPs was attended mainly by the media – not one of their 3300 staff came out. In Derby they held a lively meeting at the Derby Royal Infirmary and made a lot of declarations, but no action. At the same time we've had a strike at Ford's and by seamen on the ferries and another by NACODS in the pits. The press are speculating that it's a new winter of discontent.[2] After years of decline the unions are picking up membership again. Obviously as unemployment declines – and in some parts of the

---

1. Conservative MP for Bristol West, 1957–74.
2. The winter of 1978–9, the last under a Labour Government, was known as the 'winter of discontent' because of extensive industrial action.

country and in some trades there isn't any unemployment – they want more money. Thatcherites to a man, the working classes: lots couldn't give a damn about the old and sick. Just watch the howls if the Chancellor increases the tax on fags. Before I forget, the PM patted my hand on Tuesday after Question Time and said, 'Very good speech, that.' Ah! joy . . .

Victoria, Thursday 11 February, midnight

Golly, I'm tired. We really have been working crazy hours this week. I do not enjoy working like this and don't feel I'm achieving any-thing much. And with no exercise and a sore throat I'm putting myself at risk. For what, I wonder?

Best thing of week was vote to bring television into the Commons. I voted in favour. Margaret committed herself heavily against, which was foolish and got roundly beaten. I do not under-stand the attitudes of publicly elected representatives who want to keep television out – and there are already too many governments in the world who control the press and will not permit comment or criticism.

I was in all the press on Monday/Tuesday for the 'Woman of the Year' lunch at the Dorchester, where I was nominated in the politi-cians' category along with Margaret Thatcher, Clare Short,[1] Diane Abbott[2] and Lynda Chalker.[3] As we sat down I was told (1) Margaret Thatcher had won; (2) I was to go up and receive it. I hadn't seen the list, or Lynda, and said 'OK', but in fact she was there (looking very dowdy in a pale frumpy suit) and should have done it, as the more senior minister. Afterwards she commented and said she must get a

1. Labour MP for Birmingham Ladywood.
2. Labour MP for Hackney North and Stoke Newington.
3. Minister of State, Foreign and Commonwealth Office; Conservative MP for Wallasey.

brighter outfit. Too true. Television will make a big difference in that respect. I did feel *very* proud to be up there; maybe some day I'll get one of these in my own right!

I forgot to mention last week that the Tory lady MPs and peers took Margaret Thatcher to dinner in the Cholmondeley Room. Very nice: you could see Gill Shephard[1] enthralled; she is a lovely lady. Virginia Bottomley[2] was making notes on all the speeches – I'll bet she is keeping a diary! Best was Kay Elliot, who must be in her late eighties, celebrating thirty years as a baroness – she was one of the first lady life peers, in 1958. She was part of the Asquith family; she told me how she used to live on the top floor of 10 Downing Street as a small child. When the suffragette riots were on, she and another child leaned out of the window and pelted the protestors with teddy bears. Jill Knight plump and well-corseted; Jean Trumpington,[3] large and black-gowned, splendid, roguish, winking. She was desperate for a cigarette and held out to the Loyal Toast. Just as we were about to rise, the division bell went and we all scattered (Margaret hitching up her black velvet skirt and running down the corridor like a girl – amazing). Ten minutes later Jean had got through two cigarettes and was on her third when we came back, and was then highly embarrassed as we solemnly did the toast.

There was also a bit of a reshuffle last week as Margaret Thatcher redistributed Lord Whitelaw's Cabinet committees. John Major got 'Government communications': a very shadowy job, flagged at first as a promotion with his photo all over *The Times*, and then played down. General troubleshooter, more like, but it's a very exposed position. Oddly enough, when I think of the NHS review which is

---

1. Gillian Shephard, Conservative MP for South-West Norfolk.
2. Conservative MP for Surrey South-West.
3. Baroness Trumpington, Parliamentary Under-Secretary of State, Ministry of Agriculture, Fisheries and Food.

now underway, I trust him more to do the right thing than John Moore – and that's the wrong way round, isn't it?

Michael Forsyth told me that I can't make my Southampton speech in Scotland. Really, says I, you interfere, darling, and I won't come. I could do with a weekend off. I will change it, but let him stew a bit . . .

Victoria, Sunday 21 February, 2.30 p.m.

Back from Edinburgh this morning. The Scottish trip had been planned for months and an excellent programme set out. Friday, flew from Heathrow to Glasgow, coffee morning for Glasgow Tory ladies, lunch with the 'Publicity Club' (advertising managers) in a posh hotel, afternoon at health projects dealing with drugs and AIDS, tea with Asian ladies at the home of a GP, dinner with Glasgow University Conservatives, drove to Stirling to stay with Michael Forsyth, coffee morning in his constituency, drove to Edinburgh for a posh lunch for Edinburgh Tories, tea with Edinburgh Young Conservatives, dinner for 'Board of Finance' (contributing businessmen), stayed in hotel (North British = scruffy!) and flew home today. Ten visits, eight speeches, from millionaires to down-and-outs.

As the weekend wore on and I got more confident (daring?), I talked about those who benefit from the fruits of Thatcherism but salve their consciences by voting Labour, secure in the knowledge that voting patterns elsewhere mean that Thatcherism will continue. It went down a treat. The meetings were packed, the audiences enthusiastic and very matey, the questions lively and intelligent. I pointed out, treading on no toes, that as a non-Scottish minister I was there to learn – for example, how it was that they had the highest exports per head in Europe and the highest living standards anywhere in the country except for London – so that I could teach my Derbyshire people how to do it! That they liked very much, and clearly it had never been put to them in that way before. They should listen to their own young people, the students and the Young Conservatives, who were terrific. One student waited an hour outside the room where we ate, mingling with demonstrators (easily – he was a Sikh) to tell me quietly as I left that the demo was not representative and that he and many other students were delighted I'd come. They should listen less to the 'Sir James' and 'Sir Ian' characters, with their magnificent mansions: very pleasant people, telling me how lucky I was to be invited here and there as they didn't normally have ladies. I looked one big moustachioed dope in the eye after this had been said a fourth time and said, 'Well, Mr Cochrane, you don't need to worry. I'm no lady.' He tittered and looked alarmed.

I hope I've dropped enough hints that I'd like to speak at their Perth conference. And if the only way to get a promotion to Minister of State was to go to Scotland I'd do that willingly and have a whale of a time up there, putting Conservatism on the map and putting Scotland back on the map down here. It's a stunningly beautiful country; the loch near Michael Forsyth's home at 7.45 a.m. looked like Switzerland, with Ben Lomond snow-capped in the distance; and the castle in the crisp clear air as I jogged around it this morning was special too. The ordinary people are marvellous; with my talent for media exposure I could get to them, over the heads of the wealthy old Tories with the chips on their shoulders and their advice about what's wrong with Scotland. Not much from what I could see . . .

Victoria, Wednesday 2 March, around midnight

Been to the BMA dinner tonight, Dorchester, black tie, very nice. Got home 11.30 and did three boxes of MPs' letters.

John Moore made an interesting speech at dinner. Heavy on prevention and on linking outcomes to expenditure. Had I heard it for the first time last summer I would have been tremendously impressed. This time I noticed how tired he looks in unguarded moments: his whole face sags (though he still looks barely forty). He put forward an important policy item which is going to give no end of trouble and which had not been discussed with ministers at all, namely the 'Health Index'. He wants an index of measures of health – e.g. perinatal mortality – which will show us that the nation is getting healthier (like the tax–price index, no doubt). Problems: that is fiendishly difficult and we have no mechanisms for it; and what are you going to do with it? If health improves, do you cut the NHS? If it worsens, do you go begging for more cash? CMO[1] told me they were all very alarmed and that the Treasury in particular is horrified. What bothers me is that we (other ministers) were not involved.

John sent round a note saying we mustn't raise issues at the two weekly Prayer meetings without papers, and not to raise sensitive issues with PPSs around. Yet we have no other regular meetings; I can go for weeks without seeing him. Well, forgive me, but I think that's mighty odd. He likes doing managerial things, but has no real feel for important issues. If he cares about health, why is he so lukewarm about passive smoking? I've repeatedly asked to meet and talk about this since October, but the only meeting he's had on the topic was with the 'Tobacco Advisory Council' – i.e. the industry! And now he's looking for evidence that the Froggatt Committee[2] are wrong. He actually questioned the Committee's independence when talking to the Tobacco Advisory Council, which would be priceless if it wasn't so disgusting. Once again I

---

1. The Government's Chief Medical Officer, Sir Donald Acheson.
2. The Independent Scientific Committee on Smoking and Health, chaired by Professor Sir Peter Froggatt of Queen's University, Belfast, which advised ministers that on balance breathing in someone else's smoke ('passive smoking') was harmful.

wasn't there, nor any other minister, and it had not been discussed; I had to ask to see the minute. It turns out JM has talked to CMO (but not to ministers!) and is against any form of legislation. Of course; he voted against seat belts. The man is not suited to be a health minister.

We finished the Health and Medicines Bill committee yesterday morning, nicely ahead of time. It taught me a lot (and as I chat to backbenchers I realise how far I've come in two years – you can take for granted being on the inside till you realise how far away outside is). For example, I used to think ministers arrived with all the policy neatly tied up and amendments prepared. No: it's a seat of the pants exercise. We have been very lucky, as the Opposition led by Harriet Harman is so lackadaisical and ill-informed that they have confined their activities to reading BMA briefs. They never came close to the gaps in our reasoning – well, Sam Galbraith[1] did once or twice, since he had read the Bill and the White Paper, but his inexperience made him easy to dominate. But in overestimating them and trying to anticipate questions they might ask, we kept identifying the gaps!

Victoria, Thursday 17 March, 11.50 p.m.

Just watched BBC's *Question Time* with Brian Gould[2] – smooth! No other word for it. Malcolm Bruce[3] – bland, non-committal, rather nice, typical Liberal; Janet Cohen, (ex-civil servant, now in banking) – strong, handsome; and John Major, who was quite impressive. He needs a haircut and shouldn't point, and should get nonreflecting specs: but he was on top of his subject and visibly confident, firm and

---

1. Labour MP for Strathkelvin and Bearsden; a neurosurgeon.
2. Labour MP for Dagenham; a member of the Shadow Cabinet.
3. Liberal MP for Gordon.

pleasant. I gather he was invited to lunch by Barbara Maxwell (the editor of the programme) last summer to discuss a possible appearance, and he replied in a lordly way that he didn't go to auditions!

On Tuesday my lunchtime was free, so I phoned around for a partner and Michael Partridge accepted: I treated him to lunch in the Strangers' Dining Room and he talked very freely about the Secretary of State. He and his fellow civil servants are desperate to get some meetings with Moore: they need both a steer on his views and some decisions. Virtually everything is drifting badly, as he can only cope with one issue at a time – which he does very well, usually – but at DHSS you are always juggling ten issues a day, all of them complex. Moore moans about the volume of work and criticises staff and others constantly; he looks very tired nearly all the time and seems to lack energy. I suspect he's spending so much time on the Review – and writing lots of speeches which don't get much coverage – that he has no mental energy left. Yesterday we had our first proper meeting since the election with the regional chairmen: they had insisted on a proper discussion about the Review, and in the end we did 9 a.m.–3 p.m., which was too much. Don Wilson, who is not only a dear but a powerful man with a foot in Downing Street, said to me at dinner, 'I can't get close to him; can't figure him out. He's not going to make Prime Minister, is he?' Moore cleared off after supper at 9.30 p.m. (unforgivable; you stay and flatter them), so Tony and I drank brandy with Wilson and Jim Ackers[1] till 11 p.m. Don reckons the PM is backing off radical options for reforming the NHS and is not keen on an NHS 'stamp', which Leon Brittan[2] amongst others

1. James Ackers, chairman of West Midlands Regional Health Authority, and chairman of Ackers Jarrett Leasing Ltd.
2. Former Home Secretary and Secretary of State for Trade and Industry until 1986; Conservative MP for Richmond (Yorkshire).

has suggested; but Moore is very keen on it, on the principle that it's buoyant.[1] Ackers, wearing his CBI hat, has pointed out that it's a tax on employment and a burden on business, so employers would try to get it reduced, i.e. it wouldn't be buoyant at all. It would also be regressive and act on a much smaller tax base (the employed) than now (all of us, since we all pay VAT). So two thoughts: maybe they didn't fiddle with National Insurance contributions in the Budget, to everyone's surprise, because they want to give a bigger percentage of the National Insurance Fund to the NHS (say, from 13 up to 25 per cent), as the Fund is awash with money and likely to stay so. Or perhaps they are letting Moore get hoist with his own petard. I reckon Major certainly sees him as a rival for the leadership and it would suit him fine to have Moore shown up as a fool.

Watched B from afar this week. He looks good, but he doesn't need me now. Apart from a certain ache I'm not sure if I want or wish to ask him again. Well, we'll see. It wasn't quite so good last time – he's a bit arrogant now.

Victoria, Sunday 20 March, late evening

Came up this evening, as a meeting has been arranged for 9.30 a.m. tomorrow. Everyone seems to forget that I can't get to the office on Monday before 10 a.m. and have to come up the night before; this time Tony is chairing it, so I shall not be best pleased if he's late as usual. David Canzini, the South Derbyshire political agent, dropped round as usual on Saturday at five, looking very smart. He had been stewarding at the Central Council meeting in Buxton; said PM was brilliant, John Major excellent, John Moore lacklustre. He questioned me closely about what I'd like to do next year, to the point where I wondered if he had been put up to it.

---

1. i.e. income goes up when the economy is doing well.

The real reason I wanted to write tonight was to record the end of something very special. I wrote to B on Thursday night saying that's it, no more; posted it Friday morning, so he won't have seen it yet, maybe not till Tuesday. Because it isn't quite the fun it was – he has changed. It was best when he was restless, hiding himself, lacked confidence; he told me about his family, his early background, about being out of work, nearly being killed in an accident, all the deep things you only tell your soul. And I showed him the pain of being well known and the isolation, the pressure of being always criticised and so seldom praised: and got praise in return. He gave me no gift, only his eagerness to come and his evident pleasure when here. He wrote only once, back in 1984 before we got started, apologising for something he'd said thoughtlessly, 'I wouldn't hurt you for the world.' Once, unguarded, he answered when prodded 'I think you're lovely', but that was it. Recently, as he has done so well, he has become more confident, the doubts have vanished, and our conversations have become more like rehearsals for his speeches. I have been startled to read the same phrases, the same thoughts in newspapers a few days or weeks later. So there was nothing private! And he moves in such exalted circles now that I can't match them, the intellectual level at DHSS is nowhere near as good; I can't sparkle like that. In fact all I have to offer is moans, which is why I started this diary – and the diary is available to moan to whenever I need it, and thus has slowly taken his place. At the same time Ray has improved, particularly over the last year or so: the cigs have gone, and so has the plastic white bread, and I found a brand-new exercise gadget in our bedroom at Findern last week. He has a loose front tooth, and I offered to pay for it to be fixed for his birthday and he didn't demur, so I think he is making progress with his midlife crisis. So why did I start? Because I was unhappy with a husband forever slumped snoring in front of the television, not helpful or interested in what I was trying to do. I needed a friend. The first one on offer turned out to be a right slob, with some kinky preferences and a selfishness of such magnitude as I've never met before. I needed help and advice to get up from the backbenches, but the slob made it harder. 'I love you', he said, but his real idea of women was to keep them in their place and not upstage him. Then B came along, and he was so bloody nice and so attractive, and so quiet in public that it was a challenge to unearth the real person, and to seduce him – easy! And it was unexpectedly and spectacularly good, for such a long time. It will hurt to stop, but only occasionally. It will do no harm to devote the same amount of thought and energy to Ray, and to my job. Or even to myself. Once I lost a stone in weight so that B would have the best. (Ray never used to notice. He does now.) But why should I do it for someone else? All the best things in my life I have done for me, and that can be just as true in my forties as any other time. Rambling on: I must sound drunk. I don't have the words. I've been thinking all weekend how to write about this, but the words just aren't there. Still, the memories are, and the sweet taste, and the giggles, and the sadness at putting a stop to it all.

Tower House, Easter Sunday 3 April, 10.20 p.m.

It seems like ages since I wrote last. Too beat to do it, and too busy. I've done my forty-fifth adjournment debate and got the backlog of letters down to eight hundred – that is just over two weeks' worth, though there are still a few hanging around from January.

I seem to have been in the press endlessly in recent weeks. Harriet Harman issued a press release stating the cervical cancer service is a shambles, so my office were up till one in the morning sending out letters to every MP and I was on breakfast television saying she didn't know what she was talking about. Then a *This Week* programme, with Margaret Jay doing her socialist best to discredit the whole of private medicine. I gave a short interview arguing that we don't regard it as so outrageous to have a private market in food, housing, clothing, pensions – all once state-controlled – so why not health? And half our old people have their own property and own it outright, and might want to use it, to realise the asset, etc. They juxtaposed this bland comment with the lady who mortgaged her house, booked herself into the Wellington (of all places) and promptly ran up a huge bill. If the silly cow had taken any advice she would have been told she could have been seen in her local NHS hospital in six weeks, i.e. less time than her financial transactions took her. All the press picked up was 'Remortgage your house, old dears, and you can buy your ops', and the *Standard* even carried a story that Mum had done so (she hasn't). Then we had 'Don't screw around', an interview in *Family Circle* which I haven't seen, again on women's health, in which I said cervical cancer has a sexually trans-mitted element, don't screw around and don't smoke (based on sound medical advice, as usual). So they are all umpty about strong language. Michelle, the plump young Liverpool girl who works in the DHSS Private Office, can't figure out what the fuss is about, that's how they talk at home. Anyway it got plenty of headlines. And then there were organ donor cards – there hadn't been a cam-paign since 1984, and there was some end-of-year money – half a million it turned out – so they printed up four million cards and I went on the Esther Rantzen show to sell them. The number of dona-tion operations has been running at double the rate since her *Gift of Life* programme, compared with last year, so we are making progress, and I'm glad to praise her in public. One of my laid-back young col-leagues, Phillip Oppenheim,[1] said on Monday, 'I can't understand why you go on that terrible programme but I thought you were rather good.' Eat your heart out, Phillip, fifteen million people joined you in watching it. As a result there was a delightful story in the

1. Conservative MP for Amber Valley.

Daily Telegraph yesterday about how I've saved DHSS around £20 million in advertising, with the Esther Rantzen spot (about six minutes) being worth around £3 million. Good, that is part of the job! Thank you, Romula Christopherson,[1] thank you, Bernard Ingham.

The most upsetting event of last week was something I nearly wasn't involved in. John Moore cancelled Monday Prayers (Mary said, 'He told his office he needs a morning off', then she shrugged and grinned). On Tuesday we were up till 2 a.m. at the Commons, so he cancelled the 9.30 a.m. Prayers meeting too and we went straight into briefing for First Order Questions on 11 April (first day back).[2] At the end he asked ministers and PPSs to stay, and explained that the doctor with AIDS had died and it was proposed to take no action. I flipped. This was a young surgeon who had worked in Zimbabwe, so odds are he was infected by a patient; married, baby, fell ill at Xmas and was told it was exhaustion, died from AIDS last weekend. He had operated on over three hundred patients in Redditch and Exeter. I said that we should act at once in the interests of the public health and should contact, trace and offer reassurance and the rest. If we didn't and someone else got infected meantime, they could sue us and really take us to the cleaners – and it would get out anyway, which would destroy the credibility of Government statements. John said, the decision's taken, we've just had a meeting, we must avoid political embarrassment. And I thought, I despise you: I'd rather get the sack than put up with this. So I pitched in again and repeated the arguments, and I'm getting signals from Tony, who is looking unhappy, and John says I'm repeating what Tony has only just said in the meeting and practically accuses us of colluding (which we had not; but we do think alike on many issues). Finally, John said that if I felt so strongly about it, we'd

1. DHSS Chief Press Officer.
2. Departments have to answer questions in Parliament on a monthly rota.

better reconvene the meeting of that morning, with CMO, etc., and get the decision changed. Which we did. As we left Tony took my arm, said not a word, but squeezed it hard: I'd done the right thing. I suppose the difference between us is that he, faced with a meeting which disagreed with him, would seek a compromise, whereas I would look at them all, thinking I can convince fifteen million people in six minutes, so I'm not worth much if I have trouble with you lot – then I'd pitch in again, twisting and turning till they were convinced, or at least prepared to let me have my way. Later we had two meetings, one JM, TN and I, followed by officials. At the first, John said he was angry that I did not raise these matters in the proper way. So I put on my frozen Medusa look (copied from the PM) and said, 'Fine, but you keep cancelling meetings, so there has been no opportunity.' He backs off bloody easily! He then spent several minutes telling me how he defended my *This Week* comments to the Conference of Newspaper Editors this week, got the transcript, read it out to them, etc. (good for him; Norman Fowler would never have done that), but then John couldn't have done it with great conviction or it would have made headlines, and didn't. Anyway, Tony and I got our way – I signalled him to do the talking – and we convinced Chris France that it would be wrong to say 'no evidence of cross infection = no risk'. I shan't ever forget my November '83 question on transmission of AIDS through blood transfusion (put up to it by constituent haemophiliacs, almost certainly now infected), to which Ken Clarke[1] answered that there was no evidence that AIDS was transmitted through blood. Like Calais, it's engraved on my heart. I suppose, if I'm being totally honest, there's also the thought that if one of these liability cases goes badly wrong it could just be

---

1. Kenneth Clarke, Chancellor of the Duchy of Lancaster and Minister for Trade and Industry; Minister of State, Department of Health and Social Security, 1982–5; Paymaster-General, 1985–7; Conservative MP for Rushcliffe Division of Nottinghamshire.

me that has to defend it, sometime in future. And there are two other bits of the tale: the funeral workers told the local press about the poor doctor, so there was no chance of keeping it secret anyway – as if there ever was; and the PPSs gossiped around the House, so John Wakeham wanted to know what the row between ministers was about. But Romula looked so relieved – she had deeply disagreed with the original decision and had planned to leak it. God help us all. And maybe there will be a final sting, because John will make snide remarks behind my back – but who will he blame, Tony or me?

The girls are on holiday now. Having them at two different schools is horrendous when holidays don't coincide. Last Sunday I drove Deb to Mum's, left car there, caught 4 p.m. train to London, straight to *That's Life*, quick change, on set, finished filming 8.45 p.m., goes out 9.15 p.m., get home about 10.30 p.m., COLLAPSE! Then breakfast television on Monday morning. At times like these I feel like Houdini in chains, with only a minute or so to get out of them. Then on Thursday (after the row the previous day) I did two adjournment debates – one well (East Yorkshire where I went the previous Friday) and one badly (community care), because we don't have a policy. Ho hum, roll on summer – and reshuffle maybe – I hear rumours that I might go to the Treasury. Guardian angel at work again, I hope!

Victoria, Thursday 14 April, around midnight

The end of a very long and tricky week, but I have a feeling of triumph. We got our Bill through tonight – or the Third Reading anyway, and with good majorities on the awkward bits, dental and sight test charges. All my bits went well. I called Harriet Harman 'dim' which produced guffaws – it isn't quite true, but her little girl's style is so irritating to our side; and her habit of insisting on her rights as a mother, very ostentatiously, is so irritating to her own, that 'dim' sounds as if I'm being kind. We have our cervical cancer programme up and running, just about, so I was able to crow a bit. Late yesterday there was a short debate on contracting out led by the Scots, who don't like it; there was some discussion as to whether Forsyth should do it, and the whip David Lightbown said Tony should do it, not me, to avoid inflaming a row which could go on all night. In the end it was agreed that I should, with the strict instruction to be 'low key'. So I had a lot of fun doing some gentle teasing, it was very amicable, we finished on time and had a good majority. Brownie points all the way. Today all I had were bits – I felt like a television continuity girl – and Clause 13 on the cash limiting of (a tiny part of) the Family Practitioner Services. Now that really was an odd episode. On Monday morning after ministers' meeting John is having fits. The Clause 13 papers are awful, he says, the figures in two different tables don't match, the officials want him to say I was wrong in committee, it's all ghastly and he thinks I should do it! Then we flapped around all day, and had to bring Bryan Rayner[1] in – he must be the original Sir Humphrey, except that he has no sense of humour and is a thoroughly nice guy. I then settled down to do some work on it; it's quite technical and John was right, the papers were a mess, but he was also wrong, for the two tables were GB and England and clearly marked as such. I decided our position in committee was fine and told officials to stop messing about and in the end we had only a rapid twenty-minute debate at 9.30 p.m. and a division on it, called by the Scottish Nationalists. John was absolutely amazed, and kept saying how extraordinary my energy and optimism was; but in reality it was dead easy, it just needed a very clear head, one or two decisions and no flapping – but under pressure that's what he does, flaps. If he were a woman, or plain, he would not be getting the benefit of the doubt at all.

1. Deputy Secretary, Department of Health and Social Security.

I've found it very effective when I make an announcement at the Dispatch Box to look very serious, to say, 'I have an announcement to make', and then to read it, apparently very carefully. The language should be slightly pompous, to emphasise the official nature. And I look up to check that everyone has understood and repeat a key phrase or two. That does the trick, and stamps the debate for those few minutes with an authoritative and decisive tone!

Our boss is looking more like a sacrificial lamb than ever. He could hardly talk on his big bit, dental charges, and did what is now normal for him, spoke in a cracked whisper, with rather wild, darting eyes, with casual 'you knows' and suchlike – totally unsuitable for a formal chamber, with no one listening – chatting away on all sides, the Speaker and the Labour front bench stifling yawns: a speech full of statistics, delivered in a monotone, very fast, no emphasis, no style, no conviction, and not convincing anyone in sight. He made a nasty mistake when giving way to Tam Dalyell,[1] who was once PPS to Richard Crossman at DHSS. Had CMO agreed the charges? Now it is a long-standing convention that ministers do not reveal the advice they are given by civil servants, and John should have said so at once, firmly. Instead, he said that CMO had endorsed the White Paper. So Dalyell and others nagged away all evening and said House of Commons was entitled to know views of CMO (which it isn't). Tony had to say that his Right Honourable Friend (John) had answered that question. If I'd been asked, I'd have said that I never reveal what my civil servants say to me, and I seldom reveal what I say to them: but then, I take full responsibility for what I say at the Dispatch Box. Splat! But John didn't, and I feel that this silly little row will rumble on.

We had an 'emergency' debate yesterday on the social security

1. Labour MP for Linlithgow; MP for West Lothian, 1962–83; Parliamentary Private Secretary to Secretary of State for Social Services, 1964–70.

reforms, which became effective Monday. As a matter of fact it's a bloody good reform and I'm proud to be associated with it; of course there are losers, but you can't expect to please all of the people all of the time and in politics you're doing well if you please a few occasionally. There is room for a very robust and lively defence, indeed exposition, and Norman Fowler would have done it competently. Robin Cook[1] opened with his usual hard, elegant, humourless, accurate speech – not quite as good as his brilliant NHS opening speech, I thought this one had slightly too much reliance on individual cases and some were a bit weak. But John was terrible. He was droning on when Dave Nellist[2] kicked a marvellous own goal, by misbehaving and getting himself thrown out and named. The Labour front bench were furious and came into our lobby; most Labour MPs abstained and thirty-five voted against. But it all saved John's bacon, whereas he is supposed to be saving ours. I wonder when he'll get the chop?

Victoria, Thursday 28 April, 10.40 p.m.

Ray has gone off to Derbyshire again, as he now usually does on Thursday. He spends the evening in the Wheel, often till long past closing. He has put on weight recently and falls asleep at the least thing. I don't think he is doing himself any good at all – he's nearly forty-three and looks fifty-five. He's still looking for jobs elsewhere. When I first met him, eighteen years ago, he was so tough and ambitious, heading for a partnership, a high flyer. Other people overtook him and now are clearing the £100,000 salary mark, plus shares and money in the bank, but he still has an overdraft and is heading downwards in the salary scale. Why? He's very able, hardworking,

1. Member of Shadow Cabinet and Labour MP for Livingston.
2. Labour MP for Coventry South-East.

thorough and straight. He's also stubborn and pigheaded much of the time and reduces his capacity through lifestyle, and I suppose in the end he just lacks the instinct. Watch: he'll leave Arthur Andersen's after twenty-one years' service, with never a bean, instead of organising it to get a golden handshake which would at least pay off our debts. What happened to his get up and go? It got up and went . . .

Oddly enough I don't mind and our relationship is just as good. We each demand very little of the other. He doesn't expect dinner on the table every night and I don't expect him in the gallery every night (like Leo Beckett,[1] looking besotted!). But we each try to give, and all the giving is a bonus. So we toddle along and are content, and I ask no more, for it leaves me all my mental energy for the job, and he is pleasant, undemanding and comforting when I come home. He's a good father and a good companion. And I don't mind him sloping off on Thursdays because I can write my diary . . .

John Moore performed tolerably well in the debate on social security this week. His voice was better, though it does have an uncontrolled squeak and he's still feeling sorry for himself, but he was better for keeping it short. His responses to interventions were hopeless – he just looks so defenceless and dopey. 'Like an earnest garage mechanic' was how one paper described him, when we need a racing driver to head the team. We seem to have dropped all pretence of collegiate working in the department. John hardly bothers to come to meetings, doesn't attend Prayers. I made an *appointment* to see him today and found I was to be followed by Roger Skelmersdale – what a crazy way to run a department! I had talked about it to Tony before Easter, as everything just 'slips' and we are

---

1. Husband of Margaret Beckett, an Opposition frontbench spokesman on Health and Social Security, and Labour MP for Derby South.

constantly into crisis management, and suggested that he, I and Roger get together once a week, say Wednesday morning, with Michael Partridge and two or three key staff, just to think ahead a bit. He said he had talked to Partridge who agreed, adding delicately that civil servants also felt we had far too few meetings. Back we came after Easter and nothing had happened. That is typical of Tony! This week a series of minor uncoordinated catastrophes meant I raised it again; so we tried to fix up a meeting with Partridge, but it didn't come off . . . and unless I nag everyone sick it won't happen. 'They' are thinking about splitting the department up, putting another (extra) minister in Cabinet: JM to do health, someone else to do social security. But in my view that is the wrong way around, as the social security reforms are done (apart from a bit of tidying up) and JM is good with figures, whereas the health reforms are yet to come and will require a deft political feel, skill at communication and interest in the public health, and Moore has none of these. And the Downing Street Review won't be ready for the Party Conference, so if he has to do a health speech they would give him a *very* hard time. I can see a partial eclipse coming . . . Incidentally I requested a meeting to discuss the Review with him as he at no time has invited his junior ministers to contribute – Roger and I both had to hassle to get papers, Roger more so than me. We both feel very angry at that; Roger wrote and circulated a sharp note pointing out that he would have to sell it all to their Lordships. The only person to emerge with credit this week is Nick Scott, who did very well at a packed backbench committee meeting on Tuesday (with nothing to tell them, but he was nice, and concerned, the opposite of John) and again in debates winding up.

Victoria, Sunday 8 May, 6.20 p.m.

I've been in Essex today, Tony Newton's seat at Braintree. He is just about the only MP I would give up a Sunday for! They tried to arrange it last May, but the election intervened. Today was a damp, sticky, humid day and the function was at the Essex showground, which got very hot inside.

Next week should be quiet apart from Questions on Tuesday: I hope I don't get blasé about them, they are always an ordeal. But last week was certainly heavy going: I clocked up ninety-one hours. I had kept a check because Margaret Quinton, my new local Conservative Ladies' chairman, had commented that I didn't like doing Sunday functions; so I've sent her the diary, and now she knows why!

I overslept on Tuesday and missed two trains, so I didn't get to London till 1.30. I've never done that before (Ray was in London already), and it must have been psychological, for the first meeting on Tuesday was NHS Management Board, looking at the figures for NHS finance for 1988–9 – and very nasty they looked too, with an estimated £150–200 million extra needed for this year to avoid wholesale closures. A bid for £200 million had gone in with the Review Body bids, but had been turned down flat. All very odd: the Review Body announcements were brought forward a week which allowed no real time for argument on the rest; they were decided at an 'inner' Cabinet (not a Cabinet committee, which would have been minuted), which included Norman Fowler and Treasury but excluded Scottish, Welsh and Northern Ireland health ministers, so the numbers were stacked against John Moore.

I found myself very miserable about all this, which I pieced together during the week. John Moore heading straight for more trouble, etc. On the Wednesday afternoon I was in the Commons and all was quiet. I had had at the back of my mind for some weeks that I must alert David Waddington, as it looked as if JM was losing on all fronts. I opened a door and there was Murdo Maclean;[1] I

---

1. Chief Whip's Private Secretary, a Commons fixer.

asked if David was free, and in a trice I was in his office and sharing with him, in a very muddled way, my concerns: (1) about the under-funding for 1988–9 and imminent hooha that will cause; (2) that the Downing Street Review is failing to address the real question of the funding of health care against a background of rising demand, espe-cially from the elderly; and (3) that if there is any reshuffling to do, give JM the social security job, as he's good at money but has no feel whatsoever for health. I didn't feel the least disloyal, for JM has never made the least attempt to win my personal loyalty – which is given to the Party and to those who will help maintain the health and welfare of 'my' people (by which I mean my constituents). In any case I had put my thoughts about the NHS Review on paper (copies only to Tony Newton, Roger Skelmersdale and my friend at the Treasury) for JM – a highly elliptical document, which sets out clearly that we mess about with the NHS at our peril. He's a rather vindictive man. He won't find out about the Chief Whip, but he may take a dim view of my efforts to put him right. We'll see. The PM at a private CPC meeting recently commented on the 'woopies'[1] idea and was reported to be 'much taken with it', so maybe I'm safe. She is said to be very cautious about major reform of the NHS, and most of our backbenchers are the same (we are now having regular drinks parties with them), so radicals like John are getting to look rather isolated.

My chat in the inner sanctum had an amusing aftermath. Late on Wednesday afternoon we had briefing for Questions; after Tony asked me to come in for a chat and we talked over what we do about a useless Secretary of State. He said there are plenty around who would like him 'off the board'. Fowler for one, for trying to mess up his reforms and for being so loud-mouthed and critical

---

1. In a recent speech EC had floated the idea that well off old people – 'woopies' – should contribute more to the cost of their nursing care.

about them, and perhaps on ideological grounds. Ditto Major, whose star is rising fast and is now being talked of with Baker and Clarke as a candidate for The Job when she goes. The newspapers think Major is Thatcherite, just because he grew up in Brixton and went to grammar school; but he's much more complex than that, more pragmatist than anything else, but only too pleased to grind John Moore's pretty face in it in my judgement. I asked Tony if we should alert anyone to the problems, including the fact that as ministers we never meet, never discuss issues. Should we quietly warn the whip? Some issues coming up were real nasties, e.g. not having any money for a drugs campaign or for extra services to cope with drugs/AIDS. No, he said, that would be going behind JM's back. If we don't, said I, we will be blamed, and I don't care for that. At this point Tony was handed a letter that John Moore had written to John Major saying we are short of money, there is trouble ahead. We both felt relieved – but it is extraordinary that we did not know he was going to write and did not see a text of this most important letter until it had been sent. JM is quite mad; he has so much expertise at his fingertips and chooses not to use it. I had a quiet smile to myself. This story is not over yet.

London-bound train, Monday 23 May, 9 a.m.

It is getting harder to write this diary! The weekend before last Ray and I had quite a row – actually I picked it as I was feeling fed up – about his lackadaisical approach to getting a new job. He's been talking about it for a year, but the nearest he's got was to apply for General Secretary of the Sports Council. With his total lack of a track record in sport or in that kind of public body work, he really had no hope of it. What bothered me was that it was quite a cut in salary too, but if he was happy we would have managed. There are very few jobs in the world he's in – training accountants – and he doesn't want to start his own business; lacks the drive I suppose. He's not happy at Arthur Andersen, but not doing much about getting out. Anyway, since then he's been sloping off to Derbyshire less, attacking the field outside the house with energy and filling in application forms for squash clubs. So I'm not on my own so much. I am glad.

Despite the descriptions of John Moore in the press as 'woebegone', the atmosphere in the department is much better, mainly because they are making progress on the Review. They have decided to leave the NHS mainly intact, no more charges, still mainly to be funded from taxation – that's a relief. Moore presented plans to the PM to drop child benefit last Tuesday morning (each 10p is £40 million), and to use it to improve basic pensions instead. At Question Time she told John Cartwright[1] that there were no plans to change child benefit and gave the same promise later that afternoon to McCrindle,[2] Squire[3] and the other wets. She is not minded to risk too many 'poll tax' type defeats. However we have bounced back to a 9 per cent lead in the polls, after being neck and neck back in April when DHSS was so exposed.

There's trouble ahead, though. The NHS continues short of money. So I think we are back into closures, etc., and John Moore will have to face more rows in the House of Commons in the autumn if not before. Treasury know, but are worried that £2.5 billion has left the reserve since April (£800 million to write off British Leyland's debts for privatisation) – that explains some of the coolness towards Lord Young, as does a £2.5 million advertising campaign from DTI for the 'Department of Enterprise'! No one else can afford television advertising now, and certainly not DHSS for health promotion. Treasury asked us to muddle through at least till the Review, but it could be awkward.

1. SDP MP for Woolwich since 1983; formerly a Labour MP for Woolwich East.
2. Robert McCrindle, Conservative MP for Brentwood and Ongar.
3. Robin Squire, Conservative MP for Hornchurch.

Tower House, Thursday 2 June, midnight

Spring Bank Holiday week: Debbie went back to school yesterday, looks very grown up, nearly as tall as me now; Susie on Sunday night. Took them to London on Tuesday for *South Pacific*, which they loved but I found oddly flat, perhaps because I knew the story – it did feel old hat after *Cats* and *Starlight Express* and *Blues in the Night* – mores and tastes do change.

Previous week solidly busy: 2.30 a.m. on the Monday, 5.30 a.m. on Wednesday for Firearms Bill. The little band of Tory opponents led by Jerry Wiggin[1] and Hector Monro[2] voted against a guillotine at 9.30 p.m. then went home, so Skinner[3] et al. played silly beggars with all the amendments which the dissidents had demanded. So we were voting all night. David Waddington wrote a really nice personal note to all those who stayed and voted for Third Reading – much appreciated – Brownie points all round.[4] Total hours for week = ninety-one.

Good week for Moore, too. Standing ovation at RCN Conference on Monday, first time they have ever given a minister a standing ovation. And he got another on Wednesday at Conservative Women's Conference at the Barbican. It was slightly engineered – they were unkind to Nick Ridley first, then polite to Hurd, then friendly to John Moore. But he spoke better, from notes not a script. Melinda Libby[5] says he hates using a script, and can't use an autocue because he can't see and won't wear glasses. He can't see well enough to recognise people in the House. She intends to talk to his wife about

1. Conservative MP for Weston-super-Mare.
2. Sir Hector Monro, the long-serving Conservative MP for Dumfries.
3. Dennis Skinner, Labour MP for Bolsover.
4. EC had had a shooter's licence till this Bill, the aftermath of the Hungerford shooting in 1987, was proposed, and gave it up at that point.
5. Special adviser to the Secretary of State.

getting him specs or contact lenses. She also says he doesn't prioritise: he just ploughs through whatever is put in front of him. You cannot do a job at our level like that. I sat opposite him on the way to York, and he spent the whole journey discussing papers with his Private Secretary – not the minister opposite! Not meant as snub, I'm sure, but clear that it doesn't appear odd to him at all. He has *seven* special advisers (i.e. including ministers) and simply fails to make use of them. As a result he feels beleaguered. But it isn't satisfactory to make speeches from rough notes all the time. I feel one of the skills I have picked up this year is making good snappy speeches from carefully cleared texts: quite effective too. If Moore doesn't learn that, he'll go no further.

It should have been nicer being home this weekend, but it is no rest with kids around and I'm still painfully conscious of how much needs doing in this house and how little money I have to do it. Damp patches in round room again, and we didn't bother heating the pool because no one uses it even when it's warm. Depressing. If anything ever happens to Ray, I'll be out of here like a shot. And when I'm home I don't really adjust. The main thing I do is eat like a pig, so my weight and waistline shoot up – I can put on half a stone in a week. It's very mixed up: I feel I don't deserve to do well, so I reassure myself with cake or chocolate; I'm not busy and the kitchen is right there, so I fill my boring time with toast and sandwiches; I'm not wearing smart clothes, so 'it doesn't matter', etc. One result is that my skin looks ghastly, the asthma starts playing up and I feel even more depressed. I'm then relieved to get back to work. Perhaps my target ambition for the next two years should be to learn how to relax in a mature and disciplined manner. There must be some reason why I find it so fiendishly difficult! Similarly, I haven't really found a way of living and coping with being famous. At first it was fun and I was delighted to be approached by people. Now it is often frightening – you wonder if this next chap has a knife or gun or is going to hit you. If I'm 'on duty', then I'm all dressed up, made up and accompanied: no problem, I'm like a performer on stage and I enjoy it. When work has finished I just want to go home, change into casual clothes and relax. The problem comes during intermediate activities, e.g. invitations from constituents or friends of Ray, etc. There are very few I regard as personal friends, all the rest are 'work'. Personal friends know when to talk politics and when to stop; not to show me off to their friends; not to breathe a word that I'm coming; not to say I've been; and nothing whatever to the press. There are so few people I trust: it's sad really, though I think I've always been a bit careful, even as a kid. Taking the children out is a real problem. If I'm in jeans I look a mess and I don't think they are too proud of me! If I'm recognised (less likely if I'm in jeans), we are stared at or approached and asked for autographs. I feel much safer with Ray there, partly because people don't look at a woman accompanying a man. It's the same when I'm in a car. If Ray drives, no one notices me. If I drive, everyone waves. I don't think I've figured this bit out either! Maybe if you're well known you're always on duty?

Tower House, Sunday 26 June, 8.15 p.m.

I've been in the headlines again, twice, and not intentionally in either case, but as usual I seem to have struck a chord with the general public. First it was GPs; on Friday 3 June I went to Bristol for the twentieth anniversary conference of the UK transplant surgeons. Afterwards they flew me back to Derby in a helicopter used for transporting kidneys, etc., all very exciting! I had to make a few comments to the surgeons on the Primary Care White Paper, pointing out the need to use GPs better – if they just act as postmen (like mine, who's never examined me yet, but still sent me on to the consultant), then we are not using resources well. We have been working on this for three years, ever since the Green Paper came out – but suddenly the *Daily Mail* heard of it, and 'Edwina lashes lazy doctors' became front page news. The BMA was predictably horrified (though I had not used 'lazy' at any stage) and stormed in to see John Moore, who defended me vigorously.

Then I spoke at the annual conference of the local dental committees in Whitbread's Brewery (*beautiful* spot, lovely food). The problem was that they had a large number of very drunk dentists there who didn't want to listen. It wasn't helped by the fact that the first speaker made a very funny speech, full of dirty allusions. I warned them at the start of mine that I wasn't going to follow his lead, and as a result the evening was not a success! Several papers picked up my speech as my criticism of the dentists (which it was, and the serious papers clearly thought that wasn't worth reporting), but Peter Dobbie of the *Mail on Sunday* phoned and talked about alcohol, so I let fly about drunks at dinners, and there we are on the front page again today. They didn't reduce me to tears, whatever the headline!

There was a profile of John Moore on telly last Sunday. They went to the USA and brought back a picture of a very ambitious young man who lived in a tiny flat with his ambitious American wife, worked for the Democratic Party – well, they were in power then – and had all his subsequent rise to power planned out. I'm not surprised; the naive, vain thing is that he told anyone – these things do surface, even twenty-five years later. There were pictures of him with Michael Caine curls in the 1970s, but he is better looking now: harder, more wary, looks as if he has practised. He had a long interview (recorded in Michael Portillo's office – looked like a pink boudoir!) and talked quite well. It is difficult sometimes to figure out what he is saying: his command of language is poor, he isn't fluent, and he isn't given to metaphor or other illuminating figures of speech – he can be *very* boring and pedestrian. The strain showed, as he was sweating hard towards the end. He was asked about wanting to be PM and allowed himself to chatter on about it, saying he always tried to do the job in hand, then gave us his c.v., Transport,

Treasury, etc.! (Incidentally, I noticed this week that one of his rivals, John Major, has had his teeth fixed and has new specs which don't glint in the light. Cruel world, isn't it?)

I was very surprised to find another lunch date at Number 10 in my diary at very short notice – I suspect someone had to drop out. It was a lively and friendly event, with all of us talking nineteen to the dozen, though to no great purpose. She looked tired and flushed – recent weeks have been very exciting with summits, etc., but all that must be a big strain. The main topic of interest which came up was planning, raised by Angela Rumbold.[1] There are serious shortages of land for house building in the south and house prices are soaring – over £60,000 for a tiny flat in Angela's constituency, which makes life impossible for first-time buyers (and it will be chronic after August when the Chancellor stops double tax allowances). Meanwhile Nick Ridley (who wasn't there) is in a big row because he says there must be more building, yet he objected to planning permission near his own property! I pointed out that the NHS has property it doesn't need, including old hospitals (a National Audit Office paper had just pointed out how much land we are sitting on) and mentioned problems in getting planning permission (e.g. Darenth Park in Dartford), which can make land worth one hundred times more. Margaret suggested quite seriously that we promote a private member's Bill to give all DHAs automatic planning permission! Then Archie Hamilton,[2] Tim Eggar[3] and others with psychiatric hospitals pointed out the problems of community care, and she switched immediately, saying we shouldn't close the

1. Minister of State, Department of Education and Science; Conservative MP for Mitcham and Morden.
2. Archibald Hamilton, Parliamentary Private Secretary to the Prime Minister; Conservative MP for Epsom and Ewell.
3. Parliamentary Under-Secretary of State, Foreign & Commonwealth Office; Conservative MP for Enfield North.

hospitals in the first place, etc., and how community care was expensive, unkind and didn't work (she has this problem in Barnet). Actually I agree, though the hospitals are too big and often in the wrong places. She is going to chair meeting(s) on community care in the autumn after the main stuff of the Review is out of the way; and I think she's shaping up for a real row about it.

[A reshuffle in July led to the Department of Health and Social Security being split in two; John Moore became Secretary of State for Social Security, and Tony Newton was made Chancellor of the Duchy of Lancaster; Kenneth Clarke became Secretary of State for Health, with David Mellor as Minister of State and EC as junior minister.]

Victoria, Sunday 4 September, 11 p.m.

I've puzzled in the last few weeks about how to handle the coming year. A survey in *The Economist* last Friday helped me decide – of a representative sample shown photos of various politicians, 78 per cent could name me, which makes me the best-known politician in the country after the PM. The next was Heseltine, at 64 per cent (I think, from memory), and then Lawson, at just over 50 per cent. Ray showed me the story with the comment, 'That'll make you a few enemies' – but then spent all weekend telling everyone that I was ten times more famous than my boss. So that gives me guidance. If I'm well known, what I do is news. So don't do too much, and whatever you do, do it well and make sure it's in the public interest. Guard your health fiercely – so I've bought an exercise bike and broken my nails getting it installed here in the flat!

I suspect I just have to work hard and keep my head down. I've realised how big the chat I had with David Waddington in May was. Whatever the detail of what I said, the message was clear, that John Moore's junior ministers had no confidence in him. That's big stuff.

I've told no one else and I'm certain Waddington hasn't, for none of the whips has whispered it at all. Portillo came into my room the night he was promoted to Transport: he'd had a drink or two and was excited and talkative. He asked what I thought of the split and I said, it's good, John couldn't cope. He said, you kept your views very quiet on him, I am surprised to hear you say that; and I replied, ah well, at one time we thought he was going to be PM, and loyalty matters too. So Portillo does not know about my conversation with Waddington – and he's a recent ex-whip, usually they have no secrets from each other. That's a relief. It has weighed on my mind quite a bit and joined one or two other secrets.

The children went back to Denstone tonight, Debbie excited, Susie quietly apprehensive and a bit brazen. We've had a good summer holiday. Looking after the children is *very* hard work, both physically and emotionally, and I get frustrated intellectually, as their conversation is limited to pop groups and clothes. They will be beautiful clever women and I am so thrilled and proud of them. But I wouldn't want to spend all my time looking after them; no way!

Tower House, Sunday 18 September, 8.30 p.m.

I had an interesting talk with David Mellor[1] last week – apparently he doesn't want any of my leftover engagements – they are called 'returns' in lawyer's parlance! So if I can't do a job, I shouldn't assume he can do it – just get the private secretaries to check – and certainly not pass anything upwards to Ken (that's fair enough – I had offered one, which was in fact in Nottingham,[2] because he might just have

---

1. Formerly Minister of State at the Home Office (1986–7) and Foreign & Commonwealth Office (1987); Conservative MP for Putney.
2. i.e. near Kenneth Clarke's Rushcliffe constituency.

been interested). Mellor's diary is quite empty, not a single Conservative speaking engagement in it except for Putney. He says he doesn't like travelling – though foreign travel is OK! – but how does he expect to be leader of the party if he doesn't do the rounds of the constituencies? Still, he's trying to be nice to me, and was making an effort. I just wonder if he is basically a bit lazy, a bit under-committed; he spent five years as a junior minister and is now on his third Minister of State job and is clearly not content with that.

The NHS Review proceeds apace. Ken Clarke has been looking over all the papers; there was an agreed summing-up by Cabinet Office on 26 July (the day after the reshuffle) which is written like a White Paper, and we are expecting one in the autumn. But Ken wasn't content with the proposals and suggested another radical departure, giving GPs a (cash limited) budget for simple ops and cold surgery which they could use to negotiate with local hospitals. This is a bizarre idea in my view.

Tower House, Tuesday 27 September

Sinking feeling this week. Debbie was gated and couldn't come home for the exeat. She and the other two girls in her dorm were caught smoking. I went up to the school on Sunday afternoon to talk to her. She said she had done it before, and had her first one at eleven; so while she was busy trying to persuade Ray to stop, and grieving over the death of her grandfather from lung cancer – and she *did* cry, the only one of us – at the same time she was trying it, because all her friends smoked and she wanted to know what they enjoyed about it. She told me that she had been drunk, too, one afternoon when a group of them went to Alton Towers with some cider. She wasn't keen on that; it made her giggly, but by the time they got back to school she had a headache. Deb's ability to resist peer pressure has always been suspect – back in 1986 she went

AWOL from the Bluecoat[1] with a friend – and she does not connect consequences with actions, an immaturity which does worry me a lot. It could have been something far worse; a group at Repton School was recently expelled for drugs.

It turns out that David Mellor keeps a second, secret diary, entirely composed of lunches and dinners with journalists and important people. It's the gossip in the office, where civil servants are amazed. Ken Clarke ticked him off about it.[2] I suppose David doesn't want people to know, as they read the papers, where the hints are coming from . . .

There have been interesting developments on the ministerial responsibilities side: I have all the estate, and health and safety, and kitchens; so I called the (rather minor) officials together as a 'Clean Machine' group. Ken is a bit twitchy about it, as that's the responsibility of the health authorities, but we have cockroaches and belching chimneys (and prosecutions) everywhere, and EEC directives to come. I shall enjoy that work. I've also put all the officials for elderly/mental handicap/mental illness together in a 'Priority Care Group', which, like Women's Health, Prevention Strategy, Social Services Inspectorate and the Clean Machine, will meet me regularly. (Social Services Inspectorate may go to David – I hope so, I have enough.) The only part of my proposed endless list of responsibilities he wanted was the overseas visits!

Victoria, Sunday 2 October, late

I have to do breakfast television at some ghastly hour tomorrow – I wish it had never been invented. We're launching the new triple vaccine against mumps (first time ever in the UK), measles and rubella (first time for boys). This year we've had over seventy

1. A prep school.
2. This ticking off appears in *A Woman's Place* (1996).

thousand cases of measles so far and nine deaths from measles alone, so hopefully we'll wipe them out, as they have done in the USA.

I saw B again on Friday: I was in the area where he lives, and he and his wife offered their home for a rest, which I appreciated. It's nice, and reminded me a lot of our old house in Birmingham. Inside was a bit plain and unimaginative, but the garden is beautiful. To my horror, the magic started to work again in a very big way. When we parted he held my hand a long time and squeezed it, even though other people were there. The house and his thoroughly nice family clearly mean a great deal to him; as we stood in the garden (his idea to walk out there: but we did not touch then) he said, happily and quietly, that he loved it there and had known it was right the moment he saw it; he could not manage without it. And by 'it', he means the family too. It was uncanny how many of the things he said precisely mirror how I feel about my home. I was called to the phone at one stage, and he took me to the phone in his bedroom (pretty, flowery). I sat on the bed while he sat on the stool near the mirror – what did he think I was going to do while his wife was in the kitchen? He offered me hospitality for the night, but I said no; when he pressed me I whispered, I couldn't take it, couldn't cope. He looked puzzled, then grinned and relaxed. Maybe he'd been concerned that I'd been a bit cool till then? I didn't return his kiss of greeting or hug him. Sounds like a schoolgirl escapade or a Mills & Boon book, doesn't it? But this man is very special, and I think he finds himself equally surprised and pleased that I'm his, as I do that he cares for me. It's not just sex, it's a very high regard, too. When I went looking for a husband I chose very carefully and very well – almost too well, for I doubt if I could ever clear off from Ray. And when I needed a lover, again I chose too well, for I didn't expect to love this man – and I do, very much indeed. All weekend I've been feeling his hand on mine, and it turns my heart over. I weep for what I don't have, with the increasing certainty that I want it very much and somehow will have it again. For a long time it made me stop loving Ray – or maybe the contrast was just too stark? Maybe my innate dissatisfaction was surfacing anyway, and if it hadn't been B, it might have been someone else, someone more aggressive and less concerned at breaking up a marriage? Since the spring, when I decided the liaison with B was too dangerous, I've made a much bigger effort at home, and I think that helps. I suspect I did a lot of snapping at everyone before, and was resentful and rude. Certainly Ray seems more relaxed and has stopped job hunting and is more affectionate and friendly. We've also agreed to spend (borrow) rather a lot of money to improve Tower House, which will make it more comfortable and roomy and leave me more content. But oh, as I sit here in the flat, B is here too – in spirit! – and I wish I knew he would be knocking on the door in ten minutes, I would not have tears dripping gently off my nose right now.

Debbie's smoking ended up on the front page of the *Sun*. Unfortunately she appears to enjoy the notoriety and was seen on television waving and giggling at the cameras. I'm really very angry with the school. Then *Today* came around to Tower House and photographed the swimming pool, etc. – apart from worries about security, it makes us look like plutocrats, though I'm sure our little flat in Victoria is worth more. The *Today* man came back to the house this morning and wanted to know if Debbie was home. I shut the door in his face.

I'm cross about the fact that every speech I make is crawled over by officials, then cleared by other ministers and sent to Number 10. I know the PM saw the 'woolly hats' speech before it went out and didn't change it at all – we had nice comments back via Bernard Ingham – and it was cleared with Nick Scott who, as Minister for the Disabled, is in charge of 'Keep Warm Keep Well'.[1] At Thursday's

---

1. The Government's campaign to persuade old people to keep warm during the winter. EC's 'woolly hats' speech was part of the launch for this campaign.

Cabinet John Moore complained to Ken about it, assuming that it was my own idea, and worrying that it would draw attention to the nasty things they've been doing to heating allowances. Ken asked me about it at lunchtime, and was both startled and amused when I told him that the speech had been checked and cleared by everyone. Moore is a fool, who clearly doesn't know what is going on in his own truncated department, and doesn't remember what went on in DHSS last year either. So I sat down and wrote a memo to Ken, explaining that my extraordinary interest for the media could be a blessing or a curse: asking that he and David should read my speeches (Ken had said he didn't want to) and thus understand and endorse them. I also hinted strongly that David had to pull his weight – in September I've had seventy-eight departmental invitations and been able to accept only two.

Victoria, Friday 7 October

Busy week! The MMR launch went very well and the children were just *lovely*! Some of the nicest photos ever taken of me in the press the next day. W. C. Fields was wrong – you should always be photographed with children and animals – as the PM has found, hugging calves during election campaigns and a koala bear on her recent visit to Australia.

Most of the week seemed to be spent in cars or trains. I came up (by car) on Sunday night, caught the train to Nottingham for Trent RHA's 'personal services' exhibition (all about making NHS more consumer friendly, excellent stuff), back by train to speak in Battersea for John Bowis[1] (packed and all very matey, but once again no microphone, so a sore throat resulted); Wednesday by car to

1. Conservative MP for Battersea.

Bristol and a disorganised scrum of pressmen and a few demonstrators. We had been told to go to the wrong entrance and it was a bit scary for a while, feeling totally unprotected. I've now insisted that someone from the department – either from my office, or R/L (Regional Liaison) or Press Office – go down and case the joint for all my visits, as we are having too many disasters. I put out the proposed circular on children in hospital that day, which amongst other things says, 'parents are not visitors', i.e. they should be part of the normal running of a children's ward. Thursday morning from Bristol to Derby; evening at a mock *Any Questions* for Patrick McLoughlin[1] in Ashbourne, and lots of agitation about their little (under-used) maternity unit which we are about to close. Big room, over 150 people, and no mike. Two of my office have been off sick with colds and flu this week and I suspect I've been fighting it off, but my throat is sore all the time and I am wondering if something is wrong – nodules perhaps! Meantime there's a new instruction: no mike, no come. They all think I have leather lungs and I haven't, and it doesn't occur to most of my hosts that a mike is a courtesy *and* a necessity.

And so back to London today (and drive back to Derbyshire early tomorrow). The main thing today was the Radio Show at Earl's Court which was super, with the real *Any Questions* in the evening: Tony Benn, John Mortimer, David Steel and me. I didn't think it was the best one I've done – I was trying to be wise and sensible and probably sounded rather ponderous instead. David Steel was rather low key too – now he's a nobody again, the edge, the fight, has gone. I remember Shirley Williams on the same show in Edmonton soon after she lost in Liverpool and became SDP president: the spirit had gone. I hope I don't lose mine for a while yet. John Mortimer was

---

1. Conservative MP for West Derbyshire.

civilised and fun at supper, and witty on the show, but turned out to be a founder member of the '20th June' group, a left-wing think tank. In the first question he showed himself a unilateralist, which was a gift – that rather demolished many of the apparently lofty political points he made later. Tony Benn was his usual dotty self.

We did have a really interesting discussion before the show about diaries and autobiographies and memoirs. Benn told us that he writes two thousand words of diary every night. David Steel is just settling down to write his, while Sara Keays this afternoon got an injunction against Norman Tebbit's memoirs and is planning to sue him for libel. *Norman's Revenge* should have been the title, as he has a swipe at everyone that doesn't think he's wonderful, starting with Lord Young, then Tim Bell, etc.! But his description of the bombing in 1984 is vivid and agonising – he 'heard his guts sloshing around inside him'; he thought there was a dead body beside him and it turned out to be his own, useless arm. His wife Margaret apparently had serious bouts of depression before the accident too; one gets the flavour of a man with a sad home life getting all his needs from politics.

I couldn't do a diary every night. I don't have, and wouldn't make, enough time. Douglas Hurd does, apparently, so we have something to look forward to there as well. It suggests a more ambitious person: he thinks he is going to be worth writing about in future! Perhaps that is in my mind too as I write this. A bit like being active in the Oxford Union twenty years ago and wondering if I should have a go at the presidency – then leaving it too late, not doing it well, not believing in myself (not doing anything behind the scenes either – how naive!) and so not getting it. I have slowly come to realise, and somewhat unwillingly, that I will have a crack at the leadership as soon as I can. Partly because I am in touch with real people, partly because I can offer some leadership and view of the future. I look at rivals like David Mellor and I like me better. In between I need to gain as much experience in Government and as much support in the country as possible, so that when the time is ripe it will seem very natural and I won't feel I'm not up to it. We're lucky, there are lots of good people around who could do a really good job, so I wouldn't mind in the least if someone else got it, as long as I could play a useful part – and that is far more likely if I've stood in a leadership contest and picked up a respectable amount of support. In all honesty I'm surprised at myself, and it shows you how far I've come since Oxford. The summit of my ambition then was to be an MP, and that seemed nearly impossible for so long. Once I was on the backbenches and debating with Tony (lovely) and Ray Whitney[1] (a fool) I wanted to be a minister. Right now I'd like to be promoted, outside the Department of Health preferably, and I would like to get into Cabinet as soon as I've picked up plenty of solid experience at number two level. If you get promoted too fast, like John Moore, it shows, so I'm not in haste. By then there will be a leadership contest which will involve those in the present Cabinet: unless, of course, she decides to stay on till they've all dropped off from old age! For example, Howe is sixty-one and Lawson fifty-seven – they won't wait around another five years. Baker and Clarke will, and by then they'll have John Major up with them. Hurd will stick it out (and he is damn good). Of all these I'd vote for Baker, Hurd, Clarke and Major in that order, but it may change. Clarke is too undisciplined for my taste as a leader (and he's been around since 1970 and was a whip back in Heath's Government, so someone else thinks so too). Baker has the edge over Hurd; there's a sweetness[2] about him and a resilience I like. He has also, to be frank, been very nice to me, even when I was a back-bencher, whereas Hurd has always reacted to my activities like

1. Conservative MP for Wycombe; Parliamentary Under-Secretary of State, Department of Health and Social Security, 1984–6.
2. EC later changed her mind about Baker.

there's a bad smell under his nose. Major is brainy and tough and nice underneath, but there's a definite lack of charisma; I reckon I would run him close in a straight fight after a few more years in Government. Ah! We shall see. I'd serve contentedly under all these and others like Malcolm Rifkind, but preferably in the Cabinet, not outside.

Neil Kinnock won his leadership contest with ease at the Labour Party Conference this week, but having handed him the chalice they poisoned it good and proper, by refusing to change their unilateralist stance on defence. So they won't get elected, simple as that. They also voted to repeal every scrap of trade union legislation since 1979, and even Kinnock himself admitted on television that the electorate would not accept policies like this. They have got themselves in a real pickle. The official line – peddled both by Neil Kinnock and that wily old warrior Denis Healey – is that the policies the Labour Party adopts must be credible and attractive to the electorate. Then they can win power. Then they can get rid of Trident, etc. But they must think we're all daft to fall for that approach; and if we do, then we are.

I gather that Tuesday's NHS Review meeting was 'confused and fraught', with the PM refusing to give way over independent hospitals and saying that the only reason for the delay is that the Department of Health isn't doing enough detailed work on it. They are all agreed that they want to sort out the consultants – don't we all? – but it's hardly the stuff of which great reforms are made. The trouble is that The Lady, like Kinnock, knows what she wants. And that what she wants will lose us elections.

Tower House, Sunday 16 October

Party Conference last week was a mild and uneventful affair, even though press speculation tried to whip up talk of revolts over high interest rates, etc.; but Nigel was super, better than I've ever heard and duly got his ovation. I loved the way he linked the free market to freedom and democracy; it touched something very deep for me. Ken Clarke gave a rumbustious speech, heavily larded with more money for the nurses: an extra £138 million. And that, he said, is in full and final settlement. Stuffing their mouths with gold! After the trade unions staged another breakdown of talks on Tuesday he was ready for them. Sod the talking, he said, we'll keep our word and we'll pay it anyway. We demand to see the minister! they howled. Fine, he said, there's David Mellor, see him. No! they shrieked, we want to see you; sod off, he said, and don't keep chasing me to Brighton because I won't see you there either. I reckon Ken's approach was quite right – masterly in fact; and on *Any Questions* on Friday he said the rudest things about the trade unions in a laid-back, exasperated tone, all the things John Moore muttered under his breath but never dared utter.

I slipped out of the meeting to finalise Ken Clarke's speech to hear John Moore address Conference on social security. The man really has no personality, no presence at all. It took him ages to get his first applause, and then only when he praised the PM. He said sensible things about the half a million fathers who don't support their children, but it wasn't clear what he was going to do about them. Behind the scenes he's fighting hard to get indexation for child benefit. Last year he was talking about abolishing it. I suspect Treasury are screwing him down hard, but I sense there's something personal there too; John Major wants him off the scene.

My only Conference activity was a fringe meeting on Wednesday for the Conservative Medical Society. I talked about the philosophy of prevention of illness in a free society and how Government's role must change, how compulsion is unnecessary (or ruled out). *Guardian* readers have bean sprouts coming out of their ears; the problem is to reach readers of the *Daily Mirror.* The *Daily Mail* was tickled about this and duly put me on pages one and two; they don't realise I'm saying that their readership is too thick and ignorant to take any notice of their own health unless someone screams it at them. Oh Lord, I hope it works. It did for Ray. I wonder if Ken Clarke . . . ? Not until he's had his heart attack, if then; but he must be a prime candidate, one of these days.

One last thing: Tuesday at a loose end I phoned around for a lunch companion and ended in the House of Lords with Roger Skelmersdale (made me pay my share!). It turns out that he chose DSS over DoH; after years of being a jobbing minister in the Lords, he can ask for what he wants. He said promotion for me won't take long – I hope not, or I'm going to get bored. And I gather I have a fan in Cabinet in the person of Lord Young, who sat next to me on the platform for Ken's speech. Don't take any notice of the critics, he said, you've done more to put these ideas forward than anyone, I'm a great fan of yours.

Tower House, Sunday 23 October, 11.45 p.m.

I fetched the girls from school on Friday, then on Saturday we spent a lot of time in Burton on their favourite activity, shopping for clothes, and I zipped through £150 quite easily. I felt myself go cold in the market when a youth went up to Debbie and offered her a cigarette; she looked very puzzled and I told him to go away, then she just took my arm and kissed me and said, I love you, Mum. Sympathetic clucks from the stallholders, but it makes you fearful for the future.

John Moore has lost the battle, if there was one, over the uprating of child benefit, which is to be frozen for the third year running, with the intention of allowing it to 'wither on the vine'. It was of course John Major who, as Minister of State for Social Security, wrote into the manifesto that child benefit would continue to be paid 'as now, and to the mother'; he didn't want it switched to the breadwinner or subsumed in tax allowances, etc. Ah, but that was then, and this is now. I've always thought that the £4 billion plus paid to every family in the land was a daft way of helping the needy and I find distasteful a mental picture of all these parents holding their hands out to the Government saying, 'Gimme!'. I'd rather they keep the tax they pay in the first place. There was a very friendly story on the front page of the *Sunday Times* today, saying John Moore was never in favour of uprating at all, but wants extra for targeting and had achieved it, and had done the same last year. I'll bet that was Major's idea: it sounds just like one of his deep schemes. They are offering up Moore as a sacrifice; she can't sack too many people when the next big reshuffle comes, but he is one of them, poor little man.

The Health and Medicines Bill comes back to our House on 1 November and there will be a real humdinger of a row. John Wakeham hinted last week that there must be concessions over eye tests for pensioners (and indeed that was his written advice), but Cabinet slapped him down and we'll crack on with fresh votes to restore the charges for both eyes and teeth. Ken will have a grand time and will win it; it will have to be a good majority for their lordships to back down. I'm enjoying this! Ken is just the man to take on the BMA. He does wear his scar tissue close to the surface, and has been delighted to see just how much more aggressive the NHS is now than in 1983–5, when he was Minister of State.

As for aggression, David Mellor really laid into the social workers this week. He told them not to be so protective, 'sanctimonious' and introverted. It was very well done, and the tone was just like his comments to the Israeli major[1] – 'It won't do, it really won't do.' Amen to that. I can't imagine Tony Newton leaning on them like that. I am pleased for David, too. He seems to have got over his resentment at being moved from the Foreign Office, though his

1. On a visit to the Occupied Territories, when he was a junior minister at the Foreign & Commonwealth Office.

office is full of photos of him with robed and exotic foreign dignitaries. Very able, yes, but not very nice. Yet he obviously cares about some things, quite deeply.

Tower House, Sunday 30 October

Debbie's fourteenth birthday; I've just taken her and Susie back to school, and Ray is driving down to London. He's welcome to the drive; I'd rather take half the time tomorrow on the train. Ray had his teeth out on Thursday – the front four – and now has a temporary plate. It looks very smart, *much* better than before, but he's very conscious of it and talking funny! We went to Devon on Thursday/Friday for half term; I spoke in Sidmouth and then joined the family at Brian and Trixie's[1] new house and we had supper and stayed overnight – the first time we have ever stayed anywhere other than Medical Hall.[2] On the Saturday morning I opened the new community hospital in South Molton, which replaces the tatty place where Ray's father died of lung cancer in 1985. Both the public events went very well. Jim Cobbley, the agent for twenty-five years in the Honiton constituency, said that the tickets have been changing hands on the black market! In fact they were matey and listened carefully to the speech, which also got good coverage. In all we've had a terrific press this week. Maybe since *The Economist* poll I'm being treated more seriously.

I've been thinking about families. Anthony Clare was on the radio again, and I thought about our session.[3] Why don't I get hurt? Because I have learned to protect myself. How did you learn? Because my father hurt me very much, and after that, nothing could

---

1. Ray's elder brother and sister-in-law.
2. i.e. with Ray's parents.
3. *In the Psychiatrist's Chair* broadcast on Radio 4 in 1988.

touch me as much. Clare poked away at the events of '71–2 (when my father broke off all relations upon my engagement to Ray), but left me feeling unmoved, and I've puzzled about why. When I think about my parents (not just Dad) hurting me, it is not then that comes to mind: it's ten years earlier, when I was fourteen. My parents flipped when I started going out with a Catholic boy. I accused my father of being a racialist, and he slapped me across the face. I remember feeling triumphant: I knew what I had to do then, to live my own life (keeping it all a secret from them, and from anyone who would tell), and to leave all those restrictions and rules behind as soon as I could.[1]

My revenge came in two satisfying dollops: one, the scholarship to Oxford, which he could *not* gainsay; and the other my marriage (which put him permanently and publicly in the wrong), both of which were my 'tickets to ride'. I sure learned patience, for both had to be right for me, too. I wasn't going to give him the satisfaction of saying I'd made any mistakes.

Can I do better with my own kids? I doubt it. Debbie is moody, beautiful, elegant, easily led. Susie is very clever, charming, ambitious, stoical and organised (which is why her bedroom is a mess, since someone else will always clear up after her!). When they are being grotty I lose interest fast and I'm much too didactic with them; I suspect the Currie in them will lead to polite, superficial relationships within the family, and to make their real intellectual and emotional lives elsewhere. How l would love to be their friend and confidante too, but I'm not motherly enough for that.

Must write briefly about politics, though I've been writing for an hour already (it does make me feel much better to put it on paper. I hope I never regret it.). On Tuesday we have the Health and

---

1. Some of these incidents appear in *She's Leaving Home* (1997).

Medicines Bill – and I have six files to read after this; still no concession on charges for tests. A concession to all pensioners on eye tests would cost only £22 million and on teeth £5 million and would see the Bill through, but it's the principle: pensioners are getting wealthier, not poorer (and more numerous) and there are other things such as television licences which could be demanded as a necessary free service. I thus think that Treasury were right, but the whips are very worried. Our majority last time was seventy-five with seventy-two Labour members away; this time Labour are flying them in from all over the world, and seventy of ours have signed an Early Day Motion against us. It may help that the Autumn Statement is on the same day. Hints have been dropped about '£1 billion extra for the NHS' and in fact it is £1.6 billion, and together with cost improvements and a cut in employers' National Insurance contributions will give £1.8 billion extra next year. John Major comes out of it with flying colours, having put in staggering numbers of hours – typically fifteen hours or more with each of the most difficult ministers.

The PM startled everyone, and saddened a few, by revealing in *The Times* that she intends to be leader for many years yet, and can't see anyone ready to take her place. Now that's no way to reward the loyalty of Geoffrey and Nigel, is it? She is still in great form. If looks could kill, she'd have turned the hapless Speaker[1] to stone when he 'failed' to hear Kinnock call her a cheat over child benefit. Kinnock (to his credit) repeated it loud and clear, and then the Speaker twittered his request for withdrawal; but the damage was done, both to the Speaker's reputation and to relationships between Margaret and Neil. She really loathes him and vice versa, and nothing will budge her from the leader's seat as long as she suspects that someone else might be nice and accommodating to him or his successors! She is

1.   Bernard Weatherill, MP for Croydon North East.

a little tubbier these days, but still very smart; often a bit husky and seems to get colds frequently but she works potty hours, often after 2 a.m., and has incredible stamina.[1] In the Commons on Thursday Geoffrey Dickens[2] congratulated her on the *Times* interview; as she rose to reply she caught my eye and grinned. She is a more relaxed person since the third victory, and I suspect feels she has proved her points, has won support, and can now start all over again being radical, the way she always wanted, without trimming. Hence child benefit, and all the effort (at least) to privatise the NHS till she realised, pronto, that the electorate wouldn't have it; hence the plans to privatise steel, rail and coal, at last. I wonder what she'll do after that?

Two other bits, this week. David Lightbown[3] has told me I should have a PPS, so I started the ball rolling by writing to Ken, who pooh-poohed the idea and said I should use either his or David's. The trouble is, there's far too much work for them to do (I've just done my fifty-fifth adjournment debate, the thirty-first since the last State Opening), and Ken's is Phillip Oppenheim, whose natural twerpness and arrogance has been given a real boost by his appointment. (David's is Greg Knight,[4] who is fine.) On Wednesday I was trying to find out what time Thursday's adjournment debate would start, as we thought the business might collapse. Standing at the bar of the chamber I was trying to explain my difficulty to Phillip, when suddenly it dawned on me. 'You're the PPS, Phillip!' I said. 'You go and find out.' 'What, me?' he said rudely. 'Yes, you, Phillip! You're the PPS, and I'm the minister,' I said to him, amused at his expression of horror. But he didn't go, so I did

---

1. At this time Margaret Thatcher was sixty-three years old.
2. Conservative MP for Littleborough and Saddleworth.
3. EC's whip; Conservative MP for Staffordshire South-East.
4. Conservative MP for Derby North.

it myself, and of course shared the story with the whip. They knew, it seemed; apparently the issue of my PPS has been discussed twice at whips' meetings this week (not much else to gossip about, said Tom Sackville,[1] the Department of Health whip) and the Chief is going to talk to Ken about it. I made it clear that I haven't been doing any lobbying.

Tower House, Thursday 10 November, 8.10 p.m.

I'm not supposed to be here at all but in Madrid, preparing for a WHO conference on tobacco tomorrow and an audience with Queen Sofia. But the debate on the last stages of the Health and Medicines Bill went on till 2.30 this morning (and I had the adjournment debate afterwards), so we pulled stumps and have a three-line whip on a guillotine tomorrow morning. So: no Madrid. I have looked suitably martyred all evening, but in all honesty it was a long way to go for a meeting and I would have seen nothing of the city except a hotel room. To enjoy it I would have needed several days and Ray and/or the kids. Doesn't that make me sound boring!

Tuesday was election day in the USA. I spent part of the evening at the US embassy, along with 1700 other people. It was billed as a great party, but in fact it was *very* dull. Free coffee (if you could find it) and Coke and Budweiser, but any more respectable drink was at a cash bar, as I discovered as I asked for a gin and tonic: '£1 please!' The food was ghastly and almost nonexistent – just one small display of 'Dunkin Donuts', and cold ones at that, and somewhere there were some hamburgers. No popcorn or corn on the cob or pancakes or Howard Johnson's ice cream or milkshakes or anything much; so at 12.45 a.m. I cleared off home and watched television

---

1. Conservative MP for Bolton West.

from bed for another hour. Well, Mr Ambassador, we have much better parties than that.

The Health and Medicines Bill passed rather easily through the Lords with a majority of fifty, but only by the skin of our eyeballs in the Commons. Our majority on teeth was sixteen and on eyes only eight. Both Ken and David misjudged the mood, as a very generous Autumn Statement had been announced that day; they were rather belligerent and threatened all sorts of other cuts if these clauses should fail.

The Review has got stuck again. It should be comic – but isn't. There was a full meeting on Tuesday morning and it is clear that the PM doesn't know what she wants, except more money for Barnet. It seems that they are back to square one. She suggested that John Major should chair it in order to make some progress – that shows how he has got on! Ken would accept that, and willingly work with John, whom he regards as reasonable.

Another supper with Jimmy Savile at the Athenaeum last Wednesday. And Jimmy in a suit looking *so* normal! He talked about his 'six foot girlfriend' (Diana) and how he got her involved with Barnardo's instead of AIDS. Fascinating evening.

Victoria, Monday 21 November, 11.30 p.m.

Back in flat after eve of session dinner at Number 10. Chicken again! It cannot be said that she overdoes the food stakes. Plenty of wine, though; very little smoking; Willie Whitelaw in attendance as special guest who toddled off at 9.50 p.m. and debate on the address to be led by Giles Shaw[1] and John Maples[2] (she called him Robert) in our

---

1. Sir Giles Shaw, Conservative MP for Pudsey.
2. Conservative MP for West Lewisham.

House, and Humphrey Atkins[1] in the Lords. The dinner was curiously low key; I was seated between Alan Howarth[2] and Lord Belstead[3] who are rather alike, and I did find conversation flagged a bit. Both are elegant, nice and intelligent, neither is sly or funny or cynical. I felt I should be discussing Proust or Elgar, but the topics didn't come. Instead I felt somewhat morbidly apprehensive, as I think we are going to have a grotty year. The nurses' dispute will grumble on for months, the NHS Review is failing to deliver the goods, everyone wants community care settled but no one wants Griffiths'[4] solution of local authorities doing it; we have a relatively short session and a lot of contentious legislation, including privatisation of water and power, neither of which will go down well in the Lords. Michael Howard was on the other side of Belstead, and his views (e.g. anti-Griffiths) did not help my generally gloomy mood. Nigel Wicks (the PM's current Private Secretary) was right opposite; I would have loved to gossip with him. I remember his phone call to our house – 'PM's office here' – in September 1986, asking me to come to Number 10, and thinking it might be a hoax. I recall phoning a whip (I think that was Peter Lloyd)[5] and asking him what he would do if 'Nigel Wicks' told him to start driving down to London, and he said, 'Get in my car . . .'

I've seen quite a lot of the girls recently, as they had an exeat this week and came home. We went to a Chinese for lunch yesterday and ate fried seaweed and wonton soup; and last weekend I was summoned by Susie to watch her play hockey (which I was able to

---

1. Holder of various Government posts, including Secretary of State for Northern Ireland, 1979–81; Opposition Chief Whip, 1974–9; Conservative MP for Spelthorne, 1970–87; MP for Mitcham and Morden, 1955–70.
2. An assistant Government whip; Conservative MP for Stratford-on-Avon.
3. Minister of State, Department of Environment.
4. Sir Roy Griffiths chaired a committee which reported on community care; it recommended that responsibility be shifted to local authorities.
5. A senior whip; Conservative MP for Fareham.

do, as my new Private Secretary Meg had sent one box without the key), and she won 3–1, scoring the last goal, with me cheering her on and 'embarrassing' her. It was fun, and lovely out on the hillside with the sun shining over Staffordshire, then tea and buns with muddy teachers.

Saw B several times recently. Will try and get it going again this week: no regrets either way.

Victoria, Thursday 24 November, 10.45 p.m.

I spent this evening at IBM's HQ on the South Bank, where they presented a computer to Esther Rantzen's ChildLine organisation. It was a splendidly professional do, audio-visual, etc. The phone line set-up followed *Childwatch*, a television programme she made in 1986 which brought child sexual abuse out into the open. She has had to put up with plenty of abuse since, but they are answering a thousand calls per week, and around seven thousand more can't get through. About four hundred have been referred to the authorities. Many have queries which aren't appropriate (e.g. parents arguing or little brother being a pest), and I suspect a large number are emboldened by their conversation with ChildLine to approach a caring relative. They are goodies as far as I am concerned, and I said so. Norman Fowler arranged a £50,000 start-up grant, the PM had a reception for them and I gave them a further £100,000 grant this summer. Today we published the Children's Bill, which starts in the Lords – led, remarkably, by the Lord Chancellor – and will come to us by end January. But all the legislation in the world will not touch some children, and Esther Rantzen will: good for her.

Earlier in the day I met Princess Anne, who attended the annual lunch of the British Nutrition Foundation at the Royal Society of Medicine (second time I've been there this week. Last night it was the dinner of the Royal College of Pathologists: nice people).

Smoked fillet of fish, chicken with veg and baked apricot in fruit sauce: all lovely and *so* balanced. My driver Cliff told me with disgust that all the drivers were attended to downstairs and had greasy hamburgers, fried onions and chips – he was not impressed! HRH was smart and very slim, in a green suit dress with a big collar. She stays slim by eating very little: the fish, the spinach, toyed with the chicken, had part of the apricot, no wine, just water. She chatted in a good-natured and friendly way during lunch, about her home in Gloucestershire, teaching the children to ride with proper helmets, and sports injuries – how we look after the horses better than the riders. She is pretty and very pleasant close to, with a delightful, broad, winsome smile.

Ken Clarke's Prayer meetings are totally casual and unstructured, so there's no opportunity to raise proper issues and get a 'steer'. We tend to do that at the end, when Ken tosses off the first thought that comes into his head, without realising that some considered views (however brief) are required. In this way he has twice said to me that he is not happy about our mental illness policy, which has been decided for years between psychiatrists and the pressure groups such as MIND, and asked me to look into this. I had decided months ago that next Monday's MIND annual conference in Bournemouth would give us time to work through some ideas and duly prepared a speech, officials happy, including Permanent Secretary. Then Ken announced that our current, inadequate policy is working beautifully and is not to be challenged. I took a deep breath and said that I thought many of the criticisms of our policies in this area were well founded. (I had given him a copy of the speech to check, and pointed out with a little malice that weeks ago he had said that he would not read through my speeches and I had insisted!) Fortunately I had almost subconsciously engaged in an old trick, of producing a speech that was too long. By the time we had erased four or five paragraphs we were still left with a powerful ditty. Home Office had agreed the lot without a murmur and now we'll see what

Number 10 make of it; and I hope to heaven that Ken does not mess it about any more. We had a fierce argument, but I was very keen to win it, and tactically the best way was to make him knuckle down and adapt the text. Really I was saddened that Ken was under-informed and still spouting the same stuff as in 1983. That's the trouble with an instinctive politician – he starts off with an opinion, and is reluctant to modify it in the light of facts.

Tower House, Sunday 11 December

A lot has happened since we last met! Mostly concerning eggs. I've just written another bit of my obituary.

We have been worried for some time about a rising tide of food poisoning, mainly associated with salmonella from chickens. It is appalling to think that most of the carcasses on sale in this country are infected with this bug, but it is killed by cooking, and only poor handling (e.g. allowing a defrosted chicken to drip over cooked food) will cause any problem. This year it got into the eggs, which means real trouble. In August CMO issued a Press Notice advising against the use of cracked eggs and raw eggs (e.g. in icing, mayon-naise, mousse, etc.). By November we were getting reports of virulent infection from cooked eggs, e.g. in lemon meringue pie, scotch eggs, or egg sandwiches. I've just seen papers circulated to Cabinet, following discussion on Thursday, which linked eggs to twenty-eight deaths. 'Egg infection has the potential to be fatal,' it says blandly. So CMO issued another statement on 21 November, saying cook all eggs thoroughly and don't give lightly cooked eggs to old people, pregnant women or children. Alarm mounting, egg sales dropping, nowt from MAFF, parliamentary questions started appear-ing – and then, quite inadvertently, I blew the whole business wide open by saying we suspected that most of the egg production was infected. I based this on my knowledge of the carcasses (I've seen estimates of 60–80 per cent infected), reasoning that if the fowls are infected that end up in the fridges, then so are the laying fowls which are often the same birds. Anyway, pow!

I had in fact been looking for an opportunity to raise the subject for some weeks, turning down requests from Anglia TV, etc., looking for a big national, so when ITN came along to Chellaston and caught me up a ladder helping to insulate a house for 'Keep Warm Keep Well', I thought fine, this will do. But I didn't calculate the effect – which looks like it will bankrupt a lot of farmers. My timing could not have been better – or worse, depending on your point of view. The *Lancet* had come to much the same conclusion the previous day, based on reports from Wales, including a wedding which ended with one guest on a kidney machine. The Public Health Laboratory Service then published an analysis of eggs from one flock implicated in an outbreak and found seventeen infected eggs out of 1700 tested – that's one out of every hundred, or one in every eight boxes or so, and the infection is both inside and outside the eggs which are traditionally not washed in the UK (and not refrigerated until we get them home). The environmental health officers and 'Chickens Libbers' (anti-battery farming) lobbyists piled in, with details of what is fed to the creatures – ground-up offal, droppings, etc.! Last year MAFF inspectors found that a quarter of the feed going into those farms was infected, but no one was prosecuted. The public stopped buying eggs and started writing letters: around 10:1 in support of me, though some were chicken libbers and I'm not – the salmonella has been found in free-range eggs, too.

Clearly, however, it touched a very raw nerve. Television programmes today suggested that the farmers have now realised that this government does not regard them as having any clout, and they quoted a whole range of things which the PM has insisted on, e.g. quotas, set-aside, restriction on nitrates, etc. They feel really hard done by. They have demanded my resignation in no uncertain terms and rushed to their lawyers to sue, but they would need to prove malicious intent, and faced with a barrage of statistics about the mounting tide of egg infection they would find that difficult. The PM demanded to see all the papers, read them and then said she had scrambled egg for lunch; still there was a lively discussion at Cabinet. Ken had to do a private notice question on Monday and faced down the critics – many of them are crusty old knights of the shires, misogynists he called them to me later, and others who are jealous. I'm afraid they have made fools of themselves and they won't thank me for it at all. Meanwhile, MAFF did very well as long as Richard Ryder[1] was in charge, while John MacGregor[2] was in Canada for what turned out to be an unsuccessful GATT round. Richard was very firm with the industry, telling them to stop flapping about and get their house in order: he's consulting lawyers to see if the voluntary code he announced on Monday can be made compulsory, as I suspect it will have to be.[3] John MacGregor then fanned the flames a bit more on Saturday morning by phoning the BBC from Heathrow while changing planes to Brussels. He accused me of saying that all the eggs had salmonella – which I didn't say – and claimed that MAFF had planned their action carefully and that I'd spoiled it all. That's crap, frankly. MAFF had been discussing the matter with the industry for seven months and was planning a voluntary code, sometime in the future.

I do so get fed up with all the media attention. I now refuse to talk to the press at all, which is awful; I've always believed they are an essential part of a free state, and that people in a democracy are entitled to know what we are all up to. Susie got cross when she tried to phone several times during the week and couldn't get us to

1. Parliamentary Under-Secretary of State, Ministry of Agriculture, Fisheries and Food; Conservative MP for Mid-Norfolk.
2. Minister of Agriculture, Fisheries and Food; Conservative MP for South Norfolk.
3. There is still no compulsory scheme for the eradication of salmonella in eggs or chicken meat in the UK. Such schemes as have been developed since (e.g. the lion stamp) are entirely voluntary.

answer, so we'll have to change the number. It won't stop them camping out on the doorstop at 6.30 a.m. and chasing me on to the train; I only wish my sense of the ridiculous didn't wear so thin at such times.

Relations in the department have improved. I had a long chat with Jonathan Hill[1] and he said Ken's been like that with everyone. He's simply incapable of appreciating how other people feel and think, and is often very surprised and contrite when people complain or are upset. Well, I am, I said, and you can tell him so. We worked so hard on mental illness, and on tobacco, and I would like that expertise acknowledged, not derided or ignored. I was particularly hurt at a comment reported in the *Sunday Times* from someone in his office (whom I took to be Jonathan) that while relations between us two were 'correct', David had impressed him. Anyway, the message seems to have got across and he is somewhat friendlier now. He continues to be amazed at the media coverage I attract – so am I – and said only the PM gets anything like it: which was kinder than David Waddington, who said it was like George Brown's! But Ken still isn't quite aware. Our regular post-Cabinet lunch on Thursdays is in a restaurant or a pub and the conversation is loud and jovial. Not really the way to keep us all out of the press. Oh well. God give us a peaceful Xmas . . .

Tower House, Wednesday 21 December, 1 a.m.

A week, they say, is a long time. I'm not sure where to start, so let's start at Question Time on Tuesday. I wasn't all that good, but the House seemed friendly. I counted up my mailbag and had thirty-eight antis (mostly producers), twenty-six not sure, need more info,

---

1. Special adviser to Kenneth Clarke.

and 525 in favour, many of them very sweet. I passed on the total to Murdo Maclean. MAFF still flailing around. Monday saw a meeting chaired by the PM with Richard Ryder (MacGregor still in Brussels), Clarke, Major, Acheson and Meldrum (Chief Vet). It was decided that the Government would 'have to strike a difficult balance between giving sound advice to the public on health and convincing the egg industry that enough was being done to restore public confidence'.

However, events moved faster than that. As we voted on Tuesday night I saw the PM being harassed by Paul Marland,[1] John Townsend,[2] Sir William Clark[3] and John Carlisle[4] (the last two of whom declared tobacco interests in the members' register). Turds all. Geoffrey Dickens stood up for me, and she said, I know, I know. I realised I wasn't concentrating on anything at all, and by Wednesday morning, when I went to an Institute of Directors 'Women Mean Business' Conference, I could hardly string two words together. I wanted to drop out – so I did, caught the 1.30 p.m. train to Liverpool and stayed there till Thursday night. It wasn't just eggs that were preoccupying me. Ray had been supposed to put the girls on a train to Liverpool from Stafford on Tuesday, but he was in a hurry to get back for an Old Boys' do, so he just left them, not even on the right platform, with all their school gear too, and Susie with no jacket. They had to find some help to get themselves on the train. When they told me this on the phone on Tuesday evening, I felt angry and frightened and guilty, as it was the first time they had travelled by train alone like that. So I was somewhat distracted by all this, and once they are

---

1. Conservative MP for Gloucestershire West, PPS to the Minister of Agriculture, Fisheries and Food, 1983–6.
2. Conservative MP for Bridlington.
3. Conservative MP for Croydon South.
4. Member of the Commons Select Committee on Agriculture; Conservative MP for Luton North.

on holiday I usually switch off anyway. The only work in Richmond House was endless discussion about the Review, which I find totally uninteresting – it is all yet another reorganisation as far as I can see. So it seemed a good idea to slip away for a couple of days.

When I got back to London on Thursday evening, Meg and Steve Bird from the Press Office were waiting at Euston and whisked me off. Writs from the egg producers were flying around (though in fact they never caught us). We went to my flat but there were reporters outside, so we drove on past and ended up at Meg's house in Walthamstow. I did boxes until 2 a.m., ostensibly to prepare for a debate on abortion the following day, but by early morning I was already composing a resignation letter in my head. If you can't get on with your work; if that fact means that other people have to do it for you; if you can't get any peace or rest; and if you wish profoundly and persistently that you were somewhere else, then it's no time to stay.

Ken had a word at 8.45 a.m. and I asked to see the PM; she was free at 12.50 p.m., so it looked like a long wait. I spent part of it in David's room, while the press hovered outside my window. He did not mean to be tactless, I'm sure, but he spent those several minutes talking about himself and how difficult he found the Department of Health. I told Meg in the corridor that I planned to resign; she raised a civil servant's eyebrow and said, 'Hard cheese!' Then we went across to the Chief Whip's office, round the back of Number 12, and cleared texts with David Waddington and Bernard Ingham. I didn't realise I could help write the PM's letter and asked if a reference to Derbyshire could go in, to mollify my constituents, and that was duly done. I wrote out mine by hand, hers was typed, and in I went; we ritualistically glanced at each other's letters, then talked for half an hour. It's a bit of a jumble now, but we did talk about eggs and it was clear she knew a lot about it. She did not defend MAFF or the producers, or the falsely reassuring adverts (dreadful things, I really can't believe MAFF agreed to them, but MacGregor's Private

Secretary said MAFF thought they were just right. Prats!). She said nice things about me, but made no offers or promises, except that she suggested I might chair a select committee – no thanks. She mentioned Nick Ridley's gaffe over a letter some years ago, and 'look where he is now'.[1] She was keen to get women ministers, and had tried very hard with Marion Roe, but she 'didn't have it, and you do'. And I told her that the world had changed, and we must look after the consumers, and they trust her to ensure that the product is sound. Anyway I had been fine till the end of the interview and indeed have not felt very upset since – but then she gave me a cuddle and it creased me for a minute, and when I told her how I felt she said, 'That is because we are friends', and that was that. Out the back way again, and whisked off to Ray's office.

Then the fun began. I had phoned Ray from Number 12 and asked him to arrange for me to hole up there for the afternoon and then get me to a safe house. The children were due to arrive at Euston at 4 p.m. and they too needed to be met and spirited away. Our guardian angel turned out to be Paul Russell, a small, aggressive partner in Arthur Andersen, Welshman, ex-rugby referee at international level, who treated the whole of the rest of the day like a rugby match, planned with care, executed with skill, scored without loss. Poor Ray hadn't a clue; he proposed going to fetch the girls by Tube! We insisted on a car and driver; he hadn't figured out a way in and out of the building (we went out through the bank on the Strand while the nation's press crowded round the Surrey Street entrance. Five minutes to get out before the bank's alarms went!). Having dropped the children at the safe flat, he then went back to the office. It never occurred to him that he might be recognised and followed, but fortunately Paul got him into a van and made him lie down to

1. Secretary of State for the Environment.

get him out. I went via a partner's flat, where I was given tea and toast, and then off to a lovely flat in Hornton Street, off High Street Kensington, which turned out to be perfect. We stayed till Monday night and went home after the theatre. In fact we went to the theatre twice, and to Gerry Cottle's Circus in Battersea Park on the Sunday evening. While we were holed up in the flat both John Moore and John Major managed to get through, and both were very kind; the latter was so concerned and so nice that I got a bit creased again. Now I know who will be next PM, if the party has any sense.

Chris[1] was a brick and brought food, sleeping bags and towels, and we were really a lot more comfortable than in Victoria. The shops are better too, and on Monday morning I even went jogging in Kensington Gardens and felt much more alive than for weeks. On Monday afternoon we went to my brother Henry's new house in Fulham and met his new baby daughter, so new she has no name, and for the first time I met properly his girlfriend Louise. God knows what she sees in my brother!

Eventually we drove up to Derbyshire late on Monday night: we met the police in the lane about 1 a.m. and they said, all quiet, it's dark up there. We couldn't open the new gate, so we parked in front of it and humped bags tiredly up the lane. Ray went back to work the next day and will be home tomorrow, which is why I'm writing this in the small hours and slowly getting sozzled on port – I won't get another chance till he goes back to Holland on New Year's Day. He phoned last night, and said he'd driven down to London listening to a radio phone-in programme and everyone had spoken up for me. Unfortunately, he'd also heard Edward Pearce on the radio, describing me as 'an icon': not at all sure what he meant by that – a symbol maybe, anyway something stylised, not quite real – certainly

---

1. Christine Heald, EC's House of Commons secretary.

not an object of devotion, but that is how my husband seems to have seen it, for he said that it was very difficult being married to an icon! He says he's proud of me. I think it has just begun to dawn on him that I've spent the last few years doing something useful, which people have appreciated, and perhaps he's feeling a little guilty about teasing me so much.

I've written about everything I knew and did. What didn't I know? For example, that the executive of the 1922 Committee[1] had demanded my resignation on Thursday, the night I came back from Liverpool, so that was that, she wouldn't go against them. I wasn't told this at the time, though Ken said it had got 'very nasty last night', but he didn't say any more. It's a new, rather more right-wing executive, so perhaps they were flexing their muscles too. But I was certainly enabled to write my letter as if it was all my own decision, and everyone was helpful and friendly. Ken's letter refers to 'squabbles' between David and me, but I don't recall any. On the very few occasions when we talked, we agreed, so I don't know what David's been saying to Ken. I don't trust him an inch. Something not quite right about him . . .

Could I have got out of it? I was answering a question about the hospital catering service and knew that we had warned them on eggs (there were four public health warnings before my bit, two internal to the NHS on the topic). I had seen estimates that 80 per cent of all chicken carcasses have salmonella. And I made what may – and may not – have been a false connection. Had I said 'much' instead of 'most', I might have got away with it. In fact retraction and apology was never discussed, not at any time. As it turns out, the Government appears to have caved in to a producers' lobby, and I am seen to be the victim of an injustice. There are calls

1. The influential committee of backbench Tory MPs.

for me to be reinstated and expectations that I'll be in before the next election, etc.

Frankly, I don't want any of it. I've enjoyed the last few days, being with the kids. I've enjoyed not having to do sodding boxes, or adjournment debates late into the night. I've enjoyed not dining with boring old farts in the Commons, or listening to delegations led by smarmy MPs, who then say something different in the lobby later that night. I made a long list of the advantages and disadvantages, as I always do at any turning point, and it was almost entirely positive: mainly having more time for the family, friends (totally neglected in recent years) and for myself, and having a broader remit, being able to speak in more (different) debates – and then say anything I need to. I'll be able to use my mind more, instead of endlessly wittering on about the same things and getting to dislike it all thoroughly. In fact, I think I had been bored and fed up for months – not getting on with Ken, not happy about policy, cheesed off with having to explain and defend myself endlessly to Ken and getting fobbed off with his cheeky chappie approach. I should have moved before . . .

Most of all, I can make some money. I'll try for a couple of directorships; that is the easy money. Gordon Heald[1] has already suggested advising a PR firm which is a client, and I will ask Sammy Harari[2] if I can do some for him too. I have some ideas in the human resources field (employment of women, and occupational health, and non-pay emoluments). I shall ask Basil Feldman[3] if I can assist with work he's doing on the NHS/private link up. And there's a book to be written, on Government health policy 1986–8,[4] which only I

1. Husband of EC's secretary, Chris.
2. His firm handled some DHSS and Home Office campaigns against drugs.
3. Sir Basil Feldman, chairman of Watchpost Ltd and vice-president of the National Union of the Conservative Party.
4. Of all these plans only the book materialised: *Life Lines*, published by Sidgwick & Jackson in October 1989.

can write and is the kind of political history that's rare and valuable. I shan't do articles, but I'd like to do book reviews – I shall enjoy reading the books, if nothing else. My trivial objective is to get to the end of this Parliament with a fur coat and some decent jewellery.

1989

Tower House, Wednesday 4 January

It has in fact been one of our best Christmases ever, partly because I had no work, no pressure and loads of time, and partly because everyone has been so nice to me! We have had an enormous and very friendly postbag. Back in London, poor Chris has been swamped: one morning she was so dismayed by the number of letters that she burst into tears and had to be given brandy by the head postmaster. We paid a helper just to open the letters, and in three days she spent nearly nine hours at it. One letter from a Beatle (Ringo) made it all worthwhile for her! Now I'm getting on with responding.

Here in Derbyshire, we swam a lot and shovelled logs and walked to the Stenson Bubble[1] through the mud, and through more mud to Mrs Hewitt's smallholding in Findern to see the newborn lambs. Roses in cheeks and a tremendous feeling of relaxed wellbeing, surrounded by love and affection. Make the most of it, Edwina, it won't last. The *Daily Express* followed us to the lambs: their photo was just lovely and I was secretly pleased that it was a *farming* event. *The Times* chased us in London last night, so we're on the front page today – with Debbie looking very scruffy indeed; she wasn't too pleased at that.

On Sunday Ray went to Holland for two weeks. The last time he went there was the week of the resignation, when I had no phone

1. A pub on the Trent and Mersey Canal.

number for him (and made no effort to contact him, to be truthful); this time he has phoned twice and given me his number. Susie arranged to stay with a friend in Brum, so I took Debbie to the panto (Russ Abbott, who was great, and whom we saw after), and then drove her down to London and stayed at the flat two days. She went to the Toulouse-Lautrec exhibition at the Royal Academy while I shifted paper with Chris, then she came to Star Chamber Court and helped me pack. I didn't feel melancholy, just grubby, and threw out a lot; fortunately I've kept a lot of useful stuff from '86 and '87 which I hope to use for the book (three offers from publishers so far. Golly, I hope something comes of it: I'm £400 down in December and £11,000 down for the year. We do need that money). Debbie is just lovely on her own, away from Susie: we had a great couple of days, friendly and chatty and sensible. I took her for a treat to see Francis Durbridge's *A Touch of Danger* at the Whitehall Theatre – what a lazy piece of theatre, written just like a radio play, no acting at all and only one funny line, which I now can't remember! The panto at the Hippodrome was a real contrast: lavish, energetic and genuinely funny, even at Monday's matinée. Two thousand screaming, cheering, clapping people. I asked Russ Abbott afterwards how he managed to keep it up – he said you must do it properly, it's the only way. It was a *grand* afternoon. There were several egg/Currie jokes (they were in already, it turned out) and each one got a round of friendly applause, for we had been spotted sitting in Box A. At the last Abbott pointed at me and said, 'She takes a lot of stick, but she's a great lady' and called for a round of applause which was very warm, and Debbie hugged me!

I still can't quite believe the strange events of 3–16 December, the weird row, the Government's buying off the egg industry, the fierce passions expressed on all sides, the huge, warm, emotional postbag (on Radio 4's *Today* programme I was runner-up to Mrs Thatcher for 'Woman of the Year' and 'closing fast' – Gorbachev was 'Man of the Year', and quite right). It turned on John MacGregor: had he taken the same line as Richard Ryder, I'd still be in the job and the Government's credibility would not have taken a knock. As it is though, I seem to have encouraged friends and fans to speak up by my own silence, which they see as dignified and I see as a blessed relief; after the press have pursued me up the street asking their questions, with me ignoring them and not changing pace, I get in my car, or whatever I'm doing, and buzz off; it gives me pleasure to speak the real answers out loud as I drive away! But I meant what I wrote earlier: I am enjoying myself, I'm not bored yet, I'm rested and well and love being with the children at least for a while, and I hope the new activities will absorb me asap and keep me mentally busy. I wouldn't go back to that job, and that persona, for all the tea in China; I got to loathe the 'Another row broke out' headlines, week after week, when I'd said the most anodyne and ordinary things; and I don't like the tag 'controversial', when all I was trying to do was my job as well as I could. That makes me angry and determined to put the record straight, through the book, I hope. In all the articles written about me in the last month there has been hardly any mention of women's health or any of the good things I've done, and I don't intend just to let all that die. I do not want to be a Parliamentary Under-Secretary again. It's too vulnerable a job altogether – OK if you are part of a team which works, but hopeless if there's no team, as there wasn't after the '88 reshuffle, or if no one is interested in your views.

The NHS Review was leaked today on Radio 4's *Today* programme, fairly accurately from what I can tell. Most of it, frankly, seems irrelevant to me. We will get a one-off improvement from increased efficiency and then the funding problems will start again; partly because there's not much mention about health. They started off from the proposition 'The NHS is expensive and inefficient – can we do better?', when they should have said, 'How do we improve the health and general wellbeing of the nation?' No wonder I felt as if I was in a different department much of the time.

And my latest 'row' is a silent one, as it has come out that I have politely said 'sod off' to the Agriculture Select Committee. I don't want to speak in public and I can do without their kind of kangaroo court. Ann Winterton,[1] who is a member, was on Midlands TV at 6.30 making nasty remarks; I thought no, you spiteful bitch, I'll not give you the pleasure; I'll not dance to your tune, not any more.

Tower House, Friday 13 January, 4.40 p.m.

Tuesday was my first day back in the House, for a statement by Paul Channon.[2] I asked him a (suitably anodyne) question. My heart was racing two hundred to the minute, but I sat in the third row back, close to the officials' box, and realised I could not be seen from the Press Gallery at all (Matthew Parris spotted me on his way in – but the others missed me completely). Then it was my turn, and the PM deliberately turned in her seat and gave me her full frontal sympathetic look! And then it was done; messages from Chief Whip and Leader of the House, excellent, perfect comeback. Mark Lennox-Boyd, the PM's PPS, asked me at 1922 Committee last night if I was OK and burbled on about becoming chairman of a select committee; no thank you, I thought, but there isn't a vacancy anyway.

I have, however, made other progress. I went to the House of Commons gym on Wednesday and the adviser tested my basic fitness – golly, she put me through it! She said I was excellent, I had reached the level of fitness they aspire to. That was great, but I ached all over! She will devise some exercises which will help my

---

1. Conservative MP for Congleton.
2. Secretary of State for Transport; Conservative MP for Southend West since 1959, succeeding his father, the diarist Sir Henry 'Chips' Channon.

back, which aches quite a bit these days, and try to reduce hips and thighs which look as if they come from a different body from my skinny shoulders. Then I paid my last visit to Mr Croft's surgery in Harley Street to meet his speech therapist, Mrs Cook: she's a dumpy little Australian woman, just like the Michelin man in black, but she was sweet and says the problem is that I slump when I sit and don't resonate (I do it fine when I stand up). She had me humming 'M-M-M-Monday!' until my teeth ached. That means it works, apparently, so as I drove to Leicester this morning (slowly – in a jam – as the M1 is closed) I practised resonating by reading all the street signs . . . ! I must say the most tiring (and expensive) aspect of being a backbencher again is finding one's way around: three or four taxis a day are not cheap, so I've started using the buses.

I also found my financial prospects improved dramatically this week and now I'm faced with the puzzle of how much I'll tell Ray – because I can earn far more than him, and I wouldn't want to damage his ego. The two main contributors were Maurice Lovatt of Bass Worthington; he's their PR man, cheeky chappy type but very sharp. I had him in for lunch at House of Commons and I think it will be £17 well spent. I'm after a directorship with Bass plc, which also owns Holiday Inn, Crest Hotels and Coral Leisure (betting shops), as well as breweries, pubs, etc., and is major soft drinks producer – Coca-Cola, Pepsi and Seven-Up – I thought they were supposed to compete! He was very interested indeed. I know the drinks industry is very concerned about its image, and I'm keen to learn about some new business and the hotel and catering side could use me. How much? I've no idea, but I'll ask Norman Tebbit and John Moore. Given a choice I'd have £20,000 p.a., plus £5000 of Bass shares and a new outfit for every public appearance on their behalf and a guarantee of no more than four such per annum. In a fortnight I meet John Gorton of BP and will try for them, too; if that doesn't work, maybe Sainsbury or a good pharmaceutical firm like

Wellcome or Glaxo. But BP alone could bridge the £11,000 gap between old and new income.[1]

Then I met Hilary Rubinstein of A. P. Watt, the oldest literary agents in London. Anthony Clare is on their list, which looked serious but interesting. Rubinstein wrote me a sweet letter and very diffidently put their leaflet in. He turned out to be older than I expected (?sixty), grey wispy hair, smaller and slighter than my mental image, very pleasant but sharp too. I talked through some ideas with him and have typed them up. He said we could expect an advance of £10,000, but possibly up to £25,000 (out of which I have to pay for extra secretarial help, but it's claimable against tax), and if the book does well we should have £50,000 in total. He takes 10 per cent. Very nice! But I have to get on with it, so have scheduled February and March for main work on papers and can deliver final text by 1 May. Then it can come out in the autumn and hopefully will be in bestseller lists at Xmas. (Just for comparison, my MP's salary is £24,000.)

Then the action started, and what fun it has been. All the newspapers and magazines have asked me to write articles or regular columns; most didn't mention money. In the lobby on Wednesday David Mellor told me that the *Sun* had mentioned a figure of £50,000 to him and so had *Today*. I was staggered (I used to get £75 for an article as a backbencher). It doesn't make any difference to my decision – since to write a weekly column means swapping my present prospects, whatever they might be, for becoming Woodrow Wyatt; and no money could compensate for that. The *Today* reporter accosted me in the lobby on something else, and I told him firmly that before his editor started talking to my friends about how much cash he'd offered me, he might like to let me know first. So now I

---

1. Nothing came of this, and EC was never offered a directorship of any public company.

have, nestling in my handbag, a letter from *Today* offering £100,000 for a weekly column. They can still stuff it, but Hilary might find this useful in his negotiations!

It's done my morale such good and I feel pleased as Punch. Hilary also suggested an idea I already had in mind, i.e. interviewing for someone like LWT. I'd already put feelers out to meet Brian Tesler, the MD.[1] He paid Walden[2] £75,000 for eleven interviews. I would charge less (and do fewer), and we could do this possibly in the autumn. Maybe another £25,000? Some people have said I'll be back at the next reshuffle, but that would mean taking up where I left off, which I firmly don't want, so I'd rather wait, keep busy and make some money like this.

Murdo Maclean took me out to dinner on Tuesday night. Officially we were going to show off that I was OK, so we went to Lockets[3] – but it was empty! (L'Amico would have been better.) He's an extraordinary man, great company and got me a little squiffy on champagne. I tried to tell him about the miseries before December, but I'm not sure how much he took in. (I made a better job telling John Major on Wednesday night and got some genuine sympathy.) Murdo's job is one of the most interesting in Government. Apparently the Chief Whip's secretary was always a private Central Office appointment, and in 1924, when Ramsay MacDonald came in, the new Labour Government had to borrow this chap, who continued to draw his salary from CCO! In 1929 it was at last decided to make it a Civil Service job, but unlike other ministers' private secretaries who move on each year or so, this is permanent, and there have been only three since it started. Murdo is forty-three and has been there twenty years – and each one appoints his successor. He told me lots of lovely

---

1. He was in fact chairman, having been managing director until 1984.
2. Brian Walden, the former Labour MP, had become a television presenter and journalist specialising in political interviews.
3. A restaurant in SW1 much frequented by MPs.

stories, most of which I was too tight to remember. He can never write his memoirs as it would destroy the job; he is 51 per cent in the Government Whips' Office, 49 per cent in the Opposition Whips' Office, and they all have to trust him. He was a young Assistant Private Secretary in Wilson's office when he was PM and told me that Wilson was pissed much of the time. When the Biafran War was over, Wilson had to telephone the USA and speak to the President to arrange an aid package. The PM's comments were recorded but for some reason the President's weren't – so Murdo had to make them up – and in ten years' time when the minutes are published, the President's words will be what Murdo thought they should have been! And he started life as a sixteen-year-old clerk in a social security office. Remarkable man. (David Maclean[1] said he always has gorgeous women as companions. Once he brought an Italian opera star into the Whips' Office. He had been teaching her Gaelic songs, so they had an impromptu concert from her . . . !)

Victoria, Thursday 19 January, 11.45 p.m.

Very tired and achy, mainly because I ran for a bus this afternoon, slipped and generally had a tumble. Nothing broken and only my tights gone west, but dignity compromised and bruises tomorrow!

Another good week really, though not as euphoric as last, redolent with famous names. I did a lunch for John Wheeler, the pleasant, dignified MP for Westminster North, at the Commons. He said they were all business people, but most seemed to be lawyers – except for Sir Leslie Porter of Tesco (Shirley's husband), sitting opposite – a little, brown, wizened man with bright darting eyes, just like a little monkey; and David Sieff of Marks & Spencer, who sat next to me

---

1. Assistant Government whip; Conservative MP for Penrith and The Border. No relation to Murdo Maclean.

and is the exact opposite, tall, slim, elegant, patrician, member of Jockey Club and patron of the arts, etc. I pumped him for information about the non-executive director's role, especially Lady Janet Young who is theirs. She's excellent, he said, and clearly her independence and willingness to pipe up were an asset. That's good, for I know I can do the same. I was amused at different times in the week to get different views on how much a non-executive director should expect: £5–10,000 said Mary Archer (Anglia TV, Lloyd's), but £10–25,000 said Sir Basil Feldman (widespread interests, mostly not *quite* top drawer – Murdo said, sup with a long spoon with him . . .). I don't mind, I just want a couple of nice ones which will keep me busy and happy and help pay the mortgage!

I met Jeffrey and Mary Archer at his flat in Alembic House on Albert Embankment. It's an unattractive tower office block, quite unexceptional; you press the appropriate buzzer and in you go. The flat, however, is something else – all glass surrounds, a view for a hundred miles in any direction; you could touch the towers of Battersea Power Station and look down on the Palace of Westminster. Huge off-white sofa, glass table laden with new books and a gold plaque in the shape of a book with the title *Not a Penny More, Not a Penny Less* – bowls full of pink, open, blowsy tulips and a Renoir to match of a pink, open, blowsy girl! I had met Jeffrey in the foyer, showing out Sir Ronald Millar (PM's speech writer), an actor whose face I recognised but whose name I don't remember, and another, younger man; Jeffrey said he'd just had 'one of his lunches for about ten people and this group were the last to go' (3.30 p.m.). We started off very well, for as we went up in the lift I asked if he owned the whole block; he looked startled as if he wasn't usually asked that, then a bit sheepish and said yes.[1] As we sat down, I

---

1. It seems that this was untrue.

observed that he looked down on Downing Street and Parliament and he laughed and said harshly, 'Yes! Looking down on the lot of them!' and then wistfully, 'We're still in, you know. We were at Chequers on Christmas Day with her . . .' Most of the conversation was very businesslike, clipped, a bit loud, with him yelling for some-one to answer the phone, 'I've got three staff here, where are they?' (twice) and making phone calls on my behalf, hauling people out of meetings to talk to him, and generally being very noisy and aggressive and showing off. There's a nicer and more serious person there, evident immediately when Mary came in, graceful and pleasant; he calmed down and they 'clicked', looking at each other a lot.

His advice was sound – book fine; two directorships fine; *no* television interviews (Tesler from LWT wasn't keen, via Murdo, so we'll drop that). Always think how this will be presented and always assume the worst. Four speeches on big topics per annum, follow up with major articles (£1000 a time!), all very serious, no jokes, no side cracks. He kept quoting Leon Brittan and Michael Heseltine as good examples: but both were Cabinet and neither 'got back', whereas I'm only interested if promoted. Also speak to Conservative groups around the country, plenty of publicity OK for that, arrive early and leave late, as ministers usually do opposite. That's OK as I do so anyway, but most of my 1989 visits are *very* boring and I'm very busy till May, so it won't be a top priority this year. After the coffee, he sent me back to Westminster in his chauffeur-driven Jag – a kind thought.

I was crossing central lobby the other night and literally bumped into Jim Spicer – Sir James,[1] who had gone on television so often over the weekend of 10–11 December on behalf of his battery egg farmers. Sir James put a hand on each shoulder and held me at arm's

---

1. Vice chairman of the Conservative Party; formerly a member of the Select Committee on Agriculture; Conservative MP for Dorset West.

length as if he was looking at a picture. 'My dear,' he boomed, 'why didn't you *say* something? Why didn't you *explain*? If you had *said* something . . .' I looked at him, right in the eyes, and said nothing, and the air crackled with electricity. 'Oh!' he said, and dropped me as if scorched, and I walked on at the same pace. 'Fuck off!' I said under my breath.

Basil Feldman gave me plenty of advice over lunch at Lockets this week. Speaking at party meetings, yes, lots (he made it sound a real chore). Non-executive directorships, yes, and he mentioned a whole string of those run by his friends, *all* slightly rocky (including Blue Arrow and Next, which have been all over the front pages recently). During the course of the conversation I slowly stopped trusting him. 'Hotels? How about Hilton?' 'But they are no good, Basil, I've stayed in them' (actually one in Leicester). 'Do-it-yourself – B&Q?' 'No, I don't think so . . .' He had none of Archer's feel for style and class – Archer said, Bass OK, BP *much* more like it, *real* class. (Ray says Bass very well thought of; and IBM excellent, never mind that I know nothing about computers . . .) 'How about charities?' (this in a conversation about improving my image). 'No, I've done all that, I want something with a commercial edge.' 'Design, that's important. I can fix you up with that. That's what got John Wakeham his promotion.' 'Basil, I have no taste or judgement whatsoever . . .' and so on.

Hilary Rubinstein liked the draft synopsis and spoke quite excitedly on the phone about it. Other people have spoken well of him, especially that he's very experienced and used to be a lawyer – could be useful. I met Archer's editor, Richard Cohen (*not* a Jew – virtually the only one this week!), this afternoon: he's also a publisher, Century Hutchinson, and was *very* nice and very enthusiastic. He's tall, lanky, looks about thirty-five, has twelve-week-old baby, used to fence for UK (Archer's judgements do revolve around sporty prowess; he is such an insecure man just under the surface). He's publishing a biography of Gaitskell, and his eyes lit up when I talked about Gaitskell's diaries which I've been dipping into; and when I said I found Norman Tebbit's autobiography disappointing and felt I wanted to do better, we understood each other. He also talked a lot, as Rubinstein had done, about the launch – whereas I'm preoccupied with writing six to eight thousand words a week by 1 May. I have a girl to assist me – Clare Whelan, one of Chris's friends; and I'm close to spending £1300 on a word processor and printer, so that I can do a relatively clean text fast. I hope that will all be sorted out next week; then I can start work a week on Monday. Richard said it can be done faster: Heseltine resigned in December, had a book done by February and published in March. 'He had a ghost, but he did write a lot of it himself!' Well, I can't have a ghost, as only I can see the Cabinet papers, and I'm content with that.

All in all, a solid week. Some sourness – the Agriculture Select Committee still wants me to appear before them and answer questions, even though whips (Alan Howarth) have pointed out to more sensible Tory members (e.g. Tim Boswell)[1] that insisting on their privileges won't wash, as the Departmental Select Committees have only been around since St John-Stevas set them up in 1979, but the privileges of MPs are much older – and didn't he think I'd been through enough, etc.? Terence Higgins, chair of the Treasury Select Committee, is effectively chairman of chairmen; he came and talked, very anguished, much hand wringing about how no one had said 'no' to a select committee since 1610! Jerry Wiggin doesn't have a majority on his committee, so there is a real danger of a motion in the House and a three-hour debate. I may have to back down: invited to see John Wakeham on Monday. Debate on Tuesday by Opposition on MAFF's failure to protect consumers – I have permission to be missing! David Hunt[2] (deputy chief whip) had a chat

1. Conservative MP for Daventry.
2. Conservative MP for Wirral West; MP for Wirral, 1976–83.

too; the game plan is, that I've done everything right, that in turn they never leave me alone, there'll always be someone right there (literally!); that colleagues have been encouraged to be supportive to me (and I thought they all meant it . . . I smothered a giggle as David confided. What an odd, devious man he is). The whips are not keen to see an MP bow to these jumped-up committees, for example, because next they'll start insisting that the PM should appear. And when Enoch refused to put his financial affairs on record, he wasn't hauled summarily before the committee as I may be. So plenty of good precedents. We shall see.

Victoria, Sunday 5 February, night

A lot has happened in the last two weeks or so. I have agreed to sell the book to Sidgwick & Jackson and Pan paperbacks for £50,000, and the serial rights to the *Sunday Times* starting *after* this year's Party Conference on 22 October for the staggering sum of £75,000 – that's £25,000 per *week*, as it will be two full excerpts and an interview with snippets to start. Crumbs. I have to register for VAT and I'm about to become a tax client of Ray's firm. My earnings this year by 5 November (likely publication date) will be over £150,000. And I was worried about money! It is nice to feel I can get new shoes, and towels for the house and a new car this year. I am thrilled at the notion that anyone should want to give me that much money; it does me a lot of good.

The newspapers have been full of the book. Unfortunately I was seen coming out of Sidgwick's last Monday with Hilary Rubinstein, so the cat wasn't in the bag for very long! Richard Cohen, Jeffrey Archer's pal, had sent the synopsis to the *Sunday Times*. They snapped it up and agreed all my conditions; but I am cross with Richard for being so tactless, as I thought he could be a friend. Department of Health offered a room at Alexander Fleming House and an assistant (and, it turns out, privacy, fresh coffee and a telephone – and the room is not bad at all, very quiet and comfortable) – but then they told everyone too. I was hoping it would not have come out till after the Select Committee reported in a fortnight or so, but too bad: so on Friday I sent the synopsis to the PM with a personal note and we'll see if we get any response. (She did stop on her way out of the chamber the other week, put on her concerned face and said, 'How *are* you?') Only three seconds, but it was nice of her and cheered me up when I was feeling grim. The Select Committee, however, is furious about the book, as it means I can see private papers they can't have. They think I'm keeping quiet in order to make money out of it, but that is not true; I don't wish to say anything about eggs, that's not what the book is about, and I could make money out of anything I wrote, anyway.

I am hoping to make a speech on Thursday in the debate on public expenditure. My Treasury friend suggested this right at the beginning in December, but I had dropped the idea in favour of an Opposition day housing debate last Wednesday. As it happened Tam Dalyell started a ridiculous speech (we were moving the writ for the Richmond by-election following Leon Brittan's elevation to Europe) and went on and on about Westland. The man is quite potty. Then our backbenchers chipped in – Ian Gow[1] very funny, a real parliamentary event, the sort I used to miss completely as a minister; and hey presto, we're into a filibuster and the housing debate has gone west – so my debut is postponed. I am nervous about it, though I love speaking and do it well. May the Force be with me!

At home the major event (apart from me on the front pages daily) is the publication of the White Paper on the NHS last Tuesday.

---

1. Conservative MP for Eastbourne.

Clarke was on television at lunchtime today and did very well. He is so much more pleasant in public than behind the scenes, where he can be such an aggressive bully and make life so unpleasant. I admire the PM all the more because she stood up to him and insisted on tax relief for elderly people's health insurance. That will be popular; I will be happy to pay it for Mum. I'm getting loads of invites to do health engagements, etc., but turning them all down; after an eight-hour day writing on AIDS and women's health, the last thing I feel like doing is spouting about health again at a dinner with people I'd rather not see. The worry is that I'm enjoying the new life so much, and it is so well paid, that the temptation may be there to swap over. I hope not – I shan't earn as much another year and it can all end in the sand, as it has for Matthew Parris who I heard on radio yesterday morning: keen when he gave up his parliamentary seat and had his teeth fixed to do *Weekend World*, but now a nobody with no real future.[1]

Deb is in trouble again at school. She and some girlfriends climbed out of their dormitory window (by unscrewing the blocks) and went to the boys' house where they were found at 5 a.m. Punishment = litter patrol, a filthy job, but the school didn't think it was important enough to tell us.

Tower House, Sunday 19 February

I came home on the train on Friday afternoon. It was crowded and I sat in a four by the window. Two plain little men talked incessantly about engineering the whole way. As they got close to Derby one glanced at the *InterCity* magazine with its questionnaire on executive stress. He asked his companion, 'Do you think more about your

---

1. EC was wrong; Parris became an award-winning columnist.

family at work, or about work at home?' 'Oh yes,' said the other Mr Pooter, 'I hardly ever think about work away from the office, do you?' and his colleague agreed. I caught the eye of the older man sitting opposite me and murmured, 'It depends on the work.' He nearly fell off his seat laughing.

Tomorrow is important for me in two ways: the builders come, the scaffolding goes up, and they'll be here almost till Whitsun, by which time we will have spent nearly £60,000 on Tower House. And I meet my publisher William Armstrong and sign my contract, photos for the *Sunday Times*. That's neat timing, as the Agriculture Select Committee reports the following Wednesday and I gather will be rude about everyone. Not that I care now, at all, for eventually (since they had found out about the book) I had to go before them. I did a real *grande dame* act, wearing my best black velvet and stonewalling like mad. I read through Leon Brittan's evidence to the Select Committees on Trade and Defence and wrote down all his stonewalling replies; most of what I said came from his fertile brain, including the crack about 'if people get the wrong end of the stick, that is a matter for them'.

There was a full discussion at Cabinet the next day (9 February), and she said she was very, very pleased with the way the Select Committee had gone. Bernard Ingham then briefed the press to expect my return to Government in two years' time. Two Cabinet ministers had told me as much by Thursday evening. And Peter Morrison (deputy chairman of the party) wants a private lunch in his flat soon after Easter. When asked about the book by the press, Ingham said it would be no problem. So the little frog brooch on my lapel is looking up at present.

Other things are doing well too, apart from my back as a result of that darned bed (and working curled up on the sofa, fatal). On Wednesday I am due to meet seven Japanese from Toyota. Very exciting stuff, a bit cloak-and-dagger: they've asked for no publicity, so we must hope there are no paparazzi at East Midlands airport. I've arranged a Toyota car for myself and hope we will impress them! It is depressing to think that all our green fields will vanish under a factory, but it will revolutionise this area. All the more reason to create a proper garden in front of our house. If all goes well, 1989's money will go on reducing the mortgage, a new car (the gearbox on the Maestro has packed up again) and holidays. In 1990 it is a garden, settling some money on the children and getting the flat redecorated. I'm keen to produce another book after this one – not sure yet what – and maybe some short stories. Ray told me something very bizarre at lunchtime in the pub: that he writes too, lots of different things, but keeps them secret. The only published stuff of his I've seen was newspaper articles which seemed pompous and overwritten, with lots of rather obvious language. He is so *moody* sometimes, I could clout him: it's as if a cloud comes over his face and he looks as if he wishes he were somewhere else. So do I, then. I sent a Valentine postcard to B, and he was tickled pink. I'm still not sure if one of the cards I got was from him, but he said a kind word and left me again feeling warm and churned over inside. It's a year now since we stopped, but it is still so powerful.

Victoria, Tuesday 28 February

How very odd life is. I wanted to be 'in', yet I listened to two hours' conversation last night with two people who are very much 'in', and I didn't envy them one bit.

The dinner was with John Major and Tony Newton at Gran Paradiso, near Victoria Station. I was looking forward to it, but in the end didn't enjoy it much. I'd been to the first ever reception for Chinese Conservatives in Central Office beforehand, and then I set out to walk to the restaurant. It started to rain and the wind gusted, so by the time I got there I was feeling and looking like the original bag lady, not too dignified, I'm afraid. John Major was already there, looking terrific these days. He is so confident – he doesn't need anybody else now. I noted his comments (most of which sounded like gossip, or like choosing a future Cabinet, whichever you prefer) the moment I got home. What a limited conversation it was, too – the first time in ages that I've shared a table with intelligent adults and not heard mention of Bush, Gorbachev, Japan or Rushdie. That's why I don't envy them: I could feel the headband of restricted thought which is tied invisible to the brow of every Government minister tightening as I listened to them. John Major *claims* that he looks forward to a world beyond politics, with cricket and books, but he has firmly put it on one side for the moment. We got through two bottles of red wine – I hardly touched mine and Tony only had a glass or two, so John got quite loquacious. He said that I was a 'political original', like Quintin Hogg. Ray (when I came home) was kinder and said 'like Churchill'. Like the latter, I feel I don't have much choice about what I do, and I too have dark pits of depression. One set in today. Those two Cabinet ministers didn't mean to be unkind, but in the end I had so little in common with them. I don't wish endlessly to be grateful. Real friends (perhaps) would have taken me to a movie.

The Agriculture Select Committee reports tomorrow. Sods haven't sent me a copy, but I gather it's friendlier than it might have been. Meanwhile I've signed everything, but here we are entering March and I've not seen any money yet! I looked at H. Samuel's window yesterday and with a nice warm feeling decided *against* buying a 9 carat gold necklace. I can afford better than that.

Victoria, Thursday 16 March

It's exactly three months since I resigned. The last month or so has been really good. I feel more at ease, more rested, more usefully busy than for years, and I am enjoying myself, apart from occasional pinpricks from the gossip columns who are cross I won't talk to them (I won't talk to *anybody*). Today I paid off the £20,000 mortgage on the flat, so it is now ours outright and worth £130–150,000. We have over £40,000 in the bank (mostly committed for doing up the house) and I have over £2000 in two Halifax accounts which will pay for holidays. Next tranche goes for Ray's mortgage of £14,000 and then I buy a car. Then I'll have to set some aside for the taxman, I guess. The book is proceeding apace, so I'm on target for 1 May reasonably complete, and it can be checked by the Cabinet Secretary at the same time as by Sidgwick's. Title may be *Lifelines* (Ray's idea), but Jill Ireland has a book with this title coming out soon too (I don't think Sidgwick's are terribly professional about this!). I prefer *Game for Life* which has all sorts of nuances, but they thought it sounded too jokey and too much like *Game for a Laugh*. I'll keep it and use it for an autobiography later, when everyone has forgotten the television programme.[1] And how about *Sweets from the Trolley* for a collection of short stories? Could be! I have more than twenty titles/ideas now, though there are some serious books in there too. One problem is that Pan/Sidgwick want me to traipse around the country promoting it, including a two-day trip to Dublin–Belfast. That is firmly out, not because I'm a coward but because it will all be disrupted by bomb hoaxes and the like. I don't need to ask Special Branch, they will just say 'don't'.

I made my first speech in the House as a backbencher on 2 March, the day after the Select Committee reported. The debate was fun: just knockabout, but good practice.

---

1. It was eventually decided to title the book *Life Lines*.

Victoria, Wednesday 22 March, late

Just a few words because I am tired and it is late. Doing this book needed mental purdah and I've stuck myself away, even missing PM's Question Time and not reading newspapers. Still it does feel as if it is going well. I did another chapter this week, on the elderly, and it flowed out nicely. It seems to work if I write as fast as I can one day, revise it carefully the next, check data and read more the third – the resulting text is then virtually complete. I sleep fine, deep and dreamless, and wake refreshed but full of good ideas for improvements, a word here, a phrase there. I have noticed less of that monthly cycle of depression. Hard work is good for me, no doubt.

The children were here this week, Debbie only briefly. She had arranged to stay with a friend and I collected her from Euston at lunchtime. Very grown up – looks about twenty till she smiles, then you realise she is younger. She has dyed her hair dark and is now the spitting image of me, with a very sexy, innocent look about her.

Conversation tonight with John Major as we waited for vote. He still says he would be content to stay as Chief Secretary, but he needs a department before he becomes Chancellor (though Nigel didn't) and could well replace Channon, who has had a rotten time this week after chatting to journalists over lunch at the Garrick. It appears Paul told them in confidence that the police were on to the Lockerbie bombers. Then he denied knowing anything about such reports. So the *Daily Mirror* is calling him a liar and daring him to sue. We heard on Friday that Derby is front-runner for Toyota; Paul wrote me a very helpful letter about improvements to the local road system. How does he keep his cool? In the end because he is not very bright, and can disappear home to his family, his servants and a stiff drink! I like him very much, but there is resignation/reshuffle fever in the air and I fear he's a victim. Not Mr Major, however. In an unguarded moment he told me about the fearsome row he and Tom

King[1] had with the PM over the privatisation of Shorts in Belfast; Major and King wanted to write off the debts, on the sensible grounds that nobody buys an albatross. She argued for hours, twice with Major, to persuade him not to, saying this was no way to control public spending. Major and King won, apparently.

I met and talked to B at his request, sitting in his room drinking tomato juice. Why? He said he liked talking to me; I was amusing and nice, and underneath I was soft as butter. He started to touch, but I couldn't cope with it and got a bit upset and tried rather tearfully to explain that he must not mess me about. Either we're *on* and he must come and find time to come – which means taking too big a risk, I'm sure; or we are *not on* and he mustn't tempt me, which he interpreted as teasing. Oh! The quicker I write 'Patience'[2] and get him out of my hair, the better. Soon, I hope.

Victoria, Monday 3 April, 7.30 p.m.

Parliament reassembles (House of Commons) tomorrow – Lords in action today – but I came down yesterday to dig out some peaceful hours on the book. I can't work with the others, Ray and kids, around, and have warned Ray to keep out of my hair for the next month until it is done. As part of the research I've just been rereading the old diary: such fun, but so unkind about people. I seem to have been exhausted most of the time; perhaps this explains the vituperation.

Today was my first public appearance of choice since the resignation: at Sidgwick's request I opened the London International Book Fair at Olympia. Quite an event – books everywhere on three floors,

1. Secretary of State for Defence; Conservative MP for Bridgwater.
2. 'Patience' was an idea for a short story.

Lord Stockton (Alexander)[1] stocky, bearded, matey, carrying my handbag and piles of presented tomes, increasingly amused and pleased at how it all went. Press jamboree and how! William Armstrong and Hilary there – everyone amazed at the crush and interest and at last understanding why being a minister was such fun after all. The BBC came, so I was no. 2 item on television news saying that press attention could be a pain! My little speech was slightly high-flown stuff, sending good wishes to Salman Rushdie, and 'If you want to understand freedom, just look around you' – reminding them that photocopiers and printers are Government-controlled in the USSR, for example. There was a Soviet publishing stand, virtually empty, which proved my point.

Earlier in the day I discussed two of the chapters with my editor, Carey Smith. She feels there won't be room for all the material I want to include, which may mean abandoning the chapter on mental illness – sad, as it means losing 'Jocelyn'[2] too. He'll have to go into a short story instead, or wait for my autobiography.

We had super holiday in France – turbulent crossing, then lovely warm weather and five days of thorough enjoyment. It is the first time I've ever been there with money in my pocket, so I spent about £1200 on clothes for myself and will throw some dowdy old stuff away! I've now banked nearly £50,000 of the advances for the book, though about £20,000 is due to the Inland Revenue at some point. The Paris trip cost about £2000 in all, as I paid for the hotel too (about £500 – not bad for four of us). One avoidable expense was the hairdresser. The place we usually go, opposite the hotel, had shut, so we went a bit further down Rue Saint-Sulpice and booked in

1. Chairman of Macmillan Publishers, which owned Sidgwick & Jackson and Pan; grandson of the Conservative Prime Minister Harold Macmillan.
2. Jocelyn Cadbury, Conservative MP for Birmingham Northfield, 1979–82, who killed himself. EC had always wanted to write about this. Some aspects were included in her novel *A Woman's Place*.

there, Susie and I for a trim and shampoo, etc., but Debbie wanted a perm to make her hair curly. Well, she got what she wanted, though it destroyed her prettiness – she looks quite androgynous and rather as if she has been pulled through a hedge backwards, but *very* fashionable. The bill was over 1000 francs – nearly £100!

House of Commons, Wednesday 12 April, 12.30 a.m.

Feeling very tired – two days of bad period, plus endless rain at home and buckets on the landing, plus getting the girls off to school this afternoon, plus working right through last weekend and this – I need a holiday! I just skipped off last night and didn't bother coming down, so my whip (Michael Fallon)[1] was none too pleased. I must say, I *enjoyed* sloping off: not in defiance nor disagreement over policy – it was Third Reading of the Energy Bill, privatising the power stations with which I concur; but it was freedom and the right to choose my own timetable from time to time.

Victoria, Thursday 20 April, 7.00 p.m.

Well, Toyota came. Tuesday the announcement, lunch at the DTI with Dr Toyoda and a team of slim, pleasant, anxious-to-please Japanese gentlemen, all in virtually identical grey suits. He is different: short and stocky, Ph.D. engineer, snappier dresser, cool and confident. I must say I liked him. Their whole approach is very professional, unemotional, businesslike. They have said they chose the Derby site because of the workforce and good communications, both points on which I had done some work; it appears from what Ray Cowlishaw at the City Council told me that the points I made in my

---

1. Conservative MP for Darlington.

own piece for their advisers Braxton Associates (part of Touche Ross – and *they* really were faceless men!) had given them the clues as to which questions to ask, and the data bore me out. So Burnaston airport will disappear under a huge factory – and they have taken an option on land next door, by Atkins Garage, and will decide on the location for an engine plant (another three hundred jobs) within two months. The Derby Aero Club are none too pleased and have suggested they share the site with Toyota: talk about clueless! Toyota is real big league stuff, the biggest ever Japanese investment in Europe. The first cars will come off the line in late '92, the commercial production in late summer '93, so they are looking for a very quick development, much faster than Nissan. I think we can do it, but I need to talk to them at some stage about suppliers like Lucas, most of whom will need a kick up the backside to get them going.[1]

All this exciting stuff set me back a bit on the book and I'm now working like crazy, revising and tidying up. *I* shall be done on time, but Clare Whelan, doing the typing, won't, so hopefully I can deliver on 4 May (1 May is bank holiday anyway). I understand as I do it why writers smoke and turn to drink – it is so very difficult, especially as I get tired around 4 p.m., to keep the flow going. I get slower and slower. Facing it, psychologically, is difficult too. Last Wednesday morning, knowing I was going to have to look at Carey Smith's editing, I put it off endlessly and wasted the whole morning. In the end it was fine and I needn't have worried, but I had to stomp around the room, talking to myself, before I could get going! You really do need self-discipline. Yesterday I was determined to do better, so I overdid it – up at 7.20 (Ray away), run down to the Commons gym, forty minutes on equipment, run back, wash hair

---

1. In order for the cars to qualify under European rules for the Single Market, they were required to have 80 per cent of their content by value made within the EU.

---

and bath, etc., and then suffer with aching muscles all day and last night.

Last Wednesday I went to Norman Lamont's[1] constituency in Kingston to speak at a businessmen's lunch. No microphone again, but I wore one of the new outfits from Paris, yellow short jacket and black skirt, and looked very smart indeed. Norman gave me a lift in the ministerial Montego and chatted. I don't like him: not a nice man. We talked about Richmond, the next door seat, where Jeremy Hanley (who *is* a nice man) held it last time, with a majority up from seventy-four to 1766 (Kingston is over 11,000). How did he hang on, I asked? Well, Norman said, Hanley is a very good constituency worker. 'I couldn't do what he does. If that was what I'd have to do to hang on to my seat, I'd rather, you know, move out of politics.' He means go to the City and make his pile. People like him won't win us seats like mine! Norman also talked quite a lot about John Major, who seems incapable of putting a foot wrong these days (and is Norman's boss, and into whose shoes no doubt he'd like to step). The received wisdom is that John Major will take the Transport job at the first opportunity, and it may be sooner rather than later. The whips are already asking around about promotions. Michael Fallon asked me in the library the other night who were the four most likely backbenchers. This could mean they will be ready to go in July and it could be very interesting this time. Will she give poor Paul Channon the heave-ho? Yes, I'll bet. Peter Walker, who has been making critical speeches recently and claiming that interventionist policies are best? Maybe, but better to keep him there till the next reshuffle but one, in 1990, so he can't rock the boat too much. Golly, there'll be a fist fight for the leadership after the next election! The PM told *Reader's Digest* this week that she will hang on till new

1. Financial Secretary to the Treasury; Conservative MP for Kingston.

young people come up and are ready. She may have Major in mind, but if she really thinks he's a Thatcherite, she is much mistaken. Part of Major's power is that he is in control of Government communications. He sees Bernard Ingham every Thursday and they discuss how the Government is showing, the press polls, etc. Every so often he seeks my opinion. He would make a good PM – he thinks, he asks and he listens. We had the oddest conversation at the 7 p.m. vote yesterday. He said he had been chatting to Sir Robin Butler, Cabinet Secretary, who (apparently) is a fan of mine, and who said 'I hope Edwina doesn't blot her copybook with anything in this book'. I wish they would trust my judgement more – I'm not such a fool as that. I feel somewhat ambivalent about going back in at times. They need more colour in the Government, they are certainly looking a bit jaded. On the other hand I'm not sure I want to put up with all that hassle.

I was invited to the ABPI[1] dinner at the Grosvenor House Hotel last Thursday. I wasn't on top table but right next to it, next to the director who had done the seating plan – nice compliment! Top table was a few yards away, with Ken Clarke (not the other ministers) puffing away on a huge cigar. Golly, I *do* loathe that, it is such bad manners when hardly anyone else is smoking. We fell out for a lot of unspoken reasons, he and I, but his insensitivity to other people, his total lack of recognition for how things change, rules him out as a future leader as far as I'm concerned, and a future boss too.

House of Commons Library, Tuesday 16 May, 10.40 p.m.

A warm sticky night; waiting to vote on Euro legislation on procurement. Europe is the issue of the moment, with the Euro

---

1. Association of the British Pharmaceutical Industry.

elections on 15 June. On Sunday Ted Heath made an impassioned attack on Maggie's attitudes to Europe, which has really set the cat among the pigeons. Michael Heseltine has a book coming out, in which he sets himself up as Euro champion. We have debates twice a week now on Euro directives and the like: taxation of savings, procurement procedures: and a full-day debate on Thursday. The PM says she is all in favour of Europe – 'We are good Europeans,' she protested at the Scottish Conference last week – but she'll fight tooth and nail the changes which will bring anything more than economic union. The next generation can't remember a time when we weren't in Europe, just as I regard hankering after an Empire as slightly dotty. So we should be encouraging languages and taking the high ground, giving a lead and trying vigorously to win Euro seats, then we might like the proposals a bit better.

The book has been handed over to Sidgwick's and to the Cabinet Secretary, my whip, Gill Shephard and John Major. It will also go to Dr Elizabeth Smalls, who was a member of the Women's Health Group, and to the Treasury Solicitor. So far, so good. Hilary said very nice things about it. (NB Willie Whitelaw's memoirs just out. £300,000 advance! Unreadable: just dictated from memory. Very bland indeed.) William Armstrong of Sidgwick's wants me to beef up the last chapter and describe my appearance before the Agriculture Select Committee – no fear.[1] I can destroy them, but why should I want to? Better to use their own words and show them up, elegantly and with dry understatement, as fools.

I had a sweet little personal note from Robin Butler, asking me for tea; got all dressed up (why not?) and marched across to the Cabinet Office. In his very nice, elegant room, tea in china cups – no biscuits – he launched into quite a tirade about how badly I'd been

---

1. EC agreed to describe this for the paperback.

treated, how they had thought on the Monday/Tuesday, heads down, it will all blow over, but it didn't. I reflected so sadly how no one had asked my opinion, but really I was so unhappy at the time and feeling so friendless, tired and fed up that I didn't put up much of a fight and was glad to go. That's why I appear to be behaving with such 'dignity' now! Anyway the conversation became rather embarrassing, so I stopped him and got him to do some work for me instead. Michael Fallon was in similarly friendly mood at the lunch for the PM's tenth anniversary in the Savoy, the day before the council elections on 3 May. He said I could win elections whereas people like John Major couldn't, and I should be the candidate of the right and he would play my Airey Neave![1] Oh, terrific, I thought, feeling a bit sarcastic, but I've had these thoughts myself and I know some day I will march into the leader's office (after Margaret) and say, you need me, can I be of assistance? I told Michael Fallon that I'd really like to be a senior member of John Major's Cabinet, and that's true. Anyway the first step is to get back in, preferably after I've made my fortune: I told him I'd like to help the party next year, e.g. as vice-chairman for candidates. That could be fun and I could do it well – get more women, more ethnics and, most of all, more candidates with local accents, so that we don't have lawyers and merchant bankers, however nice, coming up from London to do us a favour.

Tower House, Thursday 25 May, 10.30 p.m.

On Wednesday (17 May) I met Hilary, Carey and William at Sidgwick's in a funny old-fashioned room stuffed with books, piles everywhere. Hilary says that's how all publishers' offices used to look, but now most of them are chrome and steel and careful

1. Airey Neave was Margaret Thatcher's campaign manager when she unseated Edward Heath as leader of the Conservative Party in 1975.

lighting. We talked for two and a half hours. They wanted a new chapter, 'to give the flavour of what it's like to be a minister in Margaret Thatcher's Government', which I'd promised in the synopsis but hadn't delivered. So I put together all the anecdotes I could think of and Clare is typing it for me now. About ten thousand words, I think, and that will have to do! I've also done a synopsis for a 'Handbook on Women' for next year and will send it to Hilary next week after the Whit Bank Holiday. And I am determined to find ten hours per week to do some more writing: that should be enough for some short stories on the word processor, which can be my bread and butter from here on. Also good news from my readers: Gill Shephard says it is lively, taking her a long time to read, because she keeps rereading bits, loves the bit about Teresa Gorman[1] and says she won't mind. John Major also said very enjoyable, Norma is deeper into it than he is and says it's very good. Fallon says he's slipping through it, very easy to read; and Chris loved it. So I feel a burden lifting: I can be a success at other things besides politics, and financially very successful too. They all think it will sell! The taxman is being kind and Ian Luder (my tax accountant) has saved me over £20,000 in tax. I'm carrying around cheques with noughts on the end in my handbag and taking weeks to bank them. My Halifax account stands at £900: I laughed when I saw it – a year ago that would have seemed a very large sum, whereas on Saturday I'll write out a cheque for £9000+ for the new car without batting an eyelid. I must say, I'm enjoying this!

The Thursday and Friday of last week (18/19th) I spent in Scotland with Micky Hirst,[2] who is now vice-chairman of the Scottish Conservative Party and in charge of our Euro campaign. We hold only two Euro seats there and are probably going to lose them.

---

1. Conservative MP for Billericay.
2. Sir Michael Hirst, Conservative MP for Strathkelvin and Bearsden, 1983–7.

It's not that the country is suffering – it's stinking rich in many places. I stayed with a lovely couple, Betty and Jack Harvie, whose house was straight out of *Dallas* – everything perfect – there was a glorious huge china parrot in my bedroom, almost alive, a Japanese piece. And yet they were so *nice*, and very supportive, as were all the people we met. The problem in part is that George Younger, the Secretary of State from 1979 to 1986, poured money into Scotland and let the Labour councils, especially in Glasgow, take the credit. The policy of the Tories in official documents like their Euro manifesto is to claim they've spent *more* than Labour, effectively endorsing a policy of dependence on public money.

The rows about the NHS continue unabated: full-day debate last Thursday (while I was in Scotland) and in Questions on Tuesday. Ken Clarke still bashing on. One of Ray's colleagues in the consultancy section of Arthur Andersen, Keith Burgess, contacted me privately last week. (It turned out he's now managing partner, having taken over from one of the partners who was so kind to me in December.) Arthur Andersen is involved in two out of the thirty-plus projects coming out of the White Paper, the self-governing hospitals and the whole IT bit. 'Do they realise what the IT scale is?' he worried. 'It's as big a project as the Stock Exchange computer and will cost an enormous amount. And no one has worked out what they want. The civil servants have a 'not written here' air about them. It needs a ministerial input fast. Otherwise reputations will be wrecked.'

Tower House, Wednesday 31 May, 11.15 p.m.

Whoops: interrupted as Ray came home unexpectedly. He was only out an hour; usually it's a long session on Thursday nights! It's now nearly a week later: peace at last, after a lovely weekend, good weather and good behaviour, the kids have gone back to school and Ray went back to London yesterday morning. To continue on the NHS: I shared Burgess's concern with the ubiquitous John Major.

Treasury are already on it. I have a nasty feeling that we will be up against the Prime Minister's prejudices and against the cry that we can't back down, we must press on. The fact that health may be improved by spending the money in other ways is not being addressed, but at least John understands the point.

Interest rates are up to an awful 14.5 per cent. We have won three elections in a row because the economy was doing well – here we are, a year before we have to start easing off, trying to engineer a slowdown of the economy, which is already happening. If we go too far, a nasty recession could badly affect our chances. Many people don't like the PM, and Kinnock's ratings are improving fast. The launch of their policy review last week was very well done, for although the policies look dated to an old hand like me, they are smoothly presented by a keen young team, whereas our guys – Peter Brooke, Paul Channon, etc. – look too laid back and plutocratic (and aristocratic), and I'm worried we are getting complacent. Too many of them have safe seats in the south: they should try fighting seats up here, they'd be more uneasy, as I am.

To my amusement MAFF has at last sent out its booklet on safer food. The *Guardian* reported that it had been redrafted so as not to blame the housewife, but it is still a bit of a joke. Meanwhile, thank goodness, they have at last banned using cow brains for human consumption. The BSE scare is worrying and we've had quite a lot of cattle sick round here; the farmers are genuinely upset. And MAFF is determined to press on with food irradiation – weird how they listen to scientists when it suits them! But *politically* that is foolish, for the moment at least. Debbie said this afternoon, as we were shopping in Derby, that I'm much nicer than I used to be, 'when you had that horrible job'. I know what she means. It does worry me that I may get to enjoy being on the outside too much – not just more money but more freedom, fewer duties (usually conflicting) and far less hassle. On the other hand I do enjoy being in the thick of it. If I'm out too long, I'll lose those skills.

Tower House, Thursday 15 June

There's another rail strike on tomorrow, so I've come home this evening. Anyway, it is so hot in London, fiercely sunny and impossible on the streets where the heat rises from the pavements. Here it's cool and quiet and breezy, though since the pool temperature is up to 82° with the solar panels alone, it must have been a scorcher here too. The pool is currently filled with children up from the village having a lovely time – shouts and hoots of laughter and much splashing.

Really I should be out 'knocking up' for today's Euro election, but (1) I'm bushed after late-night sittings in the House on both Tuesday and Wednesday; and (2) it won't make any difference as we're going to get hammered.

So here we are with the Euro campaign at an end. The count is not till Sunday, so all Europe's results will be out together. Our new agent Alison has just phoned (on a different matter) and tells me the turnout by 8 p.m. was only *25 per cent*. Central Office's approach has been truly dreadful – I've never seen such an appalling propaganda disaster. The *Independent* called it 'wretched'. A poster on the Ashbourne Road, greeting me as I drive wearily home, says 'Stay at home and you'll have a diet of Brussels'. That, to any Tory who cares about Europe, is deeply insulting: worse, it's bad advertising, for 'stay at home' is precisely what they (and I) will do tonight! Another reads 'Don't let Labour in at the back door'. The reaction is, what has that to do with Europe? Labour has had a much smoother operation. I would have preferred 'We believe in Europe. We believe in a strong Europe. We believe in a strong Britain as part of a free Europe. Vote Conservative . . .' and then they might have come out to vote. A Gallup poll on Monday in the *Daily Telegraph* showed that people have very positive views towards Europe, and yet our campaign has been entirely negative. We will come apart next week when all the results are out and it will serve us right.

Then no doubt there will be a reshuffle and a new party chairman. Peter Brooke, though universally liked, is not much good and his hesitant style and patrician accent are not attractive away from the South-East. He'll be promoted to Cabinet and someone else will be chairman, possibly Norman Fowler. The main Cabinet names – Howe and Lawson – are safe for the moment because of current crises – terrible events in China, where the students are literally rolled over by the tanks and then burned, and those who escaped are being shot after show trials. Hong Kong is understandably having a fit and the PM has promised to let some of them come here; on Thursday I warned at Question Time that this is a policy fraught with danger and followed it up with a letter to her (via her PPS, Mark Lennox-Boyd) saying (1) we shouldn't underestimate the difficulties of resettlement; (2) what about families of others, e.g. Pakistanis waiting two years or more for admission; (3) it will give Hong Kong the idea that there's an answer and Britain has the key, which isn't so.

Alan Walters[1] is back in this country, and is going to dinners and lunches spreading dissension – as the PM's official adviser! – saying Nigel is all wrong. Two years ago he cut interest rates to get the pound to 3DM. Now he's spending our reserves trying to prevent it falling to 3DM. Walters is often right but is unbelievably tactless, and that all makes it harder for Nigel to back down. On television last Sunday he refused to, and was quite firm and therefore implied criticism of Walters and the PM, so there has been uproar all week.

Best news of the week – on Monday we voted to have television cameras for a six-month experimental period by quite a big majority: 293 to 69. The payroll vote,[2] to everyone's surprise, was whipped in favour but we would have won anyway, handsomely. The

1. Personal Economic Adviser to the Prime Minister.
2. i.e. ministers and PPSs – everyone regarded as in the Government.

'experiment' starts with the State Opening and is somewhat restrictive – head and shoulder shots only, what John Biffen[1] called 'shampoo politics'. I'd like it less restrictive, but I'm so pleased that at least we've made a start. I spoke in the debate, and asked a question about the European Monetary System of Geoffrey Howe yesterday, so I'm getting back 'in' quite nicely. One reason I'm in favour of television is self-interest – it can only help incumbents. I was thinking last weekend as I trotted from meeting to meeting with constituents that if I had to do any more to stay elected, I wouldn't want to be an MP! So the television will help. Nevertheless I do have a jaundiced view of it, too. It was very easy to refuse the invitation of BBC *Breakfast Time* to join them at 7.10 this morning to read the papers, and deal with a few questions on botulism, the most recent scare!

The final stages of the book are grinding on somewhat. The last chapter to go to Butler got delayed in the post (posted Saturday morning in Findern, arrived London Wednesday morning), so it will be next week before I've cleared all alterations, which is a pity. Really very few negative comments have been made, I've been very lucky. I've also done and sent off the *Handbook for Women* synopsis to Hilary and to various possible contributors. I've got through over £80,000 since the end of February, so I need the money (paid off mortgages £35,000, paid builders £31,000, car £9000, etc.) I managed also to do all the bank accounts and tax returns which was a horrendous amount of work and have sent them off too, so I'll be writing my very own first VAT cheque shortly!

---

1. Leader of the House and Lord Privy Seal until 1987; Conservative MP for Shropshire North; an MP since 1961.

Victoria, Thursday 29 June, 10.30 p.m.

Life moves on. The book went to the printers yesterday for typesetting and now I'm ploughing through the index, feeling very flat and bored. The stories about the PM went to Number 10 last weekend, so they were in amongst her papers for the Madrid summit! All approved except (1) take out most of quotes; (2) don't mention House of Commons lunches, so the context is a little muzzy; (3) take out comment about making mincemeat of Harriet Harman; everything else OK! Most of the other people to whom Sir Robin Butler referred me also were content. John Moore wanted his bit even stronger and put in an extra sentence about hating drunkenness. What a truly miserable childhood he must have had. He talked it over with Sheila, his wife, and together they rewrote the passage. I sent Norman Fowler the piece about homelessness, all of it: yes, he said, no problems, and he liked it too. John Patten[1] OK, Ken Clarke too (only showed him one bit, on tranquilliser addiction). Murdo Maclean wanted the story about our AIDS campaign ruining his sex life out, and so it is. I'll get my own back and put him in a short story some day. Foolish man didn't realise that women judge men. Robin Butler was unintentionally funny about Murdo. He said he couldn't guess who the 'very senior civil servant' was, and proposed to have a secret competition to identify him among the Permanent Secretaries over Xmas, after the book is out. But his secretary knew immediately, and yes, said I, most of the women round here would know Murdo. An eyebrow was raised! I put in an extra couple of paras to keep William Armstrong happy, and that will have to be that. It will still be a good book – Butler said it was 'terrific'.

The only dark cloud was the Treasury Solicitor, Ms Patricia

---

1. Minister of State, Home Office; Parliamentary Under-Secretary of State, Department of Health and Social Security, 1983–5; Conservative MP for Oxford West.

Carroll, who is a pain. (If she was any good, she wouldn't be a civil servant.) She has taken three weeks over the text, distributed it to MAFF, who want major changes, and to the Department of Health, etc. Now I know Butler has already consulted all the relevant departments – as I saw Mike Abrams, deputy CMO, last night at a do, and he had seen it all, and was the source of four (sensible) comments. I told Carroll that Butler had cleared it and she said, 'Well, they aren't lawyers', to which I replied, good thing too. Her worry is that the last chapter will stimulate the pressing of the Xmas writs all over again.[1] But even if I wrote nothing provocative, the publication of the book itself would still remind them; and anyway I'm being paid more than my parliamentary salary to do one interview for the *Sunday Times* and I would have to answer questions then. I checked and rechecked: Sidgwick & Jackson will have libel lawyers on it; I only have to get clearance from Butler, and that's done, and in writing and in his own hand. Michael Fallon was amused and said: 'So what if they reissue the writs? They'll be mad if they do, and it would just sell lots more books.' He said he would back me if necessary. So off it has gone to the printers and we'll look at Ms Carroll's proposed amendments and probably ignore them. One delicious anecdote: Fallon told me he was reading the script of the book during a boring part of the Children's Bill. Mellor looked over his shoulder – 'What's that?' 'Ah, that's Edwina's book. You can't see it as she's being really rotten about you.' So Mellor is grinding his teeth somewhat.

Three short stories now done. No idea at all if they are any good, but there is a story in each one, and a point of view, and some nice background. I've tried to make them sound pretty authentic, and no doubt we'll get people claiming to be the subjects! I must write 'Patience' – she is waiting inside my head – first we'll do 'Paris' and/or 'The Journey'. And I could do with something more light-hearted,

---

1. There were no writs – there never were – as Ms Carroll might have made clear.

they are all a bit heavy going at present. Happy endings, maybe! Hilary comes back from his holidays on 10 July and they'll be waiting for him. I wonder what cash they'll bring in?

Fowler said at tea yesterday that he had bid for me to be one of his ministerial team when I was first appointed in September 1986: I wonder! I do know other friends were pushing my name, but I bet Fowler wasn't one of them; just as in December, he waited to see which way the wind blew before putting pen to paper.

There was a story in last Thursday's *Daily Telegraph* about a moratorium on closing mental hospitals – apparently ordered by a Cabinet Committee chaired by the PM. She is anxious about the discharge of ex-patients – Friern Barnet is close to her patch – I recall her saying so at a House of Commons lunch last summer. Yet Ken Clarke was so foul about it in November: he was so horrible, and nasty and *wrong*. Made me feel there were better jobs than serving under him as a minister. The department has denied the story; Freeman[1] in an empty little debate on Monday this week said the stories were unfounded, but I hope they have some substance to them. Yet how do you persuade a boss who isn't listening, and who is rewriting speeches to the point where you don't agree with what you're supposed to say?

Tower House, Sunday 9 July

The Water Bill is now law, thank heavens, and the Energy Bill soon will be. The biggest hurdle is in the autumn with the placing of shares. Electric will go well, as the Government has taken all the risky stuff, i.e. nuclear power, unto itself. Water faces real problems, as some of its profitability will depend on selling off land, but they won't be able to disburse all the proceeds. More important, the costs

---

1. Roger Freeman, EC's successor as Parliamentary Under-Secretary; Conservative MP for Kettering.

of pollution and environmental control are set to be astronomical and prices will have to rise considerably more than inflation to pay for those, making the shares riskier. Likely therefore to be offered at a considerable discount. I spent Monday morning with the South Staffs Waterworks Company, which was never nationalised, and which provides the drinking water for Findern. They showed me charts going back to the 1960s of nitrate concentrations in the water. Nitrate fertilisers came in during the war, but it was *twenty years* before they showed in the boreholes. Even if use was cut 40 per cent right now, it will be the *middle of the next century* before nitrate levels return to the 1960s figures. That really is scary. So the contaminant must be removed and that's tricky – and also poses the problem of what to do with it once removed; you can't dump or tip it, it would just get back into the water supply. One tiny plant has set them back over £1 million. The scale of doing that all over the country, and improving the sewage, makes the £3 billion requirement admitted by Nick Ridley look relatively modest.

I've seen a lot of unrealistic people in the past week or so! Jeffrey Archer came to the constituency to commemorate ten years of Tory Government on 30 June, a damp rainy day, for what turned out to be an excruciatingly boring lunch on board the Stenson Bubble,[1] followed by tea in a tent at my constituency chairman's. We should have foregone one event or the other – by 3.30 p.m. he had a distinctly desperate look about him, and was being politely ignored by all my nice ladies who had come for tea and cakes and had not read his books and didn't want to buy any! The tone was set by Jill Chandos-Pole, who owns great chunks of Derbyshire; she turned up for five minutes in a great hurry, darlinks (she talks just like Zsa Zsa Gabor), bringing with her three dog-eared copies of Archer books for him to sign! In the circumstances he was very pleasant to them.

1. A barge at the pub of the same name.

Someone must have told him that criticising people for not spending enough doesn't go down too well. There was an auction which I found deeply embarrassing, for a signed bottle of whisky (£50), a commemorative plate (£200), and a voucher for British Midlands air tickets (£200). Only the plate went for much above its value. None of my wealthy businessmen, such as Don Prime or Geoff Crocker (who almost certainly charged for putting up the marquee; he did for ours!), bothered to bid a bean. And yet: they were right, and Jeffrey, with his razzmatazz and his rhetoric (very effective), was wrong. They all work hard for the party already, at a level that brings in *votes*. Jeffrey said to me, in a quiet candid moment, that he needed a job. He means the party chairmanship and he's not going to get it. He said, 'I've got everything else I need. I've got £10 million on deposit. I've sold three million paperback copies of *Kane and Abel*. I've a new play in September and I'm wasting my time being idle!' He told me again that he was at Chequers over Xmas. Yet there's no chance of his being given anything much. Maybe a peerage, and then he might aspire to be a junior minister. That's not what he wants. We talked about him in the tea room. Colleagues who remembered him from 1969 to 1973 recall someone who was already a bullshitter, who could not clearly distinguish truth from reality. He was involved with big charity appeals in those days and the money seemed to stick a bit, never quite right. His episode with the prostitute – 'just what was he doing with a handful of used notes in Victoria one night?' said one. He was regarded as impossibly rude and indiscreet. I've no intention of ending up like him. If I can't make a go of it, I'll find something else to do, and so should he.

Another unrealistic soul is Lord Young. Is he for the chop? Maybe. He is certainly thoroughly disliked by many MPs. This week he's had talks with the brewing industry about the Monopolies and Mergers Commission Report. Though I represent thousands who work at Bass and elsewhere, the first I knew about it was seeing it in the press, with Young's bullish statement that he was minded to accept proposals for large-scale disinvestment.[1] Had he bothered to ask, we could have told him that was not on. Now he's being pushed by a concerted backbench campaign, written by the brewers, particularly those whose monopoly profits are under challenge. Lord Young, however, acts as if he is chairman of a big private company, and such subtle political considerations are not for him. At a meeting of the backbench Conservative European Affairs Committee this week, he was five minutes late, which is very bad manners since his office in the building is close. But he talked very well about Europe post-Madrid, pointing out that the most *communautaire* talkers in Europe were often the worst offenders against free trade in practice. The French try to keep out lamb, Nissan cars, etc., and have exchange controls. The Germans protect their finance, banking and insurance markets. Then someone asked a question with a political edge and Young said, 'My officials do not give me advice on political matters.' Well! This in a closed meeting, mind.

I went into dinner on Wednesday night with Gill Shephard, who in a crowd goes very quiet, but is a good pal. We had with us Charles Wardle,[2] Nick Soames,[3] the excellent Ian Taylor,[4] Hector Monro and John Patten (Hector it was who was scathing about Jeffrey). Nick Soames was fooling around as usual, sweet-talked the waitresses, told them precisely how to do his steak tartare, and drank rather a lot. He too desperately wants a ministerial job, but I think he may have missed the boat. He doesn't make much effort at Question Time, except to yell at the Opposition. Often it is very funny, but he'd do better bowling elegantly at the PM or ministers and doesn't,

---

1. Breweries controlled both the supply of beer and the outlets, from which other products were banned. Lord Young proposed that they should sell off or swap thousands of pubs, which is what eventually happened.
2. Conservative MP for Bexhill and Battle.
3. Nicholas Soames, Parliamentary Private Secretary to the Secretary of State for Environment; Conservative MP for Crawley.
4. Conservative MP for Esher.

much. His marriage broke up because he was dallying with an Italian girl. He kept loudly asking me to go to Annabel's. Taylor was interesting, talking about the Foreign Affairs Select Committee (of which David Howell[1] is chairman), which produced a balanced view of Hong Kong's problems ten days ago, in time for Howe's visit there. They must all realise by now that inward migration by millions is not on. And then there was Wardle, who also drank a lot, and who at the end of the evening, while everyone else listened to Nick's stories, insisted on telling me, for about fifteen minutes, how he used to dislike me.

That overgrown schoolboy, Phillip Oppenheim, was seated at the next table. He came over and said, 'the minister (Eric Forth)[2] wants a word with you', so I went, to find Phillip poking a knife into the poached egg sitting on the minister's plate and saying, 'Now tell him not to eat this, Edwina.' 'None of my business,' I said, 'nor yours, Phillip, leave somebody else's dinner alone', and so back to my place. Phillip came up to me in the corridor afterwards: 'You don't mind, do you?' I replied, 'Since you ask, Phillip, yes I do.' So the next day he apologised.

Victoria, Tuesday 18 July, 11.30 p.m.

Lying here, just letting thoughts flow through the mind, and thinking I should write them down (Ray in Devon with Susie). Thinking what? That for most of the time I've been in Parliament, this time of year has been spent with someone else: long hot summer evenings, eating strawberries, listening to the night sounds with the window open and the light out. Golly, I was unhappy for so much of that

1. The long-serving Conservative MP for Guildford; Secretary of State for Energy, 1979–81; Secretary of State for Transport, 1981–3.
2. Minister for Consumer Affairs since 1988; Conservative MP for Mid-Worcestershire.

time and in all those years my only joy was in talking and making love late, hours of it, several of those evenings etched in time, memorable, wanting time to stand still, just a little while longer. Not last summer, of course, but other decisions had been taken by then, and it was my will (not his) that we should stick to them. And yet the last six months have been amongst the most continuously enjoyable I've ever had, with different necessities emerging, like home, family, mental achievement and money, affection and admiration, and an absence of pressure. I'm really going soft, losing my edge, enjoying laziness almost too much. If I was asked to do a job now, I would sigh a little and regret losing this independence, this freedom, this laid-backness.

I didn't write last week, thinking nothing had happened, which was foolish. In personal terms something momentous *did* happen, for Sidgwick's turned down the new book on women, and in the snidest way possible. I felt quite light-hearted about it at the time, thinking oh, we'll get somebody else to publish, but in fact it's tricky as I'll have to keep quiet until *Life Lines* is out, or Sidgwick & Jackson could get stroppy; and then there's the question of who would do the next one and the one after that. I won't be taken for granted, they will find. On the other hand I don't want two publishers in tandem, that is not good practice. I'll talk to Hilary about it in the morning. I think the handbook on women, now retitled *What Women Want*, is important and useful, and I want to do it: never mind if it's not a blockbuster.

Trying to get started on fourth short story and getting stuck – all very psychological, as I feel I'm not practising now, but using a skill to tell a tale. This one is called 'I Saw My Lover's Wife Today', for obvious reasons. It happened last Thursday. I came home and wept, wrote some strange doggerel and then realised it was a story. Went to the Conservative Peers' Tea Party last week and saw Alexander Stockton drinking again. The gossip columns say that he's left his wife, and sold his house. No wonder presenting *What Women Want* to him and his board the same day as the Dempster story was bound to meet with failure.

[In another reshuffle in late July, Geoffrey Howe became Leader of the House with the honorific title Deputy Prime Minister, and John Major Foreign Secretary. Norman Lamont replaced Major; Paul Channon and John Moore left the Government.]

Victoria, Sunday 30 July, 9.30 p.m.

I've had a good week; last weekend my name was in the *Sunday Times* and the *Express* as a possible recall to Government and then as possible vice-chair of party. I don't doubt I was considered and might well have received an invitation had Norman Fowler been party chairman, but once Ken Baker was appointed this was unlikely, as we are not particularly close and he would not want any other lights shining near him. A slight downer, however, was the appointment of two other Derbyshire MPs – Patrick McLoughlin and Greg Knight – to Government, one as minister at the Department of Transport, the other as a whip. I am *very* pleased indeed for both of them, but it makes the appointment of a *third* Derbyshire MP (me) in future less likely.

The whole reshuffle has in fact been a mess, not just the top bit, which is such a shambles. Too much swapping around, ending up with thirteen new Cabinet ministers. Still a lot of dead wood at middle and lower rank – in the Welsh Office, for example. Overall I'm not impressed.

The real row surrounds Geoffrey Howe. I'm inclined to agree with Whitelaw's comment on this aspect of the reshuffle: 'ghastly'. The PM has been fuming for months about the Foreign Office's refusals to take her line. She won't have missed my angry comment earlier this year about the tobacco directives, that the reason we could not oppose them more vigorously was because the Foreign Office would not let us; then Ken Clarke went to Brussels, harangued everyone for three hours and got voted down. There must be lots of incidents like that. She will have picked up Geoffrey's ambition to be PM: his interview with Wogan, for example, his strong views, his refusal to be written off. He was angry when she said earlier this year that she wanted to bring the young ones on, and let it be known mainly via Harris,[1] ex-political correspondent, a useful conduit (and as PPS is, of course, Geoffrey's own choice, not hers). The Madrid summit brought it to a head. The PM simply didn't agree with Foreign Office line and wrote her own: they learned about it in the press after she had delivered it. She got her own way too, and came home determined to do something about the Foreign Office and get her own man in there. Question – who? According to today's newspapers she wanted Parkinson[2] and it's not clear why she decided to appoint the Cabinet's second most junior member (the most junior being Tony Newton – DSS, best for him and us) as Foreign Secretary. Maybe to help John Major's career – but it is a mistake: he'll be good on Europe, but there are other issues, and, as Edward Pearce put it, he's hardly been abroad except on holidays. So he's seen as her placeman, will not find the job suited to his talents and now, for the first time, has enemies.

The business about the houses is both funny and tragic.[3] It has seriously undermined her authority, instead of shoring it up. She looks vindictive, the Cabinet divides against itself and her, princes

---

1. David Harris, formerly political correspondent to the *Daily Telegraph*; Conservative MP for St Ives.
2. Cecil Parkinson, Secretary of State for Energy; Conservative MP for Hartsmere.
3. Geoffrey Howe had been deprived of Chevening, the official residence of the Foreign Secretary, but was given the use of Dorneywood, the Chancellor's country residence instead, even though he had ceased to hold one of the principal offices of state and had been given the (meaningless) title 'Deputy Prime Minister'. In his memoirs Nigel Lawson makes it clear that he did not give up Dorneywood willingly.

on one side, placemen on the other, the ageing queen presiding, using spells and witchcraft and face paint to hide the advance of time. The Labour Party looks clean, fresh and new: the young Lochinvar comes out of the west, a different accent, looking different; like a late scene in a Shakespeare play.

Loews Summit Hotel, New York, Saturday 23 September, 11.00 p.m.

I am in New York,[1] writing on borrowed notepaper with a pen I 'borrowed' from the Sub Committee on Health and Ageing of the House of Representatives. It's cold, wet and windy – Hurricane Hugo, which killed dozens of people in Montserrat, the Virgin Islands and South Carolina, is blowing itself wearily out here. On Wednesday morning I leave the sanctuary of the USA to return home: back to the hurdy gurdy, bright lights and flashbulbs, and a life which isn't my own.

Good news from William Armstrong, who rang me at 6.30 a.m. in San Francisco last week: the book is reprinting already, as WH Smith want 5000 copies. More good news from Ray: I'm to be on *Question Time* soon (with Peter Sissons) and to host *The Jimmy Young Show* on BBC Radio 2 for a whole week, from 13 November – *and* it's Children in Need week, with Friday as the big day. Terrific! And *Today* newspaper wants second serial rights, and an interview at home, with my views on everything under the sun, including how to bring up teenage daughters.

Story writing has gone tolerably well since I've been here: two nice ones which would form part of a collection, one of which would stand on its own. My own reading this summer has convinced me

---

1. EC undertook a study tour of North America, paid for by the US Information Service.

that I could never write well enough to make a career of it; I'd always be imitative, always autobiographical, and it would not be taken seriously. Meanwhile, I have twenty years of experience in politics and I'm better at that than most people; so stick to it, for the time being anyway.

I have to find an answer to the question: What do you want to do now? The answer is, learn to be patient, for that is all I can do. I won't be invited back into Government before 1991, if then. It won't happen at all if I cut and run too soon – whether that means physically or by saying the wrong thing. Yet if I say all the 'right' things I lose what makes me different – bit of a tightrope, that. After the next election is the time for decisions, really; either I'll be in Government or I won't. If not, then I'm a spectator for a year or two. It's fascinating while Margaret Thatcher is leader and PM, but I doubt if I could find her replacement so interesting (unless, of course, it is someone I know well . . .). I could still make speeches and look after my constituents, and write, but somehow I don't think that will be enough, unless by then I've become a lot lazier. I shall want to be a-doing *something* by being useful *somewhere*; and because I hate repeating myself, I can't see it being on a small scale and local. It would have to be something on an international scale. Apart from anything else, this seven weeks has shown that my dislike of travel has evaporated. I could happily spend a lot of time in planes and hotel rooms, phoning home on Sundays and reading good books in bed.

The main problem I've encountered this summer has been my weight. I must be nearly 11 stone by now; the last time I was this big was after pregnancy! Then, as now, I had been 'waiting', unable to control the passage of events, under-occupied and occasionally depressed. It is *so* easy to comfort oneself with something nice to eat. On Friday I had only one engagement – a lunch; I ate my way through Chinatown first, then paid $35 for a nice meal I didn't enjoy, then slothed around all afternoon in the hotel room (while it was hot and sunny outside), eating some more and feeling ghastly. Serve me right. In bad moments it feels as if I've lost all the things I held most precious. My children are growing up and vanishing: Debbie, my beautiful, my joy, has already gone, and Susie won't be long – they only exist now, as they were, in pictures, with only a faint teasing glimmer in Debbie's face of how she once was, which tears out my heart so. And my lover, who now soars in skies far above: but oh, it hurts still to love him and not have him, and watch him fly. And finally, maybe my self-discipline? I don't know. Tonight I bought a cheesecake at Lindy's and two hours later, disgusted with myself, threw it in a bin.

In my eyrie at Tower House, Tuesday 10 October, after midnight

Came back to find house almost done (no toilet-roll holder, couldn't find shower curtain, etc.) and have indulged myself further by moving furniture, buying rug (£299 for nice wool Wilton), and generally being lazily domestic. I'm even doing needlepoint again, a picture of Mount Vernon, so I haven't read a novel for ages. Hope to write a couple more stories this week.

All bright and calm on surface, but very apprehensive underneath. First extract of book is on Sunday next, 15 October – a week before I wanted, but it will do. I think the change was because of the *Today* interview – no extracts, according to Hilary, which seems odd: they could have come to me direct instead of Sidgwick & Jackson. Anyway that's likely to be on 30 October, publication day. So they would want *Sunday Times* finished. It all seems a very disorganised world to me! I caused a fuss last week by refusing to film an ad for the *Sunday Times*; it would be much better if they use archive film, as me speaking to camera would be *so* tacky – especially just after the Party Conference. Apparently Sidgwick & Jackson expect 25,000 sales in hardback; if more, it will need third reprint. Another

25–30,000 in paperback too. A novel makes the bestseller list after 3000 copies!

Nationally, it's a bad time for us. There's a major economic row under way about controlling inflation, the stability of the pound, and the level of interest rates; the PM (and Professor Walters) are irritated at efforts to keep the pound at 3DM and are content for interest rates to stay the same and the pound to fall. But that's inflationary. So, in the short term, is putting interest rates up, now the base rate is at 15 per cent (+1 per cent last week), mortgage costs are climbing and house owners are really worried. House prices are falling virtually everywhere – except round here, where Toyota is now exerting a big effect. The Stock Exchange is wobbly too, and after speculation about disagreements between Margaret Thatcher and Nigel Lawson in the Sunday press, the pound fell anyway.

I do continue to be concerned about our prospects at next election, though still sure we'll win. But Kinnock et al. look and sound good, have recovered their confidence, have a new style and have been winning over the centre. Enough to make the difference in marginal areas.

Since I came back from America, I've done nine speeches in nine days, all *very* silly and unnecessary. So, a decision: no more prancing around the country, though it will be Easter before this takes effect, as there are sixteen dos booked in the first three months of next year. I've discovered that saying 'yes' to all that excessive work is like being a smoker – very hard indeed to give up, 'one more won't make any difference', etc. But if the party doesn't want me as a vice-chairman, then I can't quite see why I'm speaking to sixty-five constituencies this year!

Victoria, Friday 20 October, 2 a.m.

Debbie is in trouble *again*. Apparently she had had a row with Ashley, the pretty blond boy she brought home Sunday; she was messing around in prep and, when told not to, flew off the handle and swore at them all, 'like a fishwife'. I must say I'm not too impressed with the school. They don't seem to have the right combination of firmness and affection we wanted. I don't recall phoning any parents at Bromsgrove[1] when a kid swore at me. She doesn't hear bad language at home, so where did it come from? Ray got all uppity, staring into the distance, etc. Funny how I don't get upset any more, I just feel indifferent, like when Deb was being silly in Florida; I don't care, girl, you're not going to spoil *my* holiday.

The markets this week have been seesawing badly. Everyone expected a Black Monday, and shares were marked down, but the smart money was ready and started buying in the afternoon. The Chancellor was at the Mansion House tonight, fat and expansive in a haze of cigar smoke, signalling as he did at Conference that there would be no changes of policy. Commentators afterwards were talking about hiking interest rates up even more to stop the pound sliding. So we could have, not a crash, but a slow slide into recession – growth will be under 2 per cent this year, as it is. And then we'll have our backs against the wall for a General Election. I don't like it.

Michael Heseltine is coming to the constituency tomorrow. It's a sell-out and we could have sold more. In the opinion polls about who should replace the PM, he still comes top – nearly four years after resigning. He certainly has stamina and consistency. His fringe meeting at Conference was packed too. It is beginning to dawn on us that, should we not do well in the next election (lose or win closely), Margaret Thatcher would be forced out, or at least into a fight. Michael would then be a very credible candidate, and our postbags would be filled with letters from constituents to support him. He's

1. EC taught at Bromsgrove School, 1978–81.

running in a presidential primary and is not tiring. Only if we do very well would his chances fade against, say, Ken Baker's.

Monday was a busy day. I signed the contract for *What Women Want*[1] at 9.30 a.m. (It is to come out on 21 June, and *Life Lines* will go into paperback on same date.) Later I launched *She* magazine's assertiveness course (a handy £2000), complete with red stetson hat, which then looked very smart on the top table at the 'Woman of the Year' lunch at the Savoy. Princess Margaret was the principal guest. She's nearly sixty now, and looks – well, odd, for her age. Fine, pretty skin. Bags under eyes and a rather bored, vacant expression. Pretty dark hair scraped back unflatteringly from face. Slim figure, plain paisley dress, very little jewellery, bad chest – she was coughing a bit. Tiny! I was presented to her and she chatted on about salmonella, her eyes fixed straight ahead so that she appeared to be having a conversation with my collarbone; made the same comment as most people, I wuz right, etc., but quite fulsome and rather nice. Better than her nephew Charles, who was quick to voice an opinion the other way last December.

Victoria, Thursday 26 October, 11.30 p.m.

Well, she blew it. She really blew it this time: oh dear. Nigel Lawson resigned this afternoon; John Major appointed Chancellor of the Exchequer, all that done by 6.15 p.m. Then Alan Walters announces from Washington that he's going too; Nigel's letter mentioned Walters's continuous presence as the reason for his resignation. By 7.30 p.m. Douglas Hurd is Foreign Secretary and David Waddington Home Secretary. No doubt same time tomorrow we'll have a new Chief Whip and some juniors moved around too.

1. Sidgwick & Jackson had relented and decided to publish this book after all.

I had listened to Nigel in the economics debate on Tuesday, and he was a bit subdued then. We thought it was to calm the markets. There's been a row for ten days after Walters published an article in the USA (commissioned two years ago, but he could have stopped it), calling the European Monetary System 'half-baked'. He told journalists that the PM agreed with him. Treasury started taking a very frosty line – last week's (23 October) Treasury brief, which I borrowed from Nigel Forman,[1] made it clear that in their view PM and Chancellor were in complete agreement. In a television interview on Tuesday night, Nigel (looking very fed up) said advisers were to give advice and ministers decide. But Walters isn't on the normal special adviser's contract, which would make him a civil servant and silent. Gurus can't be shackled, it appears. So the row simmered on. The moment the PM came back from the Commonwealth Conference in Kuala Lumpur, Nigel had a meeting with her: by 9 a.m. this morning his resignation had been tendered on a 'him or me' basis, presumably with a deadline. At 5.56 p.m. I was going up the stairs to Room 14 for the '22', just behind Roy Hattersley and the Labour Chief Whip, Derek Forster. The journalist Colin Brown comes panting down the stairs, grabs Hatters and tells him that Nigel has resigned (at that stage Major not announced). Consternation. Everyone running. The Chamber, pottering through some boring legislation, suddenly erupts with a huge roar as the announcement is made on a Point of Order (the House was later suspended, after a statement by – of all people! – Geoffrey Howe as Leader of the House). Labour MPs dancing in the gangways and singing 'The Red Flag'. Ours standing around dumbfounded and conversing in whispers. Some angry faces, many very upset.

What does she think she's doing? Apparently she tried three times

---

1. PPS to the Chancellor of the Exchequer; Conservative MP for Carshalton and Wallington.

during the day to persuade Nigel to stay. Not hard enough, it seems. It is unprecedented for a resignation letter to mention the cause so explicitly. There's more to it, of course. Nigel *is* tired and fed up. Thérèse hates the whole business, and as she's his third wife and he has small children and no money – he lost it all in the 1974 crash – the temptations elsewhere have been growing ever stronger. I know the feeling. And Margaret Thatcher is not the best academic brain – he must get fed up with the tenor of their discussions. They disagree fundamentally on Europe: he's keen to get us into the European Monetary System (EMS), likes sorting out problems with the best international brains, very much on his level, very enjoyable. She goes on about sovereignty, about which, I suspect, he couldn't care less. I doubt if he approved of the underhand approach to discrediting Heseltine over Westland. I expect Nigel was appalled at the handbagging (Kinnock's phrase) of Howe, the cavalier attitude to Hurd, and the loss of his country house in July: that may well have started him thinking about where he was going to live next, and realising he couldn't afford much on a Cabinet minister's salary – pay rise this year, 3 per cent. And as I know, once you start looking out of the window, the grass is definitely greener.

One curious effect. I saw B yesterday for the first time in ages. Looking well. Telling me how he was to move into his new flat today (his old one precluded visits, as he only rented a bedroom in someone else's). How about coffee, one evening after work maybe? So I spent all today thinking about it; after I'd written 'Patience' I hoped I had got him out of my system. What on earth was he planning? A quick tour, gin in hand, and here's the bedroom? What kind of risks was he prepared to run, with security staff everywhere, and why on earth run any risks at all? He can't be that desperate. All a bit odd. If he just wants to be friends, then either he shouldn't bother, I'm not that important; *or* he's a genuinely nice man, and some day that could be his downfall. Anyway I doubt if anything will happen now! And in the midst of all this, the PM writes me a very nice 'thank you' letter for sending her a copy of my book.

Coming up: book launch on Monday. Wogan in the evening, I guess. Opposition day Tuesday – could be a 'No Confidence' debate, at present it's still on the economy again. *Sunday Times* extract last week was super, nearly all from the women's health chapter, which read very well. There hasn't been any television advertising last week or this, not surprising as the ad was so dreadful. *Today* paid £7500 for extracts and interview – then just did two days of interview, lots of colour photos, text generally yucky. The second day they didn't even credit the book. I was so disappointed. *Sunday Mirror* also want 'extracts and an interview', but they don't, they just want the interview, so I've said 'no'. *Dispatches* on Channel 4 last night was also disappointing. Pick of the Day for the *Standard*. But it was all about the background to the resignation, exploring all the secret corridors of the Conservative Party.

The *Birmingham Mail* phoned this week and asked, 'Is it true that Debbie has been suspended from school?' Heart in mouth. Sometimes they know before we do. It turned out that the parent of the boy who was suspended in the drinking incident[1] had talked to the press and mentioned my daughter. It's almost a good job they assumed the wrong one. Susie was here this week (Deb is in Germany with school – but she had a fight with a teacher last week) and I questioned her in detail. Apparently the incident was not discovered until a child was sick in the dormitory. They must have been unsupervised for hours. And Susie seemed to have no clear idea why stealing drink and being deceitful is all wrong – and she attends a church school and was confirmed not long ago. It won't do. I feel the school has let both of them down.

---

1. Susie had taken some miniatures as a contribution to a school midnight feast.

Victoria, Saturday 4 November, 3.30 p.m.

In between engagements – spent all morning in Croydon at an 'Autumn Fayre' for John Moore, then at a bookshop signing. This evening it's Sue Lawley on television, followed by Channel 4's *After Dark*, so right now I'm taking a rest. I went for a run, got a terrible stitch even though I hadn't eaten anything since 7.30 a.m. (i.e. seven hours earlier), had a bite, and now I'm waiting for water to heat up for bath and hair washing. By the end of next week I'll have done some seventy engagements. It's just like being a minister all over again, sore throat and all, over ninety hours done this week by the time I hit the hay again. I don't mind doing it, as long as it has some purpose. That's what was bugging me last year. I do need to have something to do, so it is nice to know the next project (*What Women Want*) is sitting waiting. And who knows what else?

The PM and the Government are in deep trouble. Every day brings new headlines: our confidence seems to have gone, while Labour are surging ahead, with leads around 12 per cent in the polls. The SDP/SLD vote has virtually vanished, and has all gone to Labour. If that happened in South Derbyshire it would make my seat marginal – but I think I'd take some, and I doubt if they will make such an effort there when Greg and Phillip are more vulnerable. So much has happened. On *Walden on Sunday* the PM looked fine, pretty even, but there was a harsh, aggressive edge to her, a kind of desperation never there before; and she sounded several times as if she was losing her marbles. Walden even asked her views on comments that she was 'slightly off her trolley', and her responses tended to demonstrate that it was true! Only the most diehard Tories can have liked it. Then we have Lawson, cool, steely and seething, speaking in Tuesday's debate and calling Alan Walters 'the top of an ill-concealed iceberg'. He clearly thought Alan's return was a deliberate challenge by the PM to his position. Nigel said nice things about John Major, who performed predictably at the Dispatch Box twice this week, but has a hunted look about him. On the evening news on Thursday John looked tired and strained, hunched forward, talking fast: none of Ken Baker's easy bonhomie. He's not a smooth man, John, and under pressure it shows.

I had a quick conversation with him in the corridor by the library on Tuesday evening, about 9 p.m. I'd written to congratulate him, of course, warning that he should be careful of enemies, but assuring him that he has friends too. We discussed briefly who the enemies might be. Parkinson (who has been doing badly of late) wanted to be Foreign Secretary or Chancellor of the Exchequer, and Major has been both. Geoffrey Howe, for obvious reasons. Baker. And a few others. I took the opportunity to tell John my concern about the pressure to push interest rates up any further. If they go beyond 15 per cent, industry in my patch will stop dead and we can kiss goodbye to the next election, be it in '91 or '92 or whenever. John said there was enormous pressure from the bankers. Of course, said I, that's how they earn their money: we mustn't sacrifice the welfare of ordinary people to them. He felt we could hold the thing if he at least made clear that he would raise interest rates if he had to: that might just be enough – and so it has proved, for the pound has steadied this week around 2.88–2.89DM and around $1.57; the Stock Exchange rallied and in fact has been rising all week.

I said to John that he should do something about his voice – in debate it goes all strangulated and squeaky. To my surprise he said he had, and was planning to visit a voice coach, but he was anxious not to lose his soft voice, which sounds considerate and pleasant in conversation.

I had the strangest conversation with John Kennedy, John Moore's PA, in the car on the way back from Croydon. He is now our candidate in Barking, standing against Labour's Jo Richardson, who has a majority of 3000, and he has a chance, with new building, etc. He chats to other PAs, including Ted Heath's. There's a genuine plot to have a leadership contest this year. Barney Hayhoe[1] and John Biffen are possibilities. Nigel was sitting third row up with Biffen, David Howell and Terence Higgins on Tuesday (looking like Mount Rushmore, the four of them!). If they both try, there's another group which will go around urging people to abstain, just to teach the PM a lesson. Now if a hundred abstain, she wouldn't get the 51 per cent necessary. Even if she fought the challenge successfully, she would have to trounce them to destroy the threat: otherwise she could be out at Xmas. Heath is going to attack her on the last day of the Queen's Speech debate, which would be a week before the contest.

I've backed the PM in public, for she's my best bet to get back in to Government before the next election (though if we lose it, I could have some fun, especially as lots of others will go off elsewhere to make money). Anyway, she still has more electoral appeal than Kinnock. On Monday at our press conference for the book launch I muttered about 'Little furry animals leaving a ship they think is sinking. The ship of state is not sinking, it sails on!' Sidgwick's asked mournfully after the third or fourth such question whether I might mention the book at all? Mark Lennox-Boyd saw me that evening and said 'Little furry animals! Oh yes, that went down very well', so perhaps I did my bit to boost her morale. As soon as we have finished with the book I can crack back in there, making speeches in the House (like Iain Macleod), attacking the Labour Party. I feel such venom inside me and it has to be directed at someone! Best, therefore, to aim it at the guys on the other side of the Chamber.

1. Sir Barney Hayhoe, former Minister of State; Conservative MP for Brentford and Isleworth.

Victoria, Thursday 16 November, 4.40 p.m.

Well, it's been a rum sort of fortnight! Right now I'm at the flat, waiting for Peter Carter-Ruck to phone and report progress (if any) on my claim against the *Observer*;[1] and for Norman Fowler's car to pick me up to go to Eton, to speak there at a function organised by his stepson, Oliver Poole. The signing tour finished Monday and was very odd indeed: some places very busy (e.g. Glasgow), others quiet (e.g. Oxford). The bookshops don't seem to have much clue about advertising these things – only little ads in small print on the book pages. It is selling very well outside London, but quiet here.

Fifteen per cent interest rates don't help, of course, with the Tories way down in the polls – we'd do much better with the book if the Government was popular! Not in the bestseller list yet. Things may improve after yesterday's Autumn Statement. John Major revised all Nigel's forecasts downward (inflation upward), probably to take a small devaluation on board, which has already happened. And the overall package, with increased spending on the NHS, the homeless and Housing Associations, and more too on transport, all looked very good. Labour very glum indeed, and I think we are back on target for an election in summer '91. It helps that John Major was a whip. His political antennae are very acute and he's been generous – quite right – the surplus is still over £12 billion. Our side all very pleased! He said gloomy things about growth in '90 but I think that's a deliberate underestimate, again for political reasons.

The Jimmy Young Show, which I've been presenting all week, has been fun and lucrative (£1000 for the week, or £100 per hour). I

---

1. EC had brought an action for libel against the *Observer*. In an interview about the forthcoming film *Paris By Night*, the actress Charlotte Rampling was described as playing an over-ambitious Tory MP: said to be 'an Edwina Currie figure'.

think I'm quite good at it, but I wouldn't want to do it all the time. It's just like teaching, having to be in a fixed place at a fixed time. At least being an MP gives you more freedom, even if it is more demanding.

In my eyrie at Tower House, Sunday 26 November, 8.50 p.m.

Cross with myself. I seem to be so disorganised at present – leaving papers behind, not disciplining myself properly, e.g. spending the hour when Ray was taking kids back to school tonight doing house-work (necessary because we have a television crew here tomorrow), but I should have been writing this. Generally feeling angry with me!

Really the reason is that we didn't make the bestseller list. I am both puzzled and disappointed. According to William Armstrong we are quite a long way down, too. Isn't it odd? The one thing I did not expect. I guess partly because all the publicity, to my irritation, has been about me, very little about the book. Somewhere this has to be Sidgwick & Jackson's fault, this must have happened before. Then Sidgwick's seem to miss a trick in sales, and I've decided they are incompetent. I spoke at Eton ten days ago, four hundred boys with bulging wallets, and staff; yet the books (sixteen!) arrived after I'd left. I've sold them, and far more, at dinners since. On Friday I was in Norwich; I'd mentioned it a dozen times and yet when we arrived there were no books and none in the bookshop opposite the hotel. A call to a wholesaler produced fifty and a discount – but what a dis-organised shower they are! Not one of the reviews has looked seriously at the book (I haven't checked the nursing/medical ones yet). The *Evening Standard* had it reviewed by the nun whose hens had salmonella! The PR material is all pale grey and doesn't stand out in a window. In Burton-on-Trent only WH Smith has it, not the smaller specialist bookshops. Roll on the demise of the Net Book

Agreement. The Pan people seem to have more clue. We shall see. It's a bit like I feel when travelling on British Rail: wouldn't I like to run this, I'm sure I could do a better job, or at least no worse than the current shower.

It looks as if Sir Anthony Meyer, the Clwyd MP, is going to stand against the PM. She has to get 216 votes to win outright on first ballot, but in fact must get over three hundred to smash him. At present he needs only a proposer and seconder, both anonymous, to stand. To make a bid for the Labour leadership you need 20 per cent of the Parliamentary Labour Party, i.e. over forty signatures, a much better system. Today's opinion polls suggest that a majority of the electorate want her gone before the next election, and even Tories are not too enthusiastic, at least when they respond to pollsters. (I said Sir Anthony should be 'strung up by the short and hairies' and that got into the *Sun*!) She has made things worse by firstly imply-ing to the *Sunday Correspondent* that she would retire after the next election, and then on Friday saying to *The Times* that she would do two more terms – go on for ever, more like! She kept saying 'by popular acclaim I will stay on' – of course, after the *Sunday Correspondent* interview she had a big postbag saying 'darling, we love you'. If I've learned anything recently, it is don't trust the fan mail, or at least, don't regard it as the whole story. They don't mean it, Maggie: if you start to look like a liability they'll drop you just like anyone else. Yet she is still head and shoulders above everyone. The first to counsel caution in Eastern Europe. The wisest head in EEC. The most successful administration for years, with the pro-portion of GDP in public expenditure down from 49 per cent to under 39 per cent now. It is all brilliant. But the lioness is ageing and the jackals are snapping at her heels. It gives me a sick feeling to watch it.

There were lots of comments in the press about the fact that seven women Tory MPs wore red during the State Opening of Parliament. Well, it's a fashionable colour this year and I *always* wear bright or bold clothes. So does Emma Nicholson[1] now, who is popping up all over the place, ambitious lady. Virginia Bottomley looked splendid wearing a tight navy suit, the first time she has shown off her elegant bottom. The men sitting next to me sighed as she shifted her weight from one hip to the other! She is a really good Minister of State and looks and sounds it; I wonder how she is getting on with Ken, and whether he still puffs the cigar smoke around. He's embroiled in another row, this time with the ambulancemen, calling them 'silly' and saying that their leader, Roger Poole of NUPE, is on an 'ego trip'. Clarke has no idea at all how to be conciliatory. So as with Margaret, the policies are presented in an unpleasant and aggressive way and we lose votes: over 90 per cent of the people think we should pay 'em the money and inflation go hang!

Tower House, Sunday 10 December

In front of a log fire, waiting for Ray to come back from Denstone. Both girls came home today. Deb is now a couple of inches taller than me: doing much better at school but still finding life a bit tough – you say a cross word to her and she's still liable to pout or cry.

The PM sailed through her test on Monday with 314 votes, but there was a surprisingly big vote against her: thirty-three for Sir Anthony Meyer and twenty-four recorded abstention/spoiled papers. Although we all went round saying it was a great victory, it did give her prestige a knock; and no one congratulated her in Thursday's Question Time on winning the first ballot in fourteen years. There were other losers in my eyes. Apart from Meyer himself, not one person has admitted voting for him: not one, not even his (secret)

1.   Conservative MP for Devon West and Torridge.

proposer and seconder. It was speculated that Heseltine had abstained, but he didn't declare himself either. They are all shits in a minor way. In the middle of all this I had to take Elspeth Howe to dinner, as she is patron of Women into Business and I'm now the president. Angela Browning, who has just been adopted for the Falmouth seat, is chairman and leading light, so I'm not sure quite what I'm there for! Elspeth had got peeved when I was involved in October, hence the soothing dinner. But it was all quite bizarre. For a start Chris had made no proper arrangements where to meet, so three of us (the other being a Scottish businesswoman called Susan Bell who smoked heavily and had brown teeth) met in Central Lobby and then had to start hunting for Elspeth. She, meantime, had gone straight to the Harcourt Room, where she had attached herself to Virginia Bottomley's table and was talking hard, leaning forward, her face thrust at Virginia – who was leaning backwards and looking fastidious – and it was another twenty minutes before she detached herself and came over to our table. She then harangued me for half an hour about child care and was very critical of Government think-ing. How odd, I thought, she clearly doesn't know much about it, and yet she's the one whose husband is Deputy PM . . . I just avoided saying, 'Why don't you harangue Geoffrey about it?' Her conversa-tion is peppered with 'When I was in Poland . . .', 'When we were in India . . .', etc., and she is clearly stuck in a mental rut from the time when Geoffrey was Foreign Secretary and she had her eyes on Number 10. Not for me, those two: I don't like her at all.

We are improving slightly in the polls, and have pulled back three points this month: only six behind Labour, according to Gallup. Maybe this is because of television? There have been big audiences – half the nation watched the State Opening of Parliament. The PM looks good on television, but aggression by the likes of Kinnock and Gordon Brown doesn't. I made my first televised speech in the Queen's Speech debate on the Monday, and afterwards got a tape and watched it. I must stop moving around, and I ought to look more as if I'm enjoying it. Still it was OK, and I'll get better.

Geoffrey Howe fell asleep on the front bench as Tony Newton was winding up on 27 November. I nudged Greg Knight, the whip sitting beside him, but Geoffrey keeps doing it. Maybe Elspeth talks all night.

The PM has now told *Panorama* that she didn't mean it about retiring after next election. Of course she did, but it was foolish to say so. She seems to have lost just a little of her touch, and there is a feeling of an era coming to an end. I'm not sure I would be so excited about a Conservative Government headed by Douglas Hurd; it would be worthy, but not so tough. The next leadership election is likely to be in 1992. I wonder who will stand – who will win – and how I will vote then?

1990

Victoria, Monday 8 January, 12 noon

I haven't done any diary for a month. I'm getting lazier, there's no doubt about it, and less guilty about being lazy. Is that a good or bad thing? Life is certainly less frenetic. I'm a cooler, more easy-going person. But I'm slower and dozier, and everything is more effort. My only intellectual activity during the holiday was switching pocket diaries! Oh, and a review of three books (Jane Fonda, Shirley Conran and a book on colour therapy) for *Publishing News*. I did that for the stimulus and in the hope that I'll get asked to do more, for the big papers. An intellectual reputation would make a change.

To my amazement, I came sixth in the Radio 4 'Woman of the Year' poll. My appeal seems to have an enduring quality. PM top, of course; (2) Kate Adie; (3) Princess of Wales; (4) Princess Anne; (5) Mother Teresa; (6) EC; (7) Raisa Gorbachev. Her (Raisa's) husband came top in the men's, but he's now far more popular abroad than in his own country.

The Department of Health is facing a few problems, though Virginia seems to be settling in nicely. She sent a printed letter of thanks for our congrats on her elevation – not signed, just initialled, which I do regard as offhand: then a Department of Health Xmas card, personally signed, which is a bit over the top. She asked me in the corridor if we could have a chat, saying that nothing had been done on women's health since I left, could she seek my advice? Oh, Virginia, I laughed, you don't need *my* advice! She asked how Susie enjoyed boarding when she was little – answer, very much – as they are considering sending their youngest, now seven, off to school. No worries there about missing their childhood; but then Virginia is made of steel.

House of Commons, Thursday 11 January

First week back and busy. I've spoken twice this week and asked two questions, so that's four speeches since the opening of Parliament: as many as I did during the whole of the rest of 1989. I didn't expect to get called in today's debate on the ambulance dispute, but we were short of speakers, so in I went. Michael Fallon had suggested looking at Ennals's[1] statements in 1979 when the ambulancemen were last in dispute, and they turned out to be a goldmine (and dead easy to do – I just asked the library staff, who produced photocopies in ten minutes: so much stuff that I passed it on to Tim Devlin[2] as well!). The brief from CCO was terrible – short and non-political, just a repeat of the turgid technical stuff from the officials. Ken spoke for nearly an hour, yet, like all the other ministers on this topic, he never managed to mention the actual amounts the ambulance staff are being offered, only the percentage increases. A substantial proportion of the public would be less sympathetic to the ambulancemen if they knew exactly how much money we were talking about. Virginia closed the debate; she has a curious style, though very effective. For the first few minutes she appeared to have learned it by heart and didn't look at her notes at all, though seemed to be keeping her place in them and turned the sheets over regularly. She ignored the Opposition entirely and spoke straight to the Speaker, earnestly as if over a dinner table, and quite quietly. That made her very difficult to hear, but it had the effect, for a while, of quietening

1. David (later Lord) Ennals, Secretary of State for Social Services, 1976–9; Labour MP for Dover, 1964–70; MP for Norwich North, 1974–83.
2. Conservative MP for Stockton South.

the House. Labour really doesn't know how to deal with her – and she sounds so posh, just like the Princess of Wales, that our lot don't dare. I enjoy speaking from the green benches and feel very much at home there, I must say. When it goes well, it's like writing a good essay: not part of any great plan or movement, but just good in itself.

David Lightbown told me that Norman Fowler made up his mind to go back in the summer when he didn't get the party chairmanship.[1] That means maybe he wasn't even considered for the Home Office job when Waddington was appointed. No doubt he'll be party chairman some day, when he is about sixty and in the House of Lords. David was making noises about other ministers coming back after they've had a suitable time out, but it did sound a bit like a formula. I don't mind it so much now. The 16th December[2] came and went – we had a drinks party in the Jubilee Room and I felt very cheery. I've no idea how the book has gone, but since the bulk of my money (heading soon for deposit in Jersey – some plutocrat!) came from the *Sunday Times*, it doesn't matter anyway. Like my chemistry A level, I've put it behind me and am now reading hard for the next one.

House of Commons, Monday 22 January

I seem to be *so* busy. This afternoon I finished off the epilogue for the paperback edition of *Life Lines*. I enjoy writing, but sometimes feel square eyed after sitting at the word processor for hours on end. This morning I had a meeting with Ian Chapman, Martin Neild and Billy Adair from Pan. If all goes well, we'll announce the *What Women*

---

1. A few weeks earlier Norman Fowler had resigned his job as Secretary of State for Employment 'to spend more time with his family'. He returned to front-rank politics as Conservative Party chairman in 1992.
2. The anniversary of EC's resignation.

Want book on 12 February. At present I have seven contributions in; have asked Sue Harvey of Luncheon Vouchers for another; and am chasing Gordon Heald, Anthony Clare and Barbara Young. We have enough, if necessary, for a two-hundred-page book, which is about what I want. The women's issue is beginning to explode, rather as I hoped it would.

Brook Street Bureau has booked me for next Tuesday to do a press conference and open their latest office in Upper Regent Street (near the BBC), and on Thursday morning I'm on *Kilroy*, arguing the toss with Jo Richardson. In addition, *Newsnight* wanted me on the ambulance dispute, as (apparently) Ken Clarke turned them down. It doesn't seem to have occurred to Ken that he has a team, that they are all competent, and that their feelings must be hurt as mine were when he acts as if they don't exist. Nice to be in demand, but no. Even the whips are at it now, pushing me to speak in last Thursday's debate on the community charge. It was a lot of fun to do and I was not displeased, even though it was virtually off the cuff. I followed Bernie Grant,[1] who came to the Commons with such a fiery reputation; he plodded through a written speech without style or substance. Pity, really; someone else was always pulling the strings, it appears. So that's five speeches since the Queen's Speech and three since the January return. Greg Knight wanted me to speak in today's debate on social security too, but I demurred, as I must get on with *What Women Want*. It shows, however, that the effect of televising Parliament is wearing off; colleagues are no longer falling over themselves to be seen speaking.

That may well be because Tim Renton,[2] the new Chief Whip, is doing things differently. Get good speakers who can support the Government, he's saying, we must win these debates on our feet.

---

1. Labour MP for Tottenham.
2. Conservative MP for Mid-Sussex.

David Lightbown told me that the whips' weekly meetings used to spend all their time discussing the following week's votes; now they dispose of that double quick, and spend more time thinking about how to improve the party's standing. The Chief Whip is really a minister without portfolio; the only others are Ken Baker (Chancellor of the Duchy of Lancaster) and the PM herself. So we are a bit light on 'thinkers'. Baker is disappointing me – he is more reactive than I had expected, tending to wait till challenged, e.g. on the ambulance dispute and on Hong Kong. There's no feel at all of a coordinated effort to present policy in a positive way; it's too much teeth and Brylcreem. He is stealthily distancing himself from colleagues in trouble (including maybe the PM?), and has the sheen of Teflon man about him. We know what happens to them – they come unstuck! And I doubt if too many people will regret it if he does. Take the stories which appeared in the press about how he'd refused to have me as a vice-chairman. I didn't care too much either way, but on reflection it would have been appreciated if he (or his PPS, or *someone*) had just whispered, 'Ken hopes you'll take no notice of those stories: he values what you do very much'. That might have been a lie, but it would have made me feel better. His silence leaves me feeling a bit grumpy.

I had the opportunity to see Renton in action last Tuesday, when John Taylor,[1] the whip on the Broadcasting Bill Committee, told me to go over to Number 12 for drinks. I was expecting a cosy but high-powered chat. Instead a batch of MPs and whips *and wives!* were milling around, very cocktail party, with Mrs Renton, a slim dapper lady just like her husband, showing everyone how they had moved the pictures around. They have damn good taste, too, with original illustrations of *Alice in Wonderland* and some decent

1. Conservative MP for Solihull.

landscapes. The photos of the whips' cricket teams have all been relegated to a dusty corner! It was in this room that I wrote out my resignation letter. I remember feeling tired and bewildered – but also relieved that I didn't have to be Edwina Currie any more. Last week the room looked smaller, cosier, less forbidding. But the conversation was altogether less meaty – at least it was until the PM turned up. If that lady isn't on HRT, I'm a monkey's uncle. She is round and soft and sexy, very female indeed. It was hard to remember she's sixty-four – she looks better than Marion Roe, who is more than ten years younger. And she's fizzing, in a controlled, deliberate, disciplined way. Still throwing off wild remarks, chucking around her prejudices, waiting for people to argue with her. 'Well, Edwina!' she boomed at me, 'what are you up to now?' She points a lot, and when she talks the crepy skin on her neck goes pink and blows out a bit. I kept thinking of a turkey which does the same when showing off. In a conversation about the Broadcasting Bill, she went on about the BBC: 'You keep them under control, my dear!' – as if I could, or would. We talked about satellite TV, and how some councils and landlords are refusing to allow dishes. 'Get cable!' she shouted, 'Westminster Cable – only £10 per month – I watch it all the time – you can get everything on it, more than Sky – you can get CNN from America, it's so good, much better than the BBC!' and then she swept on to the next group . . .

It was drinks the next day with the Chancellor. A motley crew: Peter Hordern,[1] Michael Shaw,[2] Janet Fookes[3] – the knights I guess, other than the Finance Backbench Committee officers. Once again Major made me wonder whether he lacks personality or is just

---

1. Sir Peter Hordern, the long-serving Conservative MP for Horsham.
2. Sir Michael Shaw, Conservative MP for Scarborough.
3. Dame Janet Fookes, Conservative MP for Plymouth Drake.

excessively modest and self-disciplined. His room at the Treasury was awful, dull brown, ancient scruffy furniture, nothing personal whatsoever. His rooms as a junior minister and Chief Secretary were exactly the same. He has, however, stopped the practice of Treasury ministers leaving their families for the whole weekend to go to Chevening for their Budget deliberations. When they went this time, the weekend before last, they finished by Saturday lunch, and off he went to his Norma. Quite right too.

Victoria, Monday 5 February, 6.30 p.m.

Odd stories in the press last week, whiff of Bernard Ingham about them, that the PM was not well pleased with Baker or Clarke, or Parkinson, and was thinking of replacing them in the run-up to the General Election. Personally I think that would be mad, we've already had three reshuffles in six months. But my name was mentioned: one story said I'm to get a Government department with full Cabinet rank. Unless she's thinking of a 'women's role' job, I can't imagine what that would be. How very bizarre.

I spent an hour this afternoon trying to set up a week's holiday in Israel for Susie and me at Easter – Deb is going to Germany – but it was harder than expected, as the only packages handled by Amex and Thomas Cook are to the sunshine of Eilat, which I don't fancy! No, it has to be Jerusalem. I'm not sure I can afford it, but the whim has taken me; I've never wanted to go there before, but now I want to watch the setting sun on the Dome of the Rock, and feel the clash (metaphorical, preferably) of cultures. Susie is very clued up about Religious Studies and probably knows more than I do. Deb wouldn't appreciate it much, and anyway I am not taking the two of them away together; they fight.

House of Commons, Wednesday 14 March, 11.30 p.m.

Beware the Ides of March ... a cartoon in one of today's serious newspapers had Margaret Thatcher looking defiant, a Tory front-bencher armed with a knife lurking behind every pillar. It doesn't look good, but more important it doesn't feel good either. The opinion poll in tomorrow's *Guardian* says that Labour have a 21 per cent lead over us now (polling done last weekend). Apparently no Government has ever recovered from a 20 per cent deficit.

We lost a vote last night, and again it has an ominous feel. It's the first vote the Government has lost in four years. We changed the rules on the payment of social security for people in nursing homes and residential care. It isn't enough, and the proprietors are worried – but worse, the rules only apply to new residents and existing ones are treated under the old rules, which are unsatisfactory. A very low-key campaign has tried to persuade the Government to treat the old the same as the new. Hard luck for them that the Bill is Ken Clarke's; he doesn't give a damn and angered everyone, so I'm told, by being very dismissive and saying the matter had gone through without any trouble in committee. The debate, led by Ann Widdecombe[1] and George Young,[2] was also very convincing, though the effect would be to give the proprietors, who can be a greedy bunch, *carte blanche* with Government money. (David Lightbown said to me last week that if ever anything convinced him that I was a reasonable woman, it was the advent of Ann Widdecombe to the Commons!) Tony Newton, looking haggard as ever, had nothing to offer; this decision has all the hallmarks of a Cabinet committee in which he was in a minority. The whips were a bit too relaxed about it, too, and failed to warn people to be here; at 11.30 p.m. the vote

1. Conservative MP for Maidstone.
2. Sir George Young, Conservative MP for Ealing and Acton.

was called and we lost by three, with more than thirty Tories in the Opposition lobby. Labour, of course, are cock-a-hoop, but I think it was more cock-up than anything else.

I'd be very surprised if Cecil Parkinson hangs around much longer. He was on the same table at dinner tonight, with Tony Coombs,[1] Rob Hayward[2] and me, and made no attempt to talk to us, engaging in conversation the whole evening instead with Cranley Onslow[3] at his side. If he was planning to stay and try for the leadership, he would have been chatting us up. Michael Heseltine does! She must also be under considerable pressure to ditch Nick Ridley before the election – a real vote loser there. However right he may be in retrospect, his 'couldn't care less' handling of poll tax and water privatisation has been bad news. I am now inundated with letters about the new tax from horrified constituents who would have to pay five or six times as much as their rates. I wrote privately to John Major, telling him how worried people are about it. Those with a little money in the bank – and many of them have just recovered their loss from Barlow Clowes[4] – do not qualify for rebates, and such people are appalled that they will have to spend their precious capital, accumulated in all the ways Margaret told them to, in order to pay her tax. They are livid. For the first time, I'm beginning to wonder whether we will hold South Derbyshire.

Victoria, Thursday 22 March

Budget debate is on till Monday, so one-line whip tonight. Busy week, and I'm feeling tired: not helped by increasingly painful

---

1. Anthony Coombs, Conservative MP for Wyre Forest.
2. Robert Hayward, Conservative MP for Kingswood.
3. The long-serving Conservative MP for Woking.
4. An investment fund which collapsed in 1987–8 as a result of fraud, wiping out the savings of many investors.

periods, which leave me washed out after. I suppose the change is starting. My right hip now plays up after only an hour sitting in one place, so that I can't bear driving the whole way home. I'm having days on end with pain somewhere and I really *don't* like it. Not nice, getting older. Everything seems to creak or hurt or take longer to get better or harder to keep in good condition.

Roger Freeman in the tea room last week late, preparing for an adjournment debate. I'd done 59 in my 27 months. In the 15 months since, he's done 72 . . . awful. I bet Ken Clarke doesn't even know, he takes no interest in his juniors. But if it had been me, I'd have been ready by now to quit politics altogether. What a daft way to run a country and grind down competent people. I certainly feel grateful that I've been rescued from all that, even if the future is uncertain.

The Budget was great – no giveaways, no harshness, lots of incentives for *saving* which (if they work) will bring down consumption (and so inflation) a lot less painfully than tax increases, etc. Of course there will be some moving around of funds, but, for example, it will pay better to put money into tax-free PEPs and TESSAs, especially after stamp duty goes, than offshore as I've been doing. So we should see a net inflow of funds again. I watched the Budget debate from upstairs as usual and caught Major's eye as he started. He was determined, nervous and competent, and came across very well.

Tower House, Tuesday 17 April, 10 p.m.

We've been out canvassing this afternoon in Littleover in Derby and got caught in the rain, sheltering from the wet under flowering trees with the blossoms blown around in the wind like confetti after the wedding party has left.

The polls for us are still pretty awful, but I have a feeling now that they won't get worse. People in South Derbyshire seem to have calmed down a bit about the community charge and we are getting fewer letters. Still a fierce battle in the press. There's no doubt that a

(*Left*) With Margaret Thatcher on the stump during the 1987 election (Empics)

(*Above*) As Health Minister, promoting healthy eating in 1987

The ministerial team at the DHSS in September 1986.
(From left to right) Tony Newton, Norman Fowler, John Major, Jean Trumpington and Nicholas Lyell
(*Daily Telegraph*)

(Above) Running along the canal in Derbyshire
(Mike Stroud, Sunday Express)

(Left) Norman Tebbit, who was Party Chairman, in 1987
(Press Association)

(Below) With Tony Benn in Nottingham, June 1987

(*Above*) The women MPs who posed for the *Guinness Book of Records* in 1988. EC is second left in the back row (Guinness Superlatives)

(*Right*) With Jeffrey Archer in 1989 at the Tower House, celebrating ten years of Tory government

(*Below*) The Chairmen of the Regional Health Authorities with the ministerial team at the Department of Health, including (from left to right) David Mellor and Ken Clarke, summer 1988

(Above) John Moore, Secretary of State for Social Services, and then Social Security, between 1987 and 1989 (Press Association)

(Above right) Private Eye cover, September 1988 (Private Eye)

(Below right) EC's first book is published, October 1989 (Derby Evening Telegraph)

(*Top*) A view of 'Les Tuileries', the Curries' house in France

(*Above*) During the 1987 General Election with Ray and the children

(*Left*) At home at the piano with Debbie (left) and Susie (*Daily Mail*)

The Tower House,
Findern, near Derby

Ray, Debbie (left) and
Susie at home at the
Tower House in 1988

(Left) With the President of Toyota, Eiji Toyoda, at the groundbreaking ceremony, Burnaston, June 1990 (Adrian Heapy Photography)

(Below centre) At the adoption meeting in 1992 with agent David Canzini

(Below left) Richard Ryder, junior Agriculture Minister 1988 and Chief Whip from 1990 to 1995 (Rex Features)

(Below right) Interrogating Sir Robin Day at a Guardian debate, 1992

In 1992, the image used in the election address (Empics)

coach and horses has been driven through inflation policy when people face such huge increases – it is also knocking business sideways, as people cut their spending. And the tax is leading to higher pay demands. Inflation is now 8.1 per cent and set to rise to 10 per cent (Chancellor's own forecast), before falling to 5 per cent next year, we hope! There are still rumblings about the PM, and Michael Heseltine hovers nearby, beating his wings so we can all feel the air move – hear the careful, disciplined hum. He calls her . . . 'um, Mrs Thatcher' – always a slight hesitation before her name, never 'the Prime Minister', and sticks to the formula that he can imagine no circumstances in which he would stand against her, and he believes she will lead the Conservative Party into the next General Election and will win. Ah, but with what majority, Michael? In a way, she's wasting her time. She wanted to stay on long enough to see off Lawson and Howe and Hurd and Heseltine, then Tebbit and Baker, so that a new generation of Thatcherites can fill her shoes. But there aren't any. Only Nick Ridley is left and he can't. She has indeed outlasted all her rivals. When she goes, the new PM, whether Tory successor or Labour, will be pro-Europe and gentler on social and economic issues, more interventionist, more helpful to minorities, treading more gently in the international scene. She has already lost that final battle.

And so to the high point of the year, the visit to Israel. Susie and I flew overnight on El Al, arriving Tel Aviv airport at 6 a.m. with too much luggage, as usual. Sunny but not warm. Young people everywhere, many very dark. Soldiers carrying guns, cradling them like babies. Talking loudly in guttural accents. Girl soldiers with big bottoms in khaki trousers. Soldiers at bus stations, on street corners, so many soldiers everywhere. Going home for Passover, clogging up the buses, cramming in next to Susie on the bus to Tiberias. Nobody smiles, nobody friendly, nobody helps us with our bags on or off. Information kiosk doesn't know, shrugs shoulders, raises over-made-up eyes to heaven. Bus old, noisy, smelly, roads terrible, jolts the whole way. Orange juice freshly squeezed before us, as in Majorca: delicious. Falafels in pitta with hummus, memories of Swiss Cottage in 1969: also delicious. Dinners in hotels, pretty awful. Staff in hotels Lebanese: beautiful, but talk to each other all the time, don't explain, their English at level of 'you pay in dollar?'. Tiberias was a mistake. Bombed in 1967 and rebuilt like the worst kind of resort, plastic chairs and awnings, 'Big Ben Pub', overpriced food – St Peter's fish, a kind of carp, not bad. The mosque in the centre neglected and ignored – must have been beautiful once. Tour up to Capernaum and the Golan Heights on the Saturday much better: well-informed guide, lunch in Druze restaurant, served by young boys, earnest and for once friendly! Saw Banais, otherwise Pan-yass, established by Alexander for the god Pan at one of the sources of the Jordan, and got Jordan mud all over my new slacks. And the Nimrod Crusader castle, and the empty ghost town of Quneitra in the Golan Heights, abandoned during the Six Day War – Dayan simply occupied it, fifty miles from Damascus, and was about to keep going when the Soviets warned they would shell Israel from the Mediterranean if he didn't stop. Friday night at Kibbutz Kfar Hanassi, with an old couple who went with British Habonim[1] forty years ago and cleared the fields of stones with their own hands. They couldn't farm on the east side of the ridge overlooking the Jordan for fear of being shot. I'd hoped for proper Shabbas[2] dinner, but it's a freethinking kibbutz and there was no religious or family feel about it. That came with Seder,[3] not (sadly) in Jerusalem as I'd hoped, but in Rehovot, a suburb of Tel Aviv in the home of Rabbi Alan and Susie Levine, he Canadian, large, shambling, cheerful and she Moroccan, petite, French-speaking, bright-eyed, brown as a little bird. It still wasn't a strict

1. Patriotic Youth Movement.
2. Sabbath.
3. Passover meal.

Seder but not bad, complete with 'Ehod Me Yodayah' ('Who Knows One?') and 'Had Gadyah'.[1] On the Sunday night we met Eliahu ben-Ellisar, Israel's first Ambassador to Egypt, and his wife Nietze. He is a distinguished looking man, going grey, trim beard (could pass for Sheik Yamani) and she a Middle Eastern lady, too much jewellery, too much make-up, Western clothes not looking quite right. Both very friendly. Tea in King David Hotel, 'the height of colonialism' they said, but at least the staff were helpful! We ate strawberries and drank tea and talked politics. Impressions very mixed and not very favourable. I loved the history and archaeology, Masada was mind-blowing, and I bought Yadin's story of the dig and read it straight off. Hammat, near Tiberias, the old synagogue with a zodiac in the mosaic floor; and the mosaics at Tabgha, the church of the loaves and fishes, where the floor is Byzantine. Capernaum where Jesus chose Matthew, the tax collector. Then Galilee itself, seeing the church on the Hill of Beatitudes – somewhere I wanted to visit, but I left my Bible at home and somehow that was symptomatic of the whole trip, a sense of something missing. Maybe the love of God? Maybe the love of one's fellow man. Jerusalem: again, the history is staggering; see here, the well of Hezekiah, here the stones of Herod, here the tomb of David – in a very smelly gents' lav from what I could see, and who knows? Here the Dome of the Rock, where Abraham was willing to sacrifice Isaac and whence Muhammad rose to heaven: such beauty, such confident grace, surrounded by Arab men sitting quietly under the trees, fasting all day for Ramadan, our guide an eighth-generation Jerusalemite, gentle in his comments on the Muslims, uninterested at the Wailing Wall which was much bigger than I expected and too much an accretion of praying fanatics, clinging as if they would become lichen on the stones and never

1. Old Ashkenazi songs, traditionally sung at the end of a Seder (often now replaced by modern Israeli songs).

let go. And the church of the Holy Sepulchre, kneeling at the back close to a scruffy Coptic monk to touch and leave a candle. A day or two after we left, religious Jews took over St John's Hospice next door, initiating a riot. The soldiers threw tear gas. A court has ordered them to leave – yesterday the PLO fanatics held a demo in the church – *plus ça change.*

One last thought. It didn't make me want to go again, and it didn't make me regret any of my own history. All those religious Jews were convinced that God gave them rights – extra rights, as a chosen people; and their history is bound up with asserting those rights, without emphasising any of their obligations, a liberal view they would not recognise. The biblical promise was that if they worshipped the one true God, he would intervene on their behalf and give them victory. Christianity offers something different – free will and free choice. Much harder – much more sophisticated, especially when added to loving thy neighbour as thyself as the first commandment. The voice of Christ is heard sighing in the wind wherever he walked here. I recognise his comments and criticism, especially as I realised at Masada that he was dealing with Jews recognisably similar in their orthodoxy to those I grew up with. They wanted a leader to throw off the Romans (impossible); he came to show them the path to salvation in another world, and they were not interested. My father understood all this, but failed to come to any conclusions. No wonder he neither voted nor prayed and said he was an atheist. Well, I'm not. And though I'm glad I have a Jewish background I feel no obligations there either. Just a great deal of sadness that this exquisite little country should be in such a mess; and delight that I'm British and that my job is looking after sensible people who don't like authority of any kind and especially don't like paying taxes. It was good to get home.

Skean Dhu Hotel, Aberdeen, Thursday 10 May, 11.15 p.m.

I'm at the Scottish Party Conference, invited by South Aberdeen Young Conservatives to address a fringe meeting; but really it's an excuse to come to our Party Conference up here, where there seems to be a lot going on . . .

Michael Heseltine has been at it again, and his name kept cropping up in questions. We expected to be hammered in last Thursday's local elections, but it didn't happen; we held Derby relatively easily, romped home with huge majorities in the all-out elections at Wandsworth and Westminster, and even won control of Ealing (where Neil Kinnock lives). Michael had planned the next stage of his leadership campaign this week – he's on *Question Time* tonight, for example (the *helpful* date would have been *last* week, of course), and this morning he had a rather tendentious article in *The Times* about how he had a much better idea than poll tax back in 1981 and narrowly missed persuading his Cabinet colleagues to accept it.

Next Thursday night I'll be in Romania, as part of a two-person team sent by the Inter-Parliamentary Union. Scared a bit, to be frank. I hope it all goes off without trouble and that they elect a sensible bunch of people.

House of Commons, Wednesday 30 May

It's ages since I wrote: partly because I've done a lot of writing recently and don't feel the need for an outpouring! An article in the *Independent*, being rude about just everybody – Simon Gourlay of the NFU, Government ministers prancing around like mad cows, an industry which cuts corners: all in the hope of giving John Gummer,[1]

---

1. John Gummer had become Minister of Agriculture, Fisheries and Food in 1989, succeeding John MacGregor, who became Secretary of State for Education.

beleaguered little saint that he is, a bit of support. There had been debates while I was away, and today the French Government has banned all British beef from entering France 'until they are sure it is safe for French people' – what humbug! The Germans had taken similar steps, but it is in fact more serious than the press realise, for the disease[1] has so far been found only in Britain. Yet it seems so widespread that it must have been in breeding stock, of which we are major exporters. John Gummer told me, in a whispered aside, that ministers are just holding their breath till the first case emerges overseas which can be traced to Britain. It just shows how bloody stupid that ministry has been in the past, how lax, how foolish to encourage the feeding of cheap animal protein to cattle, chickens etc. I'd almost say, it serves them right, but it could be a long time before confidence is restored in British farming, and that would be a tragedy.

Romania was marvellous. The area around Timisoara turned out to be unexpectedly pretty, with some lovely old villages, too unimportant in days of old for rampaging armies to loot. A fourteenth-century basilica, roses around the gateway, dark and gloomy inside, gold reflecting the candlelight; the priest, a handsome fit man in his thirties, a dark-haired Richard Chamberlain, talking volubly with a knot of parishioners, his eleven-year-old son stealing away to translate for me. (I wanted permission to take some photos. In the end, I took them anyway, as the men carried on arguing and took no notice of me.) Real gypsies (they call themselves Romanies, and have their own political party), the women bright as peacocks; I moved to take a photo of one, and she pulled her little boy proudly in front of her, until her husband rebuked her for being too familiar, so my photo shows only the back of her head.

1. BSE.

I certainly liked the country areas much better than Bucharest, which may have been attractive once but is a mess now, with bombed-out buildings and a grey drabness which I suppose is the common legacy of communism: I can only surmise, as this is the only Eastern bloc country I have ever been to. Bob Wareing[1] has been to all of them, including Romania twenty-six years ago; he said that there was an atmosphere of fear then. People would only talk to him in doorways, looking over their shoulders. Not any more; like many another country which has enjoyed a false spring, the locals have discovered the pleasures of talking politics long and hard into the night. If we hadn't called a halt, we would have had no sleep at all.

The opposition parties constantly amazed me: I was struck with their innocence, their complete lack of awareness of who to vote for and against. Of course, there was no real opposition to President Iliescu; the other two candidates had not risked their lives in the way he did, and it clearly didn't matter to most people that he had been a party apparatchik for decades. So what, many of them would say, we were all forced to join the party. The Liberals, led by Campeanu, who had the most cogent economic policy, constantly talked over people's heads, and seemed ignorant of the fear of unemployment amongst ordinary workers (only too aware of how inefficient their factories are), in a country which has no social security system (they will have to create one before they go any further, or people will starve). I heard Liberal representatives, on more than one occasion and in more than one place, proclaim loudly that the peasants and workers were too stupid to understand their arguments. Now that's a good quick way of giving votes to your opponents! – and anyway, it is the job of politicians to talk in language the voters can understand;

1.   Robert Wareing, Labour MP for Liverpool, West Derby.

Iliescu did that beautifully. As for Ratiu: the Romanians were too polite (and inexperienced) to say it, but he was a joke candidate, especially with his English accent and his bow tie (so unusual in that country, that people thought he must be a queer. He didn't know that). How would we have voted in 1945, had we been offered the choice between three prime ministerial candidates, one of whom suffered with us through all the dark days, one of whom left Britain in 1931 and the other who left before the *first* war? No wonder the President got 85 per cent.

There was a lot of cross-voting, however, and there the Liberals really should have done better. Maybe they will next time, with a better leader. The parties with a clean approach, the Hungarians and the Greens, both did well. They didn't moan about ballot rigging and communists all the time, and simply argued their policies clearly. We met the Green candidate in Lipova, in Arad region; he greeted us at the second polling station we visited, and with the concurrence of the other party reps invited us for lunch. A tablecloth was brought out, napkins, flowers in a vase, chairs; we were feted most elegantly, no doubt breaking the law, as the voters filed past, casting curious glances at us.

They all had a lot of stick from international jurist observers, but I loved the way at local level the party observers and magistrates bent or ignored the rules if it meant getting a more democratic result, such as showing the gypsies what to do, or keeping the polling stations open till everyone queuing up had voted.

David Lightbown approached me on the last day of term before the recess and suggested I apply to be a member of the Foreign Affairs Select Committee. I shall make enquiries as to what they do, and may apply. It is certainly a prestige committee, with three ex-Cabinet ministers on it who might be allies in future, but the whips are concerned that it is a bit wet; my presence would help. I'm interested if they are involved in Europe, the Middle East or the Far East, but not much in Africa or South America. It would continue my education, it would keep me busy. On the other hand it would take me out of the constituency in what may be an election year. David assured me it was not a dead end: you're on your way back, he said. Nice to know, but really the excitement of endless red boxes has paled. Europe looks more attractive, especially as it seems as if we will be in the European Monetary System within the next year or so, which will sap the power of the British Government to decide economic policy – which is why MHT is against, and Labour in favour, of course. We can't still be out when the election is called as it would be a major issue, and ideal for Labour because no one understands it. And we can't go in too early, for the effects within six months will be heartily deflationary. It will be interesting to see how John Major sorts out that conundrum.

One more thing about politicians. Bob Wareing eats an enormous amount; he must have horrendous blood pressure, and I wonder how long he can carry on like that. David Owen won't last much longer, politically – his party won only 155 votes in the Bootle by-election, coming behind even Screaming Lord Sutch's Monster Raving Loony Party which attracted over four hundred votes. He's looking for a job, we all know that. He would step down now if the party could amicably decide who should succeed him as leader; but neither of the two remaining MPs, John Cartwright and Rosie Barnes, will agree to serve under the other. And we were sneering at the Romanians?

Victoria, Thursday 14 June, 10.30 p.m.

Ah, I feel so sad. Yesterday at dawn, Iliescu sent in the police and troops to clear the demonstrators from University Square. Four hundred people arrested, but of course instantly replaced by thousands more from the university. More troops, Molotov cocktails, determined efforts by the rioters to take over the television station and set it on fire, Government buildings including police HQ set on fire, and at least four people dead, hundreds injured, firing into crowd. Paratroopers sent in to retake television station. Then Iliescu goes on nationwide television last night and asks for support, so 100,000 people come on to the streets of Bucharest, running fights continue all over city centre (nowhere else – not Timisoara). This morning 10,000 miners arrive from western Romania in buses and trucks, having driven through the night, armed with staves and pickaxes and big boots. Tanks in the centre. Miners encouraged to beat up anyone they find. And Iliescu says there was a fascist plot.

So what's the truth? Maybe the demonstrators were planning something – the Molotov cocktails came so easily to hand. Maybe there's an internal political battle – the Interior Minister, responsible for police, has been sacked for being too soft with the demonstrators and not clearing the square sooner – but it was their prime minister who wanted to leave them there, as evidence of toleration of dissent. Truth: the demonstrators did not accept the result, and were loudly threatening another revolution. They did not understand how small a minority they are. Truth: there's no toleration on either side: 'We won the election, that gives us the right to crush you.' Most Romanians aren't interested in communism or non-communism: only in more basic matters like keeping body and soul together. But Iliescu has been monumentally stupid, preferring to lose all credibility in the West for a bit of peace and quiet on his own doorstep. And when his Government fails to satisfy the miners, they will dole out summary justice to him, too. What a tragedy.

I have been struggling with my annual accounts. They've taken me two days and are not yet finished. I'm in the in-between position, not so rich I can employ lots of accountants, but not so poor I can ignore the matter. Apart from books, my turnover was only £20,000, so next year I may not be earning enough to declare for VAT. That would suit me fine, as it is a chore.

It's been a long and busy day and I'm knackered, quite apart from feelings of misery over the three-week democracy in Romania. (Steve Norris[1] said it was the same in Nicaragua and Panama, no use worrying about it: smooth expansive bugger.) The review copies of the book are producing strong reactions from press and we're putting lots of interviews 'in the can'. *Today* has a piece tomorrow, for which they paid £2500. I've done interviews for *The Times* and *Daily Express*, too. No reviews yet. Launch Thursday. *Much* more laid back about this launch than the last one.

I decided not to join the Foreign Affairs Select Committee, as they are going to the wrong places, southern Africa, for example; and the SDP is no more, as Owen gave it up.

Victoria, Thursday 28 June, 8 p.m.

I came back from a visit to Milton Keynes this afternoon with a sore throat and feeling rough.

Golly, Milton Keynes is an *awful* place. No longer bare or featureless, but endless planned 1960s architecture – no fun, no style, no wit, no grace. It is the epitome of Harold Wilson's vision of Britain. No centre – no can find; even the roadworks are neatly done. No hold-ups. No litter; everything spotless, like being inside an atom. No heart . . . It drove me crazy ten minutes after arriving at the station, which looks like Birmingham airport should, except that the latter is full of life, jostling, eating, impatiently waiting, in a rush, tired, grumpy, laughing: real people, in fact. The lunch reminded me why I don't go to many Chamber of Commerce type dos. They are such macho events, with everyone on top table showing off, drinking more than they should, and being excessively familiar to the women present. My 'What Women Want' speech went down fine,

---

1. Conservative MP for Oxford East, 1983–7.

though I had to stop the two photographers flashing in my face as I spoke – don't they realise it is damned distracting? (I stop it now also because I don't like photos of me with my mouth open.) The questions went well too, mostly from the women present (about 25 per cent of the total), including a lady who said she was a secretary and only there because her boss couldn't come! Then the vote of thanks by a large, bluff, once good-looking public school auctioneer/estate agent, whose company had helped pay for the lunch. He went on and on, trying to be clever and succeeding only in sounding snide and patronising, and then launched into a string of ever sillier egg jokes (having introduced them with 'It has been suggested to me that it would be discourteous to our speaker to mention eggs . . .' and then sounding increasingly rude). One woman walked out, calling 'Get him off!' and it ended in an embarrassed silence. I was annoyed, I must say. The speech had been pitched pretty high – stats, etc. – and they had absorbed it all. Silly jokes were particularly inappropriate, and especially so in a vote of thanks, which should have been gracious.

The new book came out last Thursday (21st). It wasn't quite the emotional event of the first one, nor so lucrative. Out of the advance of £10,000 I stand to get only £3750, before agent's fees (10 per cent) and tax (40 per cent). I gather that Sidgwick & Jackson printed 5000 copies which is pretty miserable, and had to reprint another 2000 last week before the launch. I'd like to get up to 10,000, which would at least mean some royalties – a satisfying feeling. Sidgwick had little faith in the project, and I guess they would have been pleased if we hadn't finished it. That took an awful lot of determination on my part, and by Easter I was really knackered. There are rumours that Sidgwick may be folding. William Armstrong must be close to retirement age anyway. They are, in any case, leaving Museum Street (which is a bit of a hovel) to move into Cavaye Place with Pan (a good idea – make them more businesslike). In my view they need to put the new technology in place, and cut their costs and lead-in times. And they must get more efficient. I've been chasing expenses since Xmas, and in exasperation wrote to Armstrong, who wrote back, 'I don't know why you've written to me . . .' So I set it all out in detail, and now £140 is on its way and please would I send invoices for two items they've had three times already. We shouldn't have to waste time like this! If I hadn't spotted it they would never have billed *Today* for the £7500 second serial rights for *Life Lines*, and so on. I suggested to Hilary Rubinstein that we find another publisher for the short stories. Hilary wants me to write a novel. No fear. No one would review it as a novel: no one. They might, with short stories. I can't write what I would admire, I don't have the skill, and there is a strong temptation to write a political/sexy novel to a formula, like Susan Crosland's *Ruling Passions*, which I would find distasteful and tedious. At least Jeffrey Archer can tell a story.

It always amuses me when I go in to the Members' Dining Room and sit at the table by the window (there are seven seats, so often one free). Julian Critchley[1] sits there, and the two of us show off to the others assembled by talking about advances, fees for public appearances, etc. It's said that when authors get together they always talk about fees . . . it's true. I've discovered that we sold 16,000 hardbacks of *Life Lines*, and they've printed another 16,000 in paperback. So we are close to 40,000 copies of my books printed, and both hardbacks reprinted before publication. Not bad, though it would have been jolly nice to have had a bestseller (and a letter from Lord Stockton, maybe?).

It appears that Geoffrey Howe is in trouble. Stories in the press last week about getting him to go as Ambassador to South Africa with a peerage. (I bet it's been broached. Not a bad idea at all.)

---

1. Conservative MP for Aldershot; a Conservative MP since 1959.

I think his missus Elspeth is a poisonous character – snob both intellectually and socially, very Hampstead. She was with Esther Rantzen and other socialists drawing attention to the plight of the homeless by a distasteful publicity stunt of spending the night in cardboard boxes, with a few pressmen, of course. Isn't she a *fool*! Geoffrey still hankers after a crack at the premiership. He'd lose an election for us, for sure.

We are moving back up in the polls, possibly because of Ken Baker's 'Summer Heat on Labour' campaign, and a highly effective attack on the cost of Labour's proposals. Baker does know how to do this sort of thing; I'd enjoy being part of his team. The party vice-chairmen are Sir (now) Tom Arnold, Sir James Spicer, Dame Joan Seccombe, Sir Geoffrey Pattie and A. N. Other so obscure I can't remember! Not a sparkling lot. But we have gone further downhill with women voters: only 20 per cent support amongst under-twenty-fives, against Labour's over 50 per cent; even amongst older women we're either neck and neck now, or for the over-sixty-fives, Labour is slightly ahead. I'm glad I got these figures done (and I sent them to John Major), in case there is any criticism that I've caused any of the problem with *What Women Want* – which is, of course, intended to steal some of Labour's thunder. Bit difficult when they have fourteen frontbench women, when we only have four (plus the PM). She said in an interview in *Woman's Own* that we have more women ministers than they have in the Shadow Cabinet. Yes, that is true. But the perception takes in *all* ranks. The Chief Whip spoke to Jill Knight and asked if the women MPs would 'doughnut' behind the front bench, and wear bright clothes; so Marion Roe and Jill and Janet and Maureen obliged, and I've moved forward a row. But I *won't* sit on the ministers' bench until I'm entitled to. And that, of course, is up to them.

Victoria, Thursday 12 July, 9.45 p.m.

I've been up at 4.30 every morning this week to do the LBC *Breakfast Show*: a sort of local *Today* programme, all serious interviews – no music – 6 a.m. to 9 a.m. It's been fun, apart from getting up so early! And getting to bed late, either because of voting (Monday and Tuesday) or just working late (Sunday and Wednesday). Tonight we had a three-line whip at 7 p.m. then my pair Kevin Barron[1] cleared off, so I was free.

The programme has had some nice comments and is well paid – £1500 for fifteen hours' work. At that rate I'm earning more than the Chancellor, as I told him tonight at the bar of the House. He said ruefully, everyone earns more than the Chancellor does. I suspect money is not in ready supply at home, and he would certainly be pushed to send his children to private school. Right now, I wouldn't be in his shoes anyway, with inflation stubbornly refusing to come down and all the uncertainties about the EMS, etc.

The PM made a statement today about the G7 summit this week in Houston and added some comments about the NATO summit the previous week. She was on good form, bashing away like a machine gun. I was sitting next to William Powell[2] and we agreed that we'll never see her like again. He, like me, is interested in going to Europe. The PM said in passing that there will be a summit next July in London: that means, we all inferred instantly, that there will be a September election. So we won't get much holiday next August, that's for sure. I like William – he's knowledgeable and thoughtful, though with his pop-eyes and buck teeth he comes across on television as a bit loopy! If we are all trying for a tiny number of Euro seats, less well known people like himself could be in difficulty.

---

1. Labour MP for Rother Valley.
2. Conservative MP for Cowley.

Interesting article by Robert Harris[1] on Ruritanian England reflects my views – makes being a minister here seem less important.

I've decided no more books for the time being, though I'll keep on writing and certainly hope to have enough stories for at least one collection after the election. Money could be useful! But I want to spend my time in the House of Commons, not traipsing around doing silly signing sessions (Gatwick this week, harassed by delayed passengers with no money) and radio (Gloria Hunniford, or why do I bother, I don't even like the music) and unpaid speeches. I was at the Birmingham Press Club on Monday: hot, poor food, terrible mike, and collection of drunken bores not listening – and they didn't think to offer expenses and presented me with a huge bouquet, although they knew I would be going back by train – so I asked them to give it to the kitchen staff, and they were most put out! I have done ten speeches this year and served on two committees of Government Bills, but this hasn't meant much more than sitting there, and I would like to do more. If I'm going back in next year, I'll have to.

There were comments in the press that I wouldn't be invited back in because of *What Women Want*, but I know that has nothing to do with it. The decision that I must wait till the election was taken ages ago. Still, the PM wants views on the family, so I've written to her PPS Mark Lennox-Boyd, pointing out that in this country most mothers work, and really begging her to stop making silly remarks about child care and delinquent children. She is herself a working mother, daughter of a working mother, and ought to sound more sympathetic. Nor can we take any moral high ground. Saw B tonight and toyed with idea of asking him back to flat, but he looks very tired and I didn't really think about it till after. Still miss him . . .

---

1. Political columnist for the *Sunday Times*.

House of Commons, Tuesday 24 July, 11.15 p.m.

Waiting for a vote which probably won't come, feeling headachy and very bored. I must say that the European Parliament sounds more worthwhile than our backbenches. Valéry Giscard d'Estaing[1] is an MEP now, and there are numerous other ex-ministers there. So: maybe. I'm certainly going to chase a cottage next week in the Tours region. It looks as if we could get something respectable for 300,000 francs, about £33,000.

One appointment in the recent reshuffle[2] has attracted a lot of gossip and could be very dangerous: Peter Morrison has become the PM's PPS. Now he's what they call 'a noted pederast', with a liking for young boys; he admitted as much to Norman Tebbit when he became deputy chairman of the party, but added, 'However, I'm very discreet' – and he must be! She either knows and is taking a chance, or doesn't; either way it is a really dumb move. Teresa Gorman told me this evening (in a taxi coming back from a drinks party at the BBC) that she inherited Morrison's (woman) agent, who claimed to have been offered money to keep quiet about his activities. It scares me, as all the press know, and as we get closer to the election someone is going to make trouble, very close to her indeed.

Teresa also told me (couldn't wait to tell me in the cab) about Cecil and Sara Keays. I knew they had a long-standing relationship – he took her on the parliamentary skiing trips, for example. For two years she tried to break it off, and went to work for Roy Jenkins in Brussels. On her return she decided to pursue her own career and applied to go on our candidates' list. She went to the same

---

1. President of France, 1974–81.
2. Nicholas Ridley resigned after his unguarded remarks about Germany were printed in the *Spectator*; he was replaced by Peter Lilley, and the moves precipitated a reshuffle in the middle and lower ranks of the Government.

selection weekend as Teresa; who should turn up out of the blue but the party chairman (Cecil), and the relationship started again. According to Teresa, Sara was not all that keen. Then she came second in the selection for the Bermondsey seat, fought by Peter Tatchell. When the number one dropped out, it was thought Sara would automatically be asked, but no; Cecil insisted on a reselection. So (Teresa claims) he stopped Sara becoming an MP too.[1] Well, she can't have been up to much, to have been thwarted so easily – or maybe important men just overwhelm some women. Hardly my problem, at any rate not at home.

As for my action against the *Observer*: hearing is set for 26 September and they want to know who is paying my fees (i.e. am I likely to settle or not, no doubt). I do want to settle, but not for nowt, not now. I received out of the blue an invite to Edward du Cann's[2] drinks party. At the last minute James Couchman[3] warned me off – du Cann is chairman of Lonrho, which owns the *Observer*. And he was right, for Gerry Howarth[4] told me Adam Raphael[5] was there and talking about my writ. Might they have got me drunk – or in a corner? Well now, there's a thought!

France, Saturday 4 August, 4.13 a.m. (i.e. Sunday morning)

It's hot – nearly 100° Fahrenheit today. In England, where (it's claimed) the highest ever temperatures are being recorded, the roads are melting; people sitting in traffic jams are being badly sunburned

---

1. All these revelations were, in fact, in the public domain in Sara Keays' book, *A Question of Judgement*, published in 1985.
2. Sir Edward du Cann, chairman of Lonrho; a former junior minister and chairman of the 1922 Committee; Conservative MP for the Taunton Division of Somerset, 1956–87.
3. Conservative MP for Gillingham.
4. Conservative MP for Cannock and Burntwood.
5. Executive editor of the *Observer*.

through the windscreens of their cars. Thank God we're in France. The temperatures are similar, but they are more relaxed about it. No one wears a tie or a suit, and from twelve to three o'clock everything stops for a long lunch, eaten indoors in the shade. Very civilised.

Too hot to sleep. Ray and I are in one bedroom of the house we've rented near Loches. The heat is radiating from his body and he has kicked off the only sheet – the duvet was abandoned at the beginning of the week when the thermometer went past 90. Susie and her friend Sonali Banerjee have given up the house altogether, and are sleeping reasonably well in the tent we brought with us; the cool compensates for the hardness of the ground.

Debbie is back in England, having decided that yet another family holiday was beyond her powers of self-discipline, so she is staying with her friend Clare Cooper, and working in Clare's father's factory, assembling and packing for £68 per week. We spoke on the phone after the first day and she was knackered. I'm pleased that she is beginning to know how most people have to work, how tiring and boring it is; hopefully it will inspire her to get on with A levels after they return to school. In fact she and Clare were supposed to be going off to the West Country youth hostelling, but Clare's father got cold feet at the last minute and scuppered the idea, saying they were too young.

Meanwhile I'm awake at four in the morning, thinking what do I do next? What am I supposed to be doing with my time and my talents, that I haven't done already a thousand times? Current position: £45,000 deposit in various banks and building societies at good rates of interest, but all that is intended to pay my taxes. £7000 in a PEP which doesn't, to my irritation, pay me an income and probably won't show much return for many years, but which will be tax free, so OK to leave it there, but probably not add to it, as the Stock Exchange could take a real dive with the trouble in the Middle East (Iraq has just invaded Kuwait). A few water shares, and electricity shares to come, if John Wakeham ever stops messing about and privatises the business. £2000 for Deb and Susie in a National Savings capital bond, guaranteed high rate of interest, for them in five years' time. £4000 due to the landscape gardener, £5000 due to me in fees unpaid so far, and probably a bit of back tax due too! I expect the bill for the garden to total £15,000 and then we may well stop – we can't plant trees in this weather, that will have to wait till the autumn. I'm still keeping notes so that I can write it all up in due course, hopefully for a book which may pay for part of it.[1]

What else? Running up two lawyers' bills, £3000 so far from Peter Carter-Ruck for the case against the *Observer*, but I hope we can settle. I want my costs back! And an unknown amount, but hopefully less, for Andrew Lockhart-Mirams from Hempsons in the case defended against David Bookbinder.[2] Again, I want my costs back and the only way to do that is to get him into court.

I had a miserable end of term, for as usual with the children around I found it very hard to concentrate, and give them time like going to the theatre instead of ploughing on with debates in the House of Commons. Another couple of book signings too, and I am increasingly convinced that they are an embarrassment and a complete waste of time and effort. At Gatwick we were teased by Americans who had no intention of buying but wanted to show off,

---

1. EC was considering a book about the development of her garden, but this never came to anything.
2. Derbyshire County Council had brought a case for libel against EC, her fellow Tory MP Phillip Oppenheim and the *Sunday Times*. The two MPs had assisted the *Sunday Times* 'Insight' team in writing a three-week 'exposé' of the links between the council and the millionaire publisher Robert Maxwell, then the owner of Derby County Football Club, and various companies in Derby. The newspaper alleged that Maxwell had advised his friend David Bookbinder, Labour leader of the County Council, to use the council pension fund to support 'worthwhile' causes. It alleged that £2 million had been lost and another £4 million was at risk. The case was referred to the High Court, and eventually to the House of Lords in 1991. It was thrown out, on the grounds that for a local government body to bring a successful libel action would have been restriction of free speech.

and at Clulows[1] no one knew I was there except one bizarre individual who brought in the typescript of his own novel for me to read and get published for him. Shan't do any more! I'm currently tidying up some of the existing short stories and have ideas for quite a lot more; I see Hilary Rubinstein after we get back, and he can jolly well earn his keep by selling some stories before we think of publishing any more books.

The cock (who drives us crazy) has started to crow, bang on 5.30 a.m. I haven't mentioned the main things in my head, either – it always happens like this, once I start writing the pain softens – how I feel under-utilised and that I'm getting sloppy and soft and fat, losing my self-discipline, losing my talents, losing my place, if you like, and really not sure what happens next. The silly reshuffle ended up giving no clear messages at all, with people brought back in after years away, and effort by such as Nicholas Bennett[2] unrewarded.

So I am spending some time and energy looking for a little French house to buy, where I can escape from the British who want my autograph but won't buy my books, where I can feel less of a fraud, where I can concentrate and get some writing done – no excuses in such a setting – where maybe some day I could come if the relationship with Ray disintegrates, if he goes on sleeping while I'm thinking or feeling sad, if he continues to hunt for an English newspaper and look for a phone to call his bookie in England while I want to talk about long-dead intrigues and the beauty of the old houses round here. And, maybe keep on improving my French and head for the European Parliament. Who knows? I don't, not right now, anyway. And that is the hardest of all for me to bear: not knowing where I am going.

1. A Derby bookshop.
2. Conservative MP for Pembroke.

St-Jean, near Loches, Thursday 16 August, 8 a.m.

The weather has been much cooler this week, cloudy even; the girls are still fast asleep upstairs. I'm getting ready to go home and back to work, as my six-hour sleep pattern reasserts itself.

We have seen a breathtakingly cheap house nearby at Mouliherne: on offer at 220,000 francs – around £25,000 – which wouldn't buy you a garage in England now, and is no longer enough for even a tiny house in South Derbyshire. The more I see of the house the more I like it; I've figured out how to convert the main building to something very special, though the stables will give us problems if we want to convert them later as they are so small. We rounded off a lovely day in Saumur, which I hadn't seen, an attractive touristy town, not too big, with pretty squares and some splendid buildings. I suppose it missed a lot of the damage during the war because it wasn't a very important place – it was Tours and Angers which were badly knocked about. The girls fell asleep instantly in the back of the car on the way home.

Debbie, meanwhile, is back in the Tower House. She has fallen out with her friend Clare, and is now living alone, getting herself up with the alarm clock and in and out of work on the bus, and into bed by 10 p.m. each evening, watching Sky movies for entertainment. When I phone she sounds tired but content. I'm most impressed! Hard to remember I was working too, at the same age; we always think of our children as babies till they prove us wrong and out of date.

Our landlady turned up with a dinner invitation. I was irritated and described why in a story, 'The Dinner Party'. Of course, there wasn't a dinner. They would have invited everyone if I'd said yes, and then I would have been the star attraction and would have had to perform. Why don't people see that I don't choose to do that all the time? She said, they are dying to meet you. Ho, hum. I'm not dying to meet them, far from it. Had she said instead, it's X's birthday, or it's a *jour de fête*, my sister is a really wonderful cook who loves trying out her specialities, my cousin is an artist and will draw the children if we ask nicely, our neighbour is a writer, and you may know our other tenants, they come from your area, we will understand perfectly if you didn't want to come, but you would be most welcome . . . then I would have been tempted. Had they given us a discount on the rental of the house – oh, Mrs Currie, seeing it's you, just pay for two weeks and have the other one half-price . . . then I would have been under an obligation, and would have gone and been gracious. But I'm not under any obligation, not at £400 per week. The kids accepted the invitation to swim, and found out when they got there that there was no dinner party, and indeed the woman had gone out without even bothering to tell the concierge that the girls were coming for a swim. I bet she's narked that I said no. Serve her right.

France, Thursday 11 October, 11.20 p.m.

I escaped from the Party Conference, caught the boat from Portsmouth at 11 p.m. last night, emerged into a magical misty French dawn this morning, ate a comfortable lunch in a Routiers café near La Lude at noon with a pair of young English lorry drivers (one of whom wouldn't touch the food, not even the cheese), and arrived here at 2 p.m.

The house at Mouliherne is 100 feet long and 17 feet deep, and will eventually have four rooms and *cave* downstairs and three huge bedrooms upstairs, with two bathrooms and utility room (*lingerie*), all for a starting price of less than £20,000. I know the bill for doing up the ground floor alone will be more than £25,000, with fees and furniture and landscape gardening on top: but I'm ecstatic about it, really tickled pink, and now I can afford it.

I've been writing bits for the national press ever since I resigned, but since the summer – when I think Bernard Ingham must have said nice things about me – the requests have been rolling in: *News of the World* (£1000), *Sunday Express* (£500), *Evening Standard* (£500). Then a phone call from David Montgomery of *Today* asking to meet at the Party Conference, so we arranged breakfast yesterday morning. I suspected he was going to ask me to work for them again, and so it proved. Peter Wilenius, the political editor, was there, and Heidi, David's wife – very pretty, nice dark-haired girl. The two men seemed quiet and professional and normal and I liked them. So now they are talking to Hilary Rubinstein, who knows they offered me £100,000 p.a. to work for them back in January 1989. I could not have done it then; I didn't know how to put an article together or make it zappy or intelligent or interesting; but I do now. Not an hour later, I'm sitting in Conference listening to John MacGregor on education, when Robert Key[1] asks me about my new job. Then Brendan Bruce[2] asks me how I got on at breakfast. 'How do you know about my breakfast?' I ask, and he says, 'I fixed it up.' Did he indeed! I think *Today* is quite capable of having fixed it themselves; still it's nice to think CCO knows and may well approve. Its readership is young – 70 per cent under thirty-five – homeowners, share owners, C/Ds mainly, so they are Thatcher's children if not Thatcherites. Writing for *Today* may well help the party, and I look forward to it.

On Friday morning the Countryside Commission announced that the new Midland Forest is to stretch from Charnwood and Needwood across South Derbyshire to north-west Leicestershire. We are to have £100 million of new trees, most of which will be planted in the next ten years. Great chunks of South Derbyshire will become green belt, and designated for English deciduous forest. Land values will jump. I can't quite believe it yet – but oh, what good

1. Conservative MP for Salisbury.
2. Press Officer at Conservative Central Office.

news for us; Swadlincote and Gresley and Newhall to be surrounded by forest! Then, almost to wrap it up, on Sunday we had a service at Gresley church to unveil a stained glass window paid for by the UDM, in honour of the miners of South Derbyshire. It's really stunning: four miners, two young, two older, one stripped to the waist and holding a miner's lamp, are standing in a coal tunnel: and there is Christ, the light of the world. Very simple, sweet piety. A lovely service, with Gresley Male Voice Choir singing their hearts out – it brought a real lump – and Daw Mill Colliery Band in the background. Dinner after in the Miners' Welfare, surrounded by £80,000 new houses. End of one era, start of another.

On Friday evening John Major announced our entry into the ERM as of Monday, and a 1 per cent cut in interest rates. Everyone (except Nick Ridley) euphoric; Margaret with gritted teeth somewhat. But this is Major's success; my only regret is that I wasn't there this morning to see him enjoy it.

Angela Rumbold talked a lot of pompous claptrap in the Conference debate on the family and got a cool reception. There was a big row at the 300 Group[1] meeting about our muddled, confused and insulting attitudes to women at work. Not our best area.

Victoria, Thursday 18 October, 10 p.m.

On Monday evening I went into *Today* to talk shop, and saw for an hour or two how a newspaper is put to bed. David Montgomery was not there, but Peter Wilenius is clearly the boss on a day-to-day basis, even though he is called 'political editor'. He works till 9 or 10 p.m., then goes for a swim and on home (like me, they all live nearby). Then he's in early (8ish) in the morning. A fourteen-hour

---

1. The all-party group set up to increase the number of women MPs.

day, six days a week. His driver Gary said he's always been like that; even on the *News of the World*, where most of them are very laid back, Peter was always working. He's a softly spoken, slim Irishman: looks almost fragile, but his manner is polite and he has enormous powers of concentration. Next day I came in for an editorial meeting at 11.30 a.m. and met all the editors: quite a large group and very diverse: from old hacks with their bellies over their belts to Amanda Platell, a big, bouncy, black-eyed beauty from Australia, who is effectively Peter's deputy. Montgomery appeared only briefly: obviously he hadn't said anything to them, so there was surprise and a professional welcome. One embarrassment is that Wednesday is to be my day and they already have a Wednesday lady – Jane Gordon – who (in my view!) isn't very good; but then she's a journalist and I'm not. So she will have to be moved.

Just had a phone call from Ros, the publicity lady from *Today*. We spent all day yesterday filming an ad with Saatchi, but David Montgomery doesn't like it; he feels we can do better. Hard to tell, as I haven't seen the finished version, but it sounds like I lose my Sunday to redo it. We filmed in a house in Kensington – very swish – in my yellow and black suit, seventeen or so takes, to get it to eighteen seconds dead, etc. I would be surprised if any spontaneity remained after that! This morning we did lots of photos of clothes – some nice outfits, including an Arabella Pollen which looked nothing on the hanger and great on me – I fell for a Jaeger purple jacket for £199 and spent some of my not-yet-received cash on it, and a black skirt at £79!

Victoria, Thursday 1 November, midnight

Well, now I'm *really* fucking depressed. Geoffrey Howe resigned tonight. I think the whole thing is falling apart, over Europe too, which is the right issue – but it could let Labour in by default, perhaps less than a year from now.

It has been an extraordinary week. On Tuesday evening about 7.30 contact was made under the Channel between the two sides digging the tunnel. First time ever: no longer an island. Now they can get on and finish it, ready for 1993. At the weekend there was a summit in Rome – unnecessary, said the PM – ostensibly called to discuss farm subsidies and the Gulf (not a lot), but bounced by a gleeful Italian Foreign Minister into agreeing that we will go ahead with a common currency (possibly the ecu) alongside our national currencies, aiming at a starting date in early 1994. That will mean a European Central Bank (or cluster of banks) and a Monetary Fund – general view of informed backbenchers, e.g. Nigel Forman, is that the timing sounds about right. We were forewarned last Thursday with the state visit of the Italian President, who made a very robust speech about the relentless drive to economic and political union. The PM, sitting there looking frosty, should have taken more notice. Instead she exempted Britain from the agreed communiqué and marched out of the meeting to make some very strident remarks to the press. On Sunday's television Geoffrey Howe disagreed. She was challenged at Question Time on Tuesday to defend him, but didn't. Her response that a big man like him didn't need a little man – Kinnock – to defend him was funny, but beside the point. So tonight, like a wounded beast, he slips away. I wonder if he will challenge her for the leadership?

Debbie was sixteen on Tuesday: tall, not yet elegant, a bit heavy, a bit clumsy: lovely face, but all the fashions are against her and she isn't yet at ease in her 5 foot 8 inch body. She told me in the supermarket that she now knows all about *it*, and *it*'s lovely – which left me sad, that she should be so casual about sex – that's missing a lot. She has to take a low dosage Pill to regulate her periods so I have no worries for her, but I doubt if she'll ever quite enjoy it as I do; the fire is missing. She seems to want it to be a part of normal dreary life, and it isn't, or shouldn't be . . .

Today is going well: on to my second column this week and

beginning to get the feel for it. Ray showed me an article in *The Times* called 'The Rubies that must be Read' – the rubies being the top columnists. I'm being far too ambitious again, but if we lose the election (or if Mrs T is toppled), then I could be writing for them for a long time. I'm not sure I would mind, either. It is fun, and very interesting, to sit with these highly intelligent and well-informed people. Unfortunately it makes some of my colleagues, even the nice ones, sound even more stupid – like Colne Valley's Graham Riddick, who railed against broadcasters in general and Radio 4's *Start the Week* in particular for its 'left-wing bias': a preposterous performance, especially compared with the cool lucidity of George Walden.[1]

Victoria, Thursday 8 November, 11.45 p.m.

Queen's Speech and State Opening yesterday, and I managed to speak in today's debate on Foreign Affairs. I feel as if, having been shorn and left in the cold to die nearly two years ago, I have grown a new coat – both harsher and sleeker than the old one, or better suited to the climate. I only wish it covered a frame a stone lighter! (10 stone nine pounds on Wednesday.)

The dates for the leadership contest, if there is to be one, are set, and MHT put her nomination in, sponsored by Hurd and Major, at once. Nobody else would be silly enough to try. Michael Heseltine wrote an official letter to his constituency party on Sunday, saying (effectively) that we need a change, and then left for a well-publicised visit to Israel. To everyone's surprise, his constituency chairman wrote back saying no, we do not need a change. No doubt he had received a phone call from Smith Square, but Heseltine was

1. Conservative MP for Buckingham.

very silly not to have fixed all this up before leaving. It suggests real lack of judgement, and caused many guffaws in tea room.

Had lunch today with David Montgomery at the Howard Hotel on the Embankment, which backs on to Arthur Andersen and is used as an entrance for secret meetings, so I was greeted with much warmth by the *maître d'hôtel*, with David grinning that I get more attention than most Cabinet ministers. He said last week, when I was asking why so much coverage of me in first week's newspaper, 'You're better known than the newspaper', and I think he's generally pleased with my work so far. David wants *Today* to be given a bigger promotion budget (£5 million p.a.), so they can go for a larger share of the market. It sells more than the *Guardian* or *The Times* or *Independent*, but they all have top appointments, cars, and luxury goods advertising which *Today* hasn't, and the *Guardian* has cornered the market in public service jobs, teaching and now media. A tabloid can't do that. David cleared out the Bingo last year and lost 69,000 readers (more than 10 per cent), but he is glad they are gone. Recent survey (just before he contacted me) shows people like the paper once they have read it. It occurred to me that they are getting very little feedback; apparently I'm getting a bigger postbag than any other writer on paper, but still that's only a handful each week! The journalists on *Today* seem to like what I'm doing anyway, including Jane Gordon, which is a relief. So far none of my colleagues have made any comment, except Emma Nicholson, who liked it.

Getting ready for Bangladesh:[1] full of injections. Will probably write my article from there. Finding it difficult to do any other writing as my head gets so full of words each week – must revise 'Patience', must do another for *Today*, must do piece for Helsinki Conference on Health next year. No more travelling after this trip (Bangladesh and

---

1. EC was going to Bangladesh as part of a Commonwealth Parliamentary Association delegation.

Pakistan), as I need to concentrate on constituency. East Europe I hope in August, and I shall ask *Today* to contribute to the expenses. It is nice to be able to tap into their resources; for the debate today I got the whole MORI poll from last week's *Sunday Times*, no problem and no queries about why/what for/can't use, etc., and it arrived in an hour after asking. Wonderful: I could get used to this!

I am immeasurably happier than I was two years ago, and a great deal better off financially. I feel less self-absorbed too, more aware of Ray and my big beautiful girls: more aware of the world beyond Britain, more willing to stop work and partake of the fun around. I watch B perform and am so happy for him, he is doing so well. David Hunt told me that a journalist had approached him and said, 'I know all about you and Edwina . . .' which must have been difficult to stare down '. . . going to school together and all that'. He'd got him mixed up with Steve Norris![1]

House of Commons, Thursday 15 November

Ah, gadzooks, we're into a leadership contest. Howe made a truly brilliant, devastating speech on Tuesday, and Heseltine declared himself yesterday. So all other activity is off, and Labour is watching happily as we chew each other up. I got embroiled when I remarked in Kensington (John Stanley's constituency – he didn't turn up but went to the dentist instead, rude beggar!) that Heseltine could do immense damage to the PM without winning himself – thus opening up a second ballot, when all the big boys will come in, with Hurd and Major the likeliest lads. Then we could have a smooth change of leader and get reunited again to fight the General Election.

I can't write well as I'm very tired (it is only midnight). This

---

1. Norris was at the Liverpool Institute at the same time as EC, and afterwards they went up to Oxford at the same time.

leadership business is so wearing – we talk in corners all day, with no pretence of hiding the arguments or looking around to ensure no journalists or socialists might be listening. MHT's supporters are really unpleasant – impugning everyone's motives in a graceless and snide way – talking about Howe's pique and Michael's ambition, as if that didn't call into question Margaret's own motives in 1975, when she stood against Ted Heath. I particularly disliked Norman Tebbit's description of her opponents as suffering from 'mad bullock disease'. When I meet a wavering voter on the doorstep, I invite him to talk while I listen. I certainly don't tell him he's suffering from a disease. Tebbit kept it up behind the back of the Chair, pinning me to the Bag[1] as people surged around us after the 10 p.m. vote, and grinning at me like some lunatic while he explained that there was no alternative but to vote for Margaret.

Oh yes there is, and I knew it as I listened to Geoffrey Howe. He had carefully thought through a statement, mainly on Europe, also on Cabinet government (echoing Nigel's words in 1989). I agreed with every word and nuance. We have to be positive about Europe; it is changing and we have to join in, not say 'never'. He could not have done more damage if he had lobbed a grenade at the front bench; we were all gasping, and from there on a leadership contest was inevitable. Now I don't want Michael Heseltine either, even though I admired him in Liverpool and Birmingham when I was housing chairman and he was Secretary of State for the Environment. So I have to abstain.[2] Return due late Tuesday, which will make writing my column very difficult!

I went to see John Major in his room last night. 'Don't be too close to her,' I said, 'or you could go down with her too.' He said both he and Hurd had been approached to stand, and clearly he has been

---

1. The Bag which hangs behind the Speaker's Chair, where petitions are put.
2. But see page 214.

thinking about it. If they decide to go for it, they will have to persuade MHT to stand down after the first ballot.

Sonargaon Hotel, Dhaka, Bangladesh, Sunday 25 November, 8 a.m.

It was, in the end, an extraordinary week. On Tuesday 22 November Margaret got 204 votes, ten short of the number needed, and Heseltine 152. There were sixteen abstentions, so she had barely half the vote. I had thought a likely breakdown would be 150:150:72 (MHT:MH:Abs), but in the end most of those I thought might waver voted for her, so they could tell their constituents they had done so. Margaret bounced down the steps of the embassy in Paris to tell the BBC and others (she nearly grabbed the microphone) that she would go on to the next round. In doing so, she broke a promise to Ken Baker and others that she would consult them first. Gerald Howarth said on the radio that the 'No Turning Back' group had also discussed tactics with her, and they had agreed four scenarios: one being that she would declare her continued fight without waiting for anyone to interfere. It put the party into consternation – my firm view that she could *not* continue reflected the views of the 'men in grey suits' (people like Tim Renton, Chief Whip; Cranley Onslow, chairman of 1922 Committee; and Lord Whitelaw, ex Deputy PM), but they were lily-livered enough to say it was *her* decision. Wednesday was a day I would not wish to live through again: really horrible. The MHT supporters started a witch-hunt against those who had declared for Heseltine, with special venom reserved for people like me who had been critical of Margaret in the past. So the phone lines buzzed to our Swad[1] office and to Chris, very unpleasant, with 'retribution' on the

---

1. Office of the South Derbyshire Conservatives.

lips of Nick Brown in Derby (fool him, couldn't have won his seat with Margaret at the helm, not a chance), and my Association falling apart. In fact, the South Derbyshire Conservative Association made complete fools of themselves, and on my return from Bangladesh and Pakistan I will gather them in and say so! You don't have to answer the phones: their ringing creates no obligation, you can just lock the door and go home. I am eternally grateful for my *Today* contract, for it gives me confidence that if the gamble in pushing for MHT to stand down doesn't come off, I do have a job to go to, and a lucrative future ahead. I should be either a minister or a millionaire, I reckon. To make your daughters wealthy women is not a bad ambition.

Wednesday ended in tears for me, though no one saw them. On my way out, using the ministerial corridor past the Leader of the House's office as I often do, I saw Tris Garel-Jones,[1] Alan Clark[2] and Richard Ryder at the back of the Chair. I didn't know that Tris had held a 'blue chip' dinner at his house the night before (though it was in some newspapers) with Chris Patten,[3] Norman Lamont, etc., at which they had agreed Margaret could not carry on and that they must tell her. Had I known, I might have been friendlier. But Richard had a broad, vacuous grin on his face. 'Everything all right?' he asked as I went past. Prat, I thought, vacuous, unctuous prat: not like you, Richard, usually so careful. 'No, it isn't,' I snapped. 'The party is falling apart and you're just sitting there grinning.' He stopped grinning. 'I'm going out with my wife,' he said lamely. 'Well I'm going home to my husband,' I said, trying to sound gentle and not too bitter, 'but I don't feel good about what's happening. If she carries on, we will tear ourselves to pieces.' Clark said angrily, 'Why

1. Tristan Garel-Jones, a senior whip; Conservative MP for Watford.
2. Minister for Trade since 1986; Conservative MP for Plymouth Sutton.
3. Secretary of State for the Environment; Conservative MP for Bath.

don't you apply for the Chiltern Hundreds right now? Then you can have a different career.' Snob, I thought, and turd with it. 'I have other things I do now, Alan, and you don't need to be insulting to me: I'm not going to insult you. But we cannot win the election on the basis of safe seats in the south alone. We *have* to win my seat, and many others like it in the Midlands and the north.' By this stage Ryder has his eyes fixed on me and is nodding; changed sides, it looked like. I will *not* be faced down by these men, I thought, and walked off to the car park, where I cried in my car in the dark for ten minutes. Tris had not said a word. Given the discussion at his own dinner table the previous night, when the same points must have been made and accepted, he might simply have said, 'We know, Edwina' or even 'Why do you think that?' – at least inviting me to sound like an intelligent participant in the little group, instead of an unwelcome intruder. But he has views on women, apparently, and was determined that the Whips' Office should stay a gentlemen's club in the eight years he was in it. Renton didn't agree so Tris had to go, but Renton doesn't want women in there either. We will not forget, gentlemen.

What I didn't know were the shenanigans going on all Wednesday. In the morning following MHT's announcement, the whips were reporting her support falling away by the hour: MPs were disgusted that she put vanity ahead of honour and graceful withdrawal. Heseltine needed to win over about eighteen to beat her on second ballot, and by lunchtime about twenty-five had privately said 'that's it'. So he was cock-a-hoop. She, meantime, looked a little mad on television in Paris, really megalomaniac, a similar eye-rolling to Ceauşescu's on the balcony just before his own fall in Romania. By lunchtime she was back. Hurd and Major (recovering at home from a wisdom tooth operation) had both of course said they would nominate her again – Jeffrey Archer made a late-night round trip to Huntingdon to get John's signature. When I heard this, I was going to write a piece for Friday's *Today* called 'The fateful signature'. If John had refused, it would have been over a lot quicker. By early Wednesday afternoon Margaret knew she was in trouble, but leaving Downing Street she was defiant. When I saw her on 6 p.m. news I thought, oh God, she really is crackers, she means it – yet I'd watched her extraordinary performance at the Dispatch Box at 3.30 p.m. with a growing feeling that she had made up her mind to go. I said as much to Colin Brown of *The Times*, and now he thinks I'm psychic! So when I saw her on television later, I thought, Jesus, how sinister, she is going to try and win with only 187 votes, and then she is going to destroy the anti-Thatcherites. She'll do it by being coolly non-Thatcher for a few days till the voting is over. How magnificent; how fiendish and cruel. And what would she be left with? A Labour Government as an absolute racing certainty.

I went to aerobics twice last week – it really helps bouncing around with that cheery teacher, all Afro hairdo and long lean limbs, so much the sort the Tories try to ignore. Came back, made toast, didn't get to eat it . . . At 9.40 a.m. the phone goes and it's the *Derby Evening Telegraph* – she has resigned. Oh thank God, I thought, common sense at last. And I started dancing round the flat.

Major and Hurd came into the fray quickly – she hadn't left much time, as nominations closed at noon. I interviewed both Michael and John during the day (to my amusement!) on how they would unite party, how they would sort out CCO ('Would you help?' asked Michael. 'Of course,' I said, 'but I'm not touting for a job.') John said two weeks ago that I should be housing minister. That was when his becoming PM was only a faint possibility. But I think whoever wins should keep the team intact if possible. Anyway I prefer to wait so I can put money aside, get incorporated in April or it will cost £20,000 and clean me out, sort out my South Derbyshire Association, and let the dust settle a bit. Would you refuse a job, John had asked – then no, of course you wouldn't, and I'm sure Douglas would give you one as well. Nice to be wanted, and jolly nice to be relaxed about it all: what a difference two years has made. Heseltine did impress: he allowed plenty of time, listened, made a couple of notes and didn't argue; seemed to understand what I was getting at. If he wins, he'll be fine. If John wins, oh whoopee!

Now the legend starts – the godhead Margaret. Her performance at Prime Minister's Questions and in the No Confidence debate on Thursday afternoon was sheer magic. Out with a bang, not a whimper. It brought tears to the eyes of even those who wanted her out. *Magnificent* is the only word. So, for the record, this is why I felt she had to go:

1. She's wrong on Europe – in her bones she hates the whole idea. I'm keen; South Derbyshire is stuffed with inward investment because we are in Europe. That is the future and we are very lucky to be inside.
2. Her diplomatic and political methods stank. Bully, loudmouth (she reportedly told her Cabinet they 'lacked balls' on Wednesday morning. They came out looking dazed). Using patronage and pressure to get own way (Greg Knight: 'She likes you, Edwina. If you play your cards right she will probably have you back in after next election.' Me: 'I've been offered jobs by all of them, silly. And we won't win it with her.' How I *hate* being bribed – or blackmailed – like that. Horrid).
3. She failed to see change in British society under her nose, or prepare for it – she slew the old dragons, but continued to wear the same bloodstained armour. Meanwhile a nicer, gentler, kinder Britain is waking up. She wanted to handbag it.

I voted for Heseltine on first ballot, but only Chris and he know that. And before I caught the plane to Bangladesh I gave proxies for both second and third ballots to John Major.

Hotel Sonargaon, Dhaka, Bangladesh, Wednesday 28 November, 6.30 a.m.

He did it – he bloody well did it! David Seymour of *Today* phoned me at 12.30 a.m. (6.30 p.m. UK time) to give me the results: Major 185, Heseltine 131, Hurd 56. That was uncanny, as I had dreamed vividly the night before that John Major got 186, i.e. not a majority (187) – that would have been unfair, somehow; but a graceful whisker short. Hurd I thought might make 70 and Heseltine only about 120, for some of his support (like mine) came from an absolute determination to get rid of Margaret.

Today got it absolutely right, and came out for Major yesterday morning. David Montgomery told me he'd interviewed all three candidates on Sunday and John was much the 'liveliest'. This guy knows where he's going, has always known, a part of his mind working always on what to do when he becomes Prime Minister. I called him that – 'Prime Minister' – last Thursday night when I grabbed a few minutes after the 10 p.m. vote – insisted on seeing him, indeed, partly to give him my proxy votes in person, for which I received an excited kiss – and partly to take what I thought might be the last opportunity to talk to him informally. We sat in his PPS Graham Bright's[1] office, a tiny and untidy room, John with his back to the door which opened twice in the six or seven minutes. Jacques Arnold[2] was one and looked startled when he saw me sitting there, talking earnestly and very fast from a list in my hand. You must restore the vision of Europe, John, I said. We have been going backwards; Margaret has so much to answer for; we must get our people to see the excitement of being Europeans as we head for the next century. Yes, he said, and shook his head as if to say, how could she

1. Conservative MP for Luton South.
2. Conservative MP for Gravesham.

challenge me on that? And you must sort out Central Office, it is a shambles: not enough of the right sort of candidates, and no support for them either. We hand seats over to the enemy without a fight. None of our candidates, let alone our MPs, even knows how to use a microphone – it is so bloody amateurish.

(I shall have to cancel Pakistan. Too much – and too good to miss – going on at home. Decided the moment I knew John had won.)

John listened intently as I told him that CCO is staffed with young Home Counties kids, never fought an election, don't know anything about it; use your frustrated under-employed backbenchers instead. (I had said the same to Heseltine a couple of hours earlier: hedging my bets, of course.) And the third issue was the new agenda: what people want in the 1990s, which I've written about in *Today*. The green revolution, consumers, Scotland's problems (needing to be brought into the mainstream) – I had more time to go through it with Michael, but by this time with John we were being interrupted constantly and he was getting restless – so I pitched into the most important thing, the item I could tell him about better than anyone, the role of women: most of all, the urgent need to get women into the Cabinet and the Whips' Office. He knows me well enough to be sure I wasn't angling for a job; it wasn't necessary, for he had already explored that a fortnight earlier when he said the best for me would be housing: now that I would indeed enjoy, and as we have both been housing chairmen in big cities and tried hard to improve the housing of ordinary people, I could be sure he would understand what I would wish to do. He knows I would not come back as a Parliamentary Under-Secretary. I did say I'd like to help with CCO and the candidates; and as John ought to keep his Government intact if possible (with a big job for Heseltine, of course, and a new Chancellor – not Heseltine, John wouldn't trust him with public money), then I could do that for a while and then come back into Government at next reshuffle. And if God is listening, I *would* like a place in Cabinet, please, asap. I made John laugh by telling him that he should say to the Chief Whip that there must be two women in there, now – and if there are any objections, I want to know from whom so that they can be sacked: we are not having prejudice in the party, is that clear? He was a whip and understood, but I bet he won't do it.

Travelling back from Bangladesh, Saturday 1 December, 12.45 a.m.

On a plane somewhere over the Middle East. We're in first class (British Airways), and I'm surrounded by somnolent shapes. Next to me is Cherry, Baroness Strange. And we have certainly had an adventure in the last few days, though not one I should wish to repeat.

We arrived in Bangladesh as delegates of the Commonwealth Parliamentary Association on Saturday afternoon and went straight into a tour of Parliament (huge concrete building), a meeting with the Speaker (expansive, oily) and dinner (formal but scruffy; lots of empty places – now I know why). I took Sunday off and went out with Hassna Moudud, wife of the vice-president and an MP in her own right, a chubby, cheerful, talkative and very nice woman. I bought several *shalwar kameez* outfits and wore these throughout my stay, as Western dress reveals too much flesh, which embarrasses people there, whereas *shalwar kameez* are comfortable and practical for clambering in and out of helicopters. They were all very tickled to see me wearing this, and when in the sun I draped my shawl over my head, they said I looked like Benazir Bhutto. One chap said I looked like an Iranian – presumably because of my fair skin, but he was closer to home than he guessed!

But it all started to go wrong as we returned in a helicopter, arriving in Dhaka around 8 p.m. There was trouble, we were told, demos and some shooting. Stay in the airport – curfew imposed 9 p.m., streets will be quieter, we were then escorted to the hotel by police and soldiers. Next day (Wednesday) we went to Chittagong (very interesting if a bit sanitised) under the protection of the army – very pukka major-generals, Sandhurst- and Camberley-trained. On the way back the military helicopter filled with big soldiers, one with a machine gun. Expecting trouble . . . they don't fly 'copters at night, but this one did and again we arrived around 8 p.m. Curfew had continued all day, but was widely defied. One Opposition leader under house arrest, one gone underground. Unconfirmed reports that an Opposition MP had been shot; repeated stories of a hundred people injured, several dead, as troops fired on demonstrators. All phone lines and fax/telex links with the outside world cut off from 2 p.m. (why? So no one outside should know what was going on). The streets from the airport were littered with rocks and broken glass – mile after mile. Soldiers everywhere: real soldiers, red berets and flashes, elite regiments loyal to the President – road blocks, soldiers questioning anyone foolhardy enough to venture on the street, walloping them with night sticks. At the airport the Sheraton Hotel bus was waiting with a few passengers from the BA flight. Its windscreen had two big holes several inches across on the driver's side: rocks must have been thrown at him with great force. Cherry said the jeep we were in had been attacked too. The hotel eerie, half-empty. There had been a South-East Asia Conference, but the army had escorted all non-Bengali delegates to the airport and sent them home; the Bengali participants, unable to go home because of the curfew and no trains running, hung around the lobby disconsolately, still wearing their Conference badges. All our escorts (including the civilians) looked frightened and whispered to each other. We could hear shooting not far away; a man was killed just outside the hotel, and six petrol bombs exploded in the street outside. All the beggars had disappeared. During the night I heard whoosh-whoosh noises and looked out to see long convoys of army lorries heading up the road towards the university. (I opened the window to lean out for a better view, letting the mosquitoes in and got bitten all night, so now my face is a blotchy mess.) Next morning Cherry was swimming in the pool and met her Bengali woman friend, the proprietor of the *Bangladesh Observer*, which didn't appear from Wednesday, because they refused to publish the untruths the Government wanted. The curfew had been lifted for a few hours to enable people to get food, and would be reimposed at 10 a.m. at which point the army would enter the university and shoot the dissidents, and in this country no one would know. We had talked about it the previous evening, and Cherry and I were packed and ready to go. The High Commissioner, Colin Imray, said we should leave. Our first meeting on Thursday morning was with President Ershad – too good to miss: slimy toad, I thought, yuk. The gossip was that martial law might have to be imposed and that he had his personal plane ready and waiting. (He has apartments in Manhattan, London and Geneva and millions in the bank, rake-offs from aid contracts. Doesn't everybody?) A note came round during the audience saying that there was a plane on the tarmac heading for Singapore, and possibly another soon for Bangkok. Cherry and I were prepared to ditch our luggage and head straight for airport, we were so keen to get out! We tried to persuade the others to come too – but Max Madden[1] had come to see the Opposition leaders and still meant to, somehow, and silly little Harry Cohen[2] with him. Norman Miscampbell,[3] the 'leader' (we didn't need one) and a right prat, wanted to go on to Moscow, so he insisted on staying and catching his flight to Kathmandu, though there was every likelihood of the airport being closed. And Chris Butler,[4] fat, slow and stupid, vacillated and then said he wouldn't be the only man to leave. Norman said he wanted to 'see the fire-works' – ye gods! So Cherry and I cleared off, and after much hassle

1. Labour MP for Bradford West.
2. Labour MP for Leyton.
3. The long-serving Conservative MP for Blackpool North.
4. Christopher Butler, Conservative MP for Warrington South.

and waving of Amex cards got ourselves off to Singapore, where we had a lovely twenty-four hours before catching this plane to London.

Looking through the newspapers on the plane, I see that John has created a terrific Cabinet, minus David Waddington (removed to House of Lords) and Cecil Parkinson (resigned of own accord). So he had three vacancies to fill: Chancellor, Norman Lamont (good choice, continuity); Home Secretary, Ken Baker (he's been a disaster at Conservative Central Office and is replaced by Chris Patten, much better); and Transport Secretary, Malcolm Rifkind (rescued from Scotland and endless rows with Michael Forsyth). More: the old Chief Whip has been demoted (hooray, I never thought he was up to it), replaced by Richard Ryder. Heseltine is back at Environment, charged with delivering on poll tax and local government. David Mellor is the new entry to the Cabinet as Chief Secretary – he and John are old mates from London days. In all, a highly intelligent collection (though the first time in twenty-five years that there's been no woman in Cabinet), and to my delight we have moved ahead of Labour in the polls for the first time in eighteen months.

And me . . . disappointed really. The junior ranks were all done on Thursday when we were travelling, but it would have been perfectly possible to reach us in Singapore. I've no idea who has been appointed, as we only have Thursday morning's newspapers on board. John had said in one of our earlier discussions that housing would be OK for me, but I'm sure I would have heard by now. I wish him or her luck, whoever it is. £2000 per week is some compensation – a much better position than I used to be in – and I couldn't afford to manage now on just a backbencher's salary, so I hope I'm not offered something honorific which I might have to turn down (we have £200,000 in various mortgages, so I don't have a lot of choice). On the other hand, getting nothing will feel like a snub, and from a most unexpected source. And it could be risky. Miserable people have been trying to get me deselected, my constituency chairman in particular. She called an Exec meeting Tuesday night (no pretence of waiting till I got home!) and demanded my deselection. She even pushed it to a vote, and was defeated 6:1.

Victoria, Thursday 27 December, 11.27 p.m.

Susie and I came up to London this evening, on our way to France. The house at Mouliherne became ours last Friday. It feels good for all sorts of reasons – and at least partly because I can run away and leave life in Britain several times a year, to relax in a warm and easy place where no one nags or stares. And which I have to justify by working there – so I may be able to concentrate, and raise the standard of my writing closer to a level where I can be reasonably satisfied with it. The privacy has become more important, now that Toyota is heaving upwards on the near horizon: it dominates the view from the kitchen window. That thing really will be huge. The growing road interchange to the south is also much bigger than I expected and makes quite a sight from the top of the (*still* unfinished!) bank by the new pool.

The writing is a bit stuck at present – ooh, writer's block, how exciting! I haven't written any fresh stories since August, so I have promised myself one or two this holiday, especially as we don't go back till 14 January, the longest Xmas Recess in ten years. Definitely a new broom there. I have several ideas for stories, but I'll probably try the most commercial – 'Mother's Day' and 'Second Coming' (about Israel). Then it will be time for more personal stories like 'The Journey' and 'Your Daughter'. *Today* took 'Patience' at around fifteen hundred words and renamed it 'The Honourable Mistress', complete with a drawing vastly more accurate than they could have imagined. The end was expanded a bit, giving me an idea for a scene in the eventual book of short stories which I am keen to do, and which could be modestly successful. It will be a saleable property when I'm back in harness after the General Election.

It was odd seeing 'Patience' in print. That story meant so much to me, and cutting it down from four thousand to fifteen hundred words was painful. Reading it again brought a lump to my throat. The reworking done by *Today* turned the man into a completely cold and calculating brute, but of course the story is more complex than that, as he is supposed to be a thoroughly nice man with special qualities – an edge, of course; ambition certainly; but he should have preserved his dignity, humanity and kindness through all the pressures to get to the front. I doubt if the original would see it, buried in the dreadful magazine section of *Today*; he would need to be a *very* thorough reader of newspapers to have found it, but if he did, he must have had one stupendous shock. Still I do feel very proud that I spotted him so long ago, and that my judgement of his better qualities turned out to be so very accurate. Indeed it was almost creepy reading a story I'd written on 13 October 1989 (according to the computer), before Nigel Lawson resigned, with its predictions now so well borne out (predictions based on events on Budget evening of 1988 – golly, less than three years ago).

I now do so much writing for *Today* each week that there is less need to write a diary. I think hard from Saturday morning onwards what to include, though pieces suggest themselves all the time. The *Daily Telegraph* is most useful, as it doesn't turn its nose up at juicy snippets and generally has full and well-informed reports. On Sunday evening around 6 p.m. I phone David Seymour at home. Then I write on Monday night, about two and a half hours, and go in to edit on Tuesday morning, so I reckon I'm earning about £10 per minute worked. His official title is 'Executive Editor', but really he's in charge of features and doesn't write very often himself, unless Montgomery is away, when he may be doing all the headlines. His piece the Friday after John Major was elected was very good, all the more so for its rarity and for being based on conversations with me. He usually talks a lot and says very little, but we try to agree a headline, so a photo can be chosen to accompany my piece. It was easier, quicker and more professional when

David Montgomery discussed my pieces with me, as in the first week, and when Seymour was off getting wed; Montgomery has a sharper, less cluttered mind, and a marvellous ability to concentrate on the job in hand – though in recent weeks he has been somewhat distracted. The paper is very vulnerable; we are losing a lot of money, and we are suffering from the most catastrophic collapse of advertising for decades – other media companies are seeing unbelievable share falls as billings vanish into thin air. Thank goodness I have a contract. However, I would like the column to have more impact: this year, for example, I did not feature at all in the 'Woman of the Year' on Radio 4's *Today* programme. I've no wish to be forgotten! After the holidays, I'll have a chat with David Montgomery and suggest ways of getting some more notice for the column, so that it causes a bit of a stir.

End of year, just about. Momentous. I still can't believe we pushed her over the edge. Really I ought to take this opportunity to write to her, yet the moment slips away . . . Susie was coming upstairs last Tuesday evening when she bumped into MHT going down from the Ridleys'[1] with two bodyguards. 'How *are* you?' asked MHT. Susie goggled. 'How are *you*?' she replied, and they chatted for a moment. Margaret didn't know who Susie was, of course. Afterwards Susie came bursting in, very excited: '*Guess* who I've just been talking to?' What a great education she's getting, all these lovely contacts, what with Michael Heseltine on the phone on the Sunday, just before the first ballot, too. I do hope it does inspire her to follow a political career, as it would be such a waste otherwise! Deb seems to want to be an actress and is talking about theatrical studies at university or RADA. I've no idea whether she is good enough. Her looks are fine, but she's still so shallow and trivial in many of her attitudes, though

1. Nicholas Ridley and his wife had a flat in the same Victoria apartment block as the Curries.

so mature socially. Very like her Dad. We had a row over money as he now has a big overdraft again. That means I pay all the school fees by myself; he pays the mortgage.[1] I wouldn't mind if he had discussed it with me, but the first time I knew was when the quarterly account arrived and I checked it. And I mind that he won't tell me how much money he owes either. When he's around I get so frustrated – the feeling persists that if he had fulfilled all those early promises, we'd be a lot wealthier and we'd have a circle of influential friends and acquaintances. Instead his pals are local builders, retired policemen, an electrician at Rolls-Royce. Very sweet people, but I can't be friends with them, they are my job; and although my antennae are picking up signals from them all the time – and thus I'm not relaxed – the evening ends with me no further on. I get invited to hardly anything useful or interesting: dinner parties, receptions, etc. (and don't go to some I am invited to, not through laziness, but through weakening discipline, organisation and stamina). I daydream about another affair. Now, who might be interested?

1. (See also p. 220): interest rates had been running at 16–17 per cent and were cut to 10 per cent only on entry to the ERM (October). The Curries were not the only family facing financial difficulties at that time.

1991

Tower House, Wednesday 9 January, 1.50 p.m.

I'm home alone this week, as Ray has gone to Madrid. I found myself discussing him yesterday lunchtime, and it's the first time ever I've expressed dissatisfaction to another human being about him, though I've had the odd moan to this diary, and many hours thinking silently to myself. I took my secretary Chris to lunch at Overton's fish restaurant in Victoria. In return for Chris's confidences, I told her how bored I am most of the time. I lack stimuli, particularly at home. I didn't tell Chris about my escapades, and sometimes I wonder if I will ever tell anyone. I was B's mistress for four years, and the only people who know that are the two of us. I loved him very dearly, and I still do, and always will – and it hurts every time I see him on TV, or even now as I think about him, and worry about him. I doubt if anyone would believe me if I told them, and what good would it do?

This morning I had breakfast with Jane Reed, who is the publicity boss at News Corporation. She tells me that *Today* will be moving to Wapping, to the *Sunday Times/Times* site, in February, when we will lose our extra library, canteen, etc.: I hadn't known that in October, and really it is not nearly so convenient for me as Vauxhall Bridge Road. The printing has just moved there, with some being done on the presses in Manchester too. Big savings, but printing at 7 p.m., so all deadlines are earlier – editorial is at 10 a.m., for example, which means that the features editor has to be in by 7 a.m. None of the managers like that at all, though the production staff are very pleased to have their evenings off. I suspect *Today* is being printed in the evening and finished early so that other, more successful papers can then be run through the night. The rearrangement of the print schedules was done over the Christmas holiday, with David Montgomery having to negotiate over the phone from Canada. More, however, was to come, for on Monday evening forty-five people (forty-four journalists and one secretary) were called in and told to clear their desks forthwith. Even the leader writer has gone, and his corner stood mute and empty yesterday morning when I went in. Everyone was rigid with shock, arriving and finding all their friends gone, with pieces half-finished. David said that *Today* won't be the only paper losing staff this year, just the first. The main problem this week is putting the paper on to the presses, the managers in particular having to work very hard. David Seymour will have to do all the leaders, and he's not too keen on that. When I called him on Sunday evening, he was hosting a dinner party, and had been cooking himself; it was clear from the background noise that the call was inconvenient, then he told me yesterday that in fact the phone had never stopped, so he is in effect working a seven-day week. If that carries on, people will leave. David Seymour reckons that these cuts alone will save £1.5 million, and with the rest that might be enough to tip the paper into solvency, or profit when the recession eases and advertising revenue starts to flow again; with over 500,000 sales at 25p per copy, the paper is apparently making a £21 million contribution to group costs. Murdoch changed Montgomery's press release from 'future is assured' to 'future is guaranteed', but there ain't no guarantees when the banks are breathing down your neck.

They can't touch me, thanks to my contract: I'm guaranteed £50,000 between October and April, renewable after that. I noticed that Penny Chapman, the editor of the *News of the World*, sent me an Xmas card with a friendly remark inside, so if *Today* folds maybe the *News of the World* will take me up. It would increase my readership tenfold, and maybe somebody would take notice of what I'm saying. When I first started, my heart was in my mouth the whole time, for fear there would be a frightful row about what I was writing, but the only people to have noticed anything I've written are *Gay News*, when I said the age of consent for homosexuals should be reduced to sixteen. They nearly fell out of their pram with excitement, and asked for an interview. But, with due respect, it isn't them that I'm trying to reach. I know that John Major read the column the week he appointed his Cabinet, minus any woman for the first time in more than twenty-five years. But I should like it to be influential, and essential reading for all my mates in Parliament. 'She speaks, the nation listens' is the slogan; well, no they don't, and I wish they did.

I suggested to the Davids (both of them) and to Jane that we explore each week whether there are any items we could make a fuss about, by putting out a press release 'Edwina Currie says', etc., on the tapes; the earlier print time will make such an exercise easier. On a quiet day we might do very well, and just once or twice we might hit the jackpot, with *Newsnight*, breakfast TV, etc. At least it would mean that my profile hadn't disappeared, which is the current danger. Before I started *Today* I had articles in the *Standard*, *The Times*, *Independent*, *Sunday Express*, *Observer*, etc. Now I'm only in 'Atticus',[1] usually with a 'she's finished' tinge to the story. No, I'm not, but if I want to get back, I have to show myself to be still around and still useful: too good to leave on the back-benches.

Gerald Kaufman[2] has been calling for sanctions to be given longer to work before taking action to expel Iraq from Kuwait. Loathsome man: I find Kaufman particularly offensive, a Jew with no soul. I may have a reputation for being outspoken, but I prefer

1. A gossip column in the *Sunday Times*.
2. Shadow Foreign Secretary; Labour MP for Manchester Gorton.

that to being mealy-mouthed, and said so in today's column! And again, nobody noticed. Nobody reads the damn thing. I feel as if I'm an actress in a good play, with an empty theatre in front of me. Nothing whatever is coming back. Only the cash is good, and for me that is not sufficient.

Victoria, Tuesday 15 January, 11.40 p.m.

This is the last day we can be sure there is no war: the deadline is midnight, New York time, 5 a.m. tomorrow our time. It feels as if everything is ready, although BBC's *Newsnight* reported a few minutes ago from the Gulf that the ground troops aren't ready, and aren't preparing for an imminent invasion. So it may be some days yet.

Big vote in the House tonight on the Government's policy towards Iraq: 534 to 57 in favour, with 59 not voting (includes Speaker, etc.). Kinnock spoke well, as he did in September, when Kuwait was first invaded – he always makes his best speeches when he supports the Government. John Major opened and spoke earnestly, a little ponderously and too long; he is listened to with respect until the boredom factor takes over, and then Labour can't contain itself to interrupt, or try and distract him. But John has the tone exactly right – if we are to be dragged into war, he said at the dinner table tonight, it must be reluctantly, with no jingoism. The polls say about half the people are for any action including force, just over one-third for any action short of force, and about 15 per cent think we should not be involved at all. Results like these puzzle me, for like most Tory colleagues I've had hardly any letters, except from the usual CND and peaceniks. If there are loads of people out there against the war, they are keeping their heads down in South Derbyshire.

John Major won some new friends tonight. As we were gathering round, waiting for the vote to be announced (which obviously took ages as we shuffled through), there was a commotion and a burst of applause from the Labour backbenches. It was partly for a desperately sick Eric Heffer,[1] gaunt, grey and thin, eyes heavy with painkillers, who was sitting in his place one row from the back. He had come in to vote, sick as he was. John crossed over and knelt beside him, sharing a few words. The applause was for both men, almost unheard of in the Chamber. Those years as a whip taught John that everyone in the Commons matters. Margaret would never have done that; she despised the other side. It is sad really for her, too – she was listening to the opening speeches, sombrely clad in black, not as much make-up as she used to wear (not doing TV all the time), on the third row up, right at the civil service box end. From there you can't be seen by the Press Gallery, as the Speaker's Chair blocks the view. In the lobby, however, only acolytes (such as the oleaginous Gerald Howarth) chat to her and everyone else slides past, as if she's a turd on the pavement.

Victoria, Thursday 24 January, 10.50 p.m.

Feeling very low indeed tonight. I often do on Thursdays, when Ray has gone back to Findern: it's a tired, dead evening, really the end of the political week. And the flat seems even lonelier because on Thursdays I used to fill it with B, before he drove home.

I had a phone conversation with Hilary Rubinstein, who still wants a novel and pooh-poohed my idea of a book on Europe. 'Anthony Sampson's *Anatomy of Europe* did nothing' – he meant financially. But I want to do something interesting and worthwhile, to keep my mind occupied, and to add to my reputation. Hilary's motives are all financial, and he doesn't seem to appreciate that mine are very different. There are novels I could write, of course: a funny

---

1. Labour MP for Walton Division of Liverpool since 1964, who died four months later, towards the end of May.

'Lady in the House' *à la* Tom Sharpe. That would be harmless, and very different from most of the stuff already in existence. Or a Carson McCullers-style family saga, which could have childhood/ teenage/student/mistress, etc., sections and be a commentary on the events of our time. But both would need an enormous amount of work, the saga about two years probably, and aren't worth tackling now. So Hilary's offhand comments have left me in a bit of a mess.

Today is still not making money. On the night of the first Gulf attack (last Wednesday night/Thursday morning) an extra 90,000 copies were printed. I saw David Montgomery last night – we were both on late-night TV, so the conversation took place about 2.30 a.m.! – and asked if we were selling more. 'Yes, but not enough,' he said. There's some drive missing from this gentle, mild-mannered Ulsterman, who looks as if he ought to be a teacher or a priest. Stories about Murdoch's problems with News Corporation continue: between September 1990 and June 1991 he has $3 billion of his $8 billion debt due for repayment and he will *have* to sell assets, possibly at distress prices. Sky is costing a fortune still, and the coverage of the Gulf War is adding to the costs. So *Today* could simply be closed. The staff are all doing fourteen-hour days and looking grim.

What really knocked me sideways, however, was a cruel remark from Michael Colvin.[1] I've been nagging Anthony Sheen[2] to get organised once again on TIPS ('Tested Ideas for Political Success'), a booklet full of bright ideas for candidates, backed up by a series of conferences for candidates, run by experienced MPs. I went to one in 1983 run by Tony Durant[3] – now Sir Anthony – and found it great

---

1. Conservative MP for Romsey and Waterside.
2. A former whip and junior minister, active in the Conservative Party organisation.
3. Conservative MP for Reading West.

fun and very helpful. All the MPs there had fought and won marginal seats, so they were not just armchair advisers. At last we get a friendly hearing from Chris Patten this evening. Anthony is full of scatty ideas and talks a lot; Michael Shersby[1] is benign; Michael Colvin next to me on my right. I'm happy to do what I can, but pretty determined to rewrite the booklet in decent English! That will involve writing around to colleagues in marginals to ask for their ideas. 'You shouldn't do it, Edwina,' says Michael Colvin, 'some people don't like you and won't respond.' My mouth must have dropped open. John Lacey, head of campaigning, said quickly, 'That shows what berks some people are' – but I was devastated, and am still very shocked. They do this because they think I'm no one important, and that I don't have any feelings. It's become much worse since the reshuffle and being left out; it's genuinely believed that I'm going nowhere except outside (leaving) Parliament. And maybe I'm imagining things, but I can walk through the voting lobby and have no one speak to me unless I speak to them; I can walk into the dining room and find nowhere to sit (maybe I'm just losing my touch, my good timing, but it is a very humiliating feeling to have to walk *out* again!).

Maybe I'm too sensitive (and tired after a late night). When I write about events that have caused me pain and anger, they seem unimportant. But right now I feel lonely, neglected, unused and unloved! I wish my flat was filled with one big man in his blue underpants – I wish I was warm and sticky and laughing, and I wish I wanted the evening to last a long while, so we can talk (he can talk, I can listen). I can't make a joke of it. I haven't been drinking, but I'm deep in the black hole tonight and there is no one else in it here with me.

---

1. Conservative MP for Uxbridge.

I turned on the midnight news last Wednesday night and found myself listening to CNN correspondents describing the first air raid on Baghdad, which had started about twenty minutes before. The missiles were whistling in and crashing around their ears: really terrifying stuff. It was an extraordinary experience – alone again, Ray was in Spain – so I watched television till I fell asleep about 1.30 a.m., then woke at 6 a.m. and switched it back on once more.

I find it strange, as a woman, this war. I'm not appalled by it as I was by the Falklands: this time we have strong altruistic motives as well as pragmatic ones – protecting oil supplies, and wanting peace in Middle East, both of which I regard as admirable (the world wouldn't sniff so much if we were safeguarding the world's water supplies. But oil is just as essential – why do we persist in treating energy as a dispensable luxury?). Now we aren't alone as we were in the Falklands, but a leading part of an international coalition, and easily America's best, most committed and reliable ally. Shades of World War II. It's certainly the biggest logistics exercise since the Normandy landings, and the fire power is just staggering – explosives with one and a half times the power of the Hiroshima bomb were dropped in the *first sortie* (yet casualties are tiny and the first confirmed death was an old lady in Tel Aviv). So I find it, secretly, *very* exciting and can't get enough of it. There's something powerful and emotive about this war which helps me understand why men enjoy it.

I attended a meeting this week with the Israeli Ambassador and feel he needs to learn a thing or two. Apparently he's a nice man, but with his heavily accented English he came across as unsympathetic and deeply unwilling to trust anyone. He even made snide remarks about some unnamed countries in the Alliance, who would pull out when the going gets tough and sue for peace. In fact the opposite seems to be happening. Saudi Arabia says it won't be pulled out of a coalition even if Israel *does* retaliate: remarkable. Turkey has joined in, and its bases are being used to open up another front. The Israelis will have to come round a table afterwards, so they might be advised to build some bridges now, instead of setting charges underneath the few frail structures which do exist.

Victoria, Thursday 7 February, very late

Snowing outside, big soft white unthreatening flakes, gently blanketing London. All vehicles stilled, everyone gone home or sleeping on someone's floor. Three inches of snow on every parked car, and more falling gently. This evening I went out to dinner at a flat in Smith Square. As ever with dinner parties, which were not part of my upbringing, I found it very hard work, just trying to be sparkling and interested in my companions. I'd much rather be the centre of attention! Left the car in the Commons car park, retrieved my wellies from the boot and trudged home, rather too tiddly to care that I must have looked a sight!

John Major looked OK at Question Time, but was talking fast and didn't crack any jokes either.[1] Definitely IRA – they have been doing mortar bombs out of vans successfully in Northern Ireland for years. Most police stations are virtual fortresses as a result. First time on mainland. But democracies won't be beaten by terrorists, etc. Kinnock made good statement and hinted that Labour would go for 'unity with the Government' on action against terrorism, which suggests that he might put a whip to vote *for* the Prevention of Terrorism Act when its renewal comes up soon. That would be a snub to his left wing.

Later John came into tea room and sat at my table. His PPS Graham Bright and Roger King[2] to my left; David Ashby opposite, and a couple of others. He had a tray of two slices of lean cold beef,

---

1. The IRA had launched a mortar attack on 10 Downing Street that morning.
2. Conservative MP for Birmingham Northfield.

lots of tomatoes, mustard pickle *and* mustard and a glass of milk. He'll get an ulcer if he carries on like that! He was full of nervous energy (I noticed him fidgeting on TV while listening to Tom King). He told me he'd lost a stone since becoming PM, which explains why he looks so good on TV. He's now 2 stone lighter than when he was a whip, so he's about 13 stone and looks very good for forty-eight, though with just a little loose skin under his chin if you look closely.

He said the War Cabinet was meeting in the Cabinet Room at Number 10 when the mortar bomb landed in back garden. Whole window bowed in, lifting the window frame out; the glass didn't shatter, but it was a bit of a mess. Meeting adjourned to another room. John said his flat was quite badly damaged, glass everywhere and would certainly need redecorating. He went on to talk about poll tax, said he has no idea what they are going to do! Very conscious that a decision to return to rates could split party. On interest rates, usual same line, they will come down when inflation is under control.

He didn't talk about Gulf War, and as an issue it's fading. We are all waiting: waiting for the ground offensive; waiting to see what everything looks like after the war; waiting for decisions on the community charge; waiting for interest rate cuts and for the economy to improve. Heaven knows, enough Tory MPs have been slapping in the message on interest rates and business collapse to Treasury ministers. John said not to be euphoric about polls (showing us ahead, him most popular Prime Minister since Churchill). When the war is over, the economy will return as the most important issue.

I told Tony Newton all about it a week Tuesday (29th). I just couldn't suffer by myself anymore, and we had a series of three-line whips, so without more warning than a quick phone call, I went to his room at the back of the Chair and told him. His secretary kept getting in the way, even at 11 p.m.! I told him about B's days as a whip and how he hated the discipline, not speaking, having to be nice to people he hated; how we fixed up dates on front bench; how B likes to walk the edge, take a risk. (Tony was very surprised. 'Oh yes,' I said. 'He likes taking a risk.') How we had the joke on the press and the gossip columnists, why I insisted we stop. Tony suggested that I was responsible for his subsequent career, though I doubt if there is any truth in that; but he seemed to understand that most of the time it was two nice people, under tremendous pressure, who found a home in each other for a while, till it got too dangerous and had to stop. Tony said there are often strains in politicians' marriages, but I was able to steer him away from these conventional notions – and from his first question, 'Are you still in love with him?' It wasn't like that; much more a relationship of equals with similar needs, very thankful that we had found a secure and trustworthy and understanding opportunity. His wife and home he cherishes, as I cherish mine; and would do nothing to damage them. But emotionally there was (for me still is, and maybe for him, too) a gap. For home resents politics and doesn't want to talk about it, or share any precious time with it or its activists. Yet for people like us, politics *is* life and we are only pretending without it, or perhaps recuperating, ready for the next fray. With me he could both recuperate and share and philosophise and explore new talents (in bed!); and for me, too.

I didn't mention to Tony that I was getting fed up three years ago because I was getting the same philosophy as in his speeches – and that meant the public and private person were merging. Anyway, he had so little time, so few opportunities that I was having to nag, which meant the fun and spontaneity were vanishing; and I was too bloody arrogant to want gentle help and advice. Turn the clock back, girl, and dream a moment or two.

I diverted the conversation to my own position, my loneliness and hurt, my fear I was disappearing, disintegrating: we only exist in other people's minds, we public people. He said he would try and find out what my prospects are from the whips (he was a former whip). I told him about the two promises, one of which wasn't kept (housing) and the other (I'd be back in after the election). I think I was pretty confused and wept copiously, but Tony got the gist of it. And I feel much more normal now: better.

Victoria, Thursday 21 February, 10.50 p.m.

I am trying to shed weight and finding it tough! In the last two weeks I've been stuck at 10 stone 4 pounds, though that is certainly slimmer than I have been. Still, looking at others makes me determined not to slide into middle age like them: awful. If I have any appeal, it is based on looking good.

I suppose by now I've given up hope of getting back into Government. My mood has swung every which way and I have certainly been very depressed about it, but appraising my Commons colleagues with a very cool eye and listening to the discussions on what the Chancellor can and can't do in the budget on 19 March, it's more than clear that we are all play-acting. Most of the decisions are taken elsewhere, or can't be taken. In which case, heading for the European Parliament is looking increasingly attractive. No one pretends there that the MEPs have power: though over time they might acquire some, as the Westminster Parliament loses it. Only in the Council of Ministers is there any genuine bargaining, and if I can't be there, then I might as well play politics in a more congenial atmosphere where the pay and the food are better, and where I can walk in the street, go shopping, etc., without harassment (or fear, perhaps, of being blown up, like in London).[1] Perhaps I could help 'sell' the idea

---

1. The IRA mortar attack on Downing Street was followed by further bombs at London railway stations.

of Europe more to the British. Certainly British MEPs with some parliamentary experience (and there are *none* at present) could teach the European Parliament how to function more effectively. And we will be bringing in the new countries and Austria and Scandinavia, so there will be a lot more to do than in the UK. By 1995, when the Boundary Commission will have taken ten thousand of my best voters off me, Toyota will be up and running, the new M1–M6 link which I have been campaigning for should be open and even passenger rail services improved, as well as a host of other improvements, so I might just feel I've done all I can in South Derbyshire and it was time to move on. Notwithstanding all this, if I *was* offered a job in Government I'd take it, of course.

I wrote to Margaret Thatcher this week, after seeing her surrounded in the lobby by Tebbit, Ridley, Howarth, etc. She looked so forlorn. No reply, yet.

It feels so strange watching John Major at work. He is doing so well; his noncombative style (which I know is a deliberate choice, he can be very cutting when he wants to) goes down very well. Today at Question Time a Labour left winger went on about unemployment, etc. He replied that 'The Honourable Gentleman is a class warrior and I am not; that's the difference between us.' Much excitement that the previous weekend on the way through Doncaster he stopped at a Happy Eater for a fry-up – talk about a man of the people. But my image of him is getting blurred. I am so afraid I will lose the man I knew and he will be replaced by the current, public image. That would break my heart.

Victoria, Wednesday 13 March, 11.15 p.m.

I'm ashamed that I haven't written before. So much has happened in the last three weeks, too. The war is over. The ground offensive only lasted a hundred hours and the entire Iraqi army collapsed. It seems the most amazing anticlimax. Tom King told us that Bush was anxious for a ceasefire once US jets started shooting up the retreating army on the road from Kuwait City to Basra – they were completely defenceless and Bush didn't want a 'turkey shoot'. Horrible pictures of people (soldiers) burned alive during the fire-bombing, fused to the steering wheels of their vehicles. We got away with seventeen killed, including several SAS. One was Carl Moult, aged twenty-two and due to be married later this year, from Church Gresley, near Burton-upon-Trent. Brian Vertigen of the *Burton Mail* told me immediately he heard, and I went to see the family a week Friday. It seems so sad that of the handful of dead, one had to be so close to home – an ordinary, decent, cheeky lad, mad about motor-bikes, loving his life of adventure with the Staffordshires in the desert, so far from the humdrum life of home. The church was full of awkward sunburned young men in drill, just like him, I guess. The family are typical South Derbyshire: short, stocky, solid, plain, earnest and close. Their GP said they appreciated my support, a remark which made me feel really guilty as I hadn't done anything at all. I drew the line, indeed, at going to the cemetery where I gather the burial was accompanied by a volley of shots, last post, dipped standards, the lot; if I couldn't/wouldn't go to my father's committal, then I wasn't up for this. Instead I went to Gresley Old Hall where the army was paying for lunch, and chatted to the staff till they all came back, so anxious to do the proper thing, family and soldiers, hovering at the edge between propriety and grief.

Apparently the SAS engaged in 'direct action' to assassinate a lot of top officers so that the Iraqi army would be demoralised (that worked). We won't hear much of what the SAS got up to, though teams were clearly operating behind enemy lines for months, pin-pointing targets very effectively. One bunch (according to the Staffordshires) was surprised in their camp in Iraqi territory and managed to convince the Iraqis that they were POWs awaiting collection. They captured equipment – reportedly including a MiG jet – and brought it back so that radar could be examined and jammed;

and they brought back key Iraqi officers for interrogation. It is probably wisest not to ask how they got the information needed, or whether the men are still alive.

And now suddenly it is all over and we are back to normal. The Gulf has disappeared from our screens, Radio 4 has rubbish on all frequencies as before; there is absolutely no discernible 'Falklands factor' and indeed, apart from John, the main gainer seemed to be Paddy Ashdown,[1] generally reckoned to have had a 'good war'. Last Thursday was the Ribble by-election (7th) – I went up the Monday ten days before and was surprised to find myself doing cold canvassing with another visitor, a trainee agent from Kent. We had no local help and kept getting lost, though the canvass returns were OK – but they should have been done, and I should have been canvassing doubtfuls. The following weekend the returns suddenly got more alarming, and Tyrone[2] and all his colleagues on training were sent up for the last three days. He said afterwards that a lot of the canvassing had not been done, and he was getting a very sniffy response phoning supposed Tory pledges who were nothing of the kind; in his view there had been a lot of 'armchair canvassing'. So a 19,000 majority collapsed into a four thousand loss to the Liberal Democrats, whose candidate, Mike Carr, was local and had fought the seat before.

Such a decisive defeat made it clear that the poll tax cannot survive. Heseltine has been fiddling around in a very lacklustre way, and now John is back from the Gulf we are all demanding some decisions, fast. The southern Tory MPs, led by Robert Jones,[3] are threatening to resign if we have a property tax. Their constituents in valuable properties would, of course, lose out, but as Maggie backers

1. Leader of the Liberal Democrats; MP for Yeovil.
2. Tyrone Edwards, EC's South Derbyshire agent.
3. Conservative MP for Hertfordshire West.

they are determined to make Heseltine's life difficult. Damned if we do, damned if we don't!

So now we are behind in the polls again, with the Liberal Democrats having doubled their share of the vote. I feel quite secure in South Derbyshire, but there's certainly a sense of John Major having to prove himself.

Meanwhile Margaret Hilda Thatcher is being a confounded pest, as I said in my column today. She's in the USA receiving prizes and failing to keep her mouth shut, convinced there was a conspiracy against her (there wasn't – no need!) and reiterating her dotty and unpleasant views on our partners in Europe. It beats me how anyone can label the Germans militaristic, after their pathetic pacifist showing in the last nine months.[1] As for expressing fears that they will dominate Europe, the obvious question is, 'Well, what are you going to do about it?' Get in there and compete is the obvious answer – chuck signed contracts at them, not insults. The younger population regards such speeches as evidence that she's past it.

David Montgomery came into the House for a drink this evening. I can't help liking him. He's fighting to save the paper and is under instructions to take it downmarket, though he thinks that it will fail and be merged with the *Sun* (which is also losing circulation). *Today* faces all sorts of peculiar difficulties, e.g. they are very restricted on returns, so about 40 per cent of newsagents sell out and there are no more copies. That's how you lose readers. And there is no money for promotions: the main competitors, e.g. *Daily Mail* and the *Express*, are spending nearly £1 million a month on advertising and promotion. Meanwhile *The Times* is losing £25 million p.a. (good heavens, that's not widely known) – a lot more than *Today*.

The upshot, as I expected, is that he hasn't the money to continue

---

1. Germany's constitution prevented it from participating in the Gulf War.

my contract after April. I'm willing to carry on for a bit anyway, for less money; what I don't want is a reputation that the column was no good or not on time, etc. (It hasn't appeared for last two weeks because we were down to thirty-six pages and there wasn't room, would you believe?) David said he would see me right there, and planned to write to *Campaign* explaining that he could afford no contract writers at all. But the paper must surely fold soon after – his staff are all working like maniacs and can't do much more. I felt very sorry for him. The recession is biting very deep. There will be lots of casualties before the year is out and I suspect *Today* will be one of them.

Hotel Central, Tours, Thursday 28 March, 10.30 p.m., European time

Good journey – left Victoria 7.45 a.m., Hovercraft, train left Boulogne 12 noon (French time – an hour ahead), Paris 2.15 p.m.; then a tiring hop on the Metro from Gare du Nord to Montparnasse (the mainline station in both cases being a hefty underground walk from the Metro, to such an extent that moving pavements are provided at Montparnasse!) and then an hour on the TGV, all new on a service which started 30 September last, to St-Pierre-des-Corps near Tours, arriving 4.30 p.m. When the Tunnel is finished and all the trains are high speed, the journey should be a lot quicker, probably as fast as flying when check-in time and travel to/from airport is taken into account. I came first class, and on the TGV that is very swish indeed. Total cost £297, which is a bit steep for a weekend but includes a hire car till Monday morning (train = £133), so I'm toddling around in a little white Peugeot and trying to remember to drive on the *right* which feels very odd indeed.

I drove over to Mouliherne this evening to view the house ('Les Tuileries') just before it got dark. Damned impressive, really. The main living room is going to be stunning. The stable room next door will be very smart, too. There's a lot still to do: the inside of the roof, for example, and the staircase. But the electrics and new windows are in, and the bathroom/*lingerie* constructed. When this stage of the house is finished, I still won't have spent £60,000 and I'll have a seven-bedroomed property: in the UK it would be worth £¼ million.

France, Saturday 30 March, 8.30 p.m.

I have an unlimited capacity for excess, I think! Today I managed to spend nearly £500, 4729 francs to be exact: most (3885 francs) on a suit and blouse (the latter 750 francs), to wear to Pithiviers[1] tomorrow when I meet the Mayor, and probably Tuesday and Wednesday when I'm speaking in Taunton and Weston-super-Mare. My only justification is that the weather is colder than I expected and my dress will not be warm enough; though no doubt if I'd looked harder I'd have found something cheaper.

I planned to eat only bought-in food today to save money! That was OK for lunchtime when the goat's cheese, tomatoes, salad and strawberries went down well, sitting under the lime trees at Villandry and dozing off afterwards. But by the evening I was very cold and in need of hot food: overdid it, too, with a tuna salad followed by veal marsala with spaghetti at a café in Tours, so now I'm feeling very full and 101 francs poorer. Not the best disciplined person I know. Still it was a lovely day.– yesterday, too – sunny and bright, the air clear and lifting and cloudless.

My house is coming on fine. It will be very big: my first reaction on going inside is, golly it's massive, have I been too ambitious? Why do I need somewhere so big? Not for myself, I guess: it will be

---

1.   Twinned with Ashby de la Zouch near EC's South Derbyshire constituency.

much easier to let a big house and charge a lot for it, of course. I suppose I want to impress Ray, too: look what I've done . . . and if ever I do want to live there, it will be in some comfort. Mostly because the opportunity presented itself. I could have carried on looking forever and not made a decision, and that would have been the most disappointing of all.

All this food and a quarter carafe of wine tonight has made me feel woozy, which is exactly the word John Major used about himself on Wednesday night, when we talked after the vote in the No Confidence debate. He has done sixteen overseas visits since November, whereas Margaret Thatcher used to average only one overseas visit every sixty days, and used to take a lot more breaks and get more rest than ever she let on – he said this almost bitterly, as if he had only discovered it from her staff after he became PM. The No Confidence debate went very well for him, fortunately, and that was mainly because two hours before the debate the Speaker ruled that it would be limited to the subject on the Order Paper, i.e. the Government's handling of the poll tax; so much of John's speech was thrown away, as Matthew Parris noted in his *Times* sketch, and was all the better for it: crisp, punchy and a little cruel in its treatment of the Opposition. Kinnock in turn was excellent, with much less waffle than usual. Two good speeches and a draw, and everyone off to Easter holidays satisfied. Almost certainly no June election, and that's a relief.

It has been a rotten month for the Government, since the end of the war. Heseltine's 'review' of poll tax has been dragging on; sections of the party are bitterly opposed to any practical solution. We seem at a real turning point, with too much uncertainty and a fair pinch of chaos. I don't like it.

The Budget was designed to make matters better, but at least in the short term made them worse. Margaret sat there stony-faced right through the Chancellor's speech and managed to vote for his Budget, but it threw out most of her policies, including ending mortgage interest relief for higher rate taxpayers. Thanks a million, Mr Lamont. Heseltine followed all this on the Thursday with a less than brilliant exposition saying the Government had *not* decided on a replacement for poll tax and would instead be putting out three consultative documents after Easter. It's not even clear whether genuine consultation is intended, as all responses have to be in within three months. This could simply be an invitation to continued dispute, of course. I asked John when we would know the answers and he said in the next Queen's Speech, so it sounds as if he's expecting an October/November General Election.

Gill Shephard came into the Members' Cloakroom on the Tuesday just before the Budget looking very smart in bright yellow and black. 'Wonderful Budget – you'll love it,' she enthused. Saw her afterwards and told her I didn't agree. I expressed my views in a letter to the PM via Graham Bright, and afterwards he invited me to come and talk to him about it. The weekend polls were very disappointing – neck and neck or a small Labour lead, though John Major continues very popular, particularly among ladies (they disapproved of Margaret Thatcher, especially the younger ones, and now we have them back; once again, as twenty years ago, women are more likely to vote Tory than men). But such a 'brilliant' Budget should have produced a surge in the polls. Ministers were very crestfallen and puzzled to find the opposite had happened. Well, I told John in my letter, they agree with cutting taxes – not increasing them; OK, the overall macroeconomic effect this year is nil, but they start paying the VAT and petrol tax right away and never stop, so they *feel* worse off. And they like us cutting prices, not increasing them. More, they agree with the war on waste and so are appalled at the prospect of thirty-eight million poll tax bills, already sent out or ready to go, being pulped and reissued. If we knew we were going to sub the councils by £4.5 billion a month ago, in time to stop them, why didn't we say so? And if we didn't, and it was all decided virtually overnight, what a way to run the country . . . and so on. The electors are uneasy and confused, and so are we Tory backbenchers.

Nigel Lawson, arrogant, brilliant and thoughtless, decided to put the boot in on the last day of the Budget debate, Monday 25 March. I didn't hear his speech, but it was first item on the news and reverberated all week: a government which can't choose, he said, isn't fit to govern; consultation is not a substitute for decision making. Amen to that. He was all the more effective for being right, of course, but on Tuesday at Prime Minister's Question Time John was stung into saying Lawson was 'quite wrong' and that consultation was essential in an exercise designed to get majority support for the poll tax's replacement. But John was wrong, too – for consultation is usually based around a particular proposal, not an open-ended invitation of views. And he's wrong if he thinks consultation leads to a majority accepting the outcome – quite the opposite, as I said rather roughly in a backbench meeting with Michael Heseltine on Monday evening, not having heard Nigel's speech: the process is more like a planning inquiry in which everyone is rendered anxious and only a tiny minority are pleased with the result. Most of all, John was wrong to be quite so nasty about Nigel, adding gratuitously that he, John Major, had managed to succeed in doing many things Nigel had 'neglected' to do, namely ERM entry and ending mortgage tax relief. I told John he was wrong, too, as we sat in his room on the dingy sofa and argued about it for a bit. You owe Nigel a lot and you can afford to be gracious about him, I said: in the time since you've been Premier you have rubbished only two people in public, Saddam Hussein and Nigel Lawson, and that's not right. John is clearly hung up on creating his own agenda – 'In some ways I'm more Thatcherite than Thatcher – the mortgage relief she could never have done – but I'm not a Thatcherite, never have been . . .' His Central Council speech in Southport (22nd), of which he was clearly rather proud, set out his personal agenda, much of which seems to have been pinched from the socialists, including a

Consumers' Charter for better public services. Most people don't so much want choice, I said, as to be able to feel confident about the availability and quality of service. I agreed with *The Economist* that John's speech was 'wooden'; you need a more elegant and punchy turn of phrase, I said. If you have any contributions to make, please do, he replied, in that little-boy-lost way. It was the day before his birthday, so we closed the discussion with a kiss and me feeling very sorry for him. The worst sides of his character show when he is tired: a tendency to be offhand and critical and defensive and dismissive of criticism and a weakening of both good manners and judgement. Why didn't you just *decide* what to have in place of poll tax, I asked?

I really wanted, a fortnight ago, to sit down and write a memoir about John Major, before I forget all I know, and before it shades unavoidably into what everyone else knows about him and what I've learned since, e.g. by reading the excerpts from Ed Pearce's forthcoming biography. I can remember John bridling, for example, when I said to him once, 'It's easy for you, you're a banker.' 'I wasn't always a banker,' he replied. 'I left school at sixteen when my family had no money and worked as a labourer for four years. I was unemployed for nine months. We lived in a walk-up flat in Brixton' – all said with a vehemence of which this courteous and dignified chap had seemed incapable. And of his time in Nigeria, 'I had a car crash and nearly died – it helps concentrate your mind – if I do more than a few minutes' walking my knee blows up like a balloon' (he managed three hours' exercise without trouble to my certain knowledge!). I knew all this before the general public or most of his colleagues, and I'm sad that what once was special to me now belongs to everyone – it makes *me* feel much less special, of course. But he hasn't talked to Pearce about Norma being half-Jewish – he used to ask me about Jewish things, just at the end of the evening, as if he had been saving it up, something he wanted to know. And the most extraordinary moment was in the bath, when he asked if I believed in God. 'Yes,' I said, 'but not in all the ritual. I had that stuffed down my throat as a child.' He nodded and patted my back as if satisfied, as if he'd been asking himself the question a long time and had now found a satisfactory formula; we were like teenagers exploring the world together. And there's lots about him I won't write down, except to say he learned a lot and explored the edges very thoroughly and with great pleasure and amusement and skill and consideration; only he never, ever, gave me any kind of token, not even an anonymous one, so that the only gifts I have from men have come from André[1] and in the end no one else.

Something else from our Wednesday evening discussion: I said, 'You must learn to pace yourself. We want you as leader for ten years.'

'Oh no,' he said. 'Eight is ample, I shall be forty-eight tomorrow, and when I'm fifty-five I want to do other things.'

He'd fitted me in between the vote and drinks with the whips; we talked for quite a time and in the end I was the one who ended the conversation. Last time we spoke in December it was briefer, but he was more affectionate. I was wary of touching him in case Graham Bright came in.

I do find it heartbreaking to have lost him so completely. At times like this, sitting alone on the bed of a hotel room, I feel so very alone and sorry for myself. Having a capacity for great love, and for enabling someone to enjoy it too, it seems such a waste, so atrophied. I used to be more upset about losing him than about losing office, and that's so much more the case now. I hate my dreams, I hate my moments alone, so many at present, as I daydream about him in ways which just hurt all the more and make me feel so empty and useless.

---

1. André Marechal, EC's first boyfriend.

Michael Colvin sidled up to me in the lobby on Wednesday and asked me to come and speak to his 'best ward, where all the money-bags are – next to Southampton Itchen, so it would help Chris Chope, too'. I was gobsmacked – the nerve of the man. Majority 18,000, so it would have been 'no' anyway; if Chris wants me, he can ask himself and has done so in the past. And as I turned to go: 'It would help, of course, Michael, if you hadn't made that remark when we were at Conservative Central Office . . . do you remember?' Of course he did, the swine. And *if* I were ever back in Government, he would come fawning. Such a creep!

House of Commons, Tuesday 16 April, 11.43 p.m.

We are waiting to vote on the Cardiff Bay Barrage Bill, would you believe, and this could go on all night. Here we are with the legislative programme grinding to a halt for lack of business, and virtually nothing available for the Queen's Speech in the autumn, and they expect us to stay up half the night to force through a Bill which – if our antiquated procedures had been reformed – would not have required an Act of Parliament in the first place. Dotty.

If I were to go downstairs to the tea room I would find everyone talking about the Prime Minister. The press had a lovely time during the recess (which ended yesterday) examining the personality of John Major and finding it wanting. The key press material was an appallingly aggressive interview by Brian Walden on TV on Sunday (I was trying to prepare the Sunday lunch at the same time, and managed to burn the beef). Walden went on and ON about dithering, indecisiveness, failure to agree on poll tax, changing his mind, etc. John kept giving the same answer and became eventually very quiet, almost sullen, and defensive. Later his press office said that he was frustrated that Walden asked such a narrow range of questions – almost as though 'he asked the wrong questions'. That was my feeling when I was done by him in the autumn of 1988. But a 'Sunny

Jim' would have dictated the interview and decided the agenda. John convinces by rational discussion and is not used to imposing his personality, certainly not live on TV: the first time he did *Question Time*, for example, was all of nine months after entering the Cabinet. So he appears rattled and out of his depth.

On Monday (last) night *Panorama* tried to do a hatchet job on him, but in my view most of it will have backfired with the electorate, which is impressed by this ambitious young man from a very difficult background. The programme makers found the bungalow where he lived till he was twelve, in the garden of which lay the forlorn remains of the garden gnomes and other ornaments made by the family until the business went bust: wonderful stuff! Robert Atkins[1] talked affectionately about their conversation on a canal boat in 1986, when it began to dawn on John that he might some day be in the running to be leader. They decided that the best approach was not to lean to one side or the other in the party, and to be nice to everyone in order to make no enemies. I suspect John had sussed out that approach long, long before; his whole life from Lambeth days has the waft of an opportunistic silence reflecting tremendous self-discipline, but linked to an engaging, courteous manner. It also implies not having to read or think too deeply about the details of policy, and possibly not clinging to much philosophy at all; but as Margaret used to say, pragmatism is not a policy, and its results can be confusing and erratic.

One perceptive critic on Monday morning commented that John went into the mechanisms of thought well – 'I will consult, and then I will consider the consultations . . .' – but has no great thoughts at the end of it; and I suspect that is true.

---

1.   Then a junior minister; Conservative MP for South Ribble.

The *Panorama* team did establish two things: that John still won't say how many O levels he got. (Why not? Nothing to hide there, surely? Or did he fail and have to take some more than once, so he feels ashamed?) And that he cut corners to become a Lambeth councillor, by using an address he didn't live at, since he was living in Westminster at the time. Pressed at Prime Minister's Questions today, he said he was living over the road at the time, which is even odder: why wasn't he on the register at the correct address? I sneakily rather approved, I must say; I'd prefer to feel that he could do something a bit sharp, than think we had a ruddy saint at our head. But then I'm a cynical old Scouser. I was tickled by his comment in a Radio 1 interview on Monday that he resents the loss of privacy and can't now do even in private what he wants. Don't I know it!

It's now 2.15 a.m.; and I shall stop soon. We had a closure motion an hour ago and lost it: only ninety-seven votes.[1] The whips are around, but laid back as this is private business. I'm still here because the socialists are, mainly; and because there are pangs in going back to that flat and creeping in to bed beside a sleeping man. In some ways, I'm quite happy doing this. At least I'm thinking, and not simply lying awake remembering.

An idea for a novel is forming in my mind and I am curious as to whether it will get itself written and how it will turn out. If I use 'The Journey' as a prologue, I can make the theme deceit and impermanence. A section as a young teenager could follow: relationships with Dad, the deceit of racialism, the let-down of failure and disillusion, and perhaps something nastier happening to pals such as Michelle (pregnant) and Colin (killed in a car crash). These things really happened, of course. The next section could be Oxford in

---

1. A hundred votes are needed for closure of a filibustered debate.

1968, which was an extraordinary year; this and the preceding one would need some research.[1] Then we could switch to – say – London Young Conservatives in the early 1970s and so to the present day, or at least 1988–90 and the change in leader. There's no reason why the main character shouldn't be the mistress of a close companion to the PM, who might be in the running next time. It amused me to make a list of what must be included: a suicide, a rape, adultery, of course; a homosexual vice ring, operated from the Yes lobby of the House of Commons – that's true, too. I have lots of real venues from Chevening to the Banqueting House and a garden party at Buckingham Palace, and I can collect more. The challenge would be to make the book work on several levels, for the main theme would be the unequal way men and women move up, so that the marginally less able chap gets on and the lass doesn't.[2] The setting would be politics, but I don't think the themes would be political. The novel is certainly in my head a lot, but I wouldn't even to try to sell it until I'd written quite a bit.

The chap who is on his feet has been speaking for an hour, and so had the one before him. It looks as if Labour are making a determined attempt to talk the Bill out. (If they try hard enough, they will lose their supply day tomorrow, on the NHS.) I do so hate people who are opposed to change like that, who carp and whinge and moan while growth and development move elsewhere: then they want to know why unemployment is so much higher, why there is more poverty, in their areas. Perhaps in the end that's why I stay here until ridiculously late, to oppose that sort of attitude. I hope we get the Bill through eventually.

P.S. Around 4.30 there was another vote, a closure which we lost (fifty-two votes). After further debate, the Government announced it

---

1. Much of this plot was incorporated into EC's novel *She's Leaving Home*.
2. Incorporated into EC's novels *A Parliamentary Affair* and *A Woman's Place*.

would take over the Bill, which did, after all, involve £300 million of public money. A real victory for common sense.

House of Commons, Thursday 25 April, 7 p.m.

Yuk, I feel grotty. Bad period today, very crampy, a couple of days late: so debilitating. I met Audrey Wise[1] in the corridor yesterday all plastered up. She fell and broke her wrist, for the second time, so now she has to go for a bone scan and then possibly HRT. I joked that she could end up looking like Teresa Gorman and she was suitably horrified! I am *not* keen on more hormone treatment – swallowed quite enough pills in my life, thank you – but don't like feeling sick and dizzy either. Or creaky and wizened.

By Tuesday we were into Heseltine's replacement for poll tax. Grudgingly, and after much perusal, I've concluded that it's bloody good. Based on seven bands (to cover whole country – of course, five is enough in any one patch) of capital values (to be estimated by estate agents working for Inland Revenue, but that means no register needed, and no updating). Top band up to two-thirds higher than average, bottom up to two-thirds lower, so range is two and a half times. Take total spend net of all grants, divide up according to percentage of households in each band, etc., and there's your charge. Single people, students, student nurses, etc., automatically 25 per cent off, and nil for income support. This will reduce the amount of faffing around to be done by councils, so costs will be 40 per cent lower than community charge. I'll be paying twice the average and nearly four times as much as a widow in a little house. Labour's 'Fair Rates' scheme presented figures not far off, so we probably pitched it about right, even though we claimed *their* reduction wasn't possible (it is).

---

1.   Labour MP for Preston.

The best event of the week was Hatchard's 'Authors of the Year' drinks party, in the attractive setting of the Martini Terrace at New Zealand House near Trafalgar Square. No agents (I thought Hilary might be there) and no business talk. P. D. James, now Baroness, a lovely cheery lady – I'll get to know her better, I hope. Beryl Bainbridge, skinny and smoky and grubby teeth, but bright-eyed and interesting, telling me about trying to save the Liverpool Playhouse – it had sixty-three administrators before it employed a single actor! She was an Assistant Stage Manager in the days when my parents went regularly. Jilly Cooper, slim and giggly and very attractive in olive green silk, and her overweight husband, Leo Cooper. Frank Muir and Robin Day (now deaf, so difficult to talk to; and he booms back, so no possibility of private gossip!). The actor Ian Tomlinson, stuck in an armchair because he is paralysed now, calling me over and kissing my hand and talking Tory politics. Pretty dark-lashed lady with blue mascara and nice husband: she is the Royal Family's current press secretary, so not clear why she was there. Going down in the lift with John Mortimer: large and tall and mouth like a bull-dog's, slobbery and with teeth in the wrong place, but sharp mind and little beady eyes and surprising high voice; and in the other corner, Penelope Lively, tall county Hampstead and tatty hair, just like her heroines. I'm glad I met her too, as her work is so appealing.

The story about Steve Norris's affair with the journalist Sheila Gunn in the *People* is a damp squib: most people are treating it as 'nobody's business but yours'. Sheila was quoted as saying she and Steve are in love, and, yes, planning a future together. I doubt it, somehow; I suspect Vicky[1] has money and Steve is not stupid enough to spend on two households if not required to do so by law! He looked subdued all week, but turned up to events and yesterday

1. Mrs Norris.

convened a very interesting meeting which culminated in the for-
mation of the Conservative Parliamentary Group on Homosexual
Law Reform. He wrote to fifty to sixty colleagues, carefully chosen,
about reducing the age of consent for gays from twenty-one to eighteen. I've already written about this in *Today*, and would like same
age for all sexes. And it's still an offence at any age in the armed
forces, which is stupid. As far as I'm concerned, the state should stay
out of people's lives, provided there's no coercion or abuse: and
should encourage everyone to be responsible, tolerant and caring.
That includes gays. I tried this philosophy on James Cran over
dinner, very tentatively, and he admitted to being a homophobe, so
I dropped all ideas of seducing him, even though he is jolly attractive! For the record, those who turned up were John Wheeler,[1] John
Bowis, Michael Brown,[2] Robin Squire (as expected), Rob Hayward
and several others: nice bunch, and now all willing to catch the
more tolerant mood of the country and take advantage of John
Major's known sympathetic views.

Then there was a drink with the Chief Whip Richard Ryder,
skinny and youthful-looking too, hiding behind owlish glasses,
drinking Diet Coke (how amazing – whips are supposed to have iron
livers!) and pacing around a bit because of a bad back. I still don't
know what that was about. So why do you want to see me, I asked,
as the bell rang to vote after twenty minutes' gossip on the economy,
on John, on the council tax, etc. Just to gossip, he said. Ah, but had
he asked: are you happy Edwina, are you occupied, do you want to
tell me anything, he might have had a much more interesting conversation. Last week in the tea room David Lightbown said suddenly,
'You're on your way back', which made me think the whips have
been talking about me: how I loathe the obliqueness of every con-

---

1. Conservative MP for Westminster North.
2. Conservative MP for Brigg and Cleethorpes.

versation here! David is a big tease and you can't tell if he's trying genuinely to tell you something.

Well now: my gut ache has gone, but my back is giving me gyp – is that an improvement? So much effort is going into keeping Derbyshire at bay these days. Last week I kept a check of all the letters (and a few cards) which I signed. Of course, much of what I receive goes into the bin, some read. And much is dealt with by phone. Few nonconstituents get a proper reply, so there's a built-in bias: but I signed 235 letters in a light week (no campaigns, no 'death' or 'wedding' letters): of which 60 were personal to me, including 21 diary, 23 political/personal, 12 media, 4 charities; 143 were to constituents on constituency matters (NHS 16, community charge 11, schools 9, agriculture 7, planning 18 etc.); and 32 were to constituents on nonconstituency matters, such as the Ukraine, abortion and share ownership, bits and bobs. I feel I have thousands of children to look after, taking lots of time, offering virtually no stimulus, needing my help (or do they?) and leaving me very tired at the end of each day, each week. I do hope that, like having children, this is only a stage in my life, and not its culmination.

The novel is taking shape in my head. If there's an October election I could get a lot done in the summer – then either I will have a new job or I will sign a book contract, and concentrate on getting it done for autumn 1992. I would like that, actually. A book on Europe still takes my fancy, but maybe that could 'ride' with it – if Labour gets in, I will need to take any cash in fiscal year 1991–2 or it will be much more heavily taxed. I hope they don't!

Victoria, Tuesday 7 May, 10.59 p.m.

We have a whole batch of new lords, working peers, five each side: first time Labour has ever had parity, as Margaret Thatcher didn't believe in fairness. Ours include Jean Denton, former racing driver and frequent Tory feminist, and Detta O'Cathain, former head of the

Milk Marketing Board and currently struggling to turn the concrete dump of the Barbican into a thriving tourist attraction. I didn't even realise she was a Tory. And they will all be ministers in no time, according to the press briefings from Number 10.[1] Perhaps if I had stayed in Birmingham . . .

I've just come back from Scotland with a very upset tum: something I ate, probably those prawn sandwiches at lunchtime in Glasgow airport, though the 'orrible smell suggests H_2S and therefore eggs . . . ! I like egg sandwiches very much, but I wouldn't put it past the bug to attack me – of course, they don't know I'm their sworn enemy . . . People still go on so about the eggs business to me (except in Derbyshire where I've carved out a range of different subjects – in two years we have moved on somewhat, thank goodness). A letter from a Mrs Smith, headmistress in John Gummer's constituency, asked him to prevail on me to speak at her school as 'a controversial woman: a Jew married to a Christian' . . . 'and then there's the salmonella and eggs business' . . . ! Maybe I was too sensitive in finding her letter offensive, but it would be nice to be described as 'interesting – a good speaker – a charming and intelligent person', etc.

A strange tale was told to me in the dining room tonight by Robin Maxwell-Hislop, the retiring member for Tiverton. He won the seat at a by-election in 1960, caused by the resignation of Derick Heathcoat-Amory from both Chancellor of the Exchequer *and* his seat, a great mystery. When Robin Maxwell-Hislop came in, he asked Alan Lennox-Boyd (who preceded Macleod as Colonial Secretary) for the story as he wanted to defend his predecessor; and was told in great secrecy that so strong was the feeling against Macmillan in the party in the spring of 1960 – barely months after a spectacular General Election success in 1959, so presumably following the

---

1. Baroness Denton became a Government whip in 1991 and Parliamentary Under-Secretary of State, Department of Trade and Industry, in 1992.

'winds of change' speech in February 1960 – that Alan Lennox-Boyd and two Cabinet colleagues went to see Heathcoat-Amory and invited him to join a plot to oust Macmillan and take his place. The Chancellor, horrified that he could be the focus and magnet for such dissent, showed them the door, went to see Macmillan and resigned on the spot! He ended up as High Commissioner for Canada. The identity of the other two plotters, also in the Cabinet, was kept a secret by Lennox-Boyd. What a very dotty story. The young Heathcoat-Amory and Lennox-Boyd *fils* are both junior ministers now and neither too brilliant. It transpires that Churchill appointed Heathcoat-Amory as Minister of Pensions in 1957 because he thought he was related to Leo Amery . . . even dottier!

Tower House, Friday 17 May, 12.40 a.m.

Waiting for the results of the Monmouth by-election, expected in about an hour. A coachload of Tory MPs went last Thursday and came back looking puzzled – couldn't read it at all. Our 9350 majority looks very vulnerable. The late MP, Sir John Stradling Thomas, had been due to retire anyway: an old alcoholic, he used to creep around the Members' Cloakroom looking for his peg, cigarette tottering ash in his hand, a watery smile and gravelly comment the only sign of life. Pitiable really: the obituaries suggested a once-vibrant figure. His replacement, a London solicitor, booms away in true Thatcherite fashion, raising groans, a living reminder of how far we have come since last autumn. But if a big ship changes direction, the foaming wake heading elsewhere remains visible long after the turn is complete. Polls at the weekend suggested Labour well ahead and us second. *Real* gloom would descend if we were pushed into third place.[1]

1. Labour won the by-election with 17,733 votes; the Conservatives were second with 15,327 and Liberal Democrats third.

Jacques Delors[1] suggested this week that a Commons vote could be written into the treaty on the single currency, if that made the British feel happier. The implication is that we could sign up in principle but have our vote way into the future – not 'if' but 'when'. The Bruges Group[2] smell a rat, of course! John Major's problem is to ensure no rows before the election, hence another compelling reason for going in October. The Euro barometer polls show the British increasingly in favour of further unity, however; so the problem is not for the electorate but for whichever party fails to offer a positive attitude towards Europe.

Meanwhile much happening on the Currie front. I appear to be a national hero all over again, or anyway heroine. Peter Carter-Ruck kept sending me bills, so eventually I got fed up and sweetly refused to pay any more till the case was in court. Hey presto! The case came up on Monday 13th/Tuesday 14th. And I won! I can hardly believe it. It was only afterwards that I realised I'd been gambling around £50,000 (costs), and perhaps Carter-Ruck should have advised me not to bother. I got costs, an apology in court and a modest £5000 damages on top, but I'm not complaining, as any larger sum would have produced snide remarks in Derbyshire. As it was, even this small sum produced snide remarks in *The Times*, but I can live with those. George Carman QC appeared for the *Observer* and was very nasty: but no worse, though more sustained, than the unpleasantries of the Commons, so I could stand up to that fairly well. He'd lost interest by the end – his forte is crunching witnesses and he did not succeed with me. He doesn't lose very often and charged about five times as much as my chap, Richard Hartley, who was sweet and a bit slow. I'm not sure these guys are all they are cracked up to be – they

---

1. President of the European Commission.
2. A group set up to resist the UK's further integration with the European Union, named after Margaret Thatcher's 1988 speech.

don't seem to think out the questions too carefully beforehand. Carman was all aggression and Hartley jovial bumble. Judge Drake was wonderful: kind and precise and easy to follow, and he virtually instructed the jury to find in my favour, and to give 'modest' damages, as all I'd wanted was a retraction and apology, which came from both sleek Donald Trelford[1] and sly Carman in open court. Trelford's 'I am very sorry' was spat out at the end of his evidence in response to a question from Hartley; and Carman apologised on behalf of the *Observer*, Trelford and himself, saying that no impugning my honour was intended, etc. Trelford was horrid and deserved to lose: arrogant little man, so conceited. So now we have reams of newspaper and TV coverage. Why all the interest? Partly a thin week, partly the two of us, so rarely seen together in public, walking into the Old Bailey holding hands: Ray was wonderful! MPs on all sides were delighted – for them it's a blow against the press, bearing in mind that very few MPs feel able to sue and even fewer win, and often those who do win are left with dodgy reputations. In the end, absolutely by chance, I got lucky: a libel not so blatant it produced an immediate apology, not so oblique it didn't matter – and very dear to the public, hence all the sympathy. Nice feeling.

A pen portrait of Carter-Ruck shows a character out of Dickens: spidery, narrow bodied, dusty, not quite shaven, with odd whiskers at strange angles on his cheeks and watery flickering eyes and a soft whistling confidential voice; he kept whispering in court but I couldn't understand him. His ancient black jacket is coming apart at the seams . . . Not, in the end, a figure to inspire confidence, though maybe affection. If he drives a huge blue Rolls with personalised number plate, why doesn't he buy a new suit? His junior partner on this, Lindsay Moffatt, was quite impressive (except she kept calling

1. Editor of the *Observer*.

him Mr Carter-Ruck, which seemed unctuous). She graduated with a First from Manchester in 1985, and it's to the credit of Carter-Ruck that, of nine new partners, four are female. Hartley's brief was Tom Shields, aged thirty-five to forty: something wrong with him, I thought, as he seemed so restless.

'Les Tuileries', Sunday 26 May, 10 p.m.

In the new house in France – sitting in the kitchen under a naked light bulb, tapping away on the kitchen table because it's the only one in the house! I had forgotten just how primitive an empty or new house can be. This reminds me of Ray's camping out in Banbury Road during the three-day week, back in 1973–4. He lived in one bare room – we couldn't get the carpet delivered for months – and I cheered him up at weekends with daffodils in a jam jar. I managed to get pregnant with Debbie there, so we must have been doing something right.

I realise how long it is since I did any housework, and how distinctly it turns me off. The last thing I want to do this holiday is spend all my time with a duster in my hand, but it will take a lot of self-discipline to get anything else done.

I came across reasonably well in *Any Questions* from Formby near Liverpool on Friday night, but I had no luck at other engagements for the party, at Gainsborough, for example, and last week at a miserable dinner-dance at the new Hilton Hotel on the M1 for the Castle Donington branch of the North-West Leicestershire Tories. David Ashby had pulled out on the Tuesday, but really he should have been there; I don't see why I should have to put up with his constituents' wrath if he won't. He got rid of the agent, the chairman and most of the influential workers, and thinks he can run the constituency from London with a computer. But he is such a lazy beggar I doubt if he is even doing that well. The dinner was black tie at £20 per head, and not surprisingly was not well attended. A fair number were outsiders, mainly from Kent, who got drunk and abusive (they had come as guests of locals). I had a horrible sore throat – as usual, and now virtually a permanent problem – and the microphone could not compete against a loud humming from both the air conditioning and the disco equipment. I've had enough solid trifle, too. Perfectly ghastly evening.

I should record that some of my own lot were cross with me, following publication of an 'interview' in the *Sun* last Saturday week. I had lunch with a young local journalist, who turned out to be unreliable; for I do not remember being taped by him, and hope I wouldn't have been so harsh in my judgements of both Margaret and John had I realised I was being taped. I certainly did not give him permission to run stories in the *Sun*; but the quotes were accurate, so I decided just to ignore the piece. It would be much easier if I gave no interviews at all – nor met journalists for lunch or whatever. But generally I'm not wary enough of such people – they have a job to do, and some are friends – or are they? I have to decide soon whether to ask David Seymour and his girlfriend Helena for lunch or supper at the Commons, as I promised to do before I left *Today* – but perhaps he will come wired too, so it might be better to drop it. On the other hand, maybe I lose someone who is a friend, or could be. Muddle . . .

All this business of swimming around in a small pond in Derbyshire does get me down. I don't feel as if I have used my brain for ages. There's another row simmering in Westminster about Europe, and it throws my dilemma into sharp focus. In December decisions will be taken about economic and monetary union, for the rest of the EC want them. That means more power, of a sort, for the European Parliament. The public believe that it means less for Westminster, but in my view it only highlights and formalises the power already lost some time ago from the green benches. We lost it to the executive, i.e. the Government, which requires only the occasional endorsement of its policies and for the rest is content to smile benignly and take no notice. The whips use patronage in the most traditional manner to guarantee a majority – virtually every minister has a PPS these days. When I think of the row when I tried to get one between three junior ministers in DHSS! The effect of these changes, which have been going on for some time, is that the only people with any power anywhere in the EC are members of the various Councils of Ministers, and the Commission. I'm a member of neither. Even MEPs seem to have more influence. I don't want to spend the next ten years debating dangerous dogs and John Major's tedious ideas for a Citizens' Charter – nor looking at the back of his head.

Caring for South Derbyshire is definitely not a demanding intellectual job, though it does take energy and leaves little time for anything else. How in heaven's name am I to write an even moderately respectable novel if I can't settle down for six months, free of all distractions, and concentrate? I don't want to write a bad or under-researched one, and really I could do with the money this coming year, so I can't take too long over it. I do have an idea of writing the progress, or lack of it, of someone like me, an alter ego perhaps; and it could form part of a trilogy, for it would be interesting to have someone like my father as hero of a second, and my grandfather for a third. That would trace such a family from the old country right through a century later to the European context again, but golly it would require some research, and when am I supposed to have time?

House of Commons, Monday 10 June, 11.20 p.m.

Waiting to vote, as ever. And a complete waste of time. Today is the guillotined Bill on Dangerous Dogs. Following the savaging of a little girl by a fighting dog, Kenneth Baker leapt into action with a 'shoot to kill' policy. He rubbished all suggestions about muzzling, etc. (I'd shoot 'em – first thoughts were best), and then backed off, until today's Bill, which is a pale shadow of the original proposals. What we are really waiting for is a whipped vote at 1.00 a.m. on Janet Fookes' registration scheme. I'm tempted to slip off home before the vote.

The party chairman is now saying there won't be an autumn election (so I'll clear off to France instead of travelling to a wet, cold, dirty, expensive Blackpool for the Party Conference. Just to check the house is still there, of course). The electoral and economic timetables are now badly out of line. Unemployment will go on growing all autumn, with bad figures again expected this week. Inflation *is* coming down, but this isn't because of falling prices, it's just that many prices are rising less fast than this time last year. *Some* prices, e.g. seasonal food, anything with VAT and petrol inputs, and fuel bills after a hard winter, have been up considerably compared with ordinary people's expectations, thus reducing our credibility even more: we boast, and they count the change in their purses. So the April rise in pensions has been swallowed by price rises already. Only in the spring of '92, by which time we will have had a housing recession for three and a half years, will things pick up, and possibly not even then. It's not enough that housing prices have stabilised, since many families' income has dropped as bonuses and overtime have disappeared, and lots of companies are taking advantage of the climate to introduce pay freezes. So *either* prices must fall further or recovery will take longer. All of which puts our backs to the wall for summer '92 and increases the chances of a very close result. Indeed, I really think we will lose this one.

John Major had in another batch of MPs and prospective parliamentary candidates to have our photos taken on Thursday. The whole episode was quite bizarre: about eighty people crammed into the stuffy little basement, all invited to come at once like some badly run NHS clinic. John late, tired-looking, bashful, taking his cue from each candidate instead of the other way round (David

Curry[1] brought local cheese for the photo – smart, that!). I asked him, 'You OK?' He hesitated a split second, then said 'Yes, fine', but did not sound it. The Sunday papers described him as looking 'spaced out', and I suspect he is not sleeping with worry. Norma told a magazine he does his red boxes in bed and makes a lot of noise about it, so he goes to bed and then . . . ? Must be working late, and getting up early and so . . . He certainly looks as if he has lost all his confidence.

One problem is that he's trying to square the circle on Europe. We are close to decisions on currency union and all the other countries are going to sign up. Six have already got rid of border controls, anticipating 1992, and are linked to the DM (except France, of course). Britain is proposing a model called the pillars, in which the Council of Ministers is on top and the pillars upholding the roof are: (1) EC economic policy, together with European Parliament; (2) interaction at national level between other groups of ministers, e.g. interior/justice ministers on a common immigration policy; and (3) the WEU for defence and political cooperation on security matters. The Commission would be reduced to civil servants, federalism would be pushed away. The trouble is, as I told Tristan Garel-Jones at the Foreign Office on Wednesday, this leaves no role for elected members, either at Westminster or at the European Parliament: it is a straightforward transfer of power from the Commission to ministers, most of whom are appointed, not elected or serving MPs like (most of) ours, and often only vaguely answerable to their parliaments, which may be weak shifting coalitions. Chancellor Kohl says that Europe's electorate will be loath to elect another European Parliament in 1994 unless we increase its powers. I hope he is wrong in that sense, but while I can see why our ministers like the model

1. Minister of State at the Ministry of Agriculture, Fisheries and Food; Conservative MP for Skipton and Ripon; MEP for Essex North-East, 1979–89.

they are proposing, I don't like it at all: if we are to clip the Commission's wings, then increasing the power of Euro MPs to check and balance the action of the Council of Ministers seems wisest. That's not far from a system which has stood the test of time in the USA: the main and obvious social difference is one language. Pity that the label 'federalist' arouses such ill feeling – it's not half a bad model *minus* an elected President, which we do not need. Or pledges to the flag, etc. But any such changes are anathema to the Bruges Group, led in Parliament by the most peculiar Bill Cash[1] – tall, shambling, unbelievably pompous, persistent and maddening. He fancies himself as leader of an anti-Europe faction in the party after we've lost the election, I'm sure, with Margaret Thatcher hovering benignly on his shoulder. This group won't accept *any* change and will persistently try to trap John and stop him making progress. The rest of us, exasperated, keep mum in order to help John. Were there free votes on Europe, the Commons would give a more federalist future a big majority. The fuss will rumble on till 1994, and John will be very lucky if it is not a big issue in 1992. But if it isn't, there's a great big hole where our policy and its driving edge ought to be. And we footle around, talking about bloody dogs!

Victoria, Saturday 15 June, 12 noon

Yesterday I did a lunch (Cambridge), followed by tea and an evening meeting with a buffet in Gill Shephard's constituency, where the majority is 20,000 and they've never seen a socialist. The audiences ranged from forty at Cambridge to 140 at the tea, out in Malcolm Moss's lovely garden, and nearly two hundred in Thetford, where the huge hall was arranged as for an adoption meeting, row upon row,

---

1. Conservative MP for Stafford; a prominent Eurosceptic.

table up on the platform with flowers, water and microphone. Same questions everywhere: impact of high interest rates/lack of demand in high street, all very parochial – for 'small business' read 'small shops'. And the NHS, and worries over Europe and how we couldn't possibly get rid of our currency because that would mean giving up the Queen, wouldn't it? My God, Margaret Thatcher has a lot to answer for. Yet they were very receptive to a 'vision of Europe' approach, appropriately on a day when Yeltsin was voted President of Russia and the newly re-elected Mayor of Moscow pronounced that 'communism is dead'. That's what Europe is all about, I told them – keeping dictatorships out. As every other country in Europe has been either occupied or a dictatorship or both, the Continentals feel passionately that the EC is their guarantee of freedom and self-determination. That's why they want us in, too: and so we must be there. It's a viewpoint which turns on its head the usual British approach of 'What's in it for us?' and 'What are those nasty Europeans doing to us?' These party workers were very receptive and listened carefully.

I've just come back from a very stimulating trip to Strasbourg (where I was amused to discover that languages don't matter a jot!). I'm beginning to feel obsessive about Europe. Repeatedly, this week, I've contrasted the trivia we deal with at Westminster with the mind-boggling scale and ambition of the European Parliament. The changes being debated and negotiated between John and other leaders *must* lead to an increase in the power and influence of MEPs; while British backbenchers lack any. Add the ignorance of the Brits about what is on the agenda in Europe – I had a go at that sweetie Bill Newton Dunn[1] about the newsletter the European Democratic Group has started to send out to British Tory MPs – it goes on and

---

1. Conservative MEP for Lincolnshire; Deputy Leader of the European Democratic Group (EDG).

on about sausages and flavoured potato crisps, whereas the European Parliament is debating (as we saw) Albania, Ethiopia, the Baltic States; and is in a position to influence what happens there. The new countries want to join the EC, and that means they listen respectfully to MEPs (at least according to them!). Bill protested that trivia was what filled the UK press and their postbags. So educate the public, I said: help them understand what is going on here.

Decisions taken this week: (1) I will go to the European Parliament and will almost certainly try in '94 (apparently several safe seats are coming up); (2) I'll fight Westminster in '92 and possibly the one after that, but shan't be in Westminster by the end of the decade. If John Major ever fulfils his promise to give me a Government job, it had better be good (Treasury, FCO or his office) or I will turn it down. I wonder if I have the nerve to hint that he owes me something, even vice-chair of the party?; (3) I won't accept any more invites (except friends . . .) to speak at Tory dos; and (4) I will get a novel going this summer. So the future is looking clearer . . .

Victoria, Monday 1 July, midnight

I've done all I can in South Derbyshire – helping with Toyota and the road and the Ivanhoe line[1] and getting new land brought into use and talking up the neighbourhood till our unemployment at 4.9 per cent is amongst the lowest in the country. Add to that a good result for the party in 1992. I could go on solving the same sorts of problems here forever, but I'd be *so* bored. Then there are the other considerations: the MEPs certainly have more clout than British backbench MPs and are pushing for more – the transfer of power is

---

1. A new rail service from Leicester to Stoke, running through EC's South Derbyshire constituency.

all one way. They talk about more interesting subjects over a much wider field than we do, and more to come as Europe grows. Today's efforts to sort out Yugoslavia (going through a bloody break-up) show how the EC can act together – the UK couldn't have done that. Then there is the question of what I would leave behind: health and salmonella, both of which I loathe. As for eggs, I'm constantly asked my views on food safety, labelling, animal husbandry, etc., and really I have none, other than hoping that what I feed my family won't make them ill. I can't imagine campaigning on health or food, and refuse most invites to talk about either. Yet when I'm out, that's what I get all the time. I'd like to be part of a team, which I suspect is easier amongst the much smaller British MEP group than in the Commons. I do feel very sidelined here: no job, no role and nothing but backbiting and jealousy from twats jockeying for unimportant positions! The accommodation and the hours look infinitely better. I should be able to lead a more normal life in Europe, with the blessing of anonymity when I go out to eat or shopping. I might even find a lover – someone dashing, Continental and wealthy. A chance would be a fine thing, but who knows?

Most of all I don't want to continue wasting my time, trying to get in a question even to junior ministers and failing, chairmen of make-work committees being called first. I'm fed up with turning up on Fridays as requested by the whips, speech in hand, to find I'm not going to be called till 2.15 p.m., which means missing the 3 p.m. train, just because some fat oaf has droned on at the Dispatch Box for forty minutes. That happened in the local government debate on 21 June; I had a feeling I was wasting my time. I arrived at 9.30 a.m., be told gaily by Betty Boothroyd[1] that there were only six speakers on my side and of course I'd get my question in. By 2 p.m. only two

1. Deputy Speaker; Labour MP for West Bromwich West.

backbenchers on my side had spoken (plus a statement). God, what a yawn – what a pointless, silly exercise. Nothing I could do in Europe could be as silly and empty as that. And not even a word of apology from the whips.

'Les Tuileries', Sunday 28 July, 11.15 p.m.

I'm beat, but I have to write something! It's warm and quiet as I write in the kitchen; the only sounds are a glass rattling gently inside the fridge as it vibrates and a moth throwing itself against the light. The house is beginning to look lovely. Lucette has been religiously watering everything so the roses are a mass of colour, and the window boxes and pots are blazing away in pink and red, impatiens and petunia.

I received an estimate of 35,000 francs (£3500) for some internal painting and decided instead to do most of it myself. I don't have the money!

I spent an hour or two discussing tactics with Hilary. The publishing world is in dire straits, but he seemed amenable to my long-held idea, of a book of short stories *first* (we've sold seven now) and a novel to follow. If we go with the novel first, everyone will expect something different – a Julian Critchley or Roy Hattersley perhaps. 'Noncommercial' was what Hilary called my idea of tracing a young woman from 1963/4 through '68 to the modern day: my problem is making her more sympathetic than I am!

I've been reading a lot of political stuff recently, including a couple of books about John Major. Bruce Anderson's biography is a fun-packed, blow-by-blow account of Major's election campaigning, weak on his character (too adulatory) and on the other campaigns (only one paragraph on each), but first class on Margaret Thatcher's failings. By contrast, Edward Pearce is excellent on the young Major but thoroughly slapdash on the leadership contest. There's a collection by the Press Association taken from their pre-1990 cuttings file (no by-line) with almost illegible photos, a very poor piece of work; and lastly a breathy book by Nesta Wyn Ellis who has been hyping it for all she's worth. She reckons the Majors have rows and that John's very sexy. The book has upset Norma very much, and no wonder.

Everyone on our side at Westminster is convinced the election will be next summer and that we will win. The economy seems to be turning back up again, or at least not getting any worse. There's still talk of November, but I doubt it – that's designed to tire Labour out by keeping them on full alert. During the summer Cabinet ministers are taking only two weeks' holidays, and all departments must have a minister on duty; that's being touted as evidence of readiness, new broom, etc., but it's a bit of clever PR, because departments are always like that in holiday time. Shades of ruining my holiday with the kids in North Yorkshire three years ago, while Ken Clarke and David Mellor were sunning themselves – that did rankle, as it never occurred to Ken that having young children made a difference.

'Les Tuileries', Sunday 11 August, 7 p.m.

Hot, sunny, dry day; spent this morning partly at the *marché des puces* along the riverside at Montsoreau, pottering about and pricing things; came away disappointed, for everything I need (like a bath-room cabinet) was both tatty and expensive. I'll be better off going to MFI at home. Still, it was enjoyable to see a real flea market: such junk, most of it, though fun – an old accordion minus its keys; else-where a complete set of white only piano keys, real ivory; a huge brass telescope; old photo albums with some photos still in; and old music, horns, rocking chairs, school desks, wardrobes and whole beds, and every kind of old chair with the stuffing falling out. To make most of it worthwhile and usable, you'd need a lot of time, knowledge and patience – and a fair bit of money for materials, even after you'd got it home.

Ray has been here in Mouliherne for the last week, and as usual when we are together on holiday it hasn't been a great success. He never really lets go of home, trailing off to Tours to get the newspapers, listening to the cricket endlessly on Radio 4. He moans about the weather – it's always too hot, or it's still raining! And he is not noticeably relaxed or charming. The bonhomie he exhibits at home, and especially with his mates, seems to desert him when he's with me on holiday, so we spend hours together with him morose and not speaking. By Thursday night I'd had enough (he arrived on Saturday night), and laid into him somewhat after we had spent two hours in a restaurant with him not saying a word. He was friendlier for a while after that, but by last night we were both reading over a meal at Napoleon in the Place Bilange in Saumur: how can you do that in France, where a meal is an excuse for lively conversation? So when he announced that he was going racing at Deauville today and would then be catching the ferry home a day early, I don't think either of us felt like arguing about it.

To be truthful, I like my own space, and I can't work when he's here – while he's restless, bored and unhappy. I suspect that we have stayed married for so long simply because we don't see that much of each other, and come together mostly for family matters. Conversation and intellectual stimulus we get from other people. How I do envy some of those other people their warmth and friendship.

I have to steel myself tomorrow to phone Lisa at A. P. Watt and find out whether the two stories I've written on commission for *Living* magazine are acceptable or not. She has always been telling me to let go, not be inhibited, so we'll see (I hate this waiting – like exam results). The *Daily Express* wants to do an article on this house, but I'm skint after paying all these lawyers, so I said cough up first – and so far, no go. I'd like to write for the *Express* regularly: I could use the income. I have another commission to do a piece for the *Financial Times* on heaven and hell, and mean to get on with it after supper and watering the garden!

I'm supposed to be starting the novel and am scared stiff. I got lots of research stuff from the Colindale newspaper library, what a peculiar little place; they wanted to charge me the earth for photocopies and then I realised I could get them for free via the House of Commons Library. It worked, too – even posted to France. So I have no excuses left. If I want Hilary Rubinstein to go chase a contract for both short stories and the novel, I have to give him something to sell. And I need the money, so there's a fine incentive; I can't live on my parliamentary salary any more, at least not till one of our children has finished full-time education and got a job. Meanwhile, I've been reading: Julie Birchill's novel *Ambition*, which is just porn with a bit of feminism thrown in; and Bernard Ingham's autobiography, *Kill the Messenger*. He is best on his early years in Yorkshire and reporting the activities of the TUC for the *Guardian*. The later pages are entertaining when he is rude about people such as Nigel Lawson, but it has been heavily censored. He has the grace to apologise to both Francis Pym and John Biffen[1] for his off-the-cuff remarks – had he been a minister those few words would have led to his resignation – don't I know! – but he got away with it, because Margaret was happy to let him speak her thoughts, particularly the scurrilous ones, for her. In the end, as he fails to realise, she had made enough enemies, and disgusted enough people with these boorish and arrogant ways, to lose the friends necessary at her hour of need.

It all seems terribly passé now, reading the stories of the 1980s. Yet there was an inspiration, a sparkle, that British politics has lost. There have been more policy statements coming out in recent weeks, more White Papers promised, but it is all very dull and

---

1. In 1987 Ingham, briefing a group of political journalists, compared Pym, then Leader of the House, to the *ITMA* radio comedy programme character Mona Lott. In similar circumstances four years later Ingham referred to Biffen, Pym's successor, as 'a semi-detached member of the Government'.

worthy stuff. Not even the excitement of a minor reshuffle, for the first time in years. The Citizens' Charter fails to ignite a spark in my chest, I am sorry to say. We are not slaying dragons any more, just cleaning up the shit they leave behind. John Major continues in the polls way ahead of Kinnock, and the Tories trail Labour by a steady five points. That means the voters are still inclined to punish us for the mess of poll tax – this year proving even more uncollectable than last, so yet more money will have to be provided from the Exchequer, exactly the opposite of what was supposed to happen – and the economy, which still faces real problems, with the car industry now talking about big lay-offs and the banks and other institutions reporting huge write-offs for bad debts. I have a feeling we will pay the price, losing rather a lot of seats come the election. That could mean a hung parliament, or winning by only a short head. And the niggling little thought at the back of my mind is this: that I'm not sure it will make much difference who wins.

'Les Tuileries', Monday 19 August, 9.10 a.m.

Living magazine was 'delighted' with the revenge story entitled 'Teenager', so that's my second sale in a month, since *Woman* have taken 'Mother's Day' for next March (though that means they won't take any others before then). The *Daily Express* took my article about Teresa Gorman and gave a whole page to it; I've submitted a piece for the weekend *Financial Times*, but have to phone (today maybe) to find out if it's OK. The novel has got itself started and I can at least see a framework. It's fun to do, after the initial pain of the first day, when I was all prepared to call it off. It was so damn difficult letting go, both in terms of language and length: I haven't written anything with a 'page twenty' on it for more than two years. I'll try to get the earliest part of the book, up to the scholarship in December 1964, done this week; then there's a lot of revision and tidying up before I can hope to give it to Hilary in October. The rest would take almost twice as long, so we're not talking about a finished text before the end of 1992. I'd rather take my time over it, and do less chasing about the country speaking.

On board ferry to Portsmouth, Wednesday 28 August, 12.30 a.m.

Susie got two As for her French and Maths GCSE, which is super: she sounded very cocky on the phone from the USA and returns to UK tomorrow on the overnight plane. Deb got a B in her OA German and seemed to think that's OK. I don't think she'll be lining up any As for next summer. As for me, the *Financial Times* have accepted the piece on heaven and hell, but so far only sixty pages (approximately fifteen thousand words) of the novel have materialised, and I did very little last week. I can 'see my way' to thirty thousand, so I'd better get on with it, but I'm not too satisfied with myself. Deadlines and obligations suit me fine: I work much better that way. However, I've done much decorating in the house – kitchen and study finished, one coat on the beams in the stable room, and (wonderful) one complete coat on the staircase, which looks fabulous.

Tower House, Tuesday 3 September, 10 p.m.

Messing around on the kitchen table. Last night I cleared it of several months' accumulated junk which I shifted either into the bin bag or upstairs, into my 'study'. The dates on the rubbish up there indicated that I haven't used that properly since last summer, I suppose because if I work in the kitchen at least I'm close to the action and not so far from the phone.

I spent last week tackling the garden, which has grown – so have the grass and weeds – but on the whole looks much better, with many of the gaps satisfactorily filled. I can now see which bits have good natural water supplies, such as the south-facing wall of the pool room, where everything seems to have taken off, with the clematis reaching the roofline (no flowers though). Other areas are as dry as a bone, so in order to prepare them better for our 'dos' at the end of the month I've weeded and watered. After September they can fend for themselves!

Running through my mind is the possibility of getting to France in October and taking Chris with me; then I might just tell her a tale or two. Can I trust her – not now, but in ten or twenty years' time? I wonder what she would make of it all. I watch John Major flying round the world, collecting accolades wherever he goes; he's back up to 58 per cent approval rates in the UK opinion polls, still way ahead of Kinnock and now of Ashdown, too.

I did a bit more writing of the novel this afternoon and find I get into it very happily now. I think it has a life of its own. I read Julian Critchley's *Hung Parliament* last week – it really is crap, and unpleasant, too. I did not take to being in it every third page.[1] It's not even a good detective novel – he might have asked his publishers for a plot if he couldn't manage one himself. And he has a contract for a second one. Ugh: it left an unpleasant taste in the mouth. On the other hand there is Ian McEwan, who may be a conceited chap from the articles I read about him when *The Innocent* came out last year, but who writes like a dream; I think I'll devour him for a while and hope it will rub off. After some urging Ray has joined the Quality Paperback Book Club, so I shall be reading more good stuff – this month I've ordered a Jane Gardam novel, and a pile including Umberto Eco, Angela Carter and Rosamond Lehmann came as the introductory package. Better written than the Citizens' Charter, anyway.

---

1. He had asked EC whether he could call the novel *Who Killed Edwina Currie?*. She refused.

Tower House, Sunday 22 September, 7 p.m.

Sun just beginning to set over Toyota; there's a chill in the air and I've switched on the central heating. Winter isn't far away now. The girls are heading back to school and the house is quiet.

It has been a busy week for me personally, in which I earned £4400, of which some £400 will go in commissions. That really does something for my self-confidence. There were two events for Barbara Kelly,[1] both of which came to me direct; she earns her money by negotiating a £2000 fee for me, and politely saying 'no' to those who feel my job is to work all over the country for nothing. One was in Birmingham at the stunning new International Conference Centre in Broad Street, which is a zanier version of the Queen Elizabeth II Centre in Westminster, with the same grey and soft blue aluminium finish, a much kinder architectural style than the 1960s glass and concrete. The other was a grotty exhibition at the conference centre in Bournemouth on the theme of 'Today's Woman'; fortunately, local schools had sent their fifth years, so there was quite a crowd at the dozens of stands. Best was the effort of British Rail Network South-East, who had on display a magnificent blonde female train driver, and a fashion show of the latest trackside gear for women maintenance staff. That took chutzpah. I also wrote a review for the *Sunday Times* of Anita Roddick's (ghost-written) autobiography. I envy her in so many ways and said so. And her luck. If Gordon had turned out to be a dreamer and no good with money, she wouldn't be worth £75 million now, and a force for good in the world. She might just have been bashing away at her word processor in the kitchen, as I am.

The polls have been a-wobble this week, with MORI in the

---

1. Widow of the television personality Bernard Braden and head of Prime Performers, a speakers' agency.

Sunday Times today showing Labour with a four-point lead. John Major is still way ahead of his party, as Kinnock is way behind his. This week we had two Party Political Broadcasts, both of which I missed, and the launching of series of posters by both sides, as if the election campaign has started already. What a phoney war, and how very dull; it isn't anything to do with issues, or even personalities, since both men are patently decent, hard-working, patriotic and kind to the neighbours. Now we are in the ERM, the economy is on virtual automatic pilot. Neither man can fiddle with it; decisions are taken without reference to local politics at all. In that sense, it almost doesn't matter if Kinnock gets in, as he won't be able to do very much without the rest of Europe screaming at him. The political scene gets lively only when the vestiges of Thatcherism wave their tentacles and someone gets stung: the mainly useless and distracting reforms of the NHS, for example, which the hapless Mr Waldegrave,[1] oozing distaste, is stuck defending, and which are a wonderful target for Robin Cook.[2] I'd have been perfectly happy to have abandoned them along with the poll tax, and only feel a little uncomfortable that I didn't ever attack them in public. However, no one would have taken my criticism seriously, as it would have sounded like sour grapes.

The Party Conference is two weeks tomorrow. I refuse to pay extortionate sums for a dirty Blackpool hotel and terrible service (Hilary Rubinstein has just brought out the 1991 edition of the *Good Hotel Guide*, in which he is highly critical of such places). So I'll stay in Liverpool and go up just for Monday night (dinner with British Rail's chairman), Tuesday and part of Wednesday; after Norman Lamont has done his bit, I'll drive down to Portsmouth, collect Chris

1. William Waldegrave, Secretary of State for Health; Conservative MP for Bristol West.
2. Labour spokesman on Health.

from the station (if she can persuade herself that her family can manage without her), and so to France for the weekend, returning on Monday straight to London. I need to pay some bills in France and ensure that all the existing work is done before we start on the next lot. Mostly I want to give Chris a chance to talk, if she will; her illnesses have boiled down to 'irritable bowel caused by stress', and may have something to do with the children growing up and not needing her any more. And I think I want to tell her about my modest part in British history; I feel still very upset at being left out last December, for it means a decisive break with everything I hoped to do. If John had wanted to, he would have found a place for me. Waiting another year makes the chances of surviving long enough to get into the Cabinet that much more remote (anyway, there's no guarantee he will be able to form a Government after the election). I really don't want to be a fifty-five-year-old Minister of State without further prospects, wearily doing boxes at two in the morning, as the centre of politics drifts to Brussels and points east. John must have realised that I was desperate to get back in then. He must wonder – if indeed he thinks about me at all, which I doubt – what I do with myself now; maybe he thinks I'm just patiently waiting. He didn't keep his promise to me, as I understood it, that I would be offered a worthwhile post. That hurt so terribly – and I would have been useful to this lacklustre Government. I think I'd like the man to know exactly what he did last winter and how I felt. Preferably not when the knowledge could do any damage; but he won't always be Prime Minister, and it won't always matter.

Victoria, Monday 30 September, 8.15 p.m.

Busy day: started from Derby on the *Master Cutler* at 7.55 a.m., first time I've been down to London by train in nearly three months. I was going to drive down last night, but filthy weather and still feeling groggy after chest and throat infection last week made it seem like a bad idea. First meeting with Sir Bob Reid of British Rail anyway, so train travel a good idea! He's small, trim, lost right hand, dapper, Scots. No excess charm and no huge personality either – not quite sure he's the right man for a service industry like BR. We talked at my request about Toyota using BR freight to take cars from Burnaston and related matters. Thence (by train, of course) to Milton Keynes NE, a new seat; and then on to tea in Oxford East which we lost last time, just – Steve Norris's seat, Cowley car workers – and are unlikely to win back. Over fifty constituencies this year, and nobody knows but me. I'm now so cheesed off that I'm not even doing them properly. The *News of the World* improved my spirits yesterday, however, with a poll showing I was voted 'Britain's sexiest woman MP' and 'the woman MP most want to stay on desert island with'! The male equivalent was John Major!

Liverpool, Sunday 6 October, 10.30 p.m.

Last week's Labour Party Conference went off very well indeed for them, and one poll this morning showed them seven points ahead.

Margaret has indicated that she'll accept the title 'Countess of Finchley' on her retirement (no doubt this was timed for a November election which didn't happen). How preposterous: how crass and graceless. If Churchill and Macmillan and Heath all managed without peerages (until Macmillan accepted one aged ninety, which is fair enough), why does she want one? If Wilson and Callaghan were content with life peerages, why not Margaret Hilda? Is she really such a crashing snob? She has already arranged a title for Mark, with a baronetcy for Denis.[1] She insists on being called Mrs Thatcher, even though she's now a lady on account of Denis's

---

1. Margaret Thatcher's husband Denis had been made a baronet earlier in the year.

being a baronet. The whole thing is bizarre, and the thought of Mark with his earldom nauseating.

On the ferry to Portsmouth, Monday 14 October, 6.30 p.m.

This is the second year on the trot that I've played hookey from the Party Conference. Last year was easy – nipping from Bournemouth to Portsmouth to catch a late boat. This year involved belting down from Blackpool, more than three hundred miles, which I'm ashamed to say I covered in only four hours on Wednesday, since it is motorway down to Oxford and dual carriageway, mainly the A34, after that. Originally I was going to take the night boat with Chris, but she jacked (more about that in a minute). I was appalled at the long queues waiting to get into Conference on Wednesday morning for Mrs T, so I decided then and there to skip the rest of it.

Next year I think I will go properly, partly because it will be in Brighton, and Ray will come, and partly because it will be after the election and may be more interesting. No doubt there will be new ministers to watch and I will want to chat people up from possible Euro constituencies. I might have a new book out, too. This year I didn't really have a role at all, though I did lots of TV, including getting up at 6.15 a.m. for breakfast TV – just like old times. I was invited to speak at only one fringe meeting, the 'One Nation Group',[1] with which I agree in principle, but I find the people involved creepy – too many of them only want to be on the honours list and meet the Queen and Prime Minister. I gather we have accepted yet another cheque from an obscure Hong Kong businessman. Roll on the day when parties are funded by the taxpayer.

Conference seems to have gone off well, despite the odds against.

---

1. A Tory Party group founded in 1951 by Geoffrey Howe and others in support of the welfare state. The title comes from Disraeli's novel *Sybil* (1845).

Robust defence of the health service has boosted William Waldegrave's position, at least within the party; today Labour seemed to be backing off on charges that we intend to privatise the NHS, though I thought Stephen Dorrell's[1] effort on *The World at One* was a bit wet, wittering on about dictionary definitions instead of putting a strong and positive case. There was a flaming row during Jeffrey Archer's party at the Imperial (the *Sunday Times* reported the version according to Jeffrey, whom I wouldn't trust with last week's laundry list), when the PM laid into John Birt, director-general of the BBC, about bias in reporting of Conference speeches and topics. The broadcasters' view is that Labour are simply much better with the press and media. I note with interest that members of the Shadow Cabinet are better known to the public than their Cabinet counterparts; Peter Lilley is recognised by all of 5 per cent (but remember John Major was recognised by only 2 per cent back in summer 1988). David Hunt and half a dozen others must be grinding their teeth, for they were recognised by nil! What a dull lot they are.

Heseltine did well, for which I was pleased: a standing ovation, genuinely meant and responding to his rousing speech, good old-fashioned Conference stuff. He is to be given a leading role in the election campaign, and so is Norman Fowler, who is to be the PM's general supporter and factotum. Much surprise expressed at the latter, who had dropped right out of public view; no commentator remembered the team at DHSS which he ran so well. It will be complete if Tony Newton is given something to do. Chris Patten made an excellent speech on Tuesday, unscripted mostly – these little facts, like Heseltine's refusal to use the sincerity machine, the autocue, have produced highly favourable if surprised press comment. They

---

1. Parliamentary Under-Secretary of State, Department of Health; Conservative MP for Loughborough.

suggest a streak of self-confidence, of originality missing from Labour's tinsel-wrapped affair; and when they come off, as these two did, the press are most impressed and say nice things about us. On such trivia are modern reputations built.

I return to the question of what I am going to do about Chris, and tomorrow morning I hope to find out. She had asked for a pay rise, which I usually give in September. The girls are not well paid, but I don't need to rehearse again in my diary the juggling which goes on. In January and July next year a total of £30,000 tax is due. In other words there is nothing to spare, and I can't run the risk of being £2000 or £3000 adrift in March. Nor has Chris's work this year justified any extra money, and if tackling inflation means anything, it has to start at home! She asked me in a note and got a note back. So on Tuesday morning, sitting in my car, I got a right earful on the car phone, ending up with both of us very upset. On the boat over, feeling very lonely and unwanted, I typed out a letter to tell her how I just do not have the money. She was worth £20,000 p.a., she said, which is what the other secretaries get. Oh no they don't (unless they are wed to the MP, or sleeping with him). As I write, my intention is that she should take an extended sick leave and sort herself out. My new research assistant Adrian Pepper can cope while she is away, with some agency help.

It's dark out. The big boat, the *Pride of Hampshire*, hums and throbs across a black calm. The daytime journey is so boring. I managed to do a bit of writing in France – clearly I can write or decorate, but not both. 'Magical Mystery Tour', a story about an old people's day out, came out rather well; I like the bit at the end, about the body with rigor mortis being more difficult to get out of the coach than it was to get in alive. And I revised 'Patience' for the umpteenth time, remembering that A. P. Watt haven't seen it yet. In total, I have eighteen stories which could form a book. I've left out 'Journey', as that could form the prologue to the novel. I did some reading for it in Liverpool Local History Library on Monday – what a dismal place! No decorating since I was there twenty-five years ago, from the look of it.

Victoria, Monday 28 October, 10.40 p.m.

It's been an action-packed fortnight, politically and personally. Right now Parliament is in recess, with the State Opening due later this week. For the first time since I became a member I won't be there, peering on tiptoe around the neck of a fellow MP and just catching a glimpse of the Queen's spectacles (and hoping the nation is catching a glimpse of me). I'll be commentating for ITV, from Granada's Liverpool studio as part of their very popular daytime programme. That, I think, will be fun. Then I'll be flown back to London, hopefully in time for the afternoon speeches.

'Harmony' was the theme of today's 'Woman of the Year' lunch at the Savoy, organised as usual by Lady Lothian, wearing the same scruffy black cardigan as every year and much loved by everyone there. What a shindig – and what fun. When she started it with Odette Hallowes thirty-six years ago, she was told she wouldn't find as many as ninety suitable women in the whole UK. Now it's five hundred every year, including lorry drivers, film and TV stars, police, doctors (lots this year), lawyers, etc. The main speech came from the Duchess of York, who looked stunning in a smartly tailored tartan coat dress – she has lost a lot of weight and looks fresh, young and sophisticated. She was keen to emphasise that she had written it herself and clearly was trying to impress, which was rather touching: in a manner similar to John Major before he accepted some teaching, she commented on her own remarks and spoiled the presentation of some rather anodyne stuff. I'd love to take her in hand!

The issue which demanded most of my time domestically was, as I suspected, Chris. I got home to the flat a fortnight ago to find a supercilious letter from her giving me advice, and adding the postscript that she was going to work in the PM's office during the election. The next day Adrian was unable to gain entry to the House, as Chris had not arranged any passes for him (and subsequently I discovered that he could have had temporary passes anyway). I was absolutely furious, and after twenty minutes' talk I sacked her. Her constant moans about money were unrealistic and unpleasant and creating a difficult atmosphere. And to bugger off to work in the PM's office – without asking if I minded, and without even thinking I might be very hurt – was unforgivable.

I haven't replaced her. Adrian is supposed to answer the phone, which he does fitfully; he opens some of the mail, but I think I'll do most of it. I'm doing the diary and quite proud of getting it on the computer, a month ahead, which is more than Chris ever did! The agency is doing typing and I've swapped Jane's[1] work around a bit. Adrian's real forte is dealing with research material and he's written me rather a good speech for tomorrow's Reed breakfast (car coming at 6.50 a.m., ugh). I hope he stays. After the election I'll get a new secretary and then he can go off elsewhere with a good reference. The date now seems likely to be April, after an early Budget and Finance Bill (Easter is late so we could get it in before). The reasoning is that we should not go right to the end, in case the May election results are bad and result in a collapse of our vote.

John Major seems to have missed a trick, or several. He didn't reshuffle in September, so we still have the dullest bunch of ministers in recent history. The *Sunday Times* paid me a delicious compliment yesterday in a leader headed 'Dream Ticket', by saying I should be in Cabinet, helping to win marginal seats in the Midlands and North. Pigs might fly.

The South Derbyshire Conservative Association Annual Dinner on Friday was a misery, in the white hole of the Assembly Rooms –

---

1. Jane Lea, EC's South Derbyshire constituency secretary.

only eighty-five people there at £25 per head (for prawn cocktail, turkey and frozen raspberries/pavlova. Ugh).

Victoria, Tuesday 5 November, 4.45 p.m.

A substantial bunch of Tory MPs met together in the summer and decided that we needed to show a more positive approach to Europe, emphasising the benefits of membership. Last week we met Tristan Garel-Jones,[1] and yesterday the Prime Minister. Tris kept us waiting and then apologised, 'I've been on the phone to a foreigner – you know what they're like', which we all found distasteful and offensive. Polite but embarrassed laughter. Then Tris, who is not much good at listening or picking up vibes these days, launches into a tirade against Maastricht[2] and a long list of negatives and 'don'ts' and 'won'ts'. After some more of this I blew my top and told him we were there to urge a more *positive* tone on Europe, that we must stop sounding so scared, that our constituents expected us to be confident, not battling to avoid signing what would most definitely be in our interests to sign. The others nodded vigorously (Tim Devlin, Anthony Nelson,[3] Richard Luce,[4] etc.). Tris nearly fell off his chair in surprise. We explained about our group, how we felt sure we were the majority, wanted to help the Government, had kept quiet till now to avoid public splits, were delighted with announcement of two-day debate on 20–21 November, so we felt we could now go public. Tris had clearly never heard of our existence (Anthony Nelson said after that he avoided leaks by not telling the whips!), and had assumed

1. He had recently been appointed Minister of State in the Foreign & Commonwealth Office.
2. A new European Union Treaty, then in draft, which proposed an extension of the powers of European institutions.
3. Conservative MP for Chichester.
4. Sir Richard Luce, Conservative MP for Shoreham.

that a batch of Tory backbenchers coming to talk about Europe must, of course, be hostile. Rapidly he changed his tune and advised us to tell all to the PM, which we intended to do anyway; and said he would brief us weekly, and that we should meet regularly.

So, on to Number 10 at 3 p.m. yesterday. In total, eleven of us: the same group as saw Tris, plus Ian Taylor, David Harris, Tim Smith,[1] Nigel Forman, Sir Peter Hordern, Alistair Burt[2] and Ray Whitney. Quite a distinguished bunch, really – all able, intelligent and sensible (not clear what I was doing in there!) – several knights and ex-ministers, full age/experience range, spectrum of political opinion, representing constituencies from Stockton to Cornwall. We were ushered into the Cabinet Room, which has been redecorated following the IRA attack and looked gorgeous. It's the first time I've been in there. Walpole over the plain white marble fireplace gazed down benignly. A nondescript eighteenth-century landscape faces the PM – boring, bland and empty, a road disappearing into an anonymous distance: I wonder why he likes it? The clock facing the PM is set three minutes faster than the one behind him on the mantelpiece facing his troops, presumably helping to keep him on time! Deep cream walls, gold brocade curtains, brown baize table (stained) and light tan leather accessories, silver candlesticks and no ashtrays. Old-fashioned Cumberland HB pencils, brand new and very sharp, and a plain white notepad at each place. The PM's engagements in a stand-up reminder, slightly to his left. Tea in white china cups, too strong as it always is in Government departments (I think they use industrial size teabags). We explained why we were there. Each of us had our say in a forty-five-minute meeting – so very different from Margaret. I kept off detail and talked about the tone of the debate, which must be positive and confident. 'Insofar as we believe our

1.   Conservative MP for Beaconsfield.
2.   Conservative MP for Bury North.

attitude prevails in the country, we are here to help you. Insofar as our attitude does not prevail in sections of the Tory Party, we need you to help us. The party outside Parliament is very loyal, and if it gets a clearer, stronger lead from the Prime Minister, most will follow, more or less content.' John spoke fairly briefly and openly. 'It isn't in our interests to see Maastricht fail,' he said firmly at the end.

It was a super meeting. We left feeling much happier, though I think that's John's knack. I noticed he now has brown age spots on the back of his hands. We agreed in the doorway of the Cabinet Office that our group could now 'go public', and we've been doing that with a vengeance ever since: Tim and Anthony and Richard on national radio, me on *The World at One* and (I hope) BBC TV news at 6 p.m.

Certainly I feel a lot happier doing this than doing what I was asked to do by the Whips' Office, namely defend our policy on women and attack Labour, in today's debate on Rights and Responsibilities, part of the Queen's Speech debate. I am determined to speak in the Euro debate and the only way to be sure is not to have spoken before this session. Nicholas Baker[1] had asked me yesterday morning and I'd said 'yes'; then Maureen Hicks[2] told me that Gill Shephard had been appointed deputy chairman of the party, on top of her Treasury job. I'm pleased for Gill, but furious with everyone else. I'm asked to stand in for Eric Forth tomorrow: delighted, because his is a vulnerable seat. For Francis Maude[3] on Friday: sorry, already booked. Asking me to speak up for the party on women (not that anyone will notice or hear), as if I were party deputy or vice-chairman! God, it makes me wild. If that's what they want me to do, why not give me the job? Nothing makes me more

1. A Government whip; Conservative MP for North Dorset.
2. Conservative MP for Wolverhampton North-East.
3. Conservative MP for Warwickshire North.

disgusted with the party hierarchy than the way people like me are taken for granted, and our willingness undervalued.

Victoria, Thursday 21 November, morning

If I don't write something now, it won't get done this week, as tonight after the 10 o'clock vote, I'm doing Channel 4's *A Week in Politics*. Then tomorrow morning I'm off early to Darlington for a day's speechmaking in Stockton South (Tim Devlin), Darlington (Michael Fallon) and Hexham (Alan Amos): all likeable chaps in highly vulnerable seats.

We're in the middle of the great Euro debate in the Commons and it's turning out a cracker. John Major made a workmanlike and sensible speech, mostly in words of one syllable and heavily coded in places: in classic Major style, there was something in it for everybody. He pointed out that it would be 'damagingly wrong' to believe that the eleven would not proceed to a single currency without us, and such a currency, if convergence happens, would be 'the means of safeguarding anti-inflationary policies for the whole Community'. However, the same warnings were directed at the eleven – a deal might be 'genuinely unobtainable'. It was OK, not brilliant, but clear and sensible. Then Kinnock got up and made a real hash of things. When Robert Adley[1] challenged him about Labour's U-turns on Europe, Kinnock called him a 'jerk' (on live TV) and mocked John for the divisions in his party, which had us all pointing at his own side and hooting with laughter. The debate lasted till midnight, and of the Labour backbenchers only Denis Howell[2] and Calum Macdonald[3] took the frontbench pro-Europe line: most were openly

---

1. Conservative MP for Christchurch.
2. Labour MP for Birmingham Small Heath.
3. Labour MP for the Western Isles.

hostile. But then Margaret Thatcher stole the show (and the headlines and front pages), with a forty-minute *tour de force*: strong on body language and sentiment, pointing at the front bench, giving the PM a list of points he should be negotiating; sheaf of notes in her hand, but departing frequently from them and lambasting everyone in sight, Delors and 'the battleground' and calling for a referendum: 'Let the people speak!' (which of course this morning produced cartoons asking when did she ever listen?). She's against the narrow band of the ERM (yet she took us in), against creeping movement to a single currency, the convergence conditions are impossible, but don't believe they won't try and so on. In fact, it was much the same as in the summer. And so Downing Street moved in the wind, and by evening we were hearing that a referendum had not been ruled out, as we had believed was clear in the PM's own speech. That creates more headlines, and more opportunity for Labour to say she's in the back seat with her hands on the driving wheel. Better for John to ignore her, as he seemed minded to do at the time – his great strength is in *not* being Mrs Thatcher.

Victoria, Thursday 5 December, 11.10 p.m.

Dog tired: I did (recorded) the TV programme *Have I Got News For You* tonight with Ian Hislop of *Private Eye* and others – young, hip, slick, etc., and bloody hard work, especially if your period is coming on. I feel distinctly middle aged right now, as my gut aches and I contemplate with resigned distaste an early drive to Derbyshire tomorrow morning.

I sold two pieces this week: 'Dear God' to the *New Statesman* for £100 and 'Innocent Bystander' to *Tatler* for £200. My writing has come on a treat in the last year or so, and I only wish it wasn't such a struggle to find time to do it. We are still waiting for the *Express* to publish the Japanese families piece. They went to a lot of trouble taking photos, as I did to write it, so I asked Lisa Eveleigh of A. P.

Watt to press them. The paper is more likely to use what it has paid for.

I feel so resentful that Gill Shephard was made deputy chairman and not me, though I was already a minister when Gill was trying to get selected for a seat. Now I read she's invited to join Cabinet political discussions after main Cabinet on Thursday mornings, and is tipped for a seat in the Cabinet after the election. Of course I am pleased for her, and like her. But she is not outstanding, and certainly not so brilliant that at the age of fifty-one she deserves a Cabinet post within five years of becoming an MP. If John Major wants one of the new women, then Emma Nicholson had a far more impressive career before entering the House. If he wants someone with a proven track record and public image, then Virginia would be much better, and Lynda has more experience than either. I can't help feeling he just feels comfortable with Gillian, because she's a near neighbour in East Anglia and he knows her well.

I did an interview with George Lucas of the *Daily Telegraph* last week – he sounded quite distinguished over the phone but turned out to be a right little twerp, so another snide piece is on its way. 'But if you were offered your old job back, you'd accept it like a shot, wouldn't you?' he challenged. No, I wouldn't. That would be a *very* easy choice. And tossing through my mind the increasingly unlikely possibility of being offered anything by my ex-lover, I wondered what I *would* now accept. Only something leading straight to Cabinet, I guess. Party chairman? (Or deputy chairman, perhaps when Gill is promoted – that gets me into the Cabinet Room at least.) Or PPS to the PM: one would not turn that down. Financially it wouldn't be easy, but afterwards I'd have something marvellous to write: Arthur Schlesinger[1] stand aside! Something in the Foreign

---

1. Historian and author of *A Thousand Days*, an account of John Kennedy's presidency.

Office maybe, but all the excitement will be over after Maastricht next Monday and Tuesday. The European Parliament continues to look a much more interesting proposition. Power is moving, almost visibly, across the Channel.

Holiday Inn, Leeds, Friday 13 December, midnight

I've been in Yorkshire, (1) earning money – £500 last night from Yorkshire TV presenting the prizes for their Young Enterprise '92 Award to business people under thirty; and (2) earning my keep with *Any Questions* tonight for BBC Radio. The others were Gerald Kaufman, Menzies Campbell[1] and Enoch Powell:[2] 'a very strong panel', as David Cameron from the Conservative Research Department put it, but then it was the Friday after Maastricht, as I spotted a long time ago. I forestalled any attempt to move me by artlessly offering to Richard Ryder to stand aside if the Foreign Secretary (or someone else more important than me) wanted the spot instead. 'No, of course not,' says he, 'and if anyone suggests it just tell them to have a word with me.' Great! I hope I acquitted myself reasonably well, though really it was an anticlimax as so much of the action took place earlier in the week.

Kaufman was interesting tonight. He's such a slimy bastard, it comforts me to reflect that he only ever made Minister of State for Trade and Industry, that his main task was the nationalisation of aircraft and steel industries and then he watched the Tories dismantle all that hard work. He's a man I really wouldn't trust anywhere, yet the profiles paint him as a nice man underneath. Could have fooled

---

1. Liberal Democrat MP for Fife North-East.
2. Cabinet minister in the Macmillan Government and Conservative MP for Wolverhampton South West, 1950–74; Ulster Unionist MP for South Down since 1974.

me. Part of the reaction to him is anti-Semitic, as demonstrated in Huddersfield this lunchtime. I was asked to go there as the Association is having a terrible time, following the embezzlement of £12,000 of Tory funds by a long-standing councillor who appears to have spent the money doing up his house. As we are chatting over the buffet, one of the other councillors told me firmly that Kaufman's problem was that he was a typical Jew. Really, says I; I'm a Jew, too. It gave me enormous pleasure to see the pompous twat totally lost for words. The trouble with Kaufman, I offered helpfully, was that he was a typical socialist: no principles, only saying what would please the electorate. The councillor drifted off, eyes rolling with embarrassment.

Back to Kaufman. He was on safe ground telling anecdotes to us other three about MPs now dead. We talked about my predecessor George Brown, who lost the seat in 1970. Brown knew he would lose it, and discussed the matter with Wilson; the steady stream of Tory voters into the constituency made it increasingly weaker for him. Only boundary changes would save him (and indeed produced a 10,000 Labour majority in 1974), but Wilson warned him that it wasn't possible to get the changes through before the 1970 election. Did Brown want to move to a stronger seat? No, said Brown, I'll stay where I am. That says something for his character, though little for his political acumen. Maybe he knew that his career was finished, so there was no point in moving.

Such a course does not appeal to me. 1996 could be very sticky for a redrawn South Derbyshire. Maastricht has given the European Parliament a whole raft of new powers. I know where I'm going . . .

Victoria, Thursday 19 December, 11.50 p.m.

Almost the end of the year and time to start a new book.[1] I'm quite tiddly, having shared a bottle of St-Emilion with Richard Page[2] at dinner tonight in the Members' Dining Room. He had lamb, sensible chap, and I ordered 'Biftek of Beef Tyroléenne' (I kid you not), which turned out to be a hamburger, dry and tasteless, with fried onion rings and a tomato sauce. I wrote a remark in the suggestions book that it should have been titled 'Beef McDonald'.

Margaret turned up yesterday for the first day of the Maastricht debate, resplendent in a purple jacket and looking regal and then bored, and eventually slipped out. There was quite a kerfuffle over where she was to sit, as her new PPS didn't turn up for Prayers[3] and the place was packed, so eventually silly Harry Greenway[4] sat on the stairs. I noticed that today Peter Tapsell[5] made a point of coming into Prayers and took his seat, writing on his Prayer card 'Tapsell – in case M. Thatcher wants to sit here'. Silly boys, all of them. Anywhere else, in any other Parliament, we wouldn't be playing games over our seats.

As the debate was finishing tonight, Anthony Nelson spoke to me and invited me to join the pro-Maastricht plotters in the Smoking Room after the vote for a glass of champagne: he was expecting the PM to join us. And so he did, and later Lamont also (looking more like a Cheshire cat than ever – his human features disappearing under the cream of his self-satisfaction. A most unpleasant and untalented person). Peter Lilley also came in, but behaved like a PPS

---

1. EC wrote separate diaries for each calendar year in bound notebooks.
2. Conservative MP for Hertfordshire South-West.
3. MPs who attend 'Speaker's Prayers' at the beginning of each day's business are entitled to reserve their chosen seat for the rest of the day with a green card.
4. Sir Harry Greenway, Conservative MP for Ealing North.
5. Conservative MP for East Lindsey.

not a Secretary of State,[1] mute and self-effacing – a man promoted way beyond his capability. When he slipped away, nobody noticed. Michael Heseltine also breezed in as John was holding forth, thought better of it, waved regally and disappeared again. Those present included Nelson, Devlin, Burt, Jim Lester,[2] Spencer Batiste who acts as PPS to Leon Brittan, and half a dozen others (plus Graham Bright, the PM's PPS). John looked well and fit. His performance yesterday in opening the two-day debate was workmanlike rather than brilliant, as was his handling of Prime Minister's Questions this afternoon. This man is never going to be a great orator – yawns are stifled, bottoms shuffled, eyes turned up politely towards him, throats ready for next 'hear hears' of approval. Kinnock yesterday was excellent – real pounding stuff. He had done his homework for a change, and practised dealing with hecklers and interventions and kept his temper pretty well. A much more polished performance than on previous occasions, which left his side delighted and me full of foreboding.

So what did John talk about? That's hard to say. He acts like he's Chief Whip and there to listen to us. If it wasn't for the champagne, and Jim Lester talking about Ronnie Scott's, the conversation would have been very limp. What is John doing over Xmas? Chequers, where he will walk a bit, and swim in the pool. I mentioned my house in France; he was instantly interested and wanted to know if I could speak French, so I showed off a bit! I suppose the only surprising thing John said was that he hadn't eaten all day; he certainly looks slimmer than when he stretched out on my sofa, and more concentrated and alert too, and more tanned. I bet he uses a sun tan machine.

1. Since 1990 he had been Secretary of State for Trade and Industry.
2. Conservative MP for Broxtowe.

1992

Tower House, New Year's Day, 1 January, 2 p.m.

A mild, dry, windy day. Green shoots peeping through fallen leaves in the garden; I planted lots of bulbs in the autumn.

I virtually stopped making speeches in the House last year, as it seemed such a colossal waste of time, but I did get very involved in Maastricht and feel much better informed. After sitting through more than one debate and statement waiting to be called, I eventually got to my feet at 9.30 p.m. on Wednesday 18 December. The speech wasn't reported anywhere, not even in local press; I'm going to have to fax them bits from *Hansard* each morning as they are refusing to take Press Association stuff now, it's too expensive. This was my first speech in the Chamber for six months, other than adjournment debates. I no longer feel at home there – it's more than ever a rowdy bear pit, with speakers being shouted down, the very antithesis of the intelligent debate it is supposed to embody. Bush said recently that he is glad there's no American version.

We have all been marking time, preparing for an election which didn't come, and for an end to the recession – which didn't come either. We consolidated at Maastricht; John became a more solid and predictable figure, whose persistence, courtesy and courage enabled conclusions to be reached of a kind on the Gulf War and the Kurds and Hong Kong – but in retrospect not satisfactory, not complete. Ruthlessness might have served better? Saddam Hussein is still there and could still be in twenty years' time. Margaret Thatcher has become a fading old lady; as Gorbachev left office last week, she suggested that she, he and Reagan should get together, as they still had much to offer the world. Reagan must be nearly eighty[1] and I doubt if he would even understand the proposition!

And for 1992? It's the year of the monkey: variable and capricious, according to Chinese astrologers. By this time next year I could be a minister again, or at least a frontbencher, without much enthusiasm but an enhanced sense of duty. I'd certainly like to have switched from this 'waiting' mode – waiting for something to happen, and feeling somewhat lethargic. I'm less good at *making* things happen. This time last year I was talking about getting the short stories together, and a book on Europe, and maybe a novel: progress made on all three is minimal. Meanwhile my back aches, arthritis is starting in my fingers, my voice won't take over-use, and my weight is up to 10 stone 12 pounds (yesterday morning). What happened to the self-discipline and drive I used to take such pride in?

Tower House, 8 January, 11.25 p.m.

The General Election campaign started in earnest this week. I believe now that the PM will call an election at the earliest opportunity, as the pound and markets are being damaged by uncertainty. The press is full of articles about avoiding action to be taken if there's a Labour Government, as taxes are likely to go up. If Labour do get in, I'll use all my spare savings (earning 7 per cent, i.e. barely above inflation) to pay off my debts (paying 30 per cent, Barclaycard) – come to think of it, that's a good idea anyway! I should get back my costs from Carter-Ruck soon. In 1990–1 my earnings from savings topped £5,000, but with lower capital and interest rates, I doubt if we'll get near that now.

The first few days campaigning have all been about tax rates: who would make us pay more. Of course, Labour will either have to

1. He was in fact eighty years old.

renege on promises or shove tax rates up – so there's John Smith[1] pointing out that we doubled VAT (8 per cent to 17.5 per cent) and could increase it further. We have failed to pin on Labour the fact that they would *borrow* more if they could, so pushing up interest rates. It's no coincidence that both sides are chucking the same accusations at each other. Membership of the ERM, refusal to devalue or to increase interest rates are common policies: the question being put to the electorate is whom they trust with the policy, not what the policy should be.

I couldn't help noticing the different quality of presentation today. Our tax accusations were offered at press conference by Chris Patten, ushering in two junior ministers, Francis Maude and Gill Shephard. All three in grey/brown suits. Francis in a grey tie! He was shown on *News at Ten*, face contorted as if in pain, aristocratic distaste almost. He is not a populist; someone should tell him to sit up and face the camera, to look as if he means it, get his teeth fixed and comb his hair. Gill got no coverage at all, which suggests that she produced no *bons mots* or stylish soundbites of any interest to TV editors. For both of them, that is *astonishing*. Yet in reply there's John Smith, Shadow Chancellor, looking the soul of Scottish rectitude, smart and sleek and with a bright flowery tie that spoke a modern outlook and *confidence*.

Victoria, Wednesday 29 January, 12.25 p.m.

Not in the best of moods! I bought the *Sun* because an elderly chap stopped me on Victoria Street and asked me what I thought of page two. Banner heading: 'Edwina's back – she'll get a top job from Major' and a big photo from the old days. A senior Cabinet minister

---

1. Shadow Chancellor; Labour MP for Monklands East.

said – in quotes – that I would be straight back in if we won; 'the Prime Minister rates her very highly . . . the Government needs women with energy and talent and no one has more than Edwina.' I would start as a Minister of State and then go into the Cabinet two years later.

Why so cross? Not just because I now hate that sort of gossip: it makes colleagues either fawning or jealous. But if I have any talent, then I'm needed *now* (and without false modesty I think that's right), before the election, in order to help win it, not after, when life will be much duller. I'm not sure I fancy spending the next three years trying to sell the Citizens' Charter to the British nation and making the trains run on time: what sort of ambition is that? The main thing I care about now is Europe, and I doubt if I'm entirely in line with the Government – I'd be very positive about it, whereas the role of a minister would be to go slow, to nit-pick, to hold back. Not my style.

If it is true that I have more energy and talent than any other woman around (that's possible), then why make others deputy chairman, etc., and leave me twiddling my thumbs? On the other hand, if John thinks he has a debt to repay (and he has), then he should have done it in December 1990 and not left me bereft and isolated.

And it is too late. Two weeks ago I dropped a line to Tom Arnold, the vice-chairman in charge of candidates (now there's a job I would have liked and could have done very well), asking what I should do if I wanted my name to go on the Euro list. He phoned back with a cryptic message, taken by my new secretary, Clare Whelan: 'I've done what you asked.' In other words, he put me on the list, just like that. He spoke to me in the lobby and said he hoped they were not losing me from Westminster. How very kind – they should have thought about the possibility sooner. It shows how little importance the party attaches to Europe even now, how little they understand of what is happening under our noses; and how little we nurture the meagre talent we have at our disposal. But every time I try and fail to catch the Speaker's eye in the silly parliamentary games we play, I grind my teeth and think of a different future. The Speaker doesn't call me because I'm not a member of a select committee, not an officer of a backbench committee, and nothing of importance in the party: very low down the pecking order in fact. I can't even get to speak on health questions. I have now written to him to complain. It's the pettiness which really riles. I don't want to spend the rest of my life messing about like that.

I have to send off the stories to Hilary Rubinstein, and hope hope hope he finds a buyer. Not for the money – though almost anything would be very nice – but for the enterprise, for having another book, for the fun, and to show two fingers to the rest of the world. You think I am of no value? Let me show you, my dears! There now, my mood is lightening already. Outside the sun is shining, though it is still very cold. My gymnastics this morning have left me warm and glowing and looking good. On the windowsill the winter flowering polyanthuses are blazing away, pink and yellow and purple, lifting their faces to the sun. Spring can't be that far away, and in four weeks' time I'll be in France again.

House of Commons, Monday 10 February, 10.15 p.m.

Sitting in my office at the House, waiting for a vote on Northern Irish business (which probably won't happen, but we did have one at 9.30 p.m.). And generally feeling a bit down.

Partly for trivial reasons: my *FT* piece was published on Saturday and is terrible – all the references have been elaborated, and the balance is all wrong. The story at the end should have been expanded and the bit about me missed out. Not pleased. Similarly the March edition of *Tatler* is out today and my piece looks a bit embarrassing; I wrote it back in November when Mrs Thatcher was shooting off about referenda, the pound was plunging, etc. 'I wish she'd shut up,' I said, and she has, since.

Hilary Rubinstein called last week. He's off abroad for two and a half weeks and wanted to check if I was happy that *Portfolio*[1] should go to Sidgwick's. Not really, but if that's its destination, OK. (Hilary dampened my spirit by saying 'It wouldn't get published if it was by Edwina Rubinstein.') The only other person who has shown any interest is Richard Cohen, Jeffrey Archer's editor, who took me to lunch last year at the Tate. He lost his job a week later and is still job hunting, according to Hilary. Better the devil you know, perhaps. I would be *thrilled* to get another book out, and some money would certainly help. At least the *People* paid up (£1000!) quickly – for 'Cup Final' – so maybe there's scope there. The *Guardian* liked a piece I did last week and want more, while the *Sunday Times* wants another review: but neither pays well. It looks, too, as if the Europe book is quietly vanishing, for if I were to produce it in 1993 I'd need to be working hard on it now and nothing has happened.

The real reasons for feeling depressed are deeper. We are slipping behind in the polls again. The economy is in a wretched mess, with unemployment still rising steadily and many bankruptcies. There was even a Radio 4 phone-in on 'How to go bankrupt' this morning! With all this going on, being neck and neck in the polls is a bit of a surprise – but I don't think we are, anymore. The Sunday TV programme *On the Record* was very cruel in juxtaposing the Prime Minister's remarks to the Young Conservatives' Conference on Saturday with Kinnock's energetic and inspiring speech to local government activists. From the clips I saw, John was at his worst: nervous, boring, flat, uninspiring, even difficult to hear at times as he kept dropping his voice. How I wish I could take him in hand and show him how to do it!

Then there's the Ashdown affair. After projecting a wholesome 'Mr

---

1. A planned collection of EC's short stories.

Clean' image, it was risible to see him wriggling as he admitted a five-month fling back in 1986 with his then secretary Tricia Howard. The press huffed and puffed, but gave up really when she turned out to be a plain, dumpy, forty-nine-year-old grandmother, very similar to Jane Ashdown (who, of course, knew her). Ashdown had slapped injunctions on all and sundry last week to stop the story leaking: so much for Freedom of Information! You can imagine how I felt: amused, mostly.

The outcome of Ashdown is that most people in the UK – over 90 per cent – want him to carry on; there's an increase in the percentage thinking he would make a good PM (ho ho!); and the Liberal Democrats are up 4 per cent in the polls, not at Labour's expense, but at ours. Now that *is* worrying. It suggests our vote is very soft indeed.

Victoria, Tuesday 25 February, midnight

Ray is away (not sure where!) and I may not get many more chances to write before the election is called. Given the grim economic news from around the world, the quicker we get it over the better.

I'm feeling very blue today (maybe because of hormones – post-menstrual and they seem to be playing up a bit). The postbag is running at more than seven hundred per week and Clare is over-whelmed. Papers getting lost, needing to repeat instructions, silly things being forgotten. We are up to a month behind. It is worse than when Chris was around, worse even than in November, when I did it myself. How bloody depressing. I'm still working flat out doing correspondence and my own diary and I'm *very*, very cheesed off with it. The fact remains that we need a bigger staff and I just can't afford it.

To keep the earnings up (approximately £12,000 this quarter) I've worked hard doing articles, and I'll try some more stories this coming weekend in France – at least those sell, even if I get a refusal on a collection from William Armstrong. Silly things like Noel Edmonds's TV show (£500) and reviewing a sex manual for the *Sunday Times* (£400) help financially, and they keep my mind off the mess that the election campaign has become. It's now clear we have no answers to the recession: probably because we didn't expect to need any, as (of course) it was supposed to be over by now. Only at Xmas was its continuation apparent, and that was a nasty shock all round, for the Chancellor most of all. The electors are conscious that Labour's responses, especially high taxes, would make things worse. So we are being forced into the election crying that we are the lesser of two evils – and personally I find that very distasteful indeed.

Tonight I did a 'debate' in the Hampstead Waterstone's, organised by the *Guardian*. There were only a couple of Tories there even to begin with – mostly under-thirties Labour, with a couple of highly entertaining Revolutionary Socialists (whom I compared cruelly with libertarian Young Conservatives: to the latter's detriment!). But they kept challenging on what we plan to do: not what we have done, or what Labour would do, but what we offer for the next few years. They were demanding the Tory Big Idea, and there isn't one.

Victoria, Tuesday 3 March, very late

Alone at the flat. Just got in, and feeling very low. I picked up a bug in France which has given me a mild case of the squitters but mostly leaves me queasy and full of wind: that's the least problem. William Armstrong has written a nice rejection of the short story collection, saying 'a few are very good indeed' but leaning on me, as I expected, to do a novel. He mentions Shirley Conran's *Lace* as a good example. I've not read it, but I do resent being pushed into a novel at this stage, when I'm still learning; and he would want to see most of it before, no doubt, turning it down. So it could be a huge investment of time and emotional energy, to no great point. However if nothing turns up, I could carry on with what I've done on Liverpool, etc.[1] It's at least as good as some I've read and, with some sex in, would no doubt sell. I like my little stories and would be thrilled if someone would take them on board so must try again with Hilary, at what is really a most difficult point to find time to do anything.

Mostly I'm blue because the campaign isn't going well. This afternoon when I arrived back from France, I asked if I could talk to the Prime Minister about it, and eventually was invited up to the flat at 9.30 p.m. and stayed till 10.15, missing the 10 p.m. vote. Got two kisses, too . . . ! The problem is that the entire campaign is so negative, a sorry reminder of our 1989 efforts which switched off so many of our voters in the Euro election and lost us so many seats. This week's effort is two red boxing gloves with the line 'Labour's Double Whammy', i.e. increased taxes and increased prices (or is it increased interest rates? Shows you how effective it is). Most of the comment has been 'What's a whammy?' and the reaction is bemused or bewildered. *The Times* yesterday (Monday) reckoned that both Labour and Conservative are on target for 310–315 seats.

Mostly the campaign is distasteful as well as (in my view) unsuccessful. After twelve years in power we ought to be very proud of our record, appearing confident and positive and in control (not complacent) to the electorate. John gave me a gin and tonic and I told him my ideas. Some of them came from round the tea room this afternoon, but most of them were my own. I don't think it's really dawned on him that we might lose this. He said it is difficult to think it all through: a more positive approach was test marketed before Xmas, but the only ads which had any impact were 'Labour will increase taxes'. Hard to comment without seeing what was on offer, of course. John listed the problems – raising money for the party,

---

1. This became the novel *She's Leaving Home.*

stopping Cabinet ministers from squabbling. They'd always known that February was going to be a bad month for economic figures, and he was surprised we weren't 5 per cent behind in polls (we might well be next week, of course). What a defeatist approach! I ticked him off, emboldened by the gin and his friendliness: but how depressing that the main hope was that the economy would turn up and do all the electioneering for us.

He asked me what I was doing and admired my hair (trimmed this weekend in Saumur, not well, I thought). 'Earning as much as I can before income tax goes up,' I grinned. 'You think the other lot will get in, do you?' he asked, almost ruefully; and that was how the conversation started. Later I told him I was on the Euro list; he was startled and pooh-poohed it, saying there was no 'politics' there: but I don't like that kind of wheeler-dealing, and as a woman I tend to be excluded from it anyway. I asked if he'd considered what job he might have in mind for me and of course he hadn't thought about it. But I suggested being in charge of candidates, as they are terrible – and being his PPS, which brought a light to his eye. I should have said 'party chairman', as that would bring a place in Cabinet, too. But I suppose I really do want to go to Europe and the best chance is the four to five vacancies in the Midlands caused by retirements. It might be much harder in 1999; and it's 1994–9 which is going to be the really interesting time, when we MEPs will have two distinct jobs – selling Europe to the Brits in time for the single currency, if it comes, and selling the British pragmatic approach in Europe. I'd add, building/rebuilding the antisocialist majority in the European Parliament and ensuring the Parliament becomes an effective reality. All that sounds infinitely sweeter than any Minister of State job in the UK in a Government with a small majority and an uncertain air; but I couldn't say this without sounding dismissive and disloyal.

Was I interested in writing parts of his speeches, he asked? Of course, said I, you should have asked earlier; but use the ideas you've got now (scribbled as I spoke on back of a pamphlet), pretend they are your own. 'I can't do that,' he said, 'I'm not that kind of person.' 'Oh, don't be so fucking silly!' was my response. I don't think he had heard such vigorous language since working on a building site. All cathartic.

He looked thinner and his hair is almost silvery white now. Tired, but not as much as in his Chief Secretary days. Looking good for forty-nine in two weeks' time. Norma looks splendid for fifty, tossing a pancake today for Shrove Tuesday – doesn't make her own clothes any more! We talked (John Major and me) about women, and how he wanted more women MPs – then use your authority and prestige, I told him. 'I can't tell constituency associations what to do,' he protested, but I pointed out that shortlists for senior civil service posts *must* now have a woman candidate, and he could do same for the party. No answer! Not having women in Cabinet rankles, and he talked through the problem – clearly he's been over it in his mind, with puzzled regret, many times. 'You could have put us in,' I accused, and we mentioned Lynda and Angela and (by implication) me. 'Token women,' he muttered. 'No, we would not see ourselves as tokens: and you insult us in so saying,' I shot back. 'Any one of us would be doing a better job than, say, Peter Lilley.' He looked at his shoes, and murmured, 'You could well be right there!' 'And,' I went on, 'it would mean more votes. Many younger women, working, feel their effort is not appreciated. Putting that right is expensive. Having women in the Cabinet would be a lot cheaper.'

And so we wittered on. I felt better for saying it all and certainly he seemed willing to listen. If he asked me to be his PPS it would cost me a *lot*: but on the other hand I could write a marvellous book or diary about it. Most of all I would be doing my duty and I would *love* it. Junior minister? No, thank you, I'd rather write my novel. Minister of State? OK for two years and then off to Europe where the money is better, the horizons wider. Only a Cabinet post within those two years would postpone Europe. And if PPS . . . I'd be close to him all over again. 'We would have to have an agreement,' I said severely, as we moved to the door. He nodded – I think I would decide, like last time! But it's all a tragic muddle, because if he wanted, how could I refuse? I could write speeches and influence policy and get him more confident in public and help us win the next election – all worth doing. And he looked and sounded as if he needed some pillow talk, just as I do. 'How long is it?' he asked. '1988,' I answered, and faltered a bit. 'I can't believe it is all such a long time ago,' he said. Neither can I, John – it feels just like yesterday.

And oh, I weep for these things, in the dark fastnesses of the
    night
For my lost love
And for my lost hope
And for the future we are about to lose;
And for all the incompetence and stupidity I witness and can
    do nothing about
And for all the pain
All the pain
Which still grieves me so
And for all the talent I have and can't share
And all the talent I don't have, to be a success elsewhere
And for those who love me, and can't meet my expectations,
    especially Ray and Debbie
And mostly for John, because he too let me down – and is
    letting us all down
    – by being too cautious
    – by being too small-minded
    – by obeying too many rules
I taught him
    How to ignore rules
    How to take risks
    How to measure risk, and live with it, and *love* it – relish it,
    enjoy the edge we walk on; to fly . . .

I taught him to stretch out, keep stretching, go through
   barriers, push and push oneself – find oneself out in the
   stratosphere – float out there with your lover, together,
   with laughter sifting past the stars.

Tower House, Mothering Sunday, 29 March, 11 p.m.

Two minutes ago I took a phone call from the Prime Minister.
'Number 10, here,' says the young lady on the switchboard, sounding harassed and a bit tired, 'I have the Prime Minister for you,
please hold on.' And you do, and then you hear it ring, and then
John's voice comes through, sounding very ordinary. 'I'm going to
send you a crate of orange juice,' he said. 'Norma was very amused
when she read all about what you'd been up to.'

Well, what had I been up to? Nothing very serious, really. I did a
TV programme for Central Television on Friday night called *Central
Choice*; it replaces the *Central Weekend Live*, a live hour and a half
programme, 10.30 p.m. to midnight. With someone going down
from Etwall in a car, we got there in plenty of time, and I was due
to be the first on with Peter Snape, one of the West Midlands
Labour MPs (I think he's West Bromwich East), and he was late,
and we very nearly had me on my own. And he was in a very foul
mood, very jumpy, didn't seem to be concentrating properly,
allowed himself to be trapped into being critical of the Labour Party,
said rather nice things about John Major, in a forum where that
kind of remark really wasn't appropriate. And as we came off, he
seemed again to be edgy, and was loud-mouthed and aggressive,
rather in the way that he was a few months ago, when he says that
my car nearly hit his taxi, which is actually not true; both cars had
to stop dead to avoid a collision. And I suspect he'd been drinking.
Can't smell, which suggests it must be vodka, but he was very
aggressive indeed, and certainly not under control. In the Green
Room he was being very foul-mouthed, and loud-mouthed, and

generally shouting at me, and telling me I was going to be redundant. We kept saying to him, 'Put a sock in it, lay off, Peter.' He was helping himself to food, and a drink, and he wouldn't shut up at the bar for several minutes, so I tipped my orange juice carefully over him, and I watched in angry amusement as he opened his mouth, and no sound came out of it, and the orange juice dripped gently off his nose.

Well, it wasn't very lady-like, and it wasn't very accomplished, but what the heck? Being lady-like and accomplished doesn't get me very far. So I made my excuses and I left. Of course, it's all over the papers within hours. Somebody told the *Sunday Mirror*, thinking, of course, that it would knock me back. The *News of the World* had a lovely version of the story, in which Central TV said I had been seriously provoked, and had put up with it for a long time. I let the story run on the basis that this is what any girl would do if a man was being overbearing, in a pub or a club, and this was one way to stop it. A girl rang from the *Independent* to say that she had asked around their office and virtually every girl in the office had put up with that sort of thing at some time, and tipped a glass over a chap.

Snape claims that he was late because he'd been watching a football match. That seems like a very strange thing to be doing at about 10.30 p.m. and it suggests that he may well have been in a club where he has cronies, drinking. He has made it quite clear that if I say he had been drinking, he'll sue, which suggests that he must have been, and that perhaps he's been warned. There were funny comments in the *Burton Mail*, saying that he'd given up drink for Lent.

We went on then, John and I, to talk about what is happening here in our part of the Midlands. I told him that we're solid here, in South Derbyshire, and we should hold Burton, North-West Leicestershire would be a bit difficult, Margaret Beckett will hold Derby South, Greg may not hold Derby North, he doesn't appear to have done very much work.[1] A bit tricky as they've had a lot of unemployment and business failures, probably encouraged by Phillip Oppenheim to be too Thatcherite at a time when their local economic base was too weak to carry the growth. And I told him that we should probably increase our share of the vote, but our majority will go down. He was quite specific in wanting to know exactly what I thought our majority would be, so I said, 'Between six and eight thousand probably.'[2] I told him the Liberal vote is quiet here, and there seemed to be a lot of tactical voting, in the sense that if Labour is strong, then the Liberals are switching to voting Labour. It looks like Mrs Brass is not picking up much vote; we're only getting a handful of people on the doorsteps saying 'We're going to vote Liberal.' Mrs Brass being my Liberal opponent, who is a teacher in Ashby grammar school, and has been refused time off. Which is amazing; I feel it's quite wrong of her employer; they ought to give her the three weeks off, but she can only get a week off, so she's not actually fighting a proper campaign, she's got no posters up, she's got no leaflets out, got no literature from what we can see. And certainly hasn't been able to take part in any of the campaigns, and I feel rather sorry for her.

I think we're in for a hung parliament. The polls are absolutely neck and neck, with Labour just marginally ahead. Now, that means they're not going to win, and it means we're not going to win either. They can form a coalition much more easily than we can, as they have plenty of scope with Liberal Democrats, to whom they would promise proportional representation. There are the Scottish and Welsh Nationalists, for whom devolution is an issue, and I think they would find it much easier than we do, they've even got some of

1. The Conservatives held Burton, Derby North and North-West Leicestershire; Margaret Beckett held Derby South for Labour.
2. It was 4658.

the Ulster people, the SDLP, there's two votes there for them. On our side, we've only really got the remainder of the Ulster Unionists, and they would want us to scrap the Anglo-Irish Agreement, which I don't think we would do. So, unless we win 326 seats, I think John Major will be packing his bags from Number 10 Downing Street and heading off to the wide blue yonder.

Tower House, 6 April, just before midnight[1]

It looks like we're heading for an ignominious defeat in the election – the weekend opinion polls showed that we were on about 37/38 per cent, and since Labour is on about 39/40/41 per cent they've opened up a reasonable lead. It won't be enough to give them the election itself, to give them a majority, but it's enough to make them the largest single party. We will be lucky to hold on to three hundred seats. The main reason is that the Liberals have climbed steadily from the 12 per cent they were on at Christmas up to 20/21/22 per cent this weekend, and of course they've taken a great deal of that from us.

What's gone wrong? Well, a number of things. The campaigning has been based on two basic elements: (1) that the electorate trust us to run the economy and bring the country out of recession; and (2) that John Major was seen in the party as a popular and attractive figure. Now, the trouble is that every time we've talked about the economy, we've reminded people that there is a recession, and a lot of business has been very badly hit. There is no doubt that this is a raging recession, a really bad one. Far worse than anything the Treasury forecast, which therefore makes them look pretty silly. Every time Norman Lamont is on, which is of course an automatic

---

1. The remainder of these diaries were recorded on tape, as EC was too busy campaigning to write them out.

consequence of talking about the economy, he's looked like a real prat, and he's been hammered into the ground by John Smith. When they try to pull Norman Lamont off, we're then stuck with the other issue, which has been a central part of campaign, namely the Prime Minister, who has repeatedly acted as if he isn't Prime Minister, and indeed has turned out to be a very dull, wooden and incompetent campaigner.

I laugh ruefully when I think that actually one of the real reasons that everything ended all those years ago was that I got bored! I think my judgement then was more accurate than my judgement since.

In the last two elections, in 1983 and 1987, we had three things happening that we haven't got now, two of which were beyond our control. Namely, that the economy was moving, in both cases moving upwards quite fast (and that was apparent afterwards), and that the opposition was split, weak and generally incompetent and out of touch with the electorate. Now both of those factors have disappeared entirely this time, and nor, of course, do we have Margaret. She was not always a charismatic leader. I can remember back in 1975 thinking how overwhelmed she was; she was obviously doing her best, but she was not winning at that time the kind of adulation and support that she had later; I think it took her about ten years to get to the stage where she really found her feet. But John hasn't had that time at all; he's never fought an election before, even as a Cabinet minister, as he was appointed to the Cabinet, as I recall, the Saturday after the last election, and I can remember him telephoning me the same evening to tell me all about it. And to tell me about his excitement, about kissing hands with the Queen on his appointment to the Privy Council, and already they'd had their first Privy Council meeting. It seems like a lifetime ago!

I suspect if we, the backbench MPs, had all known what an incompetent campaigner he was going to be, we might have chosen somebody else. But that's hindsight, and at the time he was the only one available who could unite the party, and it certainly seemed for a long time afterwards like a very wise choice, even up to and including the start of the campaign. We went into the campaign with the approval rating, that is, the proportion to say they were satisfied with John Major as party leader over the proportion saying that they were unsatisfied, or dissatisfied, at plus fourteen. Kinnock was at a negative figure. We end the campaign with them both on plus two, which means that Kinnock's campaign has been a success, and ours has been a disaster.

The entire pattern of the campaign has been dreadful, and the Prime Minister, if he was listening at all, knows my views. I do feel insulted at the way he gave me all that time, and forty minutes in his room, and the flat, and it made no difference at all. The campaign was set long before then, the man was too cautious, too small-minded in character, too small in intellect in the end, I suppose, to scrap things and say, 'Come on, let's start again.' It doesn't work like that in John Major's world.

The campaign was negative, it was very thin, it was not credible, it had no substance, no content, it insulted the electorate. It left them after the first week saying, 'Well, that's all very well, but what are *you* going to do?' And worst of all there was no fallback plan, when it became obvious that this wasn't working. John himself pulled out of the hat this idea of jumping on the soapbox, and he clearly enjoyed it. The reaction of most professionals is that it was pretty pathetic. And the reaction of the electorate, and certainly the panel in the *Sunday Times*, was to dismiss him increasingly as somebody who didn't look as if he was on top of his job. But worst of all, of course, it was John's own idea. If it had been a good idea, it should have been tested weeks before. Most of the people in Central Office have no experience whatever of fighting elections *at all*, they're too young to have done so. They have believed their own propaganda, that Kinnock was unelectable, and that the British people would never tolerate, or even contemplate, another Labour Government.

And they seem very flat and very tired here in South Derbyshire. We've done a *massive* amount of canvassing, we totted up, we've done about 17,000 face-to-face contacts in the election campaign in the last three weeks. Taking into account what we've done in the last twelve months, which includes more of the stuff that we did last May (some of which, of course, we've repeated), that comes near to 24,000 face-to-face contacts. If you think about all the 'outs' and we got through 12,000 'sorry you were out' cards, we must be up to around 40,000. In other words we covered around half the electorate, which is fantastic. So I feel reasonably confident. The polls that we've done in the election campaign itself suggest that we've slipped back about 1 per cent in South Derbyshire. That's all right, I can live with that. Hopefully we'll get more than the 49 per cent[1] that we did last time.

I meant to mention one of the things that struck me with great force over the weekend. We had big adverts in the newspapers, they're in again today, so there's a big newspaper campaign going on. You're talking about £30–40,000 for a prime page, so we're spending money like there's no tomorrow. These are being followed up with the poster campaign. So, why are none of our campaign slogans in there? Labour's campaign slogan is 'Time for a change' – it's extremely powerful, and it's on everybody's lips, it's one of those slogans that people remember. Sounded a bit silly when they started, but it doesn't sound so silly now.

---

1. In fact, EC's vote was 48.7 per cent, down 0.4 per cent on 1987.

Index